LATIMER HIGH SCHOOL
STUDENT ID #2564031
Tommy Tate
LHS Status: The Banned
Tommy comes to LHS for a warm place, for food, and to survive to the next day. The Banned are absent from the LHS identity, culture, and press releases from the school.
LATIMER HIGH SCHOOL
STUDENT ID #2563524
Cullen Armstrong
LHS Status: Influencer
Cullen is looked up to by many students throughout LHS. His actions, whether he wants them to or not, leads his classmates on a daily basis.
Mia Fernandez
LHS Status: A Badge
Mia is the pride of LHS. She is a regular on the honor roll and her posters often fill the hallways. Badges help maintain the academic order of the school.
Rosi Williams
LHS Status: Subscriber
Rosi is a subscriber to the culture of LHS. Subscribers are the ones who give the influencers their status and maintain the social order among the students.
LATIMER HIGH SCHOOL
Administration Staff
Mr. Stallard
LHS Status: Content Moderator
Mr. Stallard is the head content moderator at LHS. He tasks himself on maintaining the academic and social order of the high school.

Originally Published <2020> <Honeycutt, Benjamin>

Illustrated by: Shelby Miller

Edited by: Pearl Sonnenschein and Anaya Walker

ISBN: 978-1-7358653-7-9

For Mom, Dad, Gibson, Natalie, Alex and Swachalika

I wouldn't have made it out without you.

(You too, Connor. EAS)

Part One: The Terror from Kind Pines (1)

Part Two: The Pride of Latimer (70)

Part Three: Before the Last Breath (205)

Well, son, I'll tell you:
Life for me ain't been no crystal stair.
It's had tacks in it,
And splinters,
And boards torn up,
And places with no carpet on the floor—
Bare.
But all the time
I'se been a-climbin' on,
And reachin' landin's,
And turnin' corners,
And sometimes goin' in the dark
Where there ain't been no light.
So boy, don't you turn back.
Don't you set down on the steps
'Cause you finds it's kinder hard.
Don't you fall now—
For I'se still goin', honey,
I'se still climbin',
And life for me ain't been no crystal stair.

Langston Hughes, *Mother to Son*

Acknowledgements

In the 15-year journey I had envisioning, crafting, and writing this novel, there are many people who helped me transform my trauma-filled journey in my childhood into what this work is today. Before anyone else, I have to thank my mom. My mom was there on my worst days and was always steadfast I'd overcome. Mom went on to read this book in countless iterations. Even when *Bleak* was close to 500 pages, her belief in my work, much like her belief in me, never wavered. This book would have never been written without my dad. My dad was the first person who suggested turning to the arts after the years of constant bullying, trauma, and targeted abuse I experienced in school. On days where I couldn't look at myself in the mirror, my dad inspired me to re-direct this energy into a work like this. During days when I would come home to a house without electricity, my parents gave me the belief that in spite of the hardships I was facing at school and at home, everything was going to be okay.

I am grateful for my illustrator, mentor, and dear friend, Shelby Miller. When I was ready to throw this work away, Shelby saw a vision for *Bleak* that I couldn't see. After reading a rough draft, she created the dandelion cover and encouraged me that this was a novel that needed to be published. I am also so thankful for my editors, Anaya Walker and Pearl Sonnenschein, who both agreed to read and edit *Bleak* before publication. Their energy, attention to detail, and ideas they gave to the story, its characters, and its message helped energize me to finally publish this novel. I am beholden to my teachers, Professor Gulley, Ms. Darnell, Mrs. Couchman, Mr. Krug, Mr. Clark, Dr. Martinez, Dr. Woolf, Dr. Joe O' Brien, Mr. and Mrs. Panthy, Pastor Gilstrap, Mr. Goodwin, Mrs. Watson, Mr. Vogel, Mrs. Klassen and my parents. I must also credit a mentor of mine, Jameelah Jones, who introduced me to the world of Langston Hughes. Hughes' work propelled *Bleak* in a new direction and continues to challenge me to be a better writer and person. You all demonstrated the power teachers can have and inspired me to become a teacher. I only hope I can have a similar impact on my students.

Thank you to Roland Hulme, a brilliant author who was kind enough to read a late draft of my work. Roland's constructive criticism, passion and encouragement made me believe that re-writing my book was possible (fourteen years into its conception). I will forever appreciate the time Roland volunteered to put into this work. *Bleak* would not have been what it was without the criticism I had from authors Hugh Wilson, John Jones, Lisa Luedeke, Johanna Parkhurst as well as publisher Judy Weintraub. Special thanks to my friends, Jack and Nancy Gilstrap, who were kind enough to take the time to offer advice to me. Jack's line by line edit of Bleak's first draft was transformative for the novel. To my unbelievable friends, Connor

Janzen, Jane Waters, Andre Daughty, Kelly Hunsaker, Vanishree Ganjegunte, Mitch Weisburgh, Scott Beye, Colin Renville, Dylan Samms, Jake Wells, and Zachary Hendrickson, whose talks I had about dandelions in high school helped shape their presence in the climax of this work. To my kindred spirit, inkling, and friend for life, Amber Schroetlin, my cousin, Christine Martin (a brilliant, published poet), my brother Gibson, and of course, my wife, Natalie. I can't count the nights Nat was willing to listen to ideas, tell me which were good, which were bad, and dream with me about a day *Bleak* would be published. I want to credit Georgia, Vince, Gus, Emmett, Cici, Tia, Tubs, Wally, Starbuck, Remy, Scout, Finnick and Kramer. When I received my life-changing spinal diagnosis in college, Kramer, as well as my close friends Connor, Pat, and Lex, were there for me through every moment. Dex's activism in *Bleak* was shaped by Bob Barker on sick days with Chicken Soup and Sprite (get your pets spayed and neutered!). I am grateful to my co-workers and regulars at the NCC, who supported me as I wrote 20 chapters of *Bleak* on unused receipts during dead times as a cashier. I also want to thank Govinda, Sudha, and Swachalika Panthy, as well as Indira, Sanat, and Sabin Acharya who, along with the community of Narayanpur, helped make Nepal my first place that felt like home. It was in the hills of Narayanpur that I found the inspiration to finish the first draft of *Bleak*. Finally, I'd be remiss if I didn't mention my soon-to-be-born son, Alex, who already gave me the motivation to finally publish this work. I want to thank the amazing students I've had the honor to work with at Lawrence Free State, J.C. Harmon, Monument Academy, HIPAfrica, The Tripur Kinder Academy, and Woodland Park Middle School. Our classes, conversations, and your passion about the world has made teaching my dream career. This book would not have been finished without your candor, insight, and support.

Bleak is published in memory of my student, Brendan (B), my childhood friend, Spencer, my cousin and gentle giant, Josh, Montré, who was always true, my aunt Jackie, who helped me find my love for Kansas City sports, and Nate, a bullfighter who championed animals his entire life.

The thought I could not run away from at 11 years old was "if life is so bad now, it's never going to get better." That thought haunted me, even as life did get better for me. If you find yourself in a similarly dark place, it is my deepest hope that *Bleak* can provide a small light in your world.

Content Warning for *Bleak*:

Bullying, Suicide, Racism, Classism, Homophobia, Ableism & Sexism

Suicide Prevention Hotline: 1-800-273-8255

Suicidepreventionlifeline.org

Recovery is possible.

Part One: The Terror from Kind Pines

Lynne Tate stepped inside her single wide trailer. The icy February air swirled through the open door and pierced her exposed skin. Lynne was tall, slender, had straight brunette hair, and her normally beige face was scarlet from the frozen night.

Lynne's voice tremored as she called through her home. "Tommy?"

The dining room light glowed over the table, illuminating two torn out pages of a journal. Lynne's black cat greeted her at the door, twisting through her legs. Lynne stepped to the table. The words "From your son" were written at the top of the torn-out pages.

Tommy Tate The Last Day 2/18

I felt fear explode inside my chest. I walked as quikly as I could. If Mr. Stallard found me on the way to the Annex it would ruin everything. The robbery, the months of planning, and the years of abuse that made this happen. I heard footsteps in a hallway behind me and the sounds immedeately put my throat in a chokehold. I threw open the annex door and pinned myself to a wall inside. No matter how much I breathed it felt like I was going to suffocate. When I felt the panic finally leave me I walked through the annex and stopped at the desk overlooking the darkened 2nd story windows of our gym. I set out my tools and I couldn't stop looking at them. I should have never come back to this school. Not after last April. I thought back to how the year started, how Mr. Austin convinced me to stay with a single can of Dr. Pepper. I was stupid to believe this year could be any different. I never should have come back. From the desk I stared through the annex windows and looked over the gym. I knew what Dexter meant when he called the Annex "The Latimer Watchtower." From these windows I could see everything. The gym, the banners for the basketball tourney, and I could see tonight. I felt the cool surface of my favorite tool, my weapon. Adam was going to be there tonight. Adam, the person who ruined everything for me. He started it out in second grade, he called me a piggy, a loser, and soon everyone called me Tommy Taint. They said it so much they forgot who I was, and somewhere along the way I couldn't remember my own name.

Today I know I am Tommy. I am Tommy Leigh Tate.

And after tonight, they'll never forget it again.

Lynne turned over the page and frantically skipped to her son's final entry. "Oh, God!" She whispered, "please, Tommy. No!"

Tommy Tate The Black Journal 2/19

I committed suicide last night. I have seen the life in front of me and it is one I do not wish to live. I was just not meant for this life.

Mom I'm sorry for what I did. I'm sorry I was the monster they always said I was. I'm sorry you wasted your time on a piss stain like me.

I am sorry to everyone who believed ~~I was worth a shi~~ in me. I just don't belong here. I am not meant for this life.

Tommy Leigh Tate

Mascara-cloaked tears ran down her face and splashed against the laminate floor. A passing train roared in the distance; it shook the trailer and echoed in Lynne's ears. Crushing the note in her palm, Lynne released a guttural, throat-tearing scream. "Tommy, I'm sorry. I'm so sorry!"

The sound of a train whirling through the trailer, Lynne collapsed against the table and cried out through the night. "Please come home, Tommy."

"Come home."

Chapter 1: *Song of I*

A tattered white blanket concealed Tommy's cramped-up figure. It covered him like a haphazard body bag, the exception being his light olive left hand, which laid out on the exposed stuffing on his mattress. A black cat roosted on top of the boy, and its yellow eyes glowed in the darkness.

A cinderblock-sized alarm clock sat on his headboard, and when it hit the top of the hour, it released a bloodcurdling screech.

The cat scurried from the room, but the boy did not stir. The alarm wailed until beams of sunlight glistened through the window.

Throwing off his blanket in protest, the boy opened his eyes and hit the top of his alarm. He then whipped his head toward the door; loud stomps were approaching his bedroom. Bewildered, the boy watched his mother shove open the door with a cup of icy water in her grasp.

The boy screamed, "No! I'm up, I'm—"

But it was too late. The mom flung the water and showered him in the face. "You're sure up now, Tommy! Your freakin' alarm rang for 28 minutes."

"You didn't have to keep time," Tommy said, rubbing his eyes.

Giving his mother the cold shoulder, Tommy rolled out of bed and walked out of his room. Running his hands over his plump belly, Tommy stepped into the laundry area.

The boy opened the dryer and gasped. There was nothing inside.

"Crap." Tommy breathed. He normally would have no problem re-wearing his clothes for a week or two, but his clothes were in bad need of a wash. He lifted his desert-dry jeans up from the washer, revealing a purple stain in their crotch.

"Freakin' jelly donut," Tommy yelled.

Running back to his bedroom, Tommy searched for clothes in a panic. He crammed a meaty arm between his wall and his mattress and extracted a pair of green gym shorts that he forced up his legs. Taking a breath, Tommy looked to the floor and knocked off a crusty doughnut from the top of a white T-shirt. The boy lifted the T-shirt, closed his eyes, and took a sniff.

"It could be worse," he thought in defeat.

Throwing on his shirt, the boy tripped over his black cat and collided into his wooden desk. He yelled in anger — the cat mewled its displeasure — and Tommy threw open the bedroom door.

He checked the time. "Four minutes. *Crap.*"

Fleeing the scents of cat pee and cigarettes, Tommy leapt from the steps of his single wide trailer.

Breaking into a sprint, the boy's sandals slapped against the gravel road. A knife slid into Tommy's lungs when he made it to his trailer park's paved road, and by that time his heaving could be heard through the neighborhood. Sweat burst from Tommy's brow and burned his eyes like acid. Seeing his bus driving away, the boy unleashed a high-pitched scream.

"Wait!!!"

The bus squealed to a stop beside the Manchester highway. Feeling like an Olympic champion, Tommy thrust his arms in the air and watched the bus door open. About to yell out a thank you, Tommy froze when he stepped inside the bus. The driver's thick, tattooed arms trembled as the boy walked up the staircase, and his classmates looked at him in a petrified silence. In an instant, the events of the last year crashed into Tommy's mind.

With the craziness of the morning, Tommy had forgotten. If only for a moment.

Chapter 2: ***The Terror from Kind Pines***

Cullen Armstrong resisted applause. Cullen was the 6'6 center of the Latimer basketball team. Opposing players spoke of his dominating presence in the paint and, despite his inability to dunk, often debated over whether Cullen could make it to the pros. Cullen didn't see a future for himself in basketball after high school, but he *was* working on the dunking.

Lesser known to opposing players were Cullen's tattoos, all of which were forcibly concealed by Latimer High School policies. Elaborate, carved out letters on his right shoulder bore the message of "Free Within Ourselves," while "Luke 10:25-37" stood out on his left. He stretched his arms out and looked at the ink on his rich Black skin tone. He heard his mom's voice. "You have your summer glow, Cullen." He smiled. In every other class he wore a white jacket to cover them up, but he didn't here. Mr. Austin wasn't that way.

Cullen had recently won the privilege of being Mr. Austin's assistant through the school year. The senior was hand-picked from his reputation alone and had the dual benefit of taking Mr. Austin's art class while assisting the teacher.

Amongst all the awkwardness that came with the first day of school, Cullen had the pleasure of witnessing Tommy Tate's Academy Award worthy performance. Five minutes before the first day began (and the school's cringe-fest opening assembly), Tommy informed Mr. Austin that he had entered Advanced Art by mistake and was just unsure if he could balance the workload of the course with his present "obligations." Tommy even added that the class was under "strong consideration" of being added to his senior schedule for next year. Cullen was confident that Tommy had guaranteed the art teacher's signature and was more than ready to add in a vote of confidence if Mr. Austin asked for his opinion.

Mr. Austin looked over Tommy's transfer form and narrowed his eyes. Mr. Austin had a notable summer tan, brunette hair and beard, a stocky figure, and dressed in a button-up shirt with a "Starry Night" tie. Cullen grinned. Mr. Austin was known to wear a different art related tie each day.

Mr. Austin stood from his chair, and Cullen guessed he was just under six feet tall. The teacher looked at Tommy. "If I give you a Dr. Pepper, will you try the class for a day?"

The question bewildered both students.

"Uh...what?" Tommy asked.

"If I give you a Dr. Pepper, will you stay here for today?"

The school policy over controlled substances (including sugar) seemed to weigh on Tommy's mind. "Are you even allowed to give that to me?"

Mr. Austin facetiously inspected his surroundings. "Well, Cullen here took a blood oath to take my secrets to the grave—"

"There was a ceremony and everything," Cullen added.

"— so if you don't tell, we certainly won't either."

"Let me get this straight," Tommy said. "I only have to stay in here for one day if I take the Dr. Pepper?"

"Look, as much as I love the sweet, gentle burn of a Dr. Pepper, I have not had soda for the past six years. The only reason I have this one is because my student teacher left it here last May, and because Cullen is dieting for some kind of team he's playing on. It's either yours or in the trash."

Tommy considered. “I mean, I like drawing comic books okay. I just don’t know if I want to take this class, you know?”

Mr. Austin smiled. “*You* get to design this class. In the first week, I’ll want you to reflect on what you want to get from it. Whether it’s working on comic books, digital design, clay, oil-based paints - it’s up to you.”

Tommy blurted, “What if I want an easy A?”

Cullen smirked. Usually Cullen might chuckle at a comment like this, but this was Mr. Austin’s kingdom, and Cullen’s response was silence.

“You have a buffet of options in front of you. Don’t eat the napkins,” Mr. Austin said.

Cullen laughed at this one. It was a bad moment for Tommy, and Cullen doubted he’d see the kid after today.

Tommy shrugged and looked at the far wall in the classroom. The word “Prizes” was written out on a golden banner. “What’s that all about?”

Mr. Austin beamed. “It’s a wall for students who turn in work that stands out, is creative, or is just weird.”

“Oh, that’s cringe.”

Mr. Austin seemed to agree. “Yeah, I wouldn’t expect someone wanting an Easy A to get into it. I guess I can throw the Dr. Pepper away then?"

Tommy paused for a moment before looking up at his instructor. “Is it in a can or a bottle?”

30 seconds later, Cullen watched Tommy chug the can of Dr. Pepper at warp speed before releasing an earthquake of a belch.

The bell rang, and Mr. Austin turned to Tommy.

“I'm happy you’re trying this class,” Mr. Austin said, his expression warm.

Tommy shrugged. “I’ll have my withdrawal forms tomorrow morning. Thanks for the Dr. Pepper.”

After watching Tommy walk away to the assembly, Cullen turned to Mr. Austin, and the teacher smiled. "He'll be back. Keep an eye out for him, will ya?"

Cullen stepped into the hallway and saw a piece of paper lying on the scuffed up, tiled floor. Bending down, he unrolled the paper.

	8/15 First Semester Schedule for Thomas Tate	Room
-	Block One - Tuesdays & Thursdays	
1	Advanced Art I - Austin	209
2	Junior English - Roberts	218
H	Homeroom- Perez (Last Lunch)	115
3	Astronomy - Gordon	114
-	Block Two - Wednesdays and Fridays	-------
4	Computer Applications - Spalding	131
5	Speech - Andrews	112
6	Modern History - Chantal (Last Lunch)	214
7	Algebra II - Demko	JW-B

Cullen wasn't surprised to find this here. Tommy was known to carry his mountain of school stuff in his arms every day in addition to his bag. Cullen glanced down the hallway and saw Tommy's tumbleweed of hair heading towards the gym.

Cullen high tailed it after Tommy and stepped through the mass of people in the lobby. A head taller than most of his classmates, Cullen watched Tommy and a rush of students make their way to the assembly like salmon in a grizzly-filled creek.

Stepping in the gym, Cullen yelled out, "Tommy!"

Tommy flipped around with his fists up. "What?"

Cullen felt a tap on his shoulder. Adam Augustine, brown haired, and just a couple of inches shorter than Cullen, was standing behind him. "What's up, bro?"

Cullen saw Rosi Williams standing beside Adam. She was maybe 5'5, had lily white skin and flowing brunette hair. Rosi brought Cullen in for a hug. "Ready for this awful year?"

"Yeah, let's get it over with."

Adam breathed. "Wanna sit with us?"

"Sure."

Cullen turned around to hand Tommy his schedule, but when he looked, Tommy was gone.

—

Mia Fernandez sat in solitude in the Latimer courtyard. Mia had a golden-Brown complexion and striking black eyebrows, one of which was raised up as she looked over her agenda.

Out behind the high school, the courtyard was surrounded by a wooden fence, and a great oak tree towered in its center. This morning, a hot red sun peeked over the horizon, splashing a scarlet glaze over the dew strewn grass. Sitting under the protective shade of the tree, Mia sketched a makeshift pirate ship on her agenda.

Yurika Panthy entered the courtyard. Yurika was slightly chubby, bespectacled, and had russet Brown skin. Mia also thought Yurika -- or as she called her, Yuki -- was blessed with curly black hair that ran to her waist. Yurika called to her best friend, "I thought I'd find you here!"

Mia held up her phone. "I texted you about it, dork."

"My phone's a little dead at the moment."

"I should have guessed."

Yurika sat across from Mia. "Ready for this terrible assembly?"

Mia sighed. "No, but at least it gets better from here, right?"

Yurika's brow furrowed. "What do you mean?"

Mia replied, "Well, we're now juniors, so we should be getting more freedom in STUCO."

Yurika released a full-bellied laugh. "More freedom? You really think Mr. Stallard is going to give us more freedom?"

Mia put a dandelion bookmark in her itinerary. "I'm hopeful, Yuki," she said, getting to her feet.

Yurika smiled. "There's your first problem. We go to LHS, remember? There's no hope for us here."

Mia shook her head and stepped towards the building. "Now you're just being dramatic."

Yurika whistled. "We'll see if you're still saying that after the assembly."

Mia pushed through the back doors of the building. "It'll be terrible, but at least our parts are painless. We don't have to do the skit, thank God."

Yurika shook her head. "I wish I had your optimism."

They stepped into the fieldhouse. Mia saw about half of the STUCO crew waiting for them. Before she could say anything, Mr. Stallard stepped through the crew and addressed her. Mr. Stallard was short and had white-pinkish skin and baby blue eyes that were oxymoronic to his character. He was equipped with a thin smile and large biceps that always seemed to be on display.

Mr. Stallard spoke in a cool, clear voice. "Ms. Fernandez and Ms. Panthy. You're both late."

Mia froze. A massive lump instantly engorged in her throat.

Yurika was fearless. "We're actually two minutes early," she said, her voice breezy.

Mr. Stallard smiled. Mia was almost afraid of his smiles. They made his lips carve into his face in a way that made him look unnatural. "Anything less than 5 minutes early is late. Now, let's go over our plan."

Yurika turned to Mia and mouthed, "Dramatic."

Looking to her feet, Mia prepared for their rehearsal.

—

Rosi Williams reclined in the maroon V.I.P section in Latimer High's John Wagner Fieldhouse. Rosi sat around the basketball team, along with everyone else who could fit themselves here. Bulky football players, several of the school's cheerleaders and select student council members crammed the V.I.P. section of the school's bleachers. The V.I.P section was in the first three rows of the fieldhouse, and they were for anyone in town who bought a season pass to see the school's basketball games.

During the school assembly, the section packed like sardines in an undersized container. The students at the corners of the VIP rows inched toward the starters from last year's basketball team, four of whom were spread out in the center row.

Adam whispered to Rosi, "Place looks great, huh?"

Rosi smiled. "Sure does, babe."

The gym's renovations had been paid in full by last year's district bond issue and sprouted off new lights from its ceiling. Each covered in a wire case, the lights shed an angelic spotlight to the banner at the far wall of the gym. Written in golden letters, the boys basketball team's third place triumph at state hung as an emblem to last year's achievements.

Rosi tapped Adam on the shoulder. "This year you're winning it all, right?"

Adam nodded. "That, and I'm taking my dad's point record."

"It's destiny."

Another basketball player named Brian shouted behind Rosi. "Hell yeah it is!"

Brian had khaki-white skin and black hair that was shaved close at the sides. Brian's hairline was slightly too narrow for his forehead, which Rosi thought split out like the top of a potato, and he had eyes too narrowly together for the size of his face. She didn't like Brian, but she could tolerate him.

Life was exciting here. Before the assembly started everyone in this section shared stories about their summer. Each party, bonfire and escape only grew in their stakes and gravitas, and the longer everyone shared their stories, the more Rosi felt at home.

Feedback screamed through Principal Elmer's microphone and shocked Rosi's attention. She had forgotten there was an assembly going on here.

Standing beside Elmer, Assistant Principal Mr. Stallard whispered something to the head principal, causing Elmer to smile.

Rosi looked to the gym floor. Principal Jeff Elmer stood over 6'5 and was one double cheeseburger away from 300 pounds. His imposing size was leveled out by a world class smile and light blue suits, which complemented his Black complexion.

Principal Elmer worked the crowd. "Are we having a good morning so far?"

"...yesh," the crowd answered. They had the excitement of cold mashed potatoes.

Elmer gave it another go. "Oh come on, you can do better than that! Let's try again."

Rosi smirked. As it turned out, the crowd could *not* do better than that.

Elmer raised his arms at the 800 or so students in the student body who responded with a dead-end enthusiasm. "Well, as I was saying," Elmer muttered, "it all goes back to the three A's: Academics, Atha'letics, and Academics—" Elmer caught himself. "Urm — Activities!"

Adam whispered to Rosi, "He's going to talk about us."

Elmer looked to the V.I.P section. "Erm, I don't know about you guys, but I believe that we have some 'unfinished business' in boys' basketball this year."

At this, the V.I.P section screamed with surprising life. Several basketball players stood up and released wolf whistles to the principal.

As Elmer continued, Rosi felt her side get elbowed by Brian Miller. She turned to Brian. "What?!"

Brian murmured, "You see Tommy Taint?"

Rosi felt her heart stop. That monster was almost expelled last year, and everyone said he had dropped out. She exhaled. "What?! You mean he's here?"

Brian nodded. "Yep. Saw his plumber's crack in the hallway."

Adam snorted. "Yeah, no one's mistaking that."

Rosi gnashed her teeth. "I hate that we have to go to school with kids like that." She turned to Adam. "Are you nervous? After everything he did to you last year?"

Adam swallowed. "Eh, I'll be fine. Got enough to worry about with hoops."

Rosi breathed. "Adam… C'mon. Don't do that. That kid is dangerous."

Brian spoke. "Adam isn't a woman about things like this. He'll be fine." He gestured behind him. "He's sitting over there, by the way. I might find him before the next class. We'll see if I can get him suspended again."

Rosi looked over her shoulder and, sure enough, there he was. He had long hair that covered up his face, a tattered T-shirt, and was someone who never should have been allowed back.

Adam sneered. "I don't know. With any luck we'll have a class together."

Cullen spoke for the first time in the conversation. "Why'd you want that?"

Adam was defensive. "Why not?"

Cullen continued, "All I'm saying is that y'all have been saying this kid might murder you since last April. What's the point of provoking him if you feel that way?"

Rosi looked at Adam. Cullen had a point. Adam thought it over for a moment and answered with his cool and confident voice.

"Because," Adam said, "it's fun."

Rosi snorted. He wasn't wrong. Watching Tommy's face redden and shrivel up like a toad was pretty entertaining. She turned around and looked at Tommy sitting alone under the flickering light of the bleachers. Tommy looked down and met her eyes, causing her heart to skip a beat. Seeing him again aroused an unmistakable fear inside her. He *was* dangerous. Cullen wasn't wrong to ask that question, and after last year, Tommy shouldn't be here at all.

Rosi tried to keep her voice level. "So why did he come back?"

For the first time all day, the V.I.P section was silent.

—

The second time Tommy woke up this morning came three fourths of the way through the school's opening assembly. Assistant Principal Stallard had started leading the school chant, causing Tommy to jolt awake. Rousing from dreams of soft skin and silky sheets, Tommy adjusted to his underwhelming surroundings.

The student body sang the school's fight song, the lyrics of which hung on the other side of the gym. Students and parents who attended basketball games were encouraged to shout the lyrics during every event. The banner in the gym hung below the windows of a darkened room, which Tommy recognized as the second story annex. Tommy wished he could be suffering through Latimer's fight song in the privacy of that room.

As the students made it through each line of the song, Tommy felt it drain him with each new line. Holding his breath, he listened as they sang the final words.

"To enemies of LHS, beware!"

Principal Stallard nodded his head in approval. "Inspiring! Thank you all." Stallard handed the microphone back to Principal Elmer, who took it with a hearty laugh.

"We have one more rule, and it's an important one. Remember, the earbuds are not your buds from 8:30-3:30 each day."

At this, Tommy saw STUCO member Mia Fernandez gliding through the gym floor with earbuds in her ears. The boy's heart fluttered; he always thought Mia was beautiful. She had curly black hair and braces. Tommy's mind wandered: "And the braces somehow made her prettier."

Mia always seemed to have a dandelion, and even now she had one in the book inside her grasp. Watching her slender figure stride cheerfully through the field house, Tommy let his daydreams carry him away.

Tommy liked Mia because she always smiled at him in the hallways, and these were not the nervous, sort of obligatory smiles that some spared to him. Mia's smiles felt real.

Principal Elmer brought the assembly to a close. "And if those rules are followed, we're going to have a great year."

The student body clapped a lifeless round.

Allowing the applause to subside, Elmer looked up to the audience. "And now, without further ado," Elmer said, casting a look at Stallard, "you...are…dismiiiiss--"

At that moment, Elmer was cut off by a song blasting through the speakers.

"Boooooooooom!!!!" the song blared.

An avalanche of wild screams swept down from the audience. Tommy recognized the beginning of "Thrash It," a song that shot to number one on Billboard's Hot Tracks his freshman year.

Elmer beckoned the crowd. "We're going to need some teachers to join us!"

Tommy snorted. They were going to do the dance. It was one thing to play the song, but "thrashing it" had become viral from the song's music video and choreography at a Lawn and Garden section of a hardware store. It was a dance that few mastered and many more butchered.

A large number of teachers joined the class officers and began to "thrash it." The student body cheering, Tommy watched the teachers squirm around like suffocating eels.

Tommy pointed up to the speakers. "Wait for it," he said to himself.

"Booooooooom!!!!

Thrash it, whip it, open up the spout,

Thrash it, pull it back, smoke it on the rack.

Booooooooom!!!!!"

Tommy had a joyous grin. He knew they would miss the radio edit.

Elmer spoke. "Let today be an example of the commitment our staff has to LHS."

The suggestive lyrics of "Thrash It" stuck in his mind, Tommy thought he'd pass.

A stern female voice rang out over the intercom. "All students, please report to your first hour classes. All students, please report to your first hour classes."

Keeping an eye on the V.I.P. section of the bleachers, Tommy plotted a course through the gym. Putting his head down, Tommy followed the exodus of students into the hallway.

—

Mr. Stallard, his eyes keen, saw Tommy's scarecrow-like hair drift down the bleachers. Stallard's expression inscrutable, the assistant principal watched Tommy make his way through the gym and disappear inside the school.

Chapter 3: *Bill's Beastin' Limonada*

Cocaine Thayne was walking. Sporting his greasy, long brown hair and his trademarked, open-mouthed smile, Thayne spat on the side of the Manchester Highway.

Tommy watched his cousin walk in from the bus stop on the outskirts of Kind Pines, the mobile home park where Tommy grew up. Thayne and his mom lived in a double wide trailer in the Friendly Acres mobile home area, but it was known as "Felony Acres," Tommy looked to Thayne. It was just like how his cousin was only known as "Cocaine Thayne." It would feel weird calling him something else.

Trudging along the highway's shoulder, several cars honked angrily at Thayne as they wheeled past. Thayne didn't glance at the passing vehicles. He dressed in a stained white tank-top, sagging jeans, and flip-flops that slapped against the side of the road. Thayne had noticeable, bulging red sunburns on his normally beige skin that was exposed outside his tank top. Straight, puffed-out scars stood out on Thayne's arms like ancient hieroglyphs, reminding Tommy of a past that was not so far away. Thayne had a scraggly beard that had such an uneven texture that it reminded Tommy of burnt toast.

Thayne ran across the highway and gave his cousin a hug. "What's good, cuz?!"

"Nothin'. Just had the worst first day of school ever."

Thayne pulled out a lukewarm can of *Darn Good Cola* and gave it to Tommy. "School sucks, cousin. See if this'll help."

Smiling, Tommy opened the can and watched the fizz explode all over his hand. Laughing, he stuck his mouth on the top and gargled down the sugary discount soda.

—

Tommy and Thayne walked through Tommy's single-wide trailer and watched Tommy's mom, Lynne Tate, plug in her George Foreman grill.

Lynne yelled to her son, "How was the first day?"

"Refried ass," Tommy said as he grabbed a ho-ho from the cabinet. "Why'd you make me go back?"

"Think I want you here, sittin' on your lazy butt all day?"

Tommy rolled his eyes. "Love you too, Lynne."

"Quit your whining. You're only 3 months from your GED."

Lynne Tate was tall, slender, and had streaming black hair which ran down to her waist. The only similarity Lynne shared with her son was the oversized nose on their faces.

Tommy collapsed onto the living room's rose-embroidered couch. His mother had done well to salvage the thing, as it was now the most comfortable place in the house. Outside of the stains on the cushions and the cigarette burns on the armrests, the couch was in perfect condition.

Tommy looked at the faded-blue withdrawal form in his hands. Grabbing a pen, Tommy signed his name but paused as he was writing out "Advanced Art".

Tommy replayed Mr. Austin's comment. "I wouldn't expect someone wanting an Easy A to get into it."

The boy's mind raced. "What the hell did he mean? I could get something on his prizes wall without trying. He's never even seen my comics before."

Tommy smirked. This was what Mr. Austin wanted. He wanted Tommy to care -- to try -- and Tommy wasn't going to take the bait.

Tommy and Thayne dove into Tommy's mess of a closet and started unearthing hundreds of Tommy's comic books. Tommy promised that Thayne would get a burger for his trouble (he would have anyway), but one of the glorious aspects of his cousin was how he was always up for anything.

By the time they had dumped hundreds of Tommy's comics in the living room, Tommy looked up to see his mother narrow her eyes.

She pointed a spatula toward the sketchpad in Tommy's hands. "What's that for?"

"I need it for some class I'm in."

"And *those* are gonna help you write it?" Lynne asked, referring to the comics.

"Yeah," Tommy said. "They will."

"Whatever you say. Burgers are almost done."

"Awesome," Tommy said, outlining a person on his sketchpad.

Tommy always started with the cover. The best comics had covers that drew him in like an insect to a light. When his mother used to work as a server, Tommy would spend her shifts peeling through comics at the bookstore across from the restaurant. His love for comics fascinated one of his Mom's ex-boyfriends, so much so that the man had given Tommy dozens of his old comics for his 12th birthday. Tommy wondered if that man knew how important that gift was, or if he even remembered it at all.

Thayne jumped on the couch and started looking through TV shows. "So, Tommy, what're you doin' all this for anyway?"

Tommy was terse. "I already explained it to my mom. This teacher is a tool."

"I smell what you're steppin' in, but why are you *actually* workin' on it?"

Tommy saw his mom crane her neck from the kitchen and decided to play it straight with his answer. "He told me I couldn't draw. So, I'm turning in a comic book that will piss him off."

"Ha! Nice!"

Tommy continued, "He said I wouldn't be into drawin' anything since I wanted an 'easy A.'"

"Well, screw that tool," Thayne said, extracting a pack of cigarettes from his pocket.

"He's gonna lose it when he sees this. I'm gonna knock his dick in the dirt."

"Why do you care what he thinks? I thought you was gettin' your GED this year."

Tommy was quiet.

Thayne pointed his unlit cigarette toward Tommy. "Here's what you do, since you're gonna be outta there in a few months anyway. You should dump all over his assignment and not do a damn thing. Uppity douches like him hate that more than anything."

"This one's different."

"Believe me, he ain't. He'll hate you if you don't try. That's why this plan is prime. You're gonna bounce in a coupl'a months, so you may as well *enjoy* yourself before you go. He can give you all the Fs he wants, but there ain't nothin' he can do if you don't try." Thayne lit his cigarette. "See cuz, my life woulda been much better if I'd learned that simple thing. I wish I could go back to high school for just one day, 'cause I'd have that place in anarchy."

Tommy grinned. He loved his cousin's tirades.

Thayne hit Tommy on the arm. "But knowin' your pansy ass, you ain't gonna do any of that."

"Eh. I just want to show him that I *could* do it if I wanted to. But on the last day we can switch classes. I'm gonna withdraw."

Taking a draw from his cigarette, Thayne coughed. "That's cold, bro, but that's what I'm talkin' about, Tommy!"

Tommy continued, "I'm tellin' you, had Rock sold me the Goldsmobile, I would have been out of LHS last year."

"Well, he's a little hard to get a hold of right now."

Lynne placed burgers in front of the boys. "Here you are."

"Yes!" Thayne blurted, pressing his cigarette into the arm of the couch.

Lynne snapped, "What the hell, Thayne!?"

"My bad, Lynne. I just keep forgettin' the couch ain't mine anymore."

"It never was *yours*, Thayne!"

"Well, my ma sure didn't mind it!"

Tommy pressed forward. "I know Rock's 'hard to get a hold of,' but Mom said he kept upping the price even before his 'situation.'"

"Well, he likes his ol' car, Tommy. He has an emotional attachment to the thing."

"It has a broken window and had ants in it."

"I know, and it kills him to see it like that." Thayne choked down a cinderblock of food. "Truth be told, you might be outta luck. Rock was bein' kind of a prick to me before he got time."

Tommy tried to sound impartial. "So why did you even hang with him?" Tommy did not feel sorry for Rock. Caught tossing a stolen car battery through the window of *Buzzard's Liquor* (for a single pack of Bill's Beastin' Limonada), Rock had been incarcerated for most of the summer. Thayne himself was harmless, but his cousin's tendency to partner with Rock Rustin had never sat well with Tommy. Everyone seemed to know Rock around town. He was a dealer, and Tommy hated how he always seemed to be lurking around Thayne. Rock was tall, skinny, and always goaded Tommy for a fight.

Thayne responded, "I know you have no love for him, cuz, but me 'n Rock go back a long way. Don't worry, I'll wet his whistle if he keeps it up."

"Wet his whistle?"

"Oh, yeah. I'll wet his whistle for sure."

Lynne entered the living room. "That's not what that means, dummy." Finally holding a burger of her own, Lynne sunk into her chair and switched the show.

As Thayne and Lynne wrestled over bad TV shows, Tommy spent the evening doing a sketch of the cover and writing out the text to his comic on a scratch pad on the coffee table. Thayne departed by the time he completed the layouts on what would be all three pages of the comic (and snacked on a galaxy brownie and two ho-ho's), and by the time Tommy designed the comic's inside page, his mother was standing by the door.

"Going somewhere?" Tommy asked, trying to sound uninterested.

"Out."

A car horn blared from beyond the trailer.

Lynne opened the door. "Time to go. There's extra hamburger in the freezer and ramen in the cabinet. I'll be back tomorrow morning."

Tommy heard an engine rev the moment she stepped onto the porch. Tossing his binder to his side, Tommy rushed to the window and peeked outside.

A '74 Ford Maverick sat in front of the trailer. A man with Ray-Ban shades and an auburn porn 'stache sat in the driver's seat and gave the horn a couple extra honks as Lynne approached.

Tommy sighed. "Great."

Turning back, Tommy reclaimed his seat. He had a comic to finish. He thought of his art class. "This is gonna knock their dicks in the dirt."

Chapter 4: ***Keep Your Eyes Peeled***

Jay Stallard poured coffee into a crimson LHS thermos with the precision of a chemist. Emptying the mug, Jay pushed it toward the end of the table and checked his watch. It was 6:00 A.M. He was sitting across the table at the North College Drive-In from a man by the name of Frances Bradford who went by "Duke." Jay first met him on the Baldridge city council, and they made it a tradition to meet here before their monthly meetings. Duke was broad shouldered with salt-and-pepper stubble and a sunglasses tan over his pale face, a tan that was a summer tradition.

A young server made her way to them from across the restaurant.

On cue, Duke's voice cracked the air like a hot whip. "I have put two dollars on the table. If my steak is not medium-well, these dollars will go back inside my wallet. If my eggs are not over-easy, these dollars will go back inside my wallet, and if my salad does not come out before my meal, these dollars— well, you get the picture."

Kit Shields looked Duke over with tired eyes. "Any dressing for your salad?"

"Ranch. And save yourself a trip and bring out extra."

Kit looked to the table's other occupant.

Jay Stallard pointed to his thermos. "Just coffee."

"Beautiful," Kit muttered, fleeing the scene.

Duke wasted no time. "Did you get the notes for Tuesday's council meeting?"

Stallard nodded. "What were your thoughts on the new ordinance?"

"Three pets per house? Thinking a yea."

"Same. There's no need for any more. Not inside city limits."

"Good," Duke bellowed. "That gives us two votes, and I know Kyle and Bruce will follow our lead."

A red-bearded manager put a salad plate in front of Duke. "Here you are, sir."

"Thanks," Duke said, not looking at the plate. "That Turner woman will be up in arms."

"Of course she will. She's a nut. She probably has a hundred cats in that hellhole of hers."

"Son of a gun," Duke spat. "Beardy forgot my ranch. Waitress!" Duke yelled, spotting Kit across the way.

Cut off from taking an order at another table, Kit looked over in surprise.

Duke snapped his fingers. "Ranch, por favor!"

Kit gave Duke a distracted nod.

"Jesus," Duke said, slipping a dollar into his wallet. "How about a little acknowledgement?"

"I told you, we should only come here on Sundays."

Duke looked over the customers around them. "Is that the only time this place isn't filled by hipsters and douchebags?"

Stallard sneered. "Monday mornings have their 'start the week off right' promotion; any student who comes to breakfast with a North College ID gets a discount."

Duke scoffed. "Jesus, no wonder it's so full. Kids these days think they deserve a medal for waking up on time."

Kit brought a bowl of ranch over to the table. "Sorry about that, sir. My manager forgot you liked ranch."

"Don't worry about it, Kit," Duke said, reading the girl's name tag. "Say, help my friend Jay and I settle something. You remember Jay, right?"

Kit smiled. "Of course, he was one of my principals for four years."

Duke gestured toward Jay. "See, I told you she remembered. Could we have 30 seconds of your time?"

Stealing a glance at her section, which was now full, Kit nodded nervously. "Okay."

"What do you think of Sunday mornings?"

Kit's lips tightened. "They sort of wear me down. I close the drive-in side down on Saturday and the turnaround can be tiring."

Stallard cleared his throat. "Kit, if I left you a ten-dollar tip, would you give us an honest answer?"

There had been a humor and understanding in his voice, leading Kit to smile. "If I gave an honest answer, I don't know if you'd leave me a ten-dollar tip."

Kit had been expecting laughter, but the cold smile on Jay Stallard's face caused the girl to shudder.

Stallard smirked. "Don't worry, I'd never leave you a ten-dollar tip."

Duke crumpled up the remaining dollar on the table. "Looks like you lost out on this one, sweetie."

Looking at the two in disbelief, Kit limped away.

Duke looked over to Jay. "You ever worry these kids will mess with your food?"

"It's why I order coffee. I don't put anything past this generation."

"Speaking of this generation, I heard the maniac decided to return to Latimer."

Stallard grimaced. "It surprised us all."

"God dang, what a shame."

"I'm keeping an eye on him," Stallard reassured.

"Well, you better keep two. He should have never been a Latimer kid to begin with. It's ridiculous his trailer park was zoned in our school district."

"You're preaching to the choir there."

Duke gritted his teeth. "The way your superiors swept what he did under the rug is making me think about puttin' my grandkids in the new charter school. That boy is nothing but a danger to the rest of the students."

"Don't worry. He won't last long."

Bradford shook his head. "Good."

—

Mr. Stallard stood with his red thermos on the second floor of Latimer High School across from a hallway clock that read 8:00 A.M. Mr. Stallard's eyes homed in on Tommy Tate, and he watched the student make his way toward Advanced Art with a clump of papers in his hand.

His movements smooth as a viper, Mr. Stallard stepped in front of Tommy between the hallway and the door of Mr. Austin's classroom. Tommy gave him a look of horror before gluing his eyes to the floor, and Mr. Stallard spoke in a cool, high pitched voice. "What are you holding there, Thomas? Start journaling again?"

Without looking at Mr. Stallard, Tommy muttered, "It's a comic book."

Mr. Stallard shook his head and smiled. "Thomas, you know better. Comic books are not taken inside classrooms if they aren't meant for school."

An acidic, ammonia-like smell wafted from Tommy and stung Mr. Stallard's nostrils. Without reacting, Mr. Stallard stood over Tommy.

Tommy kept his eyes on his feet and whispered, "It is for school, Mr.-"

Mr. Stallard cut him off. "Thomas, can you look at me when you're speaking to me?"

As he had many times, Mr. Stallard watched Tommy's head and shoulders shake before he mustered the ability to look him in the eyes. Tommy breathed in and repeated, "It is for school," before darting into Mr. Austin's room.

Mr. Stallard stood at the doorway and watched Tommy walk to Mr. Austin's "turn-in" folder and dump off his comic there. Stallard's narrowed eyes followed Tommy to his desk. The boy took off his backpack, revealing a deep, yellow stain on the back of his white shirt. His expression inscrutable, Stallard took a drink of his coffee and retreated in the hallways.

—

Mr. Stallard looked at the massive analog clock sitting beside the red and gold Latimer Lion in the John Wagner Fieldhouse. The banner sat above the school's trophy case, where Mr. Stallard could see first year teacher Matt Demko. Demko stood at an even six feet, with spiked red hair complete with a red goatee. Stallard recalled that he was known as "The Irishman" when he was a senior here. Mr. Stallard noticed that Demko's dress shirt was slightly untucked from his jeans and his hair was drenched in sweat. The time read 2:15. Stallard was just in time. He approached Demko and clocked his young colleague looking at a record on the football side of the record case.

<u>Most Passing Yards in a Single Game:</u> Matthew Demko 246

Mr. Stallard spoke. "Lost in the memories?"

Demko jumped. "I didn't hear you come in."

Stallard reassured his colleague. "For a school that's not known for football, that's a pretty impressive record."

"Thanks!"

Stallard put a hand on Demko. "I won't tell anyone that we lost that game by 35 points. How many interceptions did you throw? Three?"

Demko swallowed. "Four."

Stallard patted Demko's shoulder. "Don't worry, your secret's safe with me. How're things in the cave?"

Stallard noticed Demko grimace. "The cave" was an old, narrow classroom that was located through a door of the gym. Lacking fancy amenities such as air conditioning and wall outlets, the room had multiple power strips and a noisy window unit that blew lukewarm air on the students. This was the first year someone had to teach a general education class from the cave, and Demko drew the short straw.

"It's kinda weird to be so far from the math department, but it isn't so bad."

Stallard smiled. "You won't be saying that after Coach Hardcastle starts dodgeball."

Demko shuddered. "Well, we'll see."

Stallard looked over his shoulder and then lowered his voice to a whisper. "Has anyone talked to you about Thomas Tate?"

"Well, I heard about last year —"

"Have you read the letter?"

"Is it that bad?"

Stallard shrugged. "It's a smart thing to read if you have him."

"If Tommy's dangerous, then why is he back here?"

Stallard grimaced. "Not because of me, I promise you. I need you to keep an eye on things. Not only do you have Tommy, you have the student he's believed to have threatened last year."

Demko was stunned. "Wait. What? Who?"

"Adam Augustine."

Demko gestured towards the wall. "Adam Augustine? The kid with hemophilia who's setting all these basketball records?"

"That's the one."

Mr. Demko seemed outraged. "Why is he even in a class with him?"

Stallard shook his head. "I've offered to get him out twice, but Adam's refused."

A tall, tan, tawny-haired high schooler stepped into the gym. The student carried bright green eyes that seemed to peer inside everyone he spoke to.

Mr. Stallard held out his arms. "Speak of the devil, how was the summer, Adam?"

The student gave Stallard a smile and took his hand. "I was at open gym so much it felt like I never left."

Mr. Stallard probed into Adam. "I hope you found time for the lake. I remember you were hoping to go with the folks?"

Adam was almost a foot taller than Mr. Stallard but tilted himself in a way that made it seem like he was face to face with his instructor. "Ah, I decided to hold off on the lake until we take state." Adam changed the subject. "So how was your summer, Mr. Stallard? Get that fort built for your nephews?"

Mr. Stallard beamed. "Sure did. I can show you the splinters to prove it. Adam, I'd like you to meet Mr. Demko. Mr. Demko, Adam."

Adam, standing a few inches taller than Mr. Demko, pointed at the record books. "Mr. Demko? No way you were the quarterback with that record up there."

"Guilty," Mr. Demko beamed.

Mr. Stallard turned to Mr. Demko. "Matt, is it okay if I borrow Adam a bit before class?"

"Of course!"

Mr. Stallard watched Demko walk toward the cave connected at the end of the gym. "Poor guy," Mr. Stallard thought, watching the first-year teacher slink into the cave.

Finding a corner of the gym, Mr. Stallard looked to Adam. "Be honest with me. Are you comfortable being in this class with Thomas?"

Adam shook off his teacher. "Absolutely."

"Are you sure? After everything last year?"

Adam put him at ease. “Mr. Stallard, I’m not gonna live in fear. Look, Tommy’s had a hard life, you know? I can’t hold that against him. With any luck, this class can be a fresh start for us.”

The bell rang throughout the Jim Wagner Fieldhouse, leading Mr. Stallard to sigh. “You’re a better man than I am, Adam. Get to class.”

Flashing his teacher a smile, Adam ran to his friend, Brian, who was waiting for him outside the cave. Mr. Stallard breathed. In many ways, Adam felt like the son he never had.

Chapter 5: ***Before the Last Breath***

Tommy's mind was racing as he walked into Math class. He still didn't know what to make of Mr. Austin. Part of him wanted to withdraw from art… and yet, he got 3rd place in the Doodlelympics today and a fun-size *Crunch* Bar to go along with it.

Tommy stepped into his math class and lifted up a hand. "Hi," he said.

His teacher, Mr. Demko, responded with a wordless nod.

"That was weird," Tommy thought. "Do I already have beef with this guy?"

Settling in the math room, the scent of cat pee wafted up to Tommy's nostrils. The boy thought to himself. "I've been around that smell so much that it's caught inside my nose."

He smelled his shirt. He forgot to do laundry again, and he knew this shirt was running out of re-wears. The bell rang, and feelings of anxiety began to churn in Tommy's mind. "Was it possible Demko once worked at the fair? Because it'd make sense if Demko didn't like me if he had to put up with me and Thayne. Mr. Demko did look kind of like one of the carneys." But Tommy couldn't help but think it was something more sinister. "He knows," Tommy thought. "He's a first-year teacher and he knows. God, what will I have to do to--"

Tommy's thoughts were interrupted by two loud voices that caromed from inside the hallway. His eyes wide open, Tommy watched Adam Augustine and Brian Miller filter into the classroom. For a moment, Tommy's eyes locked with Brian's. Brian was an annoyance to Tommy, but the real terror was in front of Brian, and that was Adam Augustine.

Rosi Williams yelled, "Way to be on time, Adam!"

Mr. Demko responded, "Give them a break. They're *basketball* players."

Laughter echoing from his peers, Adam took confident, deliberate paces to Rosi's desk. Dressed in a long sleeve red V-neck and dark jeans that matched Latimer's colors, Adam flipped his hair to the side.

Tommy passed a scorching glance at Rosi. He was jealous of the way she looked at Adam, the way she flirted with him -- everything.

Mr. Demko swiped the seating chart from the back of the classroom. "Adam," he began, "you are in the back center, and Brian... is right beside you."

SEATING ASSIGNMENTS LISTED BELOW

Tommy's eyes read, re-read, and fastened onto the bolded message on the whiteboard. He focused on them as if nothing were more important. The words kept him from *seeing* the students walking toward him, from *feeling* the backpack strap chafe against his arm, and from *hearing* the two people settle in the seats behind him.

Brian whispered out to Adam, "Awesome seats, broskey."

"I told you we were set."

Tommy could feel Adam's eyes on the back of his skull. He could even see the perfect smile on Adam's face and braced for the next words.

The glee in Adam's voice cleaved Tommy like a knife. "Hey, Tommy Taint."

That statement alone sent Rosi Williams into harsh, gouging laughter.

Tommy clenched his fists, leading his veins to burst out over his arms. He hated the laughter; he was unsure if anything cut him deeper.

Tommy took a breath and prepared for the next 90 minutes.

—

Tommy escaped into the hallways the moment math ended.

A soft voice halted the boy's footsteps.

"Hey, Tommy?"

Tommy whipped around and was stunned to see Rosi standing behind him. His heartbeat accelerating, Tommy felt his inhibitions slacken inside her ocean blue eyes.

Lines of students encircled the lobby around Tommy, and he conjured the bravery to respond. "Uh...Hi."

"I'm sorry about Adam and Brian," Rosi said. "They were awful to you today. They really were. I just wondered... could I ask you something?"

Tommy nodded.

"Do you have a puppy or a kitty?" Rosi asked, her voice gentle.

Old emotions kindling inside him, Tommy unleashed a wide, goofy smile without meaning to, revealing his crooked bottom set of teeth. "I have a cat. My mom got her last year, and she's kind of a handful."

"Oh, well," Rosi said, her voice rising several decibels, "that kitty pissed on the back of your shirt this morning."

The air trembled. Then a single giggle tore through the dam of silence. Amid waves of deafening laughter, Tommy pulled around the back of his white shirt and saw the yellow stain in its fabric. His bedroom had smelled so bad that he couldn't tell the difference when he smelled the shirt this morning. His ears scarlet, Tommy's eyes filtered through the faceless people around him.

The faceless were every bit as awful as Rosi Williams or Adam Augustine. In their natural state they floated on in indifference, but at the first whiff of blood, the faceless sunk in their teeth and left nothing behind.

Adam and Brian stepped behind Rosi. "You know," Brian said, "I don't think Tommy Taint is good enough anymore. How does Piss Stain sound?"

Tommy bit his lip and dug in his heels.

"No, that's too easy," Adam replied. "What about Piss Stain Taint?"

Tommy felt the hallway around him bust. Laughter showered down at him from every which direction, and he felt his face grow a deeper shade of scarlet. Tommy glared at Adam. He was a sniper. He always stood at the outskirts, but when he struck, the whole world followed him.

With students chanting "Piss Stain Taint," Tommy stormed out of Latimer.

The next moments passed in a haze. Tommy's legs carried him onto Bus 98. The haze consumed him all the way until his mother's voice ripped him back into reality.

"Tommy!" his mother repeated.

"What?" Tommy asked, sitting on his living room couch.

"How was your day?"

"Well, I was right. School's bullshit."

Danger flared in his mother's eyes. "Watch that mouth, Tommy."

—

The day was Saturday. The time was 3:50 in the morning.

A fully awake Tommy laid on a scantily clad mattress. His feet against the bunched-up bedsheets, the boy faced the ceiling with a woe-ridden expression. His afternoon nap had been a critical error in judgment. Designed to be a thirty-minute power-nap, the four hours of hard sleep had kept him wide awake through the night.

The chasm between night and morning had never been fond of Tommy. Here the demons had free reign, looping tortured memories like a skipping tape over his eyes. He couldn't stop thinking of the day and the kids who chanted *piss stain taint.*

A pile of dead things beckoned Tommy from the space below. Lying inside a barred-up crypt, the terror of last April laid dormant beneath the boy's box springs.

It corroded like a bomb and was only a mattress away from ignition.

The boy whispered to the grave, "Only three months from my GED."

—

Tommy's mattress was overturned against his bedroom wall. There was an open slit in Tommy's box springs, and the bomb had been taken from inside.

Outside his home, Tommy carried the bomb he took from his bedroom. It rested inside the pages of the black journal in his grasp.

The Levine Library was a historic architectural marvel at the heart of the North College campus. Constructed on the city's tallest hill in 1907, the seven-story limestone castle was a staple of the city's skyline. Its image in reach of every person, home and business in the city, the structure loyally served its residents as the sentinel on the hilltop. In the time that followed, academically hungry high schoolers and proud North College graduates would look up toward the structure with dream-glazed eyes.

Two flagstaffs, adorned with the emblems of North College, gave off brilliant crimson and blue lights that beamed in alternate phases from the library's rooftop. At nightfall, the lights extended a warm invitation to the students at the university and served as a beacon for wayward travelers on the highway.

Distant in the horizon, the bright colors of the library towered over a gravel road on the edge of the city. This path, a dirt road between Kind Pines and a closed down warehouse on a set of railroad tracks, was unknown to most people in the city.

Tommy was a regular traveler on this road. Tonight, the sound of his footsteps crunched the gravel and carried through the unnatural chill of the August night. Clutching his journal, he approached the abandoned warehouse sitting in the horizon. Fashioned with broken windows, chained up doors and no entrance signs, it was left to decay away beside the railroad tracks. The warehouse had once been fenced off to the general public, but the apathy of time had caused the fence to wear away. It was at the point that now anyone could explore the warehouse through a yellow ladder that sprawled down from its second story. A bluish light flickered near the warehouse, casting an eerie glow through the abandoned parking lot on the other side of the railroad tracks. Forgotten by the city, the closed business lived as a remnant of American prosperity.

A black, yellow and bruised boxcar rested on a set of decommissioned tracks near the warehouse. Stuck in place from the property's closure, the *Railbox* faithfully awaited its final shipment for the last decade.

Accessible solely by a gravel road that led out of the city, the area was becoming known by young lovers as a haven for those who needed to be alone.

Tommy stepped into the light. Unaware and uninterested in how others used the area, he returned to the warehouse with a different motive on his mind. In a tradition that Tommy didn't understand, he was coming for his boxcar. He stepped over shattered glass and the railroad tracks that led to his boxcar. This was always a risky journey, and he had only made it a handful of times since April, but it was worth the risk of interrogation from his mother.

Tommy took a deep breath and lifted the bomb he had extracted from beneath his mattress. It was a black journal -- one no one knew of, one that no one had been able to find. He had been wise to stash it out here before the police came last year -- before his red journal had been stolen from him. Before his own words had been stolen from him. Tommy shouted in frustration. That journal entry in his red journal had caused the entire world to stop in its tracks. Tommy smiled. But no one knew about the black journal, or the fact that the first draft of that journal entry had been written in here.

Tommy exhaled and opened it to the page on his first try.

Tommy Tate Before the Last Breath 3/31

To whom this concerns, I promised the day was near, but you didn't listen, and now that day is here. It wasn't when you called me a fatass or a queer, it was when you told me to disappear. You said my life is a waste, and rightfully so, for soon my body will be without a soul.

But first they'll find your carcass hanging above your bed. Your blood will pour until there's none left to spill, and all they'll remember is how they found you killed.

I won't hear your cries or listen to your pleas, because you did none of this when you murdered me. When you've lost all that would've been, I'll die knowing you'll never be heard again.

Tommy breathed. He and Lynne told the school it was a work of fiction. No names were mentioned, and there was no proof he intended to put his words to action. They also had an anonymous letter from a teacher at the high school defending Tommy's right to create. He said sorry, too. He didn't mean the words to hurt someone. The school board voted 4-3. Re-admission. Lynne cried when it was over.

Deep in the horizon, the light of the train became visible in the distance. Tommy lifted himself to his feet. He had watched it dozens of times. The train was speeding his way. It would fly by on railroad tracks so close he could almost touch them. On more than one occasion he thought about stepping in its way. It would be easy, and there were times he thought his demise would be a gift to the planet.

"Not today," Tommy thought. He had something to do before that day came.

The sixty-ton transport sounded its horn to the city as the world trembled beneath Tommy's feet. Golden light spilled in the boxcar and Tommy extended out his arms, awaiting his release.

A wind tunnel surged through the boy and almost sent him to the floor. Feeling life pulse back inside him, Tommy collapsed, spread-eagle in the boxcar.

Catching his breath, he listened to the train carry itself away.

Tommy thought of the people, he thought of the words, he thought of the names that had been branded on his body. It all felt as distant as another dimension. Every day he stepped toward Latimer and every day he asked himself why he went, but deep down he knew why. The words his mom said over five years ago floated to his brain. The words from her drug addled, unfiltered mind were the final confirmation of what he knew from the day he stepped into second grade.

As much as he hated Latimer and everything that came with it, they distracted him from his mother's final verdict. The awful truth of it was that if he had known he would be sentenced to a chained-up life in Dead Oak, he would have ended his life years ago. He had to find a way out of here. Something that would take him far away from Dead Oak. He had one option that would do just that, and it laid beneath his bed. Tommy shook his head. He couldn't go just yet; his life could not have all been for nothing. He had to do something in this world before he met his end.

As horrible as Adam, Brian, Rosi, Stallard and all of Latimer were, what they did gave him a purpose in this world. That purpose rested in the journal inside his hands, and that purpose kept him alive.

Tommy smiled; at least for one more day.

Chapter 6: *The Latimer Watchtower*

Tommy stood in line with his mom at the Baldridge Marketplace. It was a good day. The only good Sunday of the month. Today his mom had her disability check for her back, and together they walked to the bus stop so she could get it cashed. Normally, his mom would do this during the week, but she had back spasms on Friday and finally felt up for it today. Tommy didn't used to come with her, but since April she usually didn't trust him home alone. If Tommy was being honest with himself, he didn't mind going; it was the only time he got to eat out.

"Next!" the clerk bellowed, allowing the line to move forward.

Tommy looked over and saw an LHS senior he knew walk into the store. His name was Dexter. Dexter had an amber Brown complexion and full, black locs, which ran over his fade haircut to his eyeline.

Tommy looked forward at the line. It was log jammed, and he had a ways to go.

Before he knew it, he let a memory carry him away.

—

Tommy trudged through his empty high school hallways, swaying right and left in an aimless fashion. Halloween decorations of ghosts, spiderwebs and witches were lazily arranged through the halls, and already a few of the webs had fallen to the floor. Tommy and his freshman Study Skills teacher worked out an unspoken arrangement early in the year. Sometime in class, Tommy would raise his hand and ask to use the bathroom, his study skills teacher would say yes, and Tommy would be allowed to walk around for 20 minutes. This gave his Study Skills teacher 20 minutes of class to peruse *ESPN* at his desk in peace away from Tommy. Everybody won.

Tommy turned to a dead-end hallway. It was tough for teachers to get down here during passing periods. This hallway had storage rooms for science and other classes; there had not been actual classrooms here for a long time. This is where the real world slipped into school. This place had fights, vapes, and romantic encounters. Sure enough, the "Say Boo on Halloween" sign had been altered with sharpie to read, "Say Boobs on Halloween."

Tommy heard a crash in one of the storage rooms and jumped in fright. No one was supposed to be down here. Tommy approached the door and saw the word "Annex" on the outside. Delicately, he guided open the door. A group of sophomores, garbed in black, stood inside a storage room with dusty trophies and windows to the outside world. The "Annex" sign inside the room had been crossed out and replaced with "The Latimer Watchtower."

A tall girl stood up. "Oh piss, it's a freshman."

A Black, dreadlocked student approached Tommy. He gave Tommy a look from head to toe and smirked. "Rest easy, Kit. This one's alright."

"How do you know?"

"Because he was sitting in Stallard's office today beside me -- and that earns points in my book." The boy stretched out a hand to Tommy. "I'm Dexter. You can call me Dex."

"Tommy," the boy whispered. "What exactly y'all doin'?"

"Isn't it obvious?" Dexter asked. "We're Christmas Caroling!"

Tommy's brow furrowed. "It's Halloween."

Dexter beamed. "Exactly."

Tommy was puzzled. "So where are you going?"

"The Simmons', Fays', and Stallards' to get started."

Tommy was aghast. "They're all douches. Why would you even go there?"

Dexter smiled. "Because of how much they hate it."

"Wait, what? Really?"

Dexter nodded. "In the past, I imagine Halloween was Stallard's favorite day of the year on the neighborhood watch. Two years ago he called the real police on Kit," Dex said, gesturing towards her, "simply because he was suspicious her and her friends were about to egg a property."

Kit laughed. "We weren't, we were just wanting candy. The whole thing was terrifying."

Dexter continued, "So last year, we got the idea to sing Christmas Carols at his house. We started at my boy Jay's, and he hated it so much and admitted he would prefer we'd TP-d his property, probably because then he could snitch to the real police. We hit up some other teachers, too. Funnily enough, Principal Elmer was the only one who liked it. He liked it so much he gave us the last of the candy he had for the night. We then decided to make it a tradition and this year ordered outfits and everything."

Tommy was in disbelief. "This is amazing."

Dex checked the time. "Bell's about to ring, y'all."

Kit nodded. "Phones out, dudes. We'll start with Holy Night."

Dexter turned to Tommy. "You want in? We have an extra outfit."

Tommy shook his head. "I gotta pass. After going to the office today I'm feeling turd brown."

Dexter looked Tommy in the eye and for a moment, and Tommy felt like Dex was truly seeing him. Dexter spoke. "Screw Stallard. Today is golden, Tommy."

The bell rang, and in unison, the students departed and started singing, "O' Holy Night…"

From hallways away, Tommy heard the angry screams of Mr. Stallard. "NO! It is NOT Christmas!!"

As the rest of the group sang, Dexter retorted back. "We'll see you at your place, Jay!"

"Oh no you won't, Dexter!" Mr. Stallard yelled, his voice echoing in the hallway.

Dexter gave Tommy a wink and lead the carolers from the school.

—

Tommy and his mom were next in line.

Lynne gestured to Tommy. "Do you know that kid? You can hang out with him if you want. I'm okay here."

Everything in Tommy wanted to say yes, but he couldn't. "Nah. He goes to my high school, but I don't really know him."

Lynne nodded. "Alright."

"Next!" the clerk yelled.

—

Tommy was blank. He was staring at the television without comprehending what it was playing. He had been determined to cling to Sunday's freedom for as long as possible, but like every school night, he had checked the clock at 4:15, and a minute later it was half past ten.

"Tommy?" His mother said, breaking the silence.

The boy turned, recognizing a tenderness in her voice.

"Sorry 'bout the water the other morning. That wasn't cool of me."

A smile found Tommy's expression for the first time that day. "No, it's okay. I'da slept till noon if you hadn't done it."

"Say," she began, "you wouldn't of happened to see a dusty trophy lyin' around here, would you?"

"A trophy?" Tommy asked, creasing his brow. "No. What is it for?"

Tommy's mother brushed it off. "Aw, nothin' important. I bought it for 50 cents at a yard sale, and I just like the way it looks."

Giving a discerning look to Lynne for an extended time, Tommy wondered if there was more to this trophy than she was letting onto.

Turning back to the TV, Tommy and his mom lost themselves in the TV's white noise for the remainder of the night.

—

Tommy waited until his Mom was asleep before making it to his bedroom door. He had been uncharacteristically lazy after the previous night. Taking a key from his pocket, Tommy opened his door and pushed into his room. The boy looked over his overturned mattress and the slit that rested over his box springs. He lifted his black journal from his rolltop desk. Tommy didn't know what it was. Today hadn't been a bad day, and yet he couldn't bring himself to throw this journal away. In fact, he couldn't get it out of his mind. His heart missing a beat, Tommy opened it to the last entry, and read what was inside.

> Final Draft: Hamartia
>
> The Murder of Adam Augustine

Closing his journal, Tommy stuffed it in his box springs and taped the slit above. It was planned out to perfection, and today he was moments away from putting it in action.

There was only one thing that stopped him. Tommy laughed. It seemed corny, even to him. But in those exhilarating moments where the west-bound train passed him by, he wondered if there was something more in this world. The rush of emotion he felt and the comedown after the train moved away… it was unlike anything he had felt in his life. It made him truly wonder if he had a higher purpose in this world than putting Adam in the grave.

Sliding his mattress back over his bed, Tommy collapsed into sleep.

—

Tommy stepped into art class Monday morning and stopped in his tracks. Mia Fernandez, *the* Mia Fernandez, was sitting at his desk. Tommy ran a hand through his hair and caught a knot. He wasn't ready for this. His mind raced. "What do I say -- should I move to another seat? Should I turn around and run?"

Mia turned and looked at Tommy, causing his heart to stop.

"Yep," Tommy's mind concluded. "Another seat it is."

Mia spoke to Tommy. "Oh, is this your seat?"

"Huh?" Tommy replied.

Mia repeated herself. "Am I sitting in your seat?"

Tommy spoke at warp speed. "Well, I mean, I do sit there but it's not *mine,* technically. I guess it's Mr. Austin's? Anyone in Mr. Austin's class can sit there, and, and -- seeing that you're there--"

Mia raised an eyebrow. "If you think about it, it's likely owned by the school. It just happens to be sitting in Mr. Austin's room."

Tommy's eyes widened and his mind raced. Did she just save him? The boy spoke. "So I guess Mr. Austin would be renting his classroom and the seats in it? So I guess it's inaccurate to say that teachers 'own' their classrooms."

Cullen butted-into the conversation. "What in the hell are you talking about, Tommy?"

Tommy turned a shade of scarlet. "Nothing! Desks. Mia, you can sit there, I'll go somewhere else."

Tommy moved to a seat on the other side of the multi-seat, rectangular desk, but paused behind Cullen. "Jerk," he whispered.

Cullen smirked.

Mr. Austin spoke. "Cullen, do you know where Dexter is?"

Cullen perked up. "You mean Dex is in here today?"

Mr. Austin raised an eyebrow. "He officially transferred in here and is presenting about the Mickey Ryan scholarship. You mean to tell me you didn't know that?"

"He didn't say nothin' to me."

Mr. Austin looked skeptical. "So you have no idea where he is?"

Cullen put on his poker face. "Nope."

Mr. Austin wrinkled his brow. "Bull. You two are like an old married couple."

"Aw, you're trippin'. You sure he's actually in this class?"

Dexter Allen crashed through the classroom door. "I am now!"

Surprised breaths and stifled laughter filtered through the room. Confident and unhurried, Dexter strode into the room with four limeades and a sack from the North College Drive-In.

Mr. Austin folded his arms. "I hope you brought something for me."

Without hesitation, Dexter tossed the brown paper sack toward his teacher. "Six 'Atkins-Friendly' breadless chicken tenders with bleu cheese on the side."

Mr. Austin caught the bag. "Did you pick my favorite order by chance or did someone tip you off?"

"There are perks to having a girlfriend at the drive-in."

"How could I forget?" Mr. Austin asked, "I'm assuming *Kit's* the one I should thank for this?"

"Yeah, she got it to me right before class."

Smiling in spite of himself, Mr. Austin dispatched the tenders into his mini fridge. "You sure you didn't make the trip yourself? At any rate, you ready to talk about the Mickey Ryan scholarship?"

Tommy wasn't sure what it was, but something about Dexter's demeanor made him feel at home. Dexter was just under six feet tall and sported a pink V-neck. He wore wide, retro framed glasses and massive white headphones which harmonized with his look. Though his sandals might lead one to believe the outfit was randomly thrown together, Tommy got the impression that everything about his look was intentional.

Dexter yelled, "Well, the Mickey Ryan scholarship is an art-based, $20,000 scholarship handed out by an art foundation in the city. Mr. Austin won the award when he was in high school, and now he runs a program that has Latimer students send in a submission every year. Four years ago, one of Mr. Austin's students won it with photography of urban decay. This year, I'm creating a documentary called '30 Days in the Life.' You know how animals are usually given 30 days in an animal shelter before they're euthanized? Well, I'm creating a documentary that covers six of these animals' lives in the Baldridge shelter."

Mia raised her hand, floored. "How do you swing something like that in high school?"

Dexter gestured to Mr. Austin. "Outside of this guy? Well, when I was younger, I found out over a million animals were euthanized every year. I was so young that I didn't understand why that happened, but since then I've always wanted to do something about it. With Mr. Austin's help, I reached out to a shelter and completed a script for a documentary."

Mr. Austin was smiling. "What are you going to do if you win?"

"I'm going to use the money to attend the Film Institute of California. In fact, it's the only school I'm even applying to, because I know if I apply anywhere else, I'm not going to have the courage to make the leap."

Mr. Austin spoke to the class. "Round of applause, everybody."

The class clapped enthusiastically; Dexter waved them off. "It wouldn't be possible without Mr. Austin, y'all. When you're about to enter your senior year, all of you should submit your creative ideas and apply. It could change your life."

Mr. Austin laughed, “Speaking of creative ideas, I have an announcement. We have our first work that's worthy of the prize wall." The teacher flipped on the projector, where he revealed Tommy's comic on the big screen.

Mr. Austin (called the "Tool of Latimer") was sketched out and laughing maniacally on the comic, while all of his students cowered in fear. There was a stunned silence in the classroom, but a small chuckle rang out from the students, and soon the entire class was laughing.

Mr. Austin turned on ceremony music through his speakers. "I've been called a lot of things in my career, but rarely am I called out so creatively. Congrats to Tommy for his comic reaching the prize wall."

Embarrassed, Tommy stood up as the whole class clapped. But what Tommy couldn’t believe was Mia was laughing, actually laughing, at his comic.

Tommy muttered, "I mean, if you're all just going to make fun of me, I don't feel I earned anything."

Mr. Austin beamed. "Students -- does anyone think they could sketch out a comic like this?"

"No," Dexter said. "This is legit amazing."

"It is," Cullen added. "You earned this, Tommy."

Mr. Austin pinned the comic to the wall. "Come up for a prize, Tommy!"

Tommy met Mr. Austin at his desk. “Really, I don’t need a prize. It’s okay.”

"Are you sure?" Mr. Austin asked, "I have handerpants. Check ‘em out. They’re like whitey tighties for your hands."

Tommy looked with a dumbstruck expression.

Mr. Austin smirked. "Interested?"

—

Dexter had brought four drinks for his friends in art class. His fourth drink had been intended for Lee Wackerman, but Dexter said he was unaware Lee had transferred from the class earlier in the day.

His hands cloaked in handerpants, Tommy took a triumphant drink from his strawberry limeade and spoke. "So if my grade falls below an 80 at any time I'm automatically kicked out of this class?"

Cullen shook his head. "That's always been the word about this class, but if we're being real, Mr. Austin lets you work in his room after school to get your grade up if it falls below an 80."

Tommy's brow furrowed. "Why would anyone want to do that?"

Dexter laughed. "Tommy, allow me to hand you the keys to academic excellence. In this room Mr. Austin has several computers, tablets, clay, two high production cameras, and all of it is available to rent and work on after school. I'm applying for a major scholarship this year, and none of it would have been possible without him."

Tommy considered. "Huh. I mean, I'm still planning on withdrawing from this class on Monday, but that does sound interesting."

Cullen raised his eyebrow at this. "Really?"

Tommy didn't reply, opting instead to drink from his limeade.

Chapter 7: ***Rust Jobs***

Mia sat beside Yurika beneath the big tree in the Latimer courtyard.

Yurika yawned. "Do you have any interviews for STUCO today?

"Kind of. I'm watching a presentation by Dexter Allen in Mr. Austin's room. You know anything about him?"

"Yeah! He's the Annex kid. We often kick him out of the Annex for our debate practice. Why?"

Mia answered, "Is the Annex like his lair or something? Have you ever wondered what the odds are that our classmates are future murderers?"

Yurika laughed. "Does he give you a murdery vibe?"

Mia smirked. "Heh, no. He was actually pretty funny when I talked to him."

"Same. He's an awesome guy. Stole a key from Stallard to get access to the Annex, I think. He often has pizza rolls ready for us in the microwave that he smuggled in."

Mia smiled. "I know I've said no dating for the next five years, but that's one of the most attractive things I've ever heard."

Yurika sighed. "He's taken. Dating a freshman at the NC if I'm remembering right."

"That figures."

"Why are you sitting in on a presentation of his?"

Mia responded, "His project is Latimer's submission for the Mickey Ryan scholarship."

"Well, let me know if any of these people you're seeing are worth writing a story about."

"I wouldn't hold your breath. These interviews have been snoozers."

Yurika frowned. "You'd think one of these organizations would be story-worthy."

The bell rang out through the courtyard, causing both girls to sigh.

Before getting up, Yurika took one last look. “I’m surprised more people don’t come out here. It really is beautiful.”

Mia lifted herself to her feet. “I’m happy more don’t know about it. This place feels like my home.”

—

Mia stared at the wild, brown-haired boy who everyone knew at school. He was the kid who was going to murder everybody. Tommy Tate. Mia checked the time. During next period she was an aide to Mr. Dickert, the head of the school’s college preparedness program.

Mia grimaced. “If Tommy is going to kill everybody, it’d be nice if he could get on with it before I have to work with Dickert.”

Truth be told, this was the first time she remembered being in the same room with the kid. He was nothing like she thought he’d be. He had been geeking out about his limeade for the past thirty minutes and was wearing handerpants, for God’s sakes.

Listening in to their conversation, Mia’s thoughts whirled. “Like, he full on hero-worshipped Dexter for getting him a soda. It’s like Dex lended him an organ or something.”

She looked at Tommy. "Huh,” the boy pondered aloud. “I mean, I'm still planning on withdrawing from this class on Monday, but that does sound interesting."

Cullen asked, "Really?"

Tommy took a drink from his limeade. After a moment, he changed the subject. “Thanks again for this, Dex. It’s the best.”

Dexter smiled. “As I said, dude, it was not a problem at all. I’m glad you liked it.”

Mia bent into the conversation. “So, Dex. Is there any chance I could interview you about the scholarship?”

Dexter responded, "Of course. Where are you going next period?"

"I'm an aide for the honor society."

Dexter laughed. "For Dickhurt?"

Mia snorted. "That's the one."

"Does he randomly leave about ten minutes into class and disappear for a half hour?"

Mia's eyes sparked. "Yes. Literally every class. He gives us a pile of work to do and then just vanishes into thin air. We never know where he goes or when he'll come back to the room."

Mia noticed that Tommy and Cullen were talking amongst themselves and not paying attention at this point.

Dexter leaned in close. "That's because he goes out to his car. Turns on his radio, opens his sunroof and eats a cup of ice cream. Every. Single. Day. Some days, he even has a second cup."

Mia laughed. "You're joking."

"Nope. I'm convinced it's the only 'me time' he gets as a teacher. I have a top-secret room that lets me see the whole parking lot."

"Would that room be the Annex?"

Dexter corrected himself. "So I have a not-so-secret room that lets me see the whole parking lot. So in class today, head to the Annex for our interview right after he goes to eat his ice cream."

Mia was skeptical. "But what if he finishes his ice cream early?"

"Then you'll have full view of him getting out of his car and will beat him back to class. If he eats one cup, you'll have ten minutes. If he goes for a second, you'll have 20-30. I did this every day starting in November last year. He never caught me. Nothing is important enough to interrupt Dickhurt's ice cream time. I'm convinced certain death awaits anyone who does."

Mia was sold. "Fine, but you better be right, Dex."

—

The Annex was a dusty, forgotten room that even *smelled* like the past. It had a musty, lingering mildew smell that quickly settled in Mia's nostrils until she didn't notice it anymore. Old, yellow analog clocks were stacked on the far-right side of the room, and as Dexter promised, at the left-hand corner sat two windows, one overlooking the John Wagner Fieldhouse, the other the staff parking lot. And sure enough, Mr. Dickert had just opened an ice cream cup from the school cafeteria.

Mia was in disbelief. "Incredible."

Dexter pointed to a big white truck sitting on the side of the road adjacent to the staff parking lot. "See that hot-rod over there?"

Mia nodded. "That truck, yeah."

"I don't want to make things weird between us, but that beauty is mine. It has a custom rust job on the side and 60 mile-an-hour air conditioning."

Mia smirked. "I had no idea you drove such a hot-rod."

Mia seated herself at a railroad sign that stood between a box of dusty trophies and old class photos in the Annex. Sitting in full view of Mr. Dickert through the windows of the Annex, Mia chewed on a pizza roll. "As STUCO's junior vice-president, part of my responsibilities are interviewing the head of every organization or committee."

"Sounds terrible."

Mia rolled her eyes. "You have no idea."

Dexter grinned. "Is your name pronounced Me-ah, or My-ah, by the way?"

"My-ah, thanks for asking. I always have to correct all seven of my teachers on the first day of school."

Dexter nodded. "Of course. So you're telling me that the Mia, who is known to belt out Tom Petty on open mic nights, is afraid of breaching 'school policy?'"

Mia's face flushed to a ruby red color. "Did your girlfriend give you that intel?"

"She says you're delightful."

"Tisk, Tisk," Mia muttered playfully. "I have to hand it to you, I didn't think anyone here knew about that."

"Anyway, are you eventually going to try to make it as a singer?"

"Don't laugh, but I actually want to write children's novels."

"Why would I laugh at that? Do you know what you want to write about?"

"Well, I've started a book called *Captain Spudz and Her Bologna Boat Fleet*, but I've put my writing on hold for now. I just have too much to do with school, work and STUCO."

Dexter threw a pizza roll up into the air and caught it in his mouth. Chewing for a bit, Dexter swallowed. "Do you need any more info for the scholly I'm applying for?"

"I need a mission statement for the STUCO newsletter."

Dex gave it a second of thought. "I created a documentary to help save the lives of animals. Three million get euthanized every year, and together we can change that."

Mia nodded her head, impressed. "With that, I think I have everything I need. It's amazing what you're doing."

"Thank you, I'm hoping it saves a lot of animals."

Mia picked up her journal with a dandelion bookmark inside. "Honestly, I asked to meet you for another reason."

Dexter raised an eyebrow. "So it's not only for pizza rolls and a lovely conversation?"

Mia responded, "As lovely as it is, I'm also wondering if you'd be up to be interviewed for the student paper by my friend Yuki?"

"Another interview? Is print journalism even still a thing?"

Mia laughed. "Give her a chance. She's wanting to use your work to go for a *Scholastic Award.*"

"Oh really? Yeah, I guess I could make time for that."

Mia smirked. She knew how to hook a boy like Dexter.

Dexter sat back. "Mia?"

"Yeah?"

"A lot of people can say they were in student council in high school, but not many can say they published a children's story while they were there. If I were you, I think I would focus on *Captain Spudz*."

Mia thought about it. "Maybe so, but I don't want to be the children's novelist who works at the greenhouse."

"And I don't want to be the film director who works at the Riverfront Brewery, but that's not where either of us are gonna end up."

Mia narrowed her eyes. "I don't think we'll end there either, Dex, but we both have to go our own way."

Dexter looked out the window. "Dickert alert. He finished his ice cream."

"Crap," Mia uttered, "that hungry a-hole is already done?"

Dexter calmed her nerves. "You have a four minute head start on him. Just pretend like you're meant to be in the hallways and no one will question you."

Mia scarfed down her last pizza roll. "Will do. Thanks for this, Dex."

Mia walked into the hallway and fired off a message to Yurika.

—

At the end of the school day, Mia stepped into the LHS parking lot and looked over her work schedule.

P/T Schedule	Mia F.	Lee W.	Jimmy C.
Mon	—	4-9	9-2
Tues	—	—	4-10
Wed	5-10	4-9	—

Mia smiled. She had enough time for a pre-shift coffee. Gliding up to her Geometro, Mia pulled out her keys and froze.

A ripped-up piece of paper had been shoved beneath her windshield wiper. Feeling her heart race, she quickly looked over her surroundings. Closing her eyes and taking a breath, Mia picked up the paper and looked it over.

It was blank.

Sighing in relief, Mia scanned her surroundings one more time before driving to the greenhouse.

Chapter 8: ***Bubble-Gum Toothpaste***

Most points in a Single Game:
Cody Augustine
45
Most Points in a Single Season:
Cody Augustine
502

Rosi stood beside her boyfriend, Adam, and looked at his father's records beside him.

Cullen's voice echoed through the gym. "Plannin' on showin' up your old man?"

Rosi turned around to see Cullen striding over to them. He waved to her. "Hey, Rosi." He rustled her hair, something he'd done every time they met for the past few years.

"Hey!" Rosi said affectionately.

Adam spoke. "Have I ever told you about when I was diagnosed with hemophilia?"

Cullen paused, and glanced a look of surprise toward Rosi, who gave it to him in return. Adam rarely talked about this, and only told her this story last year.

Adam continued, keeping his eyes on the records. "I was six when I found out and it killed me. Basketball was my dad's and I's *life*. It was our *language*. The doc said I'd have to quit the YMCA and never play again. My grandpa must have begged my doctor for hours, and the doctor finally signed a waiver that allowed me to finish the season."

Cullen laughed. "Well, you ended up doing way more than that."

Adam nodded. "I was told all my life that my opponents would get too strong and too physical. Well you know what, Cullen? On February 18th, my dad's going to be inducted into the school Hall of Fame. That day I'm going to break his single game record and show up everyone who ever told me that I can't play ball."

Cullen responded, "Does your old man know you wanna take him down?"

"No, but he'll be the first to congratulate me once I do."

Cullen nodded. "I appreciate you sharing that with me."

"Of course." Without another word, Adam took a 50-foot shot from the trophy case.

Rosi always said Adam had a "magic touch," and it was epitomized by this shot. Adam was fading backwards and was slightly behind the basket, but as Rosi expected, the ball swished through the net.

Rosi turned to Cullen. "You still smoke the ganja?"

"Nah. I have random drug tests to look out for at the home. Why you wanna know?"

Adam smirked. "We met my dealer here before you showed up."

"Are you effin' with me?"

"Nope. He got me a new vape kit," Rosi replied.

Cullen shook his head. "Aren't y'all worried you'll be caught?"

Adam brushed off the question. "My man Rock is discreet, and do you think this school would actually do anything if they caught me?"

"Well, not to your golden boy ass. What about you, Rosi?"

"You really think my dad would care? If he got mad that'd be the first time he acknowledged my existence since he asked me to buy him smokes at Bill's Gas and Bait last month."

Cullen breathed. "Fair enough. Anyway, I gotta bounce. Have to grab something from my locker before work today. Y'all goin' joyridin' later?"

Rosi shook her head. "You know how I feel about that."

Cullen smirked. "Oh yeah. I'm sure Adam will keep it nice and slow."

—

At the end of the school day, Rosi dabbed her bubble-gum toothpaste on her electric toothbrush. She had used this brand of toothpaste since age 6, and since that time, the once unknown wonders of the world corroded into life's realities.

After counting to thirty, rinsing her mouth, and washing off her toothbrush, Rosi placed her brush in her backpack. Rosi departed from the bathroom and out the backdoors of the school, but she paused when she reached the courtyard.

When they were in eighth grade, Rosi and Mia shared a belief that they would be best friends forever. Forever, as it turned out, lasted a little under six months. Volleyball, key club, new friends, boyfriends and the arrival of high school would soon prove to be much stronger than the promises of two fourteen-year-olds.

It was why Rosi hesitated when she saw her (former) best friend forever. Rosi considered making a U-turn, but the two had made eye contact for so long she knew she had to say something.

"Hey!" Rosi bellowed.

Placing her dandelion bookmark into her copy of *Grapes of Wrath*, Mia smiled. "Hi."

Rosi beamed. "So, uh, congrats on the STUCO election!"

"Thanks," Mia responded. "Did volleyball practice end early today?"

"Oh…yeah. I'm not doing v-ball this year."

"I'm sorry, I didn't know--"

Rosi's lower lip trembled for a moment. "It just wasn't for me anymore…"

Mia changed the subject. "You look really nice!"

"Thanks. I actually started dieting this summer."

"Nice," Mia said. "Congrats on sticking with it."

"Thank you. I really love your bookmark."

"Thanks. I have about a billion more back home."

Rosi looked to her feet. "Well," she stammered awkwardly.

Mia picked her up. "We really do need to catch up sometime. Maybe I could visit you at Bee's?"

"Nah. I quit the Bee's too."

Mia shook her off. "No big deal; we'll just have to go out sometime."

Rosi perked up. "We do! Do you still have the same number?"

Mia nodded. "I do."

"I'll text you sometime."

"It was great seeing you."

"You too," Rosi responded.

Rosi frowned as she walked away. For a moment, she debated turning around and getting real with Mia. Mia was someone she knew would understand her, but after a moment, the impulse passed.

—

The engine of Adam's Mustang roared in the night. The back of Rosi's head glued itself to the passenger seat as Adam spun to a dirt road. Her face white and her stomach feeling like jello, Rosi latched onto the car's handle and closed her eyes.

"I found a new place. It'll be perfect." Adam said.

Rosi opened her eyes. "Are you sure about this, Adam?"

Adam's lips morphed into a smile. "More than sure, Rose. We won't be getting caught again."

The girl shook her head. *Rose.* No matter how agitated she was with him, her heart melted a little every time Adam called her by that name.

Turning onto a dirt parking lot overtaken by weeds, trash, and cigarette butts. Adam switched off the engine and turned off the lights.

"Where are we?" asked Rosi.

"A friend told me about this place. It should be much safer than the pasture park. So…" Adam whispered, "where were we?"

Unbuckling his seatbelt, Adam began to pivot himself above his middle console. He looked deep into the blue of Rosi's eyes and moved his hands to the sides of her face.

"I have missed this, babe."

"Adam," Rosi whispered.

Closing his eyes, Adam kissed her.

"Adam," Rosi whispered again, closing her eyes.

Rosi felt Adam kiss her cheek.

"Adam!" Rosi yelled, pushing his hands away.

"What's up?" Adam asked, dazed.

"Is it okay if we just talked today?"

Adam looked cross. "Just *talked?*"

"Well, I did want to *talk* to you. I've felt like poop today, and I just—"

"It's fine," Adam said, his voice as blunt as a knife.

Disentangling himself from Rosi, Adam plopped back into his driver's seat.

Rosi spoke. "I just wanna catch up, you know? We haven't talked in forever."

A noticeable flicker burst across Adam's eyes. "Okay."

Like Rosi had anticipated, Adam was a little short at first, but he was soon more than willing to talk hoops. "Technically, it's illegal in the offseason, but there's nothing anyone can do if four of our team's starters 'happen' to be shooting around at the wellness center with a retired coach who 'volunteers' as an instructor there part time."

Rosi laughed. "So who's the holdout?"

"Cullen, but he's lazy. Everyone knows that. C.J.'s being a girl about them, too."

"What's up with C.J.?"

"He said he wants to rack up volunteer hours for a scholarship he's applying for at the NC. Luckily, Coach has hinted that he'll be conducting offseason evaluations to determine his starting line-up."

Rosi snorted. "But who could slide in for C.J.? Brian?"

Adam released an untempered laugh. "You never know. Brian wanted me to tell you that we are invited to shoot paintball with him next weekend."

Rosi cackled. "God, he's such a douche."

Adam's brow creased. "You really do hate him, don't you?"

"Yeah, he was horrible to Mia."

Adam shrugged. "Eh, I dunno about all that."

Rolling her eyes, Rosi changed the subject. "So, what's Coach doing about Cullen?"

"Cullen's been gay about everything since our state run last year. I guess he'd rather clean old men's balls than practice for a state championship team."

"Well, it's not like you can replace your 6'6" center."

"Yeah, 6'6" and can't dunk," Adam breathed. "Truth be told, Coach has asked me to push Cullen. Asked I keep him on his diet and stuff like that. He even wanted to know what he ordered when we went out the other night."

Rosi raised her eyebrows. "Did you tell him?"

"I told Coach he ordered wings."

"Wow. Adam I wouldn't expect you to snitch like--"

Adam cut her off. "I wasn't snitching. It's for the team, alright?" He shifted the conversation. "How are things with you?"

"Alright," Rosi said. "Dad's been a prick lately."

"I haven't seen my dad in months."

"But he got you this car."

"That's true," Adam acknowledged, his voice glum.

Rosi shook her head. "My dad doesn't get me crap. Even when he's sober, he -- oh my God! Adam! Someone's here."

Adam looked outside.

Rosi's heart raced. There was a man, and something was in his hands. She gasped. "Oh my God!"

"What?!" Adam asked.

"That's Tommy."

Adam whispered, "Tommy *Taint?* What in the hell is he doing?"

"Is he creeping on us?"

Adam slammed his fist against the steering wheel. "I am going to kill him."

Rosi bear hugged Adam. "Wait! I don't think he's seen us. We parked in a good place. I think he's going into that boxcar."

Adam spat. "What is wrong with that kid?"

"I don't know. Why would anyone come out here?"

The two looked on as Tommy turned around and jumped into the boxcar.

Rosi looked over to Adam. A curious, unsettling smile had fallen over Adam's face, and there was something in his eyes that Rosi had never seen before.

Rosi slid a hand over Adam's cheek. "Everything okay?"

Looking down to Rosi with his traditional confidence, Adam nodded. "We're okay, Rose. More than okay."

"Piss Stain Taint. It's perfect, Adam. And I can't believe the picture you got of him this summer."

"Well, I didn't see it. But I have it on good authority."

Rosi frowned. "I thought you were gonna show it to him this week."

"We have a long year in front of us, Rose." Adam continued, "I like this place. We need to come back soon."

The horn of a coming train echoed in the distance.

Rosi looked toward the lights approaching in the horizon. "Train's coming."

Adam looked at Rosi. "Yep, and it's perfect timing."

Rosi watched the train lights glide from the horizon and pass over the boxcar.

Adam combusted his Mustang into life. "Let's roll."

Spinning out of the gravel lot, the two sped off in the night.

Chapter 9: ***A Friend at Night***

Cocaine Thayne spat a tar-like substance into his can of *Darn Good Cola.* He was only wearing a pair of worn out, checkered boxers that hung loose on his snow-white legs, and a giant bowl of microwaved chicken nuggets sat on his lap.

"These nuggets are the bomb!" Thayne yelled. "Where'd you get 'em, Ms. T?"

"Mitch drives a food truck for a living and said he could sneak me some frozen foods when they clean out each Monday."

"Damn!" Tommy yelled. "Ring that bastard, Mom!"

"Watch that mouth, Tommy."

"Thayne cusses all the time!"

Lynne replied, "Thayne is a lost cause."

His mouth full of nuggets, Thayne turned to Tommy. "Sheth's righ, Thommy." Thayne swallowed. "Is Mitch the guy with the porn 'stache? Tommy was tellin' me all about him."

"Dang it, Thayne!" Tommy whispered, flipping his cousin the bird.

"I saw that, Tommy, and yes, Mitch is the one with the porn 'stache."

"Hot damn!" Thayne yelled. "I need to meet this man!"

Lynne carried a plate of mozzarella sticks into the room. "Jesus, Thayne, how many cans of *Darn Good* did you have today?"

Thayne spat a chewed-up nail in his can. "Three or four. I'm goin' for a record."

Lynne opened a can. "You can go for the record with your own pack, freeloader!"

Holding back a smirk, Tommy pulled out a small piece of paper resting inside his pocket. Those two had been at each other's throats all Saturday, and he wouldn't be surprised if they combusted soon. Tommy checked the time. It was almost 10; he had five minutes before he had to move.

Thayne looked over at Tommy. "I need a pair of those myself. What'd you say those were called?"

"Handerpants," Tommy said.

Thayne continued, "Good stuff. Ya know, I used to be scared to death to come over here."

Lynne placed her can of soda beside Thayne's. "How come?"

"When I was like five years old, I think, you whipped me with a belt after I ate a slice of cheese from your fridge. You remember that?"

Lynne responded, "No, but remember the time you tried to crap in our litter box?"

Thayne spat into his can. "You ever gonna let that go? Dang, that was years ago."

"You were fifteen and *missed.*"

Thayne grinned. "That was a crazy night. No need for you to be a high ridin' bitch about it."

Lynne held up a dangerous finger toward her nephew. "Call me that again and you'll go home in pieces," Lynne turned her attention to her son. "Watcha readin' there, Tommy?"

Tommy hurriedly pocketed the note. "Nothin' important. Just a note from school."

Thayne snorted. "Nothing important? Tommy's been lookin' at that like it's a swimsuit mag."

"*Men,*" Lynne said.

"I gotta take a dump!" Thayne announced.

Sensing his opportunity, Tommy spoke to his Mom. "I'm gonna take out the trash."

Tommy's mom looked like she was about to pass out. "What kinda wild hair do you have tonight?"

Tommy shrugged. "I know it's not somethin' I normally do, but it's the least I can do after such a good meal."

"Ah, get the heck outta here," Lynne sputtered. But Tommy noticed a reluctant smile settle over her expression as he tied up the trash bag.

Tommy stepped under the dim porch light of his single-wide trailer.

Now standing in comfortable solitude, Tommy lifted out the piece of paper in his pocket. Filled with as much pride as he was when he saw it yesterday afternoon, Tommy drank in its contents.

The Tool of Latimer/Week 1 Participation 8/23

Advanced Art

Tommy Tate: **A+** **5/5**

After throwing out the trash, he turned as the front door of the trailer slammed open with such force that Tommy dropped his paper. An underwear clad Cocaine Thayne leapt into the front yard.

"Tommy! You--"

A can of *Darn Good* torpedoed from the trailer, missing Thayne's head by inches. Thayne's eyes widened in panic, and Tommy heard a demon-like wail echo from inside the trailer.

Thayne screamed, "Gotta go!"

Turning around, Tommy watched his mother leap to the edge of the road.

"You better run!" Tommy's mother heaved a second can in her nephew's direction, missing her sprinting target by a matter of feet.

Tommy laughed. "Nice throw, Ma."

"Your *idiot* cousin spat my pop full of chaw."

Now under the streetlights near Green Oak, Thayne flashed her the bird. "Not my fault you drank from the wrong can, ho!"

Tommy's mother was quick to return the favor. "I know where you live, you mouth breathin' jackass!" Lynne turned to her son. "I swear to god I'm gonna kill him someday. You comin' in?"

Tommy shrugged. "Nah, I need some fresh air."

Nodding to her son, Lynne marched back to her door, but Tommy noticed her linger before going inside. He wondered if she had again noticed the piece of paper in his hands, which now rested inside his pocket. After an uncomfortable moment, he watched her go inside the trailer. Tommy felt the paper in his pocket. Monday was the last day he could transfer, but he wondered: "Is this class something I actually want to do? Is it something I actually could do?"

Without realizing what he was doing, Tommy felt his legs carry him to his boxcar and he pulled himself inside. He knew the trouble he would get in at home for coming out here, but somehow this all felt worth it.

Tommy heard the train's horn whirl in the distance. It carried through his ears, shook his boxcar, and glided through the dead end of red oak. Tommy watched the train speed towards him, and felt a strange, unfamiliar purpose kindle inside him.

By the time the train vanished in the horizon, Tommy was gone.

Part Two: The Pride of Latimer

Mr. Stallard took deliberate steps through the empty hallways. The John Wagner Fieldhouse was about to hold a rally for the first day of the sub-state basketball tournament, but that felt like a world away. An arctic energy pulsed through Stallard's veins and electrified his senses. While on the neighborhood watch he learned how to choke away emotion in times of crisis. That skill allowed him to bury his panic and fury beneath an icy resolve. A trail of blood glistened in the hallway. Stallard's movements were as silent as a vulture's glide, and he moved with a crimson gleam inside his eyes. Tracking the scarlet ravine to a darkened classroom, Stallard strangled the handle beneath his adrenalized grip.

A ravenous expression on his face, the assistant principal vanished inside the Annex.

Stallard stood in the doorway of the Annex. It was an oversight to leave a place like this unlocked. He made a note to talk to the custodial staff about this at the first opportunity. Garbage, dusted-up antiques, and overturned desks reached the assistant principal's eyes. It was like a crime scene in here.

Blood was spattered all over the floor of this room. Feeling panic seize his insides, he flipped out his phone. For some reason, every detail was sticking in his brain. His phone read back that it was February 18th, 2:36 P.M. Stallard moved past the home screen and texted the office staff.

"School Lockdown. *Now.*"

It took only seconds. High pitched sirens screeched out in terror as a computerized voice filtered through the school.

Panicked teachers, quickened footsteps, and surprised cries from students joined the alarm in a broken harmony. The words rang out through the intercom. "Lockdown, lockdown, lockdown."

Chapter 10: ***A Night in November***

A mix of blood-red and golden leaves whirled through the Latimer courtyard. A scarlet sunset sent contrails through the skies like strokes from a paintbrush. The smell of burning firewood traveled through the evening's breeze, settling over the city.

It was the first cold night of the year, and Tommy was not dressed for the occasion. The November air nuzzled up against his hands, making it difficult to hold his pencil.

On a normal day, Tommy would have been inside Mr. Austin's toasty art room after school, but today was not a normal day. Tommy had always loved the fall, and today he realized it almost passed before he appreciated it being here.

Tommy was happy -- happier than he had been in a long time. He scored a 99 on his stop-motion project in art, and even checked with Mr. Austin to make sure the score was accurate.

"Actually, yeah!" Austin said. "I graded it twice to make sure it was right. Way to go, Tommy!"

Tommy had not been told "way to go" since he had knocked over an aisle of tic-tacs while hanging with Cocaine Thayne. The comment felt better from Mr. Austin than it did from Thayne.

This encouragement was why Tommy was determined to make Mr. Austin proud.

The boy looked at the rubric in his palms.

Fall Project: The Artist in You

Mr. Austin's voice rang in Tommy's ears. "With this project, I don't care if you want to create a bookshelf, host a concert, or beat a paint can with a sledgehammer over a 4x8 poster board. If you put in effort, anything will work. The top three submissions will be recognized in the Latimer student showcase for all of the second semester."

Tommy remembered standing in admiration to Dexter's "LHS Survival Guide" that made the showcase last year. This semester, he wanted to do something worthy of the Pride of Latimer showcase -- something that would be seen by everyone at the school.

A student named Lee Wackerman had seen Tommy holding the project syllabus in the hallway. "It's going to be an experience," he told Tommy.

He agreed with Lee. It was going to be.

Tommy watched the breeze whirl a collage of multicolored leaves past his feet. He was happy he came tonight, as the leaves would have died if he waited any longer.

Tommy loved everything about the months of fall. The way the leaves would rustle against the ground and the way the smell of a fire would snuggle inside his nostrils, and above all else, he loved the mystery that accompanied nights like tonight. When he was in grade school, Tommy would disappear into these long nights, creating imagination-fueled adventures which took him far away from home. The boy used to love how, if only for a fleeting moment, these nights felt like they might last for eternity.

Looking over Latimer's wilting courtyard, Tommy felt a melancholy settle over his heart.

The nights never did.

Chapter 11: ***Dandelion Girl***

A cacophony of noise blared from an antiquated, brick-like cell phone. This particular alarm was called "Hot Jazz" but labeling this hot noise "jazz" was akin to labeling a 25-cent pack of spicy ramen as five-star cuisine. Blasting a computerized symphony that sounded like a chorus of underwater trumpets, the phone sent vibrations through a wooden coffee table.

Mia had cycled through two new phones since she used The Brick. However, The Brick had the only alarm in existence that always woke her up. Its sole purpose relegated to pissing Mia off each day, the girl shut off the steaming hot jazz and tossed her phone across the bedroom.

Reaching over her bed for her real phone, Mia turned it on and found the cheery voice of Yurika in a voicemail she left last night. "Hey, girl! Just calling to let you know that Mr. Stallard is a Bald. Headed. Douche! As predicted, the a-hole liked none of what the night crew did last night. Though he was conveniently missing until the end of our shift, he pleasantly informed us that the morning crew would have to tear everything down and rearrange EVERY single banner. KCN News will be here at 5:30 tomorrow to interview Adam after basketball practice and Stallard wants all of the banners done before then, assuming I don't murder him with a hammer before that. Hehe, anyways!" Yurika muttered, her voice losing its sarcastic, gum-like flair. "Good luck this morning, babe, love you!"

Mia sighed, "I can't wait."

—

A sticky sweat stuck on her brow, Mia looked over the "School Pride" posters that were now tacked across the John Wagner Fieldhouse. A golden "Take State" poster sat in the center, while posters featuring "inspired" phrases like "Hear Us Roar" and "One Game at a Time" were strewn throughout the gym. Ladders were up around the gym under the posters. It was a lot of work, and Mia was willing to guess that no one watching the KCN news broadcast would even notice the posters when it aired. Mia turned to Mr. Stallard. For the last hour, he had provided no assistance as they were doing the job. Stallard chose to ask questions such as "what do you think?" and "is that what you think is best?" throughout the process. She started feeling comfortable that he'd let them out early, with how hands-off he was. But as Mr. Stallard now stood with his back turned to the students in the fieldhouse, Mia and her STUCO classmates watched Stallard with nervous anticipation.

Stallard let out a dramatic sigh. "Do you all believe this is… 'satisfactory?'"

Mia felt a trickle of rage drip into her stomach. She exchanged nervous looks with her STUCO classmates.

Being met with silence, Mr. Stallard turned around to the students. "We are hours away from being the top story on KCN News tonight. Do you think this is the best way for us to showcase our school to the community?"

Chad Hinez, an honors student with blonde hair and vanilla hued skin took a step forward. He had competed with Mia for the Top GPA of their class since freshman year.

"I think," Chad started nervously, "I think, while it might be satisfactory, it's not up to the "LHS" standard."

Mia glowered at Chad with a look of fury.

Mr. Stallard nodded. "I agree with you, Chad. Let's try this again. How about we meet back at 3:15 with the next shift and figure it out at that time?"

Mia looked at her feet. She didn't know why she expected this to go any differently.

—

Mia sat with Yurika at a table in the corner of the cafeteria. Mia spat fire. "He's the worst."

Yurika sighed. "STUCO isn't worth this, girly."

Mia shut that down. "Be real with me. You don't even have a strike against you. You're a year-and-a-half away from being done with it. Why not just get through it?"

Yurika laughed. "The only reason I don't have a strike and you do is because I'm privileged enough that I don't need to work a job. But I don't care about strikes, Mia. This isn't worth it."

Mia waved her off. "It's worth a letter of reference, Yuki. It's worth a scholarship."

Yurika took a fork full of pasta and pointed it to Mia. "You need to be careful with that. You give him that kind of leverage, and there is nothing he won't get you to do."

Mia snorted. "Leverage. Your dad would be proud."

Yurika pushed back. "Your mom never talked to you about leverage? Business jag-offs never stop talking about it. They say it's key to everything in that world. Who you know, who you can leverage to get ahead, yada yada yada. I'm surprised your mom never mentioned it, with her running the flower shop and everything."

Mia breathed. "It's not that she doesn't want to talk to me about those things. I just don't want to run a flower shop."

"Well. You need leverage if you're going to get an inch on Stallard, and that's the problem. Students don't have any actual leverage over an educator like Mr. Stallard."

Mia narrowed her eyes. "Under your definition, students don't have leverage over any teacher."

"Nah, some teachers actually care about kids." She gestured over to Principal Elmer, who was standing at a table in the cafeteria and miming a tuba with a group of band kids. "A principal like Elmer gives kids leverage just by being the person that he is. They actually care about kids and give up leverage to kids to help them because those teachers want kids to succeed. Other teachers can get swayed by an angry parent or some BS like that if they can't handle the heat. Everyone can be leveraged. Teachers too. Just some can't be by students. I can't even get Stallard to put up the article I wrote about Dex in the student showcase."

Mia sighed. "So how do we leverage a guy like Stallard, a teacher who doesn't even care about kids?"

Yurika gestured toward Elmer, who was now miming a tuba solo to the laughing band kids. "Stallard doesn't care, but maybe his boss does."

—

At 3:10 that school day, Mr. Stallard inserted a silver key in the "Pride of Latimer" student showcase sitting in the school's lobby.

Mia relished the moment. Mr. Stallard had told Yuki "no" on hanging the story up twice in the last week. All it took was one conversation with Mr. Elmer for that to change.

Yurika held out her article for Mr. Stallard. "Make sure it's level," she said, feigning innocence.

Narrowing his eyes, Stallard swiped the article from her grasp. Yurika winked at Mia. This was amazing.

Jeff Elmer's voice boomed from behind them. "Looking good!"

Mia beamed; she was so happy. Yurika had sat down and interviewed Dexter at her suggestion. Her article about Dex's animal shelter project had made the front page of the *Air Capital Star*. They even included a god-tier picture of Dexter with the Shepherd mix he'd adopted after filming the documentary.

Mr. Elmer paused beside the showcase. "Thanks for doing this, Mr. Stallard. These two came to me with a perfect idea. With the news coming for Adam today, they said they thought it would be perfect if LHS's best and brightest were on display."

Locking down the showcase, Stallard gave a wordless nod.

Mr. Elmer continued, "Is it okay if I borrow these two from STUCO tonight? Yurika asked if she could interview Mr. Austin and myself about the scholarship as part of a follow up interview, and I think that's just a wonderful idea."

Giving another wordless nod, Mr. Stallard turned from the lobby.

Yurika flashed the thumbs up to Mia and mouthed, "Leverage."

Principal Elmer asked, "You said the story has been nominated for a Scholastic award?"

Yurika nodded. "Yeah. It's pretty unbelievable."

"It's deserved," said the principal; "What you and Dex have done is more than worthy."

Yurika responded, "I just hope it helps him out with his scholarship."

"I have a good feeling about that. To my office?"

Mia went to follow the two but heard a devastating voice ring out behind her. "Jeff?" Mr. Stallard said, "On second thought, is there any way I could borrow Ms. Fernandez? We need to be ready for Adam's broadcast, and I just had someone cancel a STUCO shift on me."

Mia flashed a look of panic at Yurika, who gave it in return.

Mr. Elmer considered. "What do you think, Mia? Is the work with me a job Yurika can handle on her own?"

Mia considered, cycling through her next words carefully. "I... I think so. I can help Mr. Stallard. No problem."

Mia turned to Stallard and couldn't help but notice a thin yet present smile on his face. Putting her head down, she followed him through the hallway.

Stallard spoke. "I'm glad you're here. I was going to ask if you could cover the 3:30 shift tonight. Kate had to go home with a cold."

"Is there any way I could leave by 4:30? I was going to see if I could pick up a shift at the greenhouse tonight."

"Well, Mia. I'm not going to make you stay, but I can assure you, when it's time for me to fill out my end of the year evaluations, I'll remember those who went the extra mile, and those who did the *minimum.*"

Thinking through a mire of dark comebacks, a smile superglued itself onto Mia.

"Well, I certainly don't want to do the minimum."

"I knew I could count on you," Stallard answered, his voice given new life. "I don't know what it is, but the crew seems to work *much* harder when you're around, Mia."

"Only naturally would something be so natural," Mia said sardonically.

Mr. Stallard smirked. "See you at 3:30."

—

The brisk afternoon was evident by the rosiness on Mia's cheeks. Shivering as she walked toward the school courtyard, she paused when she saw someone already there. Without seeing his face, she knew exactly who he was from the tumbleweed of brunette hair on his head.

Mia spoke. "Is this seat taken?"

She watched Tommy turn around and freeze. "You mean th-this one?" The boy stammered, pointing to the empty space.

Mia smiled. "Yes, goofball, I mean that one."

"Oh then, knock yourself out," Tommy said. "So, uh," the boy continued (Mia noticed his voice lowered several decibels), "what's crackin'?"

Mia raised an eyebrow. "What's crackin'?" She repeated. She watched Tommy recoil a bit when she did, but she couldn't let him get away with that question without him feeling a little embarrassed. She continued, "Well, Mr. Stallard voluntold me to prepare for the "big night" tonight, so I'm guessing I'll be here until 6 at the earliest."

Tommy narrowed his eyes. "I didn't think the game was until tomorrow."

Mia nodded. "It's not, sadly. I'm so ready for it to be over."

Tommy looked surprised. "Really? Not big into the rivalry?"

Mia laughed. In the city of Baldridge, every family on the northwest side of the Manchester highway sent their kids to become Latimer Lions, while those on the southeast belonged to the Baldridge Brinehawks. Both schools were on Salem Street. Baldridge downtown, and Latimer in the "burbs." It was why the upcoming game was called the Salem Street rivalry, and somehow why everyone at Latimer hated the Baldridge players despite living in the same town.

Tommy continued, breaking her from her thoughts. "So what's Stallard so uptight about?"

"He wants the gym finished in time for the… basketball team's news story today." Mia had paused mid-statement and opted against admitting the story was centered on Adam, especially after what she had heard last year. "The whole thing has made me see what the dude actually cares about."

"Isn't Stallard the best?"

Mia pulled an apple from her purse. "He's bad news bears, man." Mia pointed at "The Lottery", a short story in Tommy's grasp. "Is that for Roberts' English class?"

"Yeah. Just her Regular English, though, not her Honors."

Mia snorted. "Her honors course is tough. Her test on short stories was rough."

"How did you end up doing?" Tommy asked.

"A 90. Honestly, I was a little disappointed."

Tommy facepalmed.

Mia smirked at that reaction. “What?”

“You’re one of *those* people.”

Mia narrowed her eyes. “Those people?! Haha, how do you do on her regular stuff?!”

“I don’t want to say,” Tommy breathed.

“You have to tell me!”

“...On her last test I got an 84.”

Mia laughed. “Oh, that’s great! Don’t feel down. One of my friends is in her regular English class and ended up with a D+.”

Mia’s hot jazz alarm rang from her phone. She sighed. It was 3:25 already.

Tommy spoke. “I really like your alarm. It’s classy. Is it like freeform or something?”

“It’s something, alright. Well, I should get back before Stallard notices I’m gone.”

Tommy nodded. “Have fun.”

“I’ll try. Was this your first time in the courtyard? I’ve never seen you out here.”

“I started coming here last week. I like catching the later bus. My early one smells like sandwich-ass."

This term broke Mia. She broke into several heaves of laughter. "Sandwich-ass?! I'm stealing that one, Tommy."

Beaming, Tommy kept going. "Plus, I really like fall and decided to start coming out here before the season changed.”

Mia caught her breath. “It’s beautiful, isn’t it? STUCO's had me so tied up I hadn’t been out here in weeks. Anyways, you should keep coming out here, Tommy. It would be.... nice to have someone to talk to.”

“Really?” Tommy said, his voice confused.

"Tommy, every day I have to deal with people who would probably kill me if it meant some extra credit points. I'm not allowed to speak my mind to people like Stallard, and pretty much let those people run my life. Coming out and hearing someone describe a smell like sandwich ass... I don't know, it's nice. I'll see you later, Tommy."

Tommy looked up at her in a punch-drunk way. "Yeah, you too"

Mia stepped from the courtyard. She could tell Tommy had it bad for her, but she hoped they could be friends. She didn't know how to explain it, but she meant everything she told Tommy before she walked away.

Chapter 12: ***A KCN Exclusive***

Rosi stood at the side of the John Wagner fieldhouse. A group of three people from KCN News were standing at the gym's center. They were all dressed in suits, and from the way they looked, the way they answered questions, and how they carried themselves, it felt like they thought the cameras were always rolling. Rosi admired it, in a way.

The cameraperson was the exception to the rule. He was dressed in a single t-shirt and had a pencil behind his ear. His massive camera in a bag beside him, he held his hands up like he was looking through a lens. He seemed to plan for Adam to stand in front of the "Lion of Latimer" banner; a banner Rosi drew that had Adam's design sketched out to the side.

Adam walked over to her and poked her in the stomach.

Rosi looked to him. "How are you doing?"

Adam replied, "It's like there's a cinderblock in my ribs. It's the same way I feel before a game."

"You'll own it. Just like you always do."

"It's not a game, though. I'll be talking about my diagnosis."

"And can you imagine? Everyone is going to know you as I know you," Rosi reassured. "You're going to own it, babe."

A female newscaster called over to Adam, "Are you ready?"

Kissing her on the head, Adam glided over to the newscasters.

Rosi looked on at Adam, the banners, the bleachers, and the lights assembled around them. There was a kingdom within Adam's grasp, and all he had to do was take it.

—

The next day, Mr. Demko turned on the classroom television with a flick of the remote. Rosi watched with major anticipation. Normally she ignored the school's LHS broadcast, but after Adam's interview last night she couldn't help but watch.

"Hey, everyone?" Demko blustered. "You'll want to pay attention to LHS news today."

Rosi responded, "Listen to Mr. Demko, everyone!"

Triggering eyerolls throughout the room, the students begrudgingly turned toward the TV.

"Thanks, everyone," Demko whimpered.

LHS News anchor Ann Suzuki filled Mr. Demko's television screen.

Rosi heard Brian whisper over to Adam, "We hanging at Grant's after the game?"

Adam answered, "Yeah, his parents will be out of town."

"Dope."

Demko pointed to Brian. "No talking, please!"

Much to Rosi's annoyance, Brian continued whispering. "Are you worried at all about Baldridge?"

"No," Adam answered. "They couldn't even beat us with Ridge Winter last year."

"Seriously!" Demko yelled. "No talking, guys!"

Brian tapped Rosi on the shoulder. "Is he on the rag today or what?"

Suzuki's voice began to rise. "And now, it is our pleasure to re-air last night's KCN broadcast about Adam Augustine. We're proud of you, Adam!"

Rosi knew most of the class had already seen the story. Heck, almost everyone in the entire school was watching the previous night's KCN broadcast, but no one was complaining about watching it a second time.

Emotional piano played in the background while Adam's voice radiated through the television's speakers.

"They told me I could never play basketball again."

Footage of Adam alone in a darkened John Wagner Fieldhouse faded into the newscast.

"I was diagnosed with type B hemophilia when I was five years old."

Brian whispered to Adam, "I am so happy for you, dude."

"Thank you."

"I somehow didn't know this was even happening yesterday. I guess I-"

Rosi felt her frustration boil. "Seriously, shut the hell up, Brian!"

The students around the room laughed. Brian flashed a hurt gaze toward Rosi, but she didn't care. She was halfway certain Mr. Demko heard her too but didn't intervene. If anything, he probably supported it.

After Principal Elmer explained the extra medical precautions Latimer took on gameday in the newscast, they cut to Coach Hardcastle. "Adam's a class act. He's a genuine kid. Whenever someone is having a rough day or if I've been hard on a kid one practice, he's always there. He cares about people and always lifts people up when they're down."

Rosi turned around and smiled at Adam. This was finally his moment.

The scene cut to Adam. "After everything I've had to go through with having hemophilia, I told myself I would always be there for anyone."

It was a small sound, one that would pass unnoticed under regular circumstances. It was a single, muffled snort. Rosi may have been one of the only people to hear it, but to her, it was heard around the world.

Rosi turned around and looked Tommy in the eye. "Was something funny about that, Piss Stain?"

Several heads turned in Tommy's direction.

Tommy was quick to reply. "I just coughed, I'm sorry."

Brian's voice rose. "It sounded like a laugh to me, Tommy Taint."

"It was just a cough!"

Demko yelled, "Tommy! Keep your voice down!"

Despite Demko's warnings, Rosi saw all the eyes in the room find Tommy.

Adam's voice flowed from the television. "I wouldn't be who I am today without God and my father. My dad was always there to push me, and to let me know that *nothing* was outside my reach."

Brian continued, "Never knew hemophilia was so funny."

"It was *just* a cough."

Rosi saw a smile appeared on Adam's expression. He was back on his game. This was his class, his school, and his year.

Adam spoke from behind Tommy. "Don't lie, Tommy. Let it out, *before my last breath.*"

Brian's eyes lit up. "You're a *fatass* and a *queer*, Tommy Taint."

The sugary voice of a female news anchor completed the KCN exclusive. "Known around the league for his electrifying, one handed dunk, Adam says it's his goal to bring home Latimer's first state championship, and besides opposing players, could anyone root against him?"

Rosi saw red splotches appear through Tommy's face. The sound had fallen out of his mouth like fizz from a shaken soda can. Rosi breathed. The hounds were going to rip him to shreds.

Coach Hardcastle stepped into the cave and spoke to Mr. Demko. "Hey, Matt, can I talk to you about something?"

"Sure! I'll be back, everyone. Don't go crazy while I'm gone."

The moment Demko stepped out of the room, Brian began. "Tommy Taint, if I told you to disappear, would my family *find me killed*?"

Tommy turned to Brian. "No. I don't care about you. You're only Adam's boytoy."

Brian recoiled, but Adam stayed on point. "What kind of moron brings a journal like *that* to school?"

"You know," Tommy answered, "wh-which one of you took it from my backpack last year? I never found out."

Brian laughed. "Oh, that was me. Good job leaving your bag for me."

Adam whispered, "What're you gonna do, Tommy? Call your deadbeat whore mom to come save you? Oh yeah, is she single again?"

Jolting laughter burst through Rosi's lips. "Awww, I think the fatty is about to *snap*, Adam."

Rosi watched Tommy ball his hands into fists.

"Are you broken, Tommy?" Adam asked. "Were we the ones that *broke* you?"

Tommy slammed his fists into his desk. "Seriously!"

A stunned silence choked the classroom. He had the eyes of everyone in the room. Tommy yelled, "What did I even do to you guys?"

Rosi was quick to respond. "You smell bad."

A throng of laughter sloshed out from the sides of the room, and Rosi saw Tommy's expression break.

Adam considered. "What did you do? You exist."

Much to her enjoyment, Rosi watched Tommy hurl his face into his hands.

Rosi drove in the final nail. "Cry somewhere else, loser."

—

The scents of chemical body spray and teenaged odors waged war outside the boys' locker room.

The combination burned the edges of Rosi's eyes. Anxiety crept up on Rosi as she gazed at the entrance of the locker room. She was beginning to have doubts about Adam's plan.

Rosi's mind wandered. "Maybe this is too much, even for Adam."

Adam walked out of the locker room, his face brimming with confidence. "We're on," he said confidently. "Rock's in."

Rosi whispered, "Babe, I..."

Adam cut her off. "This is going to be legendary, Rose. People are going to talk about this forever."

Rosi choked down her doubts. "I know..." She breathed. "I know it'll be amazing."

Cullen stepped from the locker room and joined her and Adam. "What's good?" he asked.

Adam replied, "Nothin'."

Cullen turned to her. "So what all went down in your math class today?"

Rosi stepped back. She didn't appreciate his tone. "Uh, Tommy made fun of Adam's hemophilia."

Cullen turned to Adam. "What? Bro, that's messed up. What exactly did he say?"

She and Adam were quiet for an uncomfortable moment. Tommy didn't actually *say* anything, but Rosi was quick to recover. "He laughed. He laughed when they talked about Adam's diagnosis."

"Wow," Cullen uttered. "That's wild. The other people I talked to must not have heard that."

Rosi raised her voice. "What are you asking us here?"

Adam's cool voice joined the conversation. "Since when did you and Tommy get so close, Cullen?"

"What do you mean?"

"With the way you're defending him, I wondered when you became friends."

Rosi smiled. Adam had a way of coming in like a sniper on conversations like this.

Cullen clarified. "I wouldn't say we're friends. Mr. Austin just asked me to keep an eye on him. He ain't that bad of a kid."

Rosi jumped. "That bad of a kid?!"

Adam cut her off. "No worries, dude. Anyways, if y'all are interested Grant is throwing a party after the game tonight. His sister will supply the drinks if we all chip in five dollars."

Cullen nodded. "Sounds good. I have work the morning after so I'll likely just be in and out."

Adam smiled. "No problem, man! Just swing by if you can."

Watching Cullen walk away, Rosi turned to Adam. "He has no idea that he's about to be a part of a legendary night in the Salem Street Rivalry."

Adam smirked. "You're in on the plan then?"

"Always was."

—

Rosi sat breathless in the stands. There was a wild energy pulsing inside the John Wagner fieldhouse. The crowd of crimson and gold surrounded the fans of the blue and gold Brinehawks. Rosi screamed the Latimer fight song with the Latimer crowd to drown out the visitors, and she gave it a venom and vigor reserved only for the Salem Street Rivalry. An old man in a blue polo stood cross armed in a row beside her. Rosi smirked. He was probably like all the Baldridge old timers she used to serve at Applebee's who were all still seething that Latimer broke away from Baldridge 40 years ago.

There was one minute until game time.

Rosi watched Adam inch toward Isaac Segal. Rosi knew they had been friends since grade school, but right now it looked like they wanted to kill each other.

No one was sitting in Latimer's student section; everyone was on their feet, smashing their fists against the bleachers and chanting the fight song so loudly that Rosi could feel her heart pulse against her rib cage. The chant was so loud that she missed the opening whistle.

Adam was ready, though. The ref threw the ball in the air, and Adam leapt above Isaac and tipped it to his teammate, Jonah's, outstretched hands.

Jonah sprinted down the court, drove into the gold and blue Baldridge defender and passed the ball to Adam at the three-point line. Without hesitation, Adam threw it to Cullen; the 6'6 center was streaking toward the basket.

Baldridge was ready, though. A blue and gold opponent tipped it out of bounds.

Adam looked up to the stands. That was her cue. Rosi pointed toward Rock Rustin, whose group lifted a massive poster toward the Baldridge side of the court. Rosi heard gasps and frenzied reactions rang from the visiting side of the gym.

Go Lions! **Wipe Up the PEASANTS.**

From behind the poster, Rock Rustin launched a roll of toilet paper and arched it toward the Blue and Gold crowd. Like the opening arrow to an assault, Rosi watched multiple people stand up and launch dozens of rolls to the Baldridge side. Chaos ensued, toilet paper smacked the Baldridge parents, and Rosi watched the young, 20 something officials look to each other in shock as outrage poured from the Baldridge crowd. Rosi watched Rock and his contingent bolt from the stands, and several players on the Baldridge bench had to be restrained from giving chase.

Piercing screams came in waves from the Baldridge parents. Rosi gasped. The crowd felt inches away from a riot.

She didn't hear a whistle, but Rosi watched Jonah throw the ball into play. None of the Baldridge players looked ready, distracted by what was going on in the stands, but Adam was sprinting toward the basket and pointing up to the skies. Watching Jonah loft the ball in the air, Rosi watched Adam leave his feet and snag the ball with a single hand.

Rosi bit her lip. Isaac had snuffed out Adam's plan. Leaping into the air, Isaac collided with Adam beneath the basket.

Call it brute force, call it sheer will, but even as Isaac's elbow smashed into Adam's face, Rosi watched Adam find a way to slam the ball in the rim. Landing back on earth, Adam released a bellowing roar that caused the Latimer crowd to erupt in crazed, animal-like shouts. Rosi listened as the Latimer crowd resumed the school's fight song, drowning the outraged boos on the Baldridge side.

The refs whistled the play dead, calling Isaac for a flagrant foul. Rosi gasped. Streams of blood flowed from Adam's nose, but he kept his smile and pointed her way.

He screamed, and Rosi wondered if he was talking to her. "All game, baby, all game!"

—

Her eyes ravenous, Rosi watched Adam make his way through the student parking lot from the door of his Mustang. Her breath blowing out billows in the night, Rosi shivered as Adam stepped from the Latimer staircase.

"What'd you think, Rose?!"

"Ad-Adam! We crushed them. You were unbelievable. You had -- what -- 26 points?!"

"27!" Adam corrected.

Truth be told, Rosi knew it was 27. But she knew Adam would love to correct her for a point more. Rosi's voice broke. "I was so worried about you. When I saw the blood I just--"

Adam shook her off. "The nurse has meds I can take whenever I start bleeding. It ain't no thing. Did Stallard notice anything?"

Rosi's teeth chattered through her answer. "He noticed me signal Rock. I thought he was going to ki-kill me, but he *barely* seemed to care."

Adam laughed. "Paying off Rock was the best $200 I ever spent. Did he ask about Rock?"

"He did, but I relayed the story you told me to tell him, and said I only looked at them when I saw the sign."

Adam looked at her, concerned. "Did he buy it?"

Rosi shook her head. "I don't think so, but he didn't ask me anything after that."

"Did the police officer ask you any questions?"

Rosi nodded. "He said that they'd press charges if I ever did anything like it again."

"Excellent."

Rosi continued, "Apparently Elmer was really upset and is going to have an assembly about it. He even had to give an interview about it to the newspaper tonight."

Adam asked, "What happened to Rock?"

"He and his buddies slipped ski masks on and found a way out of the gym before any of the officers caught him. Apparently, an old fart chased them seven blocks before giving up.

Adam laughed. "That's classic."

Rosi shook her head. "You were amazing today. What had Isaac so mad at you?"

"Before the game, I told him we were shoving it down his damn throat."

Rosi stepped back in surprise. "Haven't you two been friends since grade school?"

"I played Y ball with him for God's sakes. I don't know what came over me. I just -- I have one goal this year, Rose. I am getting my dad's records, and anyone standing in the way of that is a problem."

Rosi tilted her head. "Adam... I…"

Adam cut her off. "It worked out, didn't it?"

She looked at Adam. He wasn't even looking at her now, but at the high school -- and she watched him extend a hand toward his self-anointed kingdom.

It was all inside his grasp, and for the first time in her life, she didn't know how she felt about that.

Chapter 13: ***Perfumes of Arabia***

The room was still.

A body was on the bed, its eyes open, arms extended, motionless.

A drop of blood trickled from Tommy's hand.

Hatred pulsed life into his body.

Blood dripped against the floor.

Tommy's mind wandered to the basketball game tonight.

And soon it went to a place far away from here.

—

Tommy closed his eyes on Friday night and when he opened them, it was Monday morning.

At least it felt that way. Tommy took a big bite of his *Galaxy Brownie.* He stood in front of a grimy, drop-splotched mirror with a crack along the center. He was running late for his bus, but he didn't care. His shirt was stained, his hair was everywhere. Tommy stitched a coat of Kevlar around his body. He had every class on Mondays. The boy swallowed. He had to go.

"Just keep breathing," Tommy told himself. "Just breathe."

When Tommy stepped out of the bathroom, his mom was waiting.

Lynne spat. "So, you plannin' on tellin' me what happened to that hand?"

Tommy looked up defiantly. "Nope."

The boy forced his way past his mom and to the entrance of his trailer.

Tommy felt his mom following him close, close enough he could smell the cigarettes on her breath. Tommy tried to open the door and felt his mom slam it back shut the moment after it opened.

Lynne lowered her voice. "If you don't tell me, I'm gonna find out a different way."

Tommy looked at his mom and thought of the lock barricading his door. He breathed. "Good luck."

Opening the door again, Tommy stepped onto Red Oak road and made his way to the bus stop outside of Kind Pines.

—

Tommy stood outside the gym and tried to find the energy to go into Mr. Demko's math class. He was already tardy, and he found he couldn't go any further.

Without realizing what he had done, he found himself dislocated from his math class altogether and now somehow sat in Mr. Austin's room. Inside an enormous black hoodie that looked like a trash bag, he put his head against Mr. Austin's back wall.

Tommy could hear Dexter and Mr. Austin's voices swirl from the hallway. Tommy looked outside Mr. Austin's window. They had been playing a game of HORSE with wadded-up papers and trash cans in the hall.

Mr. Austin's voice trickled from the halls. "How's the doc coming?"

Tommy heard Dexter's reply. "Great! I have a rough cut of the footage I took at the shelter and the interview I took with Pat Hendrickson, our district representative. Once I get an interview with that council member and the shelter's staff, filming should be complete."

Tommy was increasingly aware that the longer the two talked outside, the more awkward it would be when they walked into the room. But he didn't care. There was not a chance he was stepping foot into math today. Not after what happened last class.

Dexter's voice filtered in. "How are you so good at playing horse with wadded up pieces of paper?"

Mr. Austin laughed. "I'm a teacher. I've had so much practice I'm pretty much Steph Curry when it comes to making baskets with wadded up paper."

Mr. Austin led Dexter into the classroom and stopped when he saw Tommy.

"Hey, Tommy!" Mr. Austin said, as if he were expecting him. "What brings you in?"

"I was wondering if I could spend the period in here?"

"Who's your instructor?" Austin asked.

"Mr. Demko."

"Hm," Austin murmured, walking over to his desk. "I think we can arrange that."

Tracing the math teacher's extension on his wall, Mr. Austin made the call.

"Yes, Mr. Demko? This is James Austin calling to inform you that I will have Tommy for the day and excused him through the system. Sorry -- it's very important he finish his Claymation project today. Uhm, yes, no, thank you!"

Mr. Austin flashed the thumbs up, and Tommy mouthed a "thank you."

—

Tommy crumpled up his half of a Hershey's wrapper. "Thanks for the candy bar."

Dexter smiled. "Don't mention it. I'm heading out. I'll pick you up at your place tomorrow. Cullen, Kit and I usually grab a bite and study together at the North College Library. You're gonna love it."

Tommy beamed. "I can't wait."

Waving to Dexter, Tommy turned his eyes to Mr. Austin's windows. Almost a week ago, Mia told Tommy she would like to see him in the courtyard more, so naturally Tommy had not gone anywhere near the courtyard since that time. Tommy was looking at Mia from the safety of Mr. Austin's art room.

Mr. Austin spoke from his desk. "You can't make today a habit, Tommy."

Tommy sighed. "I know."

"Why didn't you go to math today?"

Tommy bowed his head. "I don't want to talk about it."

"Fair enough," Austin replied. "So, let's talk about your hand."

Tommy exhaled. "How did you notice?"

"You're not the first one to wear a hoodie like that. C'mon, let's see it."

Taking a breath, the boy pulled back his sleeve. Tommy's right knuckles were blown open and soaked in oozing, scarlet blood. The boy flinched as the open air penetrated his mangled hand. An engorged vein, painful at the touch, rested in the center of a massive purple bruise that extended from the knuckle over Tommy's pinky to the space halfway down Tommy's hand.

Pulling out his reading glasses, Austin examined the damage.

"This isn't good, Tommy."

"I'll be okay."

"I once thought the same thing," Austin muttered, "but $4,000 dollars later I was singing a different tune."

Tommy's face fell. "You don't think it's broken, do you?!"

Standing up, the teacher walked to his filing cabinet. "Best case? Let's hope it's just bruising and swelling. My older brother once popped a blood vessel and it looked a lot like this."

Mr. Austin extracted a slender white bottle and an unopened roll of gauze from the top of his cabinet. "Be sure that's wrapped up and doesn't get infected, Tommy, and after a week or two it should be cleared up. If it's not, then you're going to need to see a professional."

"What if that's not an option?" Tommy asked.

"Worst case? It has to be. In my senior year of college, I didn't think it was an option either."

Tommy was blown away. "You did this your senior year in college?"

"Punched a door? Oh yeah. Things got a little complicated when my dad decided to move in with my roommates and me. Two months later I was so caught up in his life that I forgot why I was going to school. It all came crashing down when he decided to total my car."

Tommy gasped. "What?!"

Mr. Austin released a dark smile. "Yeah, he crashed head on into a bridge. He was fine, of course, but I can't say the same for the car. I snapped that day, and I broke both my bedroom door and my left hand in the process. The only transportation I had to school and my job had been totaled."

"What did you do?"

"I did what I should have done years before. I cut ties with my dad. I filed a restraining order the next day."

"I'm surprised that kept him out."

"The Glock 17 in my nightstand may have helped too."

Tommy laughed. "I wouldn't have thought you were a gun owner."

"There's a lot you might not guess about me," Austin mused. "My dad made sure I knew my way around a Glock when I was in first grade. When my dad would get liquored up, it was my job to hide his weapons so he wouldn't kill someone. He gave me a Glock to protect myself after someone followed him home after a knife fight. I don't think he ever thought I'd use it to protect myself against *him.* He was eventually arrested for driving without a license, and one day I found his name in the obituaries of the town paper."

Tommy was dazed. "Holy crap. I don't even know what to say."

"There's not much that can be said, but it goes without saying that you need to remove these destructive forces from your life."

Tommy shook his head. "I can't."

"Can't get out of Algebra II, huh?'

"It hangs over everything I do like a.... a shadow. No matter how my day is going, they are *always* there. I've fought back, I've turned the other cheek and taken every single blow they've given, but they are not going to stop no matter what I do."

Mr. Austin leaned back. "So you need an outlet. I have art, karate and meditation for my outlets -- what do you have?"

Tommy thought about it. "Well, everyone knows about my writing."

Mr. Austin sat back. "How's that going?"

Tommy gave his teacher a suspicious glance. The question felt genuine, but that topic was dangerous to talk about in this school.

Tommy breathed. "I have to be careful there. You know what happened last April."

"You mean when the school board decided you wrote a work of fiction? I know a lot of kids write fiction, Tommy, but none of them stopped writing because of it."

Tommy shook his head. "That's not what I mean. When I start writing about certain topics, I start going down a road I can't control."

Austin gestured toward Tommy's hand. "And that's you under control? If you're flirting with thoughts like these, I guarantee that me, your friends, and the school board would want you to find another outlet."

Tommy smiled. "You don't even know."

"You'd be surprised. So what is it? Revenge? Plans where each kid in that math class begs for your forgiveness?"

Tommy cut across him. "More than that. Plans where that math class, this school, and this entire damn town never forgets my name."

Mr. Austin narrowed his eyes. "I think people know you, Tommy."

"No," Tommy countered. "They know me as Piss Stain. I want this school to remember me as Tommy. Tommy Leigh Tate."

Mr. Austin shook his head. "Then why aim only for this school? Tommy, when I see your projects, I see creativity that could inspire generations of people. You don't need revenge to do that. You don't need a manifesto. Don't be Shakespeare, just be Tommy, and people will never forget you."

"I want to do something cool for the *Artist in You* project." Tommy said.

Mr. Austin's eyes lit up. "Really? Like another comic?"

"No. Something more." Tommy wondered aloud, "I thought about going freehand, but the first drawings I've made have been crap."

Mr. Austin raised an eyebrow. "Ever tried working on my classroom UTablets?"

"You mean your UTabs? No."

Mr. Austin picked up a UTab from behind him. "Sure. A UTab ya whippersnapper. Take it home with you tonight and see what you think."

Tommy leaned back, surprised. "I couldn't."

"Yes, you could. It's one of my personal ones. It's okay if you don't like it. But it's been gathering dust since Dex finished using it for his doc. The apps on here are killer. Just give it a try, okay?"

Tommy looked over the device. "This is more than I deserve."

The activity bell rang through the school.

"That's your ride. Take this charger, too. Just get these back when you're done," Mr. Austin said.

Tommy was baffled. "I don't know what to say."

"What everybody has forgotten is that the school board decided you didn't do anything wrong." Mr. Austin revealed a thin scar across his hand. "It's a bleak road. Some never make it out, but every once in while someone fist fights long enough and can claw their way to survival. I believe I'm looking at a survivor, and I can't wait to see the day you make it out of here."

Tommy looked up at his teacher. "Thank you."

Mr. Austin opened his classroom door. “And, Tommy? I don’t mean to lecture you, but revenge? I don’t think it’s for you.”

Tommy looked at the tablet in his hands. “I’ll see what I can do with this.”

Mr. Austin smiled. “I’m happy you're in my class.”

“I’m happy you had a Dr. Pepper.”

A newfound color filling the boy’s expression, Tommy departed from the classroom.

Chapter 14: ***Bolt Cutter***

Cullen turned his Dodge Stealth into the Latimer High School parking lot. It was an early morning workout season for the basketball team, and while attendance wasn't mandatory -- it still was. To his surprise, he saw Dexter sitting alone in the bed of his white truck.

Cullen pulled into the empty spot beside Dexter and jumped out of his car. "What's good, bro?"

Dexter flashed a wan smile. "You'll be happy. Kit broke up with me last night."

Cullen's eyes went wide. "Whoa, *what*?"

"I'm as surprised as you. A year and a half down the drain."

Cullen pushed back. "Not down the drain."

"C'mon, you think I'm lucky."

Cullen put a hand on Dexter. "Naw, I think you're *hella* lucky."

"Well. Thank her manager Luke for that."

Cullen gasped. "Woah! Like 35-year-old Luke? My-uncle-is-the-owner-so-I'm-the-manager Luke?"

"That's the one."

"Sorry, Dex. The feeling is never easy."

Dexter turned to Cullen. "Can I ask you something?"

"Shoot."

Dexter continued, "Why didn't you like Kit anyway?"

"It's not that I didn't like her. It's just she wasn't the one for you. Know what I'm sayin'?"

Dexter shook his head.

Cullen sighed. "Remember the day the animal shelter gave you permission to film your doc last year?"

Dexter nodded. "Yeah."

"The day that happened, Kit told me that you were never going to slow down for her."

"Maybe I should have," Dex conceded.

"Dex, I'm about to knock you silly. If you're caught bein' choosy between your dreams and a person's expectations of you, then that ain't the person for you."

"Maybe. If I win the doc, it'll all be worth it."

Cullen raised his eyebrow. "Only if you win?"

Dexter was firm. "Yeah. Otherwise what was the point of all this? You know where she was during my night shoots at the shelter?"

Cullen was livid. "Bro, I don't give a speckled crap about where she was. I care about where you were--"

Dexter cut him off. "Yeah, I was tryin' to win a dumb scholarship--"

Cullen spoke up. "You ain't seein' this right. You remember how you got involved in this whole thing? It wasn't about a damn scholarship -- it was 'cause you got tired of seein' animals get put down -- animals you got to know while volunteering cleanin' turds up at the shelter. You got in this to help dogs get adopted and cats find homes, and you're gonna do that whether you win or not."

Dexter breathed. "I know. It's just hard to see right now, you know? Anyway, enough about me. You hear back from North College yet?"

"Naw, I probably didn't get in to the NC. I don't know, just trying to plan on bein' outta college for a year if I don't make it."

Dexter pushed him. "C'mon, dude. You're in, and you're gonna do great."

"Maybe. Wish I felt like you did." Cullen pulled out a BON energy drink from the pocket of his letter jacket and tossed it to his friend. "I'm guessing you're gonna need this more than I will today."

Dexter smiled. "Thanks, bruh."

Cullen patted Dexter on the back. "Stay strong."

—

Cullen absentmindedly shook his creatine infused shaker at a lunch table. On the lunch menu today was a rectangular pizza, one that featured cheese and a watery red sauce that was spread thin over blackened crust. Cullen pulled out a jar of peanut butter and a spoon from his backpack, a staple on pizza days. Cullen took a swig of his vaguely fruit punch flavored beverage and scanned the cafeteria. Tommy was sitting alone at the table behind him. He was wearing the handerpants he won in Mr. Austin's room and chewing on the cardboard crust of the school lunch pizza.

Cullen yelled out to Tommy, "Yo, Tommy. Quit being antisocial and sit over here."

Tommy probed him. "You're sitting alone, too."

Cullen stretched out his hands. "Someone's gotta be first to the party. Come on over here, Tommy."

Tommy murmured, "Alright."

Cullen pointed at Tommy's hands. "Like the handerpants."

"Thanks. I finally remembered them on a cold day. First time I've had gloves in a while."

Cullen noticed heavy bandages under Tommy's right hand. With a pang, he remembered what happened in math on Friday. "So Tommy, I uh--"

Mia's voice ripped through the cafeteria. "Are those your HANDERPANTS?!"

Tommy and Cullen looked up to see Mia running towards the table, clad in handerpants of her own.

"We're twinning, Tommy!" Throwing a hand up, Mia clapped Tommy's hand several times.

Tommy flashed Cullen a look as if to say, "is this actually happening?" to which Cullen gave him a wink.

"Handerpants?" a boy asked from a table away.

"They're like whitey tighties for your hands," Tommy replied.

"That's awesome!" the boy yelled.

Creating a flurry, Cullen watched Tommy and Mia field questions about their cost, comfort and support for the next five minutes. Cullen wondered how often Tommy had found himself in the center of attention in a good way or if he had ever even been there before.

When the bell finally rang, Tommy looked disappointed the fanfare was leaving him and Mia. Getting up with his empty tray, Tommy grabbed his backpack and departed for his next class.

Mia spoke. "Hey, Tommy?"

"Huh?"

"Where's your next class?"

Tommy looked to his feet. "In the cave. I have Algebra 2."

"That works! I'm in Evans' AP History class. I'm right across from the gym."

"Sweet!" Tommy answered. "Well, I'll see you tomorrow. "

Cullen cut into the conversation. "Seems like you two could walk together then."

Tommy looked over to Cullen in shock. "Uh, I mean, only if Mia would want, I mean."

"Well, yeah!" Mia sputtered. "Let's walk together, dork!"

Cullen smiled as he watched them walk through the cafeteria and stretched out his legs on the lunch table. There were surprised faces through the cafeteria as student eyes followed Tommy and Mia; several folks even craned their necks to get a better view.

Brian Miller walked up to Cullen's table so quickly he bumped into Cullen. Without moving his legs, Cullen looked at Brian.

Brian gestured to Tommy and Mia. "So uh, what was that about?"

Cullen smirked. "Looks like Tommy and Mia are walking together."

"Oh?" Brian said, trying to play it cool. "Why's that?"

"Don't worry about it."

Brian had a too-wide smile on his face. "I'm not worried. I just want to know."

"Seeing how it's none of your business, I think this conversation is over."

The sides of Brian's temple cracked, and Cullen heard a tremor in Brian's voice. "You should know the *only* reason people like you is because of basketball, douche."

Cullen let out a confident laugh. "Anyone ever tell you your face is hard to look at?"

"Huh?"

Cullen continued, "Because you should know you *and* your pancake ass face weren't welcome the second you came up to me. Now go away, stalker."

His palms shaking, Brian pointed at Cullen's chest. "I'm gonna remember this."

Rolling his eyes, Cullen stretched out at the table and sighed.

—

After the final bell signaled the end of the school day, Cullen glided through the hallways without thinking about where he was going. He was a head taller than everybody else, and sometimes he felt himself go on autopilot through the barrage of beige complexions at Latimer High. Though he was 6'6, sometimes it even felt like they didn't notice him at all. Cullen got out to the bus stop and saw Tommy's hair sticking up in the crowd. Cullen smiled and ran up to pat Tommy on the shoulder. "Are you a wizard, Tommy?"

"Huh?"

"Don't you play dumb. You and Mia Fernandez?"

Tommy responded, "We just walked in the hallway."

Cullen raised his eyebrows. "Aaaand..."

Tommy laughed. "Does it really mean much?"

"Are you kiddin' me? It's time to make a move!"

Tommy looked to his feet. "Look, there are a lot of five-year-olds who love Dodge Challengers, but that doesn't mean they know how to drive one."

"Screw that. The kids just have to take the wheel!"

Tommy gestured toward his stomach. "Have you seen all of this? I don't think all of this has a chance with the Mia Fernandez."

Sensing Tommy's hopelessness, Cullen put a hand on his shoulder. "Alright, hear me out."

"Oh," Tommy said, his voice glum. "I have to catch the bus."

Cullen scoffed. "Catch the activity bus, then."

Tommy raised an eyebrow. "Seriously?"

"Be real. What's gonna be more important to you, the hour more you got to spend at home or the advice I'm gonna give you?"

Tommy laughed. "Okay, fair point."

Cullen continued, "Girls -- hell, *people* like confidence. Hella confidence. Remember that simple fact and you'll go a long way. Now when I look at you-" Cullen gestured toward Tommy's gym shorts and hair, "-I ain't seein' a lot of confidence."

Tommy rolled his eyes. "I know. Girls don't like nice guys; girls like cocky a-holes."

Cullen snorted. "That ain't been my experience. Girls, and everyone, really, like people who bring something to the table. It's true for me too, you know? Hang with me here, but I've always looked at it like a group project. You ever get stuck with someone who does nothing in a group project?"

"Sure, who hasn't?"

"Well, I was once paired with a girl who had it bad, and I mean had it *bad* for me, Tommy. I thought it was gonna be awesome, but it *sucked.* She didn't do anything but talk about how much she loved watching me play basketball. It was annoying. I didn't want her to fawn over me, I just wanted someone to do their part of the mole day project."

Tommy looked confused. "And this relates to girls… how?"

"Look at relationships like a group project. If you ain't bringing anything to the table, just worshipping the other person is gonna get old, fast."

Tommy sighed. "Okay, but what can I even bring to the table?"

Cullen pulled out a stick of Berserk deodorant from his bag. "Start here. I am trusting you with one of my most treasured secrets. That stick has helped me into some of my best and worst relationships, and the worst ones were of no fault of the deodorant, but I digress. It's gonna help you, Tommy. Remember, girls ain't gonna fool around with a guy who doesn't care about himself, so lose the gym shorts, get that hair under control, smell fresh, and wear something that makes you 'Tommy.'"

Catching the stick of deodorant, Tommy grimaced. "I don't really have a lot of 'cool' things I can wear."

"That's okay. Just do what you can and the rest will figure itself out."

Tommy looked up. "Thanks, Cullen."

Cullen tapped his head. "Confidence, Tommy!"

—

Cullen, sweat still hanging on the sides of his face, set a playlist to shuffle chopper rap before his drive home. Cullen soon lost himself in thoughts about his city. The Manchester Highway (U.S. 86) carved a thin line through Baldridge; the town stood at the center of waving wheat and rolling hills as far as the eye could see, and the highway stood as the city's primary artery. Beginning a northeast curve to Chicago at the city center, the highway was the demarcation line between the new and old Baldridge. There were only two parts of Baldridge's old city that crossed into the Latimer school district. One was found on the two blocks of mostly dilapidated homes beneath the third street overpass, while the other was the trailer park of Kind Pines. Most students who lived beyond the third street overpass opted to go to Baldridge despite being in the Latimer district. Cullen and his sister, Tamira, had been exceptions. Their dad wanted them to stay in the Latimer district. Cullen could hear his dad's voice: "Students who go to Latimer go to college." But Cullen and his sister never were selected for the college readiness programs when they went to Latimer's Prairie Range Middle School. Cullen heard Tamira's voice at the end of her 7th grade year: "We ain't welcome at Preppy Heights, Cullen. I'm out. You should go too if you know what's good." Cullen sighed. He didn't know what it was. Maybe it was being in Dex's class since Kindergarten, maybe it was playing on the same b-ball team since elementary school. He didn't know, but there was something that kept him at Latimer for all this time.

Cullen's radio station shifted from a track from Shawnna into an ad for North College, which blared through his car's speakers.

"Your future is our mission. Everyone is welcome to North College to fulfill one goal, one dream, and one--"

Cullen muted the radio with a frustrated look on his face. Looking up at the abandoned buildings that lined the road under the third street overpass, Cullen sighed and turned towards his home.

He drove through the boarded-up businesses and into the two blocks of residential neighborhoods on this side of 3rd street. Many of the homes featured tattered paint and boarded up windows. Cullen stopped at a four way stop on Cheeseboro lane.

Cullen quoted his grandfather: "It's all 'cause of that damn Cheeseboro." Cullen was told several times over about Samuel Cheeseboro, the brother of John Cheeseboro. John was the home developer who built all these homes. Unfortunately for John, the Great Depression came a couple of months after he finished, and it ended his grand plans for the neighborhood overnight. Samuel ended up with the homes.

Cullen heard his grandpa's voice: "And Sam destroyed the neighborhood!"

Cullen looked down Cheeseboro road. It was fitting. There was nothing left but foundations of old buildings and wheat fields off in the horizon. He drove up to the blue and white house that he, his dad, and his sister had given a fresh coat of paint.

"But Cheeseboro didn't sell any of the houses," Cullen's grandfather's voice continued. "He and his family bled them out until this whole block was unlivable. But not our house. This house here is an Armstrong house."

Cullen stepped out of his Dodge Stealth and walked toward the mailbox at the corner of the driveway. He was still foggy on the details, but somehow his granddad bought the home on a land-contract, and it stayed in the family until today. There was no chance to sell it, though. Homes didn't cost anything out here. Cullen reached in the mailbox and pulled out an envelope from North College, addressed to him.

Cullen's heart skipped a beat. He wasn't ready for this. Taking a breath, Cullen tore the envelope open and saw the unmistakable, bold "**Accepted**" near the top. There were other words, too. Happy ones.

Depositing the letter into his pocket, Cullen opened the door and stepped into his house.

His dad was passed out in the lazy chair in the living room. His sister, Tamira, was cutting up apples for Uncle Warren's dinner at their wooden dinner table. Warren was on top of his electric wheelchair, which he had decorated like the iron throne.

Cullen smiled. "Love the throne, Warren."

Warren replied, his voice measured. "Hi…jackass."

"Hi to you, too, Uncle."

Tamira looked up at Cullen. She had a rich Black complexion and was wearing a silver bonnet over her hair. "What's good?"

Cullen looked at his younger sister. "Eh. BS day."

Tamira smirked. "BS at the Latimer Prep? You're kiddin'."

Warren let out wheezes of laugher. Cullen looked at his sister. "Does Baldridge still want to burn our school down?"

"Eh, they're calmin' down. Russ is still pissed you didn't transfer over. He sees you as a sellout, just bein' honest."

Cullen nodded. "Yeah, he's been comin' after me on social."

Tamira shrugged. "He'll be alright. He's just mad you held him to 5 points. I don't think any of the team has any beef with you. They hate Adam, though."

"What else is new?"

"Another early mornin' tomorrow?"

Cullen nodded. "Meetin' Dex early. You'll be happy to know that he and Kit broke up, so we're gettin' some guy time."

Tamira sputtered, "Psh. Dex is a suburb boy."

Cullen laughed. "Girl, you've been mackin' on him since pre-school."

Tamira waved him off. "He's too short."

Cullen rolled his eyes. "He's what, an inch shorter than you? Whatever, sis. You know I got in trouble today for only being three minutes early for mornin' practice. According to Hardcastle, being less than 5 minutes early is late."

Tamira raised an eyebrow. "That's so bougie. He ever get on Golden Boy Augustine about stuff like this?"

Cullen laughed. "Adam could walk in with a *Cheech n Chong* sized joint and still be on the starting team."

Warren spoke. "Cullen… you hear anything from the… NC?"

Cullen looked to his uncle. His sister was looking up at him too. Cullen shook his head. "Nah. Nothin' yet."

Tamira tapped her brother's shoulder. "Ah, you'll get in. I know it."

Chapter 15: *The Predator*

Lynne grabbed the metal lock outside of Tommy's door. The lock was through an iron latch and was one of the three locks guarding Tommy's bedroom. The door was also locked at the door handle, and Tommy was right to think his mom had a back-up key to that in her room.

Lynne put a hand on Tommy's bedroom door and closed her eyes, thinking through what she was about to do. She had ignored the signs last April. She had seen a few, of course. But it wasn't real until the phone call she got and the cool, arrogant voice of Jay Stallard informing her that her son was in custody. She thought of her son's swollen hand. It all could be about to happen again.

She remembered the moments of elation when Tommy was allowed back at Latimer on a 4-3 vote by the school board. The board president read a letter from an anonymous teacher defending their right to teach Tommy and Tommy's right to be a writer. She didn't think Tommy would have come back without that letter. Mr. Stallard was not swayed. She remembered what he told her like it was seconds ago.

"Your son is a predator," he said out in the parking lot.

Lynne opened her eyes. There was no other way. Lynne stepped outside their single-wide trailer and walked around the edges of Red Oak road. She rounded the corner of the trailer and stepped over the Riggs and Sutton mower that had been dead in their yard for three years.

Lynne approached Tommy's outdoor window and felt along the outside casing. She remembered these windows. They were installed by some government program to better insulate all the trailers in Kind Pines and keep the electricity bills low. The windows were okay. But they tended to fall apart after a couple of years. With a good landlord (like the one she heard about at Friendly Acres) this wouldn't have been a problem. But the only windows Richard Cheeseboro was willing to repair were the double-wides on Green Oak road. Those who lived on Red Oak were out of luck.

"Frickin' Dick Cheeseboro," Lynne whispered.

It was nice to have good windows for a while, but as she looked at Tommy's window now, the screen had been torn out two years ago (like most in their trailer). What Tommy didn't realize was that all she needed was a little room.

Lynne took a flat tipped screwdriver from her back pocket and inserted it into a small crease on the right side of the storm window. The storm window popped out with very little pressure and gave access to Tommy's inner window, which she pushed open with ease.

Tommy never locked his bedroom window, and he couldn't. The lock for it had broken soon after the screen was torn apart.

Lynne thought of Tommy's complex locks on the outside of his door and smiled. "Amateur."

Lynne climbed in her son's window and scanned the insides of his room. While she was here, she figured she looked for her old trophy, too.

"I told him I bought the trophy at a yard sale. He probably didn't think it meant anything to me." Lynne stumbled up to her feet. "I bet he thought it would look good on the top of his roll top."

She could see it clear as day inside her mind. A half a foot long, the trophy had a blue hilt that bared a golden Baldridge hawk at its top. She could see its inscription: "Baldridge High School's vocalist of the year: Jaime Lynne Tate." She was itching to find her trophy.

Dust-clogged sunlight streamed through Tommy's bedroom windows. It wasn't at the top of his roll top. Lynne continued to scan the room. There were several holes in his wooden door, including small blood-stained droplets on the exterior of the holes.

"He wasn't fighting someone, so that's good," she mused. She opened a drawer to his rolltop, and Tommy's green journal was right below her sight.

A misguided, dangerous understanding was forming inside her mind. "Could it be happening again?" She wondered. Could all her answers be in here? She had thought Tommy was done with journaling. She *warned* him to quit.

She moved her right hand to her face.

And then it happened.

Lynne's phone rang from inside her pocket. Gingerly lifting her phone, Lynne's greatest fears were confirmed. *It was from the school.* Could she have been a step behind again?

Lynne braced for the voice of Mr. Stallard. "…Hello?"

A man answered, with a warmer tone. "Yes, Ms. Tate?"

"This is her."

"Excellent. I'm Mr. Austin. I saw this cell phone was added to your parent account and I was wanting to make sure it would work. I apologize if I disturbed you. I wanted to let you know that your son is rocking my honors art class. I even heard from Principal Elmer that's he in line to win Latimer's most improved student this year."

"Huh?" Lynne answered, taken aback.

"Your son is doing great. Killin' it, as the kids say."

Her mouth open, Lynne didn't know how to respond.

"Ms. Tate? Are you there?"

Lynne was in a different world. Tommy -- her Tommy -- could win most improved student.

Mr. Austin continued, "Ms. Tate?"

Lynne snapped out of her daze. "Please, call me Lynne. Uh, thank you for this. Feel free to call me about Tommy any time."

"Of course. Have a good day!"

Feeling jarred, Lynne ended the call.

Her thoughts ran wild inside her mind. "He's the most improved student, but where in the hell did *that* come from? He was wanting his GED this year, but had he even mentioned the GED since the year started?"

Resting in Tommy's rolltop desk, her son's green journal sat beneath the light.

A rueful gaze colored over her features. "He'll never tell me why he's changed."

Lynne's hand remaining on the journal, a dangerous idea entered her mind.

"He wouldn't, but something else might." Settling into the boy's chair, the mother continued to reason. "I should at least make sure he ain't in trouble." She looked at the front cover of the journal, and saw that Tommy wrote UNSORTED in all capital letters on the front. She laughed. Her whole life felt unsorted, so she could empathize with her son.

Swallowing, Lynne opened Tommy's journal and began to read.

The Unsorted Texts: *November 15th*

I used to think I was like a poster on a classroom wall. Though bright and laminated, after a while I forgot what they said, I forgot what they looked like and I forgot they were there at all. Now I think I'm below these posters. It's not that people don't see me, it's that they wilfully unsee me, and when I'm not seen people forget that I can see at all.

....But I see everything.

I see where Rosi's looking when she tears into to me, I hear the whispers into Brian's ears before he turns the barrel on me.

He is the master pupeteer. It all begins and ends with Adam Augustine. Sometimes I get so close to crashing down the path I did last April. But no one understands. People haven't seen the Adam that I have seen for the last ten years. Hell, people aren't even looking.

But all in all? The year's been better than I exspected. Much better. I have found a gang of defectors. Mia, Dexter, Cullen, and I'd even throw Mr. Austin in there too. I don't really know if they're my friends, but I like being around them, and they don't seem to mind when I'm with them. There are days I can imagine life differently when I'm around them, and days where it feels like an ilussion.

I gotta go. I'm drawing up ideas for Mr. Austin's art project. It's funny to think that the only reason I'm in art is because of a Dr. Pepper.

Lynne read and re-read that last line several times. "What the hell?" Out of everything her son wrote, that confused her the most.

Sliding the journal back inside the rolltop. Another idea crossed Lynne's mind. Lynne reached for a small drawer at the corner of the rolltop and multiple copies of chained up keys slid in the drawer. Taking a breath, Lynne pulled out the keys and planned to copy them at the first opportunity.

"No more climbing through windows."

—

When Tommy made it home, Lynne watched him shed his backpack and make a break for the kitchen pantry. Stepping over a couple of cardboard boxes, Tommy opened a kitchen cabinet and looked inside.

Lynne, watching her son from the corner of the living room, thought over what to say. "How was school?"

"Okay," the boy muttered, dragging a Ho-Ho from the cabinet.

The mother looked at her son and tried to sift through her emotions to say something.

"Lynne?" the boy asked.

"Yeah?" she replied, her voice hopeful.

"We're out of Ho-Hos."

"Oh, I'll have to buy some more."

"Cool," Tommy said, walking to his bedroom.

Uncertainty plaguing her, Lynne watched her son depart into the room.

—

An hour after hearing Tommy's lamp go off, Lynne tiptoed through her trailer and sidled up to Tommy's unlocked room. Her palms trembling, she pushed open the door and peeked inside.

He was fast asleep. The only thing visible was his left hand, and it hung exposed out of his white blanket.

The yellow eyes of the black cat stared back at her.

Staring at their cat nestled in her place atop the boy, Lynne whispered, "Thanks for keeping an eye on him."

Chapter 16: *Where the Roaches Run*

"My name is Tommy Tate, and I am seventeen years old."

Tommy snorted. This sounded like the beginning of an orientation activity.

"My name is Tommy Tate, ~~and I am seventeen years old."~~

Tommy had been trying to write an outline for the "Artist in You" project for the last few days.

"My name is Tommy Tate, ~~and I am seventeen years old~~ I like pizza rolls."

Tommy was hoping to do this to figure out what he wanted to do for the project. But so far, he was stumped.

The lights of Dexter Allen's white truck appeared at the entrance of Kind Pines.

Cramming his journal into his bag, Tommy jumped into Dexter's vehicle.

—

The next morning, Tommy stood beside the Manchester Highway. In truth, he didn't get much done with his project the night before, but that was okay. He spent the entire night clowning around with Cullen and Dexter. Tommy hadn't had a night like that in…

He couldn't even remember. Besides, he was going to design something that would blow Mr. Austin out of the water. He just needed to find the right idea.

Tommy looked across the Manchester highway. It was the first morning of Latimer's Thanksgiving break and, more importantly, Thayne's birthday.

His home across the highway from Kind Pines, Tommy tucked Thayne's gift in his jacket and stepped onto the road.

—

Tommy stood in the shadow of his aunt's double wide trailer. Four years ago, Cocaine Thayne left high school and decided to start up a house painting business. Thayne had big plans back then; he was going to use the job to "blow outta this pop stand" and promised 12-year-old Tommy that he could join the business once he was ready. Thayne started his company by giving his mother's double wide the paint job she always wanted. He encountered numerous problems right away. His co-founders split after two hours on the job, and he had neglected to lay tarp beside the home, causing paint drops to remain on the concrete to this day.

Tan-colored primer rose about five feet from the trailer foundation before yielding to a white paint which had been peeling for two decades or more, creating a juxtaposition that exposed the halted dreams of those inside the home. And now, through the inevitability of time, Thayne's tan coat of paint had begun to peel from the house as well.

Tommy stepped on the trailer's porch and saw the front door was slightly ajar. Unsure if he needed to, Tommy knocked and waited. A roach came from beneath the door and crawled over Tommy's shoe. Not hearing a response, Tommy pushed inside.

Clothing, pots and pans, and garage sale worthy memorabilia had been sorted in a bizarre system around the living room. Two cats roosted atop of the piles of clothing and seemed to have sprayed over the pile until the odor had caked into the fabric. For the last five years, Thayne had talked about his mother's intentions to participate in the annual city-wide yard-sale, but to this day it never happened.

Holding his breath, Tommy yelled for his cousin. "Thayne?"

A gunshot blasted out from outside, shaking the trailer at its foundation. Tommy leapt in surprise and heard a female voice cackle behind him.

He turned to see his aunt, Grace. Grace was only three years older than Lynne, but she looked as though she could be nearing her sixties. Grace's

stark white skin hung down like worn out elastic, while strands of grey, matted hair drooped around her skull like dying branches. Unlike his mom, Grace still carried her Tennessee drawl, which Tommy only heard from his mom after a couple of glasses of wine. He wished he heard it more, to be honest. Grace and Lynne's childhoods in the Smoky Mountains were rarely talked about at home. Grace tapped a cigarette into an ashtray and bellowed to Tommy, revealing three missing teeth in the front of her mouth.
"Thayne's tryin' out his new birthday gift."

Tommy was bewildered. "You got Thayne a gun?"

"No, but Rock found him one on the *Craig's list.* They're out back havin' target practice."

Tommy's heart sank. "Thayne didn't tell me Rock was going to be here."

"Well, he's here, and you know where to find 'em if you still care to see my son on his birthday."

Tommy resisted the temptation to roll his eyes and maneuvered between piles of cardboard boxes that lined the sides of the hallways. Touched with splotches of multicolored mold that covered the boxes like an abstract painting, the mountainous piles reached a height even taller than Tommy.

Tommy stepped outside and took a breath again. A massive, yellow field stood behind the trailers in Friendly Acres. Rock and Thayne stood tall at the field's edge and had built a makeshift target practice about fifteen yards from the fence along the boundary. Charcoal clouds swirled in the afternoon skies and bitter winds spiked in an intermittent fashion. Walking closer toward Rock and his cousin, Tommy saw they had bound a child-sized mannequin against a wooden fence.

Thayne took aim and screamed out to Rock. "Watch this, bitch."

Thayne fired. The bullet blasted out of the revolver and blistered the fence about five feet to the side of the mannequin.

Close behind him, Tommy called out to his cousin. "Looks like you missed by a bit."

Thayne turned around, beaming. "Hey, Tommy!"

"Happy birthday, Thayne."

Standing a foot over Tommy, Rock glowered down to him. "Sup, Tommy Taint?"

Thayne showed off his gun. "Look what Rock got me! It's a .45 with 10 shots."

"Nice," Tommy muttered through his teeth.

Rock spat on the yellow field. "Nice? Orgasmic is what it is."

"Well, I didn't get you a gun, Thyane. But, I got something for you, too."

Tommy handed the small envelope to his cousin.

Opening it up, Thayne looked up excitedly. "A gift card to Hooters? Hell yeah!"

Rock smiled. "Thank your mom for him, Tommy."

Tommy glared. "Will do."

"God dang," Thayne burst out.

Tommy looked to his cousin and saw a roach walking out on the front of his hoodie.

"How many of those do you and your ma put up with?" Rock spat.

"Just a few," Thayne responded, his voice defensive. "Tommy has a few, too."

"Nope," Tommy said, in no mood to pamper Thayne. Lynne despised roaches, in large part because they infested her home back in her childhood. Tommy could say a lot about his mom, but she kept her home roach free.

"Well, I don't get that," Thayne said, his voice childlike. "Why aren't they in your trailer, Tommy?"

Rock smirked and put a hand on Thayne's shoulder. "Have you seen that pile? Even the roaches run from Dead Oak."

A dormant rage awoke inside Tommy. The boy directed a glare to Rock Rustin's gaze, and Rock responded in kind.

"Heh, yeah," Thayne breathed, squashing the roach against his neck. "Now watch this."

Thayne fired another shot, this one ricocheting off the trees behind the target.

Rock laughed. "He hasn't hit a single shot."

Thayne got defensive and held the gun to Rock. "It's not like you'd be any better."

Sneering at Thayne, Rock took the gun.

"Where'd you pick up the mannequin?" Tommy asked.

"Swiped it and a sensormatic from *Discount Clothing* before it closed," Rock said.

"Oh really?" Tommy asked. "Was that before or after *Buzzards*?"

Looking at the mannequin, something glazed over Rock's expression. "After. Otherwise it would have been shot up months ago."

Tommy's mouth curled. "Is this something you do often?"

Without a word, Rock pointed the gun at Tommy.

Tommy felt his heart race. Staring down the barrel of a gun, panic seized his body.

"Yes. Wanna know why?" Rock sneered.

Tommy kept his mouth shut.

"Ask me why, Tommy Taint."

His legs shaking, Tommy asked in spite of himself. "Why?"

"Say my name when talking to me, Piss Stain."

"Why, *Rock*?

"So when fat bitches throw shade, I know exactly where to aim." Keeping the gun pointed at Tommy, Rock continued, "How long would it take a pig to bleed out?"

Tommy kept his mouth shut.

"How long would it take, fatty?"

Keeping his mouth clamped, Tommy stared into Rock's eyes, daring him to shoot.

Without another word, Rock turned the .45 to the mannequin, and fired. The bullet blasted through the mannequin's ribs and created a baseball sized crater over its heart. Sneering down at Tommy, Rock held the revolver out to him. "Wanna go next?"

His body quivering, Tommy swiped the revolver from Rock's grasp. His right hand was still in the makeshift cast, meaning he'd have to shoot with his left.

"Don't get your clam juice on it." Rock snickered.

Tommy's eyes flared up, determined, he pointed the gun at the mannequin and fired.

The blast snapped Tommy's arm back and smashed the revolver into his face. Bent over in pain, blood poured out of Tommy's nostrils as Rock and Thayne doubled over in laughter.

The laughter rolling through his ears, Tommy felt a rage boil over him. Tommy, standing up, advanced toward the target and fired, missing again. The boy strode closer, undeterred, and fired another shot that grazed the side of the target. Spitting the blood from his mouth, Tommy stepped closer and looked into the eyes of the child.

Aiming the revolver, the boy fired. The shot blasted into the face of small mannequin and caused it to explode, pieces splintering out in each direction and some even ending up on Tommy.

His face contorted into an uncontrolled fury, Tommy turned back toward Rock and his cousin. Neither were laughing now, and Tommy kept his eyes locked on Rock until the two were face to face.

With blood spurting down his face, Tommy held his voice in a deadly whisper. “If you ever threaten me again, no one will ever find your body.”

Throwing the emptied gun at Rock’s feet, Tommy departed in a rage.

—

Hours later, the green journal laid beneath Tommy’s gaze.

"My name is Tommy Tate, ~~and I am seventeen years old~~ I like pizza rolls.

And I come from where the roaches run."

Looking oddly satisfied with his creative decision, Tommy stowed the journal in his rolltop desk.

Chapter 17: *Wicked Game*

Rosi sat on a barstool at the edge of a kitchen counter. Beer bottles had accumulated on each surface of the dining area. Commentary from a football game filtered in from the living room.

The male voice of the commentator drifted into Rosi's eardrums. "It's Thanksgiving, and there's nothing better than sitting down with your family after a big meal and watching a game between these two classic teams."

Rosi looked at the remnants of the hot pocket on the plate before her. "What a meal," she thought ruefully. Rosi carried the small plate to the sink and carefully set it on the leaning tower of dishes in the kitchen.

She turned from the kitchen and walked through a corridor into the living room. Her dad's sizable crack was visible above his red shorts, and he himself was passed out on the floor face down in front of the TV.

Rosi felt a vibration from her phone. Adam was video calling her.

Gasping, Rosi stepped outside of her double-wide and carefully positioned herself under a tree. She dressed up in a smile and answered. "Hey, babe!"

Adam smiled. "Hey." He was decked out in a blue dress shirt and a basketball tie.

Rosi beamed. "You look so handsome."

"Psh. It's Thanksgiving. It's what you do."

Rosi rolled her eyes. "I'm dressed in sweatpants and a hoodie. How're your folks?"

"Not here yet. I was thinkin', you know, if you were done eating, maybe you'd like to join us?"

Rosi's eyes widened. "Really? Is everything okay?"

"Yeah, yeah. I just know you'd said Thanksgiving wasn't a big deal and what not and maybe you'd like to join me?"

Rosi glanced back to her double wide. "I'll have to see if my dad will let me borrow his car, but that... shouldn't be a problem."

"Tight," Adam replied. "See you soon, girl."

Rosi ran back inside. Changing her clothes in rapid fashion, she lifted her dad's keys from his room and made to walk out of their home. Before exiting, she paused. Looking at her dad, Rosi closed her eyes. Worried he might vomit in his sleep, she walked over and whispered to him. "Let's get you on your side, okay?"

—

Rosi watched Adam strike a match against the corner of a match box. He guided the light to a vanilla candle on the kitchen table and kindled it to life. Rosi smiled. He was being so precise with everything, which was a big difference from his typical demeanor. He had vacuumed his grandparents' shag carpets and scrubbed the open surfaces. The aromas of ham and apple pie wafted from the kitchen, while the sound of Bing Crosby's "Mele Kalikimaka" carried in from the stereo. Rosi sat back. Everything about this home stood in direct contrast to her own. It was spacious, but didn't really seem to know what to do with all its extra space. It had shag carpets, flowery wallpaper, and discolored wooden tables all around it.

Adam's grandfather was tall and blessed with a full head of snow-white hair. Dressed in a #8 blue jersey, he rested his hands on his belly and stretched on a recliner in the living room. "You finish scrubbin' the toilet, Adam?"

Adam smiled. "Sure did. You'll need to pick up more toilet cleaner when you can."

"Thanks for doing that," Adam's grandpa said. "It's horrible for my knees. Hazel!" he yelled, looking to Adam's grandmother. "Why are you playing Christmas music?"

Hazel smiled. "It's never too early to get started."

Rosi jumped in. "Besides, there's not a whole lot of Thanksgiving music out there."

Adam's grandfather held up his hands. "That's a fair point. Adam, did Cody say he was coming?"

"Dad said he would be here at 7:00. So about thirty minutes?"

Adam's grandpa held out a hand. "Well, guess it's time for me to get cleaned up then."

"What, you don't think a jersey is appropriate for dinner?" Adam asked, lifting his grandpa to his feet.

"Not when I haven't seen my son in over a year."

Hazel yelled from the kitchen. "It's only been six months, Dennis."

Adam's grandpa replied, "Still too long. Adam, you may want to get a couple more chairs 'round the table."

Rosi jumped in. "Here, I can do that."

Rosi walked into the kitchen, and instantly Adam's grandma Hazel squeezed her cheeks. "Don't let this one get away, Adam."

Rosi watched Adam turn a bright shade of red. "Stop, Mimi."

Rosi laughed. "She's not wrong."

Hazel changed the subject. "I don't think we've seen Lindsey or Junior in two years. Junior must be getting big!"

Dennis grunted. "He turned five last Saturday. Adam, I think we have a couple extra plates in the garage. Since Rosanna is grabbing the chairs, can you fetch the plates?"

"Definitely."

"Alright," Dennis muttered; "be sure to get them set. They'll be here soon."

Unintentionally beaming, Adam departed toward the garage.

—

Rosi shivered in the darkness. She sat at Adam's empty Thanksgiving table, a room now illuminated only from a waning candle at the table.

Adam stepped into the living room, and Rosi couldn't help herself.

"Adam. I am so sorry."

Adam turned away from her and moved to the fridge. "It's alright! It makes sense. Junior got sick after breakfast today. It ain't a big deal. It would have been miserable for him to come here feeling that way."

"But Adam, you haven't seen your dad in--"

Adam held up a hand. "He's a busy guy, and you should have heard him over the phone. He felt worse about it than I did, Rose."

"Couldn't he have come alone?"

Stepping into the dining room, Adam blew out the candle. "And leave Junior alone sick? I couldn't do that to either of them. Plus, that means more banana pudding for us."

Swallowing her retort, Rosi watched the candle's smoke billow to the ceiling. Overwhelmed with conflicting emotions, Rosi watched Adam open a tub of leftovers and assemble a plate from the pudding dish. "So, uh," Rosi started, "were you wanting me to stay for any reason specifically?"

"I already told you that. I know how your dad is and just thought you might want a proper Thanksgiving."

Rosi pushed back. "Adam. Talk to me here--"

Adam cut her off, his voice firm. "Fine," he said, letting the interjection hang in the air. "I just... I just want you here tonight, that's all."

Rosi nodded. Though she knew there was something deeper, she retreated her interrogation and allowed Adam to dictate the conversation. The two talked about the night's football games and Adam's next b-ball game against the Pawnee Tigers. She wasn't sure how it happened, but eventually Adam led her by the hand from the dining room to his bedroom. The only light in the room was shed from the street light down the block. Rosi settled beside Adam and pulled him close.

Adam pulled back. "Rose?"

"Yeah?"

Adam whispered, "Can we just lay together tonight?"

"Of course."

"Thanks, babe."

Rosi looked at the ceiling, grasping for something to say. "Hey, Adam?"

"Yeah?"

"Is there any chance… any at all, that I could spend Christmas Break with you?"

Adam sighed. "Well... you know I would if I could. But I'm just... my head isn't in the right place for that right now."

Rosi nodded. "No, no. It's okay. I get it."

Adam continued, "--and with basketball."

Rosi cooed, "Adam. It's okay."

"Thank you. I knew you'd understand."

"One more thing?"

Adam looked at her suspiciously.

"Remind me what's gonna happen on February 18th?"

Adam grinned. "I'm gonna take my father's all-time single game record."

Rosi smiled. The conversation was almost muscle memory now. "Why?"

"Because it's destiny, Rose."

Pulling Adam in close, Rosi fell asleep.

Chapter 18: *Tommy T.*

Tommy woke up and laid in bed for a few minutes longer than normal. It felt like a normal day. That's because in the past, it was a normal day.

Today was his birthday. December 3rd. He was two weeks late when he was born (his mom liked to remind him), and he felt like he was two weeks late in his life in general. When he was younger, he'd always ask to stay home. He never had big parties like his classmates or much to mark the occasion. His mom always sent him to school anyway. She usually worked on this day. If he was lucky, she would bring home a dinner and cake from the drive-in. He always wanted a shared party with Thayne when he was younger, but Thayne's birthdays were too special to share, at least according to Thayne.

Tommy stopped in his tracks when he made it to the living room. His mom was holding a box, carefully wrapped for the occasion. It already didn't feel like a normal birthday.

"Tommy?" she said. Tommy could feel the nervousness in her voice. "I always promised that when you were 18, I was gonna tell you everything about your pa. I'm going to keep my word about that, but I thought today I could give you something small. From him."

Tommy felt himself shaking when he stepped up to the box. He had never known anything about his dad, other than the fact that his name was Terrance.

Very carefully, Tommy peeled back the wrapping and opened into the box, revealing a suede leather jacket that looked like it may have been new. Tommy saw the name "Terrance" written on the tag and ran over it with his fingers.

Lynne whispered, "Try it on."

Without hesitation, Tommy lifted the jacket from the hanger and threw it over his body. Tan tassels swayed from the jacket's chest as Tommy strode around the living room, and he wondered if this was the first thing he ever owned that was "one of a kind."

Tears in her eyes, Lynne asked, "What do you think?"

Tommy looked at his mom. "This is...... the most badass thing I've ever owned."

"Happy birthday, son."

—

The name's Tommy, the boy thought. *Tommy T.*

There was something new in his step -- a purpose his classmates in this town had never seen. The boy felt like the man with no name from *The Good, The Bad, and The Ugly*, and the newfound pride even stole the voice from his traditional antagonists.

Brian and Rosi were walking in Tommy's shadow, but even they seemed to struggle to find any noticeable blemishes. Aiming to sweep the confidence from Tommy's step, Brian spewed the only insult he could find.

"Nice dandruff, Tommy Taint!"

Stopping to turn around, Tommy addressed Brian with a slow, cocky salute that seemed to take him off guard. Around the corner of the hallway, Mia walked into Tommy and knocked the boy off balance.

"Tommy!" Mia yelled, wrapping her arms around him to keep him steady.

Halting the traffic behind Tommy, Brian watched the scene unfold with a look of terror.

Her arms on Tommy's shoulders, the girl surveyed the boy's attire. "Wow! I love the jacket, Tommy!"

The boy fumbled his response: "Th-thank you."

"Are you ready for your test on short stories?"

"Yeah. I think it's going to be the cat's pajamas."

Mia reached up and gave Tommy a handerpants-covered high five. "I can't wait to hear about it."

Tommy looked back at Brian and saw a murderous look in his eye. Brian turned around so fast that he almost knocked Rosi over, and he pointed a finger inches away from her throat.

"Not a freakin' word!" he screamed to Rosi.

Tommy felt Mia turn around beside him. She spoke to Rosi. "Are you okay?"

Rosi nodded. Her eyes wide in surprise.

Mia dropped her voice to a whisper. "Get away from him. He's dangerous, Rose. C'mon, Tommy."

After sharing an odd look of confusion with Rosi, Tommy followed Mia's footsteps in the hallway.

—

The smell was overwhelming.

The perpetrator was a skinny, balding man at the front of Mr. Austin's classroom. Donned in a loose-fitting salmon-colored suit, he flaunted an open can of barbecue vienna sausages, emanating an aroma like dollar store cat food. The man forked down the sausages with a discolored toothpick. Choking down his third vienna sausage, the man stuck the toothpick behind his left ear and addressed the students.

"Now that we've all made it, my name is Mr. Good. You can call me Peter, Pete or anything else really. I am fond of the nicknames. I will be substituting for Mr. Austin as he tends to a family issue. I would not call myself an 'art expert,' but my brother just gave me a painting he found on the world wide web. I am not a great person to ask questions about this class, but I will be here if you need me." Lifting his sausage can as if it were a glass of wine, Peter toasted his students and slurped the remaining water from the can. With his free hand, Peter lifted a book titled *The Rugged Cowboy* and retreated into literary seclusion.

His mouth gaping open, Cullen turned to Tommy. "Can you believe this?"

"I could be wrong," Tommy began, "but it looks like we have a week vacation in front of us. I guess that means Mr. Austin's submissions for the showcase are pushed back too."

Dexter cut into their conversation. "That jacket is fire, Tommy!"

Cullen nodded. "He ain't kiddin'. When I told you to find your thing, I didn't expect you to have somethin' like that lying around."

"Thanks, guys! It was a surprise birthday gift."

Dexter shook his head. "You mean to tell me it's your birthday?! Happy birthday, kid!"

Cullen hit Tommy on the shoulder. "Happy birthday."

Mia asked, "Where did your mom find a jacket like that?"

"It was my dad's I guess. I uh… don't actually know anything else about him."

Cullen jumped in. "Damn, Tommy. I had no idea."

"It's alright. I feel like I'm someone out in a western in this thing. Like I'm Tommy T."

There was a momentary silence at the table before everyone bust up laughing. Cullen patted Tommy on the back. "Whatever you say, T."

Dex spoke to Cullen. "Any idea where Mr. A is?"

Cullen shook his head. "I know as much as you do."

"My mom was meaning to ask him something -- she might need to call him."

"Do you know him outside of school?" Tommy asked.

Dexter nodded. "He painted our house last summer and did a bang-up job. He's wantin' to do some paint work for an uncle of mine this summer."

Tommy was puzzled. "He painted your house? Just for fun? Or....?"

Dexter laughed. "Heh, no. He runs a house-painting business in the summer."

"Really? I had no idea."

Mia pointed to the tablet in front of Tommy. "Are you working on your project for the showcase?"

Tommy nodded.

Mia continued, "Can I see what you have so far?"

Tommy shook his head. "I'm stuck. I honestly don't know what I'm going to do for this project."

"I was thinking," Cullen said, "if you guys are up for it, maybe we could meet at the Riverfront Brewery to study for our finals on Saturday? I could pick you up, Tommy."

Tommy nodded. "Works for me."

Dexter replied, "I'm on the clock that day, but as long as you leave me a good tip y'all can chill in my section."

Mia chimed in. "I'll see you losers there."

—

Unsorted: December 13th

I get why people love women, but why do people love men? I've thought a lot about this lately and I think I now know less about women than I thought I did. Last week should have been a crappy week, Mr. Austin's showcase project is now due at the end of the semester, but everything I've tried has been refried ass, I got a 63 on my Algebra II test, and Adam coined the phrase "Taint Jacket". But, even with all that I'm happier than I've been in a long time and it's all because Mia has started to walk with me through the hallways. What is wrong with me? How can a five minute walk every other day make me feel this way? Am I going crazy? Even if Mia did like me, it's not like I can do anything about it. I have no phone, no internet, and no car. There's so much I want to know about her. We can only talk about so much during our walks each day. She's told me a lot, but I feel like I don't know who she really is. I wish I knew what she put in her hair, what she wants to do with her life, and why she carries around a dandelion. I asked her about the dandelions the other day, and she told me that she just liked the way they looked. I don't buy it, and I wish I could find out the real reason.

As long as I have those five minute walks, I'm unsure if anything could bring me down again... Women. I understand the craze.

A somber residue hung over Lynne's expression. It had become a daily ritual for Lynne to peer into her son's most guarded secrets, but today's entry had left her feeling morose. There was something so defeated in her son's writing. When she talked to Grace and Thayne about this, they were both convinced Tommy had a girlfriend, or maybe even a boyfriend that he hung out with after school. Tommy didn't have either. He had a five minute walk.

"Women. I understand the craze."

Lynne chuckled at her son's final line.

"You're gonna be disappointed, kid."

Gingerly returning her son's journal to its resting place, Lynne relocked his room and stepped back into the living room.

Chapter 19: ***Cold Death of the Earth***

Mia set out a massive sketchbook on an oversized booth at the Riverfront Brewery. There was a big plate of spinach and artichoke dip set at the corner of the wooden table, complete with four small plates to its side.

Dexter dropped a large glass of iced coffee beside Mia. "Anything else you need?"

Mia looked at the glass inquisitively. "Don't you normally say glasses this large require a lifeguard?"

"In my experience, older folks are the ones who find that funny."

"I just want to make sure I'm safe to drink this."

Dexter laughed. "I did get state runner up in the Butterfly. You won't find a more prestigious loser in swimming on our staff." Dexter knocked on the table. "Cullen and Tommy just walked in."

Mia held her arms out for them. "I got spin dip, fools!"

Tommy yelled out excitedly, "All right!"

Dexter gave Cullen a fist bump. "And she gave me strict instructions to keep you stocked up on chips through the evening."

Dexter walked to another table as Cullen took a seat. "Evening?" Cullen said in surprise. "What's Stallard havin' you do?"

Mia rolled her eyes. "Mr. Stallard told us at 3:05 on Friday that he wanted us having completed posters for a new campaign by Monday freaking morning."

"You have no way out of it?"

"None. We only have two projects like this we can be excused for, and I've worked too hard to not have his recommendation by the end of this."

Tommy slid into his seat. "What's the campaign?"

"We are supposed to tell the 'True Story' of LHS by creating social media profiles of what different kids get from LHS."

"Different?"

Mia smirked. "It's the word he uses for 'diversity.'"

Cullen laughed. "He is such a crouton."

"It gets better. We're supposed to make it look like a social media profile by using 'common phrases from social media.'"

Dexter turned around from the end of his section. "Common phrases from social media? Damn -- Mr. Stallard's *coool.*"

Tommy's brow furrowed. "So this is a project to make LHS look awesome or whatever. Did any of the students on STUCO choose to do this?"

Mia responded, "Did we choose this bougie project? I'm insulted."

Cullen pushed Tommy. "It's like you don't even know Mr. Stallard."

Mia changed the subject. "Any luck with your art project?"

Tommy responded, "Nah, I just don't know where to start."

"What about your jacket?"

"Nah, the jacket still doesn't feel like mine. It feels like my dad's, a person I don't even know."

"So what do you have that no one else has?"

"I have a boxcar," Tommy said.

"A boxcar?"

"Yeah, it's on a set of unused railroad tracks about a mile behind my trailer. Ever since I was ten years old, I've watched the trains go by and tell myself that one day, I'm gonna find a way out of here. There's a yellow ladder to an abandoned warehouse above the boxcar. I climb up that ladder when I think about... Well, just to think."

Mia beamed at Tommy. "Tommy…"

A fire sparked in Tommy's eyes. "Oh my God -- that's it, isn't it?"

Mia smiled from the excitement in Tommy's voice. There was something that made her happy when she saw it from him, because it was often rare to see.

A guy with a heavily stained tank top came into the Riverfront Brewery. Mia sat back and looked him over. The guy's hair was strewn all over the place, and he looked like he hadn't slept in years. He looked over, and for a moment, Mia thought he was looking at her.

The man yelled excitedly and walked over the table. "What's up, Tommy?!"

Absolutely thrilled, Mia turned to Tommy. "You know this person?!"

Tommy was beet red, adding to Mia's excitement. Tommy whispered, "He's more like a force of nature."

The guy sat at the empty space beside Cullen. "Damn straight. Name is Thayne." Without asking, Thayne grabbed a notecard-sized chip and took a healthy scoop of spin dip, leaving Mia speechless. With his mouth full, he explained, "I'm this loser's cousin."

Tommy turned towards her. "He's known as Cocaine Thayne."

Thayne snapped at Tommy, his mouth still full. "yer bedder known wit' my fist in your face. Aaaah." Thayne swallowed. "So, you're the crew who's got my cousin thinkin' school is cool."

Mia snorted. "You have the wrong crew."

"Really?" Thayne asked, putting a greasy finger on Mia's sketchpad. "Then what's this?"

Tommy spoke up. "Quit bein' a tool, dude."

Mia looked at the orange fingerprint on her sketchpad. "Been eating cheese puffs, Thayne?"

"Balls. Cheese balls. Got a whole tub in the outdoor smokin' area if you want some."

Cullen tilted his head. "Ain't that area just for staff?"

Dexter walked to the table. "He's 'friends' with a lot of the staff too - and all the cooks know Thayne."

Thayne took Dexter's hand. "Dex! How you doin'?"

"Oh, I'm over the moon now that I know you're related to Tommy."

Mia sighed. The cheese ball fingerprint had ruined her sketch. "Well. Now I got to start again."

Thayne needled her. "That ain't a problem. This time I'll help do it right."

"Oh really? You're going to help me make a sketch to show how 'all students succeed at Latimer'?'"

Thayne held up a hand. "Can I tell you a secret?"

"Hit me."

"Alright, I usually don't hand out this advice for free, but school is not for everyone. For kids like Tommy and I, it's not meant to be anything more than lock-up."

Cullen exhaled. "Lock-up?"

Thayne's eyes got really big. "That's exactly what it is. A warm place that gives us food each day."

Mia mused. "That sounds like child-care."

"Y'all may not know this still bein' in high school and all, but once you're in your teens, the word for child care is lock-up. In adulthood, the word becomes prison. Eventually it's a retirement home for everyone. The older you are, the worse the words become."

"What benefit is there in imprisoning kids like you and Tommy?" Mia asked.

To Mia's surprise, Cullen was the one who answered. "It lets kids go to day care so their parents can get to work."

Mia thought it over. "That free day care is probably really expensive. Think of how much it costs for childcare, busing, lunch and what not?"

Cullen pushed back. "Yeah, but it's hella cheaper than helping folks in their communities. We don't offer free childcare, but we do if you call it school. Kids can't get their eyes checked, but they do if it happens at school. You really think school lunch is food anyone wants? Nah, it's food no one else is buyin'. Our society offers nothing for free unless someone else gets a cut. Think of all the elementary, middle and high schools in the country - and all of that money they're paying farming companies to get that low-quality food. A bunch of people benefit with kids in lock-up."

Thayne snorted. "Settle down there, comrade."

Cullen turned to Mia and mouthed, "What the…"

Mia looked at Thayne. "Alright. So school's lock-up. But I gotta make it a term that works for social media."

Dexter rejoined the conversation, sitting in an open spot around the booth. "You're now the only table in my section. Mind if I sit here?"

Mia nodded. "Of course. You had a plate until Cocaine Thayne stole yours. We're coming up with a term for Thayne's crowd in school."

Cullen spoke. "What about banned users?"

"I like it! It's like being banned on a platform." Mia wrote out "The Banned" on one side of the paper. She turned to Thayne. "And you like being called The Banned?"

"Hell yeah. It's the truth. I could never do the after-school programs, try out for a sport, a club -- nothin' like that. My ma didn't want me on the grid. But you know what, I liked that. I was able to get out of school early on so I could work on blowing out of Felony Acres."

Mia finished up her sketch of Tommy and added a description below.

Tommy Tate - Banned

Mia was satisfied with her work. "Alright, next challenge. What's a student like me called?"

Dexter laughed. "You're a gold star, Mia."

"And you're a jackass, Dex. It has to be related to social media, remember?"

Thayne smiled. "What about badges - like those famous people have on social?"

"Yeah - like a verified badge," Dexter added.

Mia nodded. "I hate it, and I'm all about it. Badges are perfect."

Thayne agreed. "Badges are important. Y'all are the ones that make the system look like it's working. It's your posters they put in the halls, your stories they put in the paper. You sell the story that if kids work hard enough, school can be for everyone."

Cullen asked Thayne, "So we're just gettin' into cliques now? Kids get to school, and they choose the crew they want to hang with--"

Thayne interjected, "No. I never got to choose." He looked at Mia. "What would happen to you at home if you stopped getting good grades?"

"Honestly? My parents might disown me from shame."

Thayne held out his hands. "See?"

Mia sketched out her self-portrait on her notepad. "I agree with Thayne. It feels more like a pseudo-society than a clique."

Tommy raised an eyebrow. "What's the difference?"

Dexter answered, "Well, in the real world you always have say over what cliques you choose. But with these categories, I agree they're closer to a pseudo-society because your identity in school can have zero bearing over your identity in the real-world."

Mia grinned. "Gee, Dex. You just put it a lot better than I would have." Mia wrapped up her self-portrait and looked over the results of her sketch.

Mia Fernandez - A Badge

Tommy pushed back. "People like Adam Augustine get terrible grades - and he's still looked up to. I don't think you can call him A Badge."

Dexter thought it over. "That's because Adam's an 'Influencer.'"

Mia laughed. "Oh my God. He has status 'cause he has a rich dad and did nothing to actually earn that status."

Cullen interjected, "Hey, now."

Dexter elbowed Cullen. "C'mon, you know it's true. You ever see Adam on the Honor Roll?"

Thayne took the last chip from the basket. "You know why this comrade is hot and bothered, right? It's because he's an Influencer, too!"

Cullen shot back. "My name's Cullen, pothead. I grew up on 3rd street. Ever hear the phrase 'don't take 3rd west of Salem'? That's my neighborhood, fool."

Thayne gestured toward Cullen. "So you grew up in one of the two run-down neighborhoods that sends kids to Latimer? The other bein' the hellhole my cousin grew up in, of course."

"Damn straight."

Thayne was insistent. "Still an Influencer, though."

Cullen looked over at Tommy. "Man, how have you not killed this dude?"

"I think about it every day."

Thayne replied, "Hear me out. Some Influencers' status is earned. I respect you all the more knowin' you grew up in that pile and now walk all in mighty. All in mighty for my cousin, anywho." Thayne turned to Tommy. "You should hear how much he talks about the Cullen Armstrong."

Tommy whispered, "Thayne..."

Thayne pushed the empty chip container to Dex. "You mind gettin' me a refill?"

"Ha. Swerve. I work for payin' customers only."

Looking across the table at Cullen for inspiration, Mia wrapped up her sketch.

Cullen Armstrong - Influencer

Cullen pushed back at Thayne. "So, if I'm an Influencer, does that mean people like Rosi Williams are Influencers too?"

Tommy whispered under his breath. "She wishes."

Thayne laughed. "But she wants to be right? She's an Influencer Wannabe."

Cullen snapped his fingers. "So, like Brian Miller?"

Dexter laughed. "Exactly."

Mia tisked. "I need a phrase, remember?"

Tommy answered, "Subscribers."

All of the table shouted out in unison, "Yes!"

Thayne continued, "But, see, they're the most important ones. What would Influencers be without their followers? The only thing that gives people influence is because they have someone following them. They're even more important than that, they're like..."

Tommy cut his cousin off. "Enforcers."

"Exactly!"

Mia looked over at Tommy. His ears were fire red. She whispered, "Are you okay?"

Tommy didn't answer.

Dexter got up from the table. "I'm running to the back. Lemme grab you your chips, a-hole." Picking up the empty basket, Dexter headed to the kitchen.

Mia held up the poster. She was nervous. Everything from the title to her drawings were scathing about the project. "*The True Stories of LHS*" was written at the top. She finished up her sketch of Rosi and looked it over.

Rosi Williams - Subscriber

Mia nodded. "I have one more spot left on this poster canvas. What's the last piece?"

Thayne snorted. "Girl who are you foolin'? You ain't turnin' this in."

Tommy yelled, "Why're you being such a douche?"

"I'm just bein' honest." Thayne turned to her and looked Mia in the eye. "You've dumped all over this assignment. There is no chance they'll hang this poster in the hallway - and you're smart enough to know this. You ain't turnin' this in."

Mia looked at Thayne defiantly. "Oh yeah? Watch me."

Tommy changed the subject. "So where do teachers fit into all this?"

Thayne replied, "They're nothin' but the 5-0."

Cullen pushed back. "Not all of 'em."

Thayne was adamant. "Yeah. All of 'em. They're mandatory reporters. If they catch any whiff of a crime they report it right to the police. Teachers are nothin' but cops."

Cullen disagreed. "Admin staff, principals, and most teachers, sure. But you can't do 'em all dirty like that."

"So would they be the Content Moderators?" Mia asked.

Thayne hit his fist on the table. "That's exactly what they are! If you step a toe out of line with them, whether it's the work you turn in, the things you say, hell, they won't even let you use the dang bathroom. But worst of all?"

Thayne held a finger over Mia's drawings. "They'll do everything they can to keep order in place."

Mia finished a sketch of Mr. Stallard and looked over her work.

Stallard: Content Moderator

Her last drawing complete, she held out her notebook for the table to see. "How does it look?"

Her poster said, "The Real Stories of LHS," and had drawn out The Banned, The Badges, The Influencers, The Followers, and Content Moderators.

Thayne smiled. "It's savage, girl."

"It's perfect," Cullen agreed.

Mia put the canvas down. "Tell me something, Thayne?"

"Yeah?"

"Now that we know your secrets, how'd it end up for you? You get out of Felony Acres?"

Thayne froze, and shot her a dirty look that caught her off guard.

Cullen cracked up. "Don't be that guy."

Thayne was defensive. "What guy?"

Cullen continued, "You invite yourself over to our table, eat our food, dump all over us and now we give you a little bite in return and you can't take it? You been talkin' down what we do since sittin' here with us -- it only makes sense that we'd ask how it ended up for you."

Thayne's eyes wandered around the table, and, for a second, it felt like he wasn't even here anymore. Dexter brought over a refill of chips and salsa and set it out for everyone.

Mia corrected. "I wasn't trying to hurt you. From the way you were talking I thought you getting out of there was where you were going with this whole thing."

Thayne smiled. "I'm workin' on gettin' out of there. One day at a time. I do gotta run, though." Thayne stood up at the table and took one last chip with a healthy scoop of dip. "It was good to meet y'all."

Mia nodded. "Likewise. You can crash our table any time."

Mia watched Thayne stride through the brewery and toward the back. Smiling, she looked over at Tommy. "In small doses, I'd love to have him around more often."

Tommy was surprised. "Really?"

Cullen nodded. "Yeah. I mean, he pisses me off, but that's what cousins do."

Tommy looked at the table. "I'm gonna go find him before he bounces."

Mia spent the day perfecting her poster. Tommy wasn't right when he returned. He didn't open up about his talk with Thayne, and Mia wasn't one to press. Eventually Cullen and Tommy departed, leaving her alone.

Tommy encouraged her before he left. "This is amazing, Mia. It's going to knock Stallard's dick in the dirt."

Cullen waved. "See you around."

Waving goodbye, Mia looked over her final product. It was perfect. Just what Stallard deserved after putting this assignment on them on a Friday afternoon. Taking a breath, Mia tore out the page and looked at the self-portrait she made for herself. Closing her eyes, she crumpled up the piece of paper and threw it to the side.

Mia's phone buzzed inside her pocket.

Mia froze. She was hyper aware of her surroundings. She felt a bead of sweat break from her brow and slide down her face. She felt her clothes begin to choke her skin. Sheer panic stole the oxygen from her body, and she struggled to find a way to breathe. Indiscernible conversations from tables away filtered in her ears like static. A coldness descended on her insides. Mia looked out in the parking lot. Darkened windshields stared back at her. Dozens of darkened cars. No. Maybe hundreds.

"He could be anywhere," she thought. She felt his gaze plunge into her like a knife.

She could hear his whisper. "Mia."

The voice got louder. "Mia?"

She looked up, and Dexter was standing beside her.

Dexter asked, "Anything else I can get you?"

Mia took a deep breath. "What time do you get off tonight, Dex?"

Dexter checked his watch. "Around ten, if I'm lucky. What's up?"

"You got any plans?"

"Yeah, meetin' back up with Cullen and catchin' a movie with his sister. Why?"

"A movie?"

Dexter nodded. "Yeah. *Marauders of Time.*"

Mia looked up, confused.

Dexter clarified. "It's a superhero movie."

"Ah."

Dexter laughed. "Not your thing?"

"Eh, it'll do. You okay if I tag along?"

Dexter was surprised. "That's fine. You gonna stay here until then?"

"Sure, but is it okay if I pull down the blinds?"

Dexter shrugged. "Knock yourself out."

Mia pulled down the blinds and looked over the empty canvas in front of her. Breaking out her flowery gel pens, she started on a new design for her poster.

Chapter 20: *The Boxcar*

Tommy and Thayne sat in the patio furniture in the front yard of Tommy's trailer. Tommy heard Thayne light a cigarette as they both looked up at the twilit winter horizon. Tommy watched a plane fly above them, leaving a contrail as it sliced through the sky.

Tommy looked down at his journal and saw the words he wrote looking up at him.

The Yellow Ladder

Tommy looked back up at the skies and saw a new airplane leaving a contrail as it flew by. "Thayne, do you ever think about the actual people in the planes up there?"

"Nope."

Tommy pointed toward the plane. "Just think about it. There are over a hundred people on one of those things at once: a hundred different stories, going to a hundred different places, and for a moment, I can see all of them passing over me."

"What do you even know about airplanes, Tommy?"

Tommy laughed. "Not a thing. I just see them in ads and stuff. People under the blue lights of an airplane bar. They look like they have a purpose, you know? That they're doing something that matters. I want to do that."

"You're such a phony, Tommy. Anyone ever tell you that?"

Tommy narrowed his eyes. "A phony?"

"Ya heard me. A phony."

"What, 'cause I want to fly on an airplane someday?"

Thayne spat. "Nah, 'cause you was embarrassed of me in front of your friends. Because you're ashamed of where you came from and want to run away in the sky someday. Just admit it, you were embarrassed of me, cuz."

Tommy snorted. "Well, sure. Aren't you embarrassed of me around Rock's crew?"

"That ain't the point. I get embarrassed because you're a derp. You get embarrassed of me because you think I'm an idiot. It ain't cool, Tommy."

Tommy argued, "I don't think you're an idiot; I think you're an a-hole. Why would I defend you in front of a group of people you kept attacking? You never once stuck up for me to Rock, and that a-hole makes fun of me everywhere I go. You wanna talk to me about shame? You're so insecure about yourself you had to insult all my friends, people you didn't even know."

Thayne stood up and hung menacingly over Tommy. "Whatever, cuz. I'm gonna bounce. You wanna know a secret, Tommy?" Thayne pointed at the sky. "All those people you so badly wanna be, people who are flying way outta here or whatever? It's all a lie. They're not doing anything important. Most are working for a system that doesn't give a crap about you and me, and you know what -- it doesn't give a crap about them. You think if one of those planes crash the government would cry over 'em? Nah, they'd throw in another faceless stiff who'll sign their life away to do the same thing in a week's time. You can find somethin' important right here. You don't have to leave everything behind just to get away."

Tommy looked at Thayne. "Step away from me, cuz."

"Alright. That's all I gotta say."

"You demand total loyalty from me, but we both know you'd throw me under the bus in order to score a dime bag from Rock."

Thayne looked at Tommy. "You know what? Come to a party Rock and I are goin' to on the 30th."

Tommy cringed. "Thayne… I don't know if I wanna..."

Thayne put a hand on Tommy's shoulder. "For your family, Tommy. Please. There ain't nothin' to be ashamed of, and if Rock tries anything, I'll put him in his place. Promise."

"I'll think about it."

Thayne laughed. "I'm sure you will. Love ya, cuz."

"Love ya, too."

Watching Thayne depart, Tommy got to his feet and looked at the train tracks sitting in the horizon.

The Yellow Ladder

Tommy had written about it repeatedly in his green journal so much that it gave him no other choice. Mia had the perfect suggestion -- his boxcar and the yellow ladder that laid behind.

The ladder was affixed to the closed down business directly behind his *Railbox* -- the boxcar that he had visited several times in the last two years. Tommy had almost climbed the ladder behind it many times since last April. The protective cage that had once sealed the ladder had broken away with time, and up the climb was a platform that stood two stories above the boxcar.

Tommy had thought about climbing to that platform every day last April.

The boxcar, the building, and the ladder.

They were begging to be drawn, and he would do it tonight.

—

For the second time in his life, Tommy walked to the other side of his boxcar and approached the abandoned factory. The sterilized light flickering on and off from the railroad tracks, Tommy reached out and gripped the cold metal bar of the ladder. If he was going to paint a picture of this, he'd have to find a vantage point that revealed everything -- the boxcar, the building, and the ladder.

Tommy turned on the tablet.

It was time to blow Mr. Austin away.

—

12 hours later, Tommy was clad in sunglasses, his old jacket and grey sweatpants. Tommy hid from the afternoon sunlight inside his boxcar. He had been up until 8:30 in the morning using the paintbrush tool on the tablet, but it was worth it.

He stared up at the cloud-strewn ceiling in the sky.

Mr. Austin's *Artist in You* project was finished, and it was perfect. He had included the flickering blue light, the rusty boxcar, the warehouse, and the yellow ladder that extended toward the sky.

And best of all, it even had something for Mia Fernandez. Tommy thought it was the greatest thing he had ever done.

He was ready for Wednesday.

Chapter 21: ***Dreams***

"Thank you for coming to the North College Drive-In! My name is Luke. Can I start you off with a grapefruit juice or a cup of joe?"

Duke Bradford looked up with a frown. "Jay and I requested for Kit."

The manager bristled. "I'm so sorry, but Kit is too busy to assist you. Do you mind if I cover for her today?"

Duke checked his watch. "It is 6:15 on a Wednesday morning. I count -- what -- two other tables here?"

"Gentlemen, she's had some uh.... 'run ins' with you in the past."

"Are you going to let her incompetence dictate your managerial decisions?"

The manager rubbed his beard. "If she's so incompetent, then why do you want her--"

"To serve us? Because we believe in second chances."

"Guys, I just don't think she's who's best for--"

Duke clenched his teeth. "I will be the one to decide who's best for me. Lemme clue you in. I have been friends with Lewis Wilson, the owner and your uncle, since we graduated together 30 years ago. I take my staff here and rent out the private room once a month, and I have a feeling he might wonder why we start going elsewhere."

The manager swallowed. "Do you want me to pick up your drinks when I fetch her?"

"And finally we get some service! Fetch a hot tea for me and a black coffee for Jay. Thanks, buddy."

His face red, the manager evacuated from the table.

Stallard eyed the manager as he slinked into the kitchen. "How long do you think she's been giving the ol' spit and shine?"

Duke smiled. "A couple weeks. Any longer and Mr. Manager wouldn't have thrown such a tantrum."

"I haven't seen a fit like that since I last saw the in-laws."

Laughing, Duke changed the subject. "How's Nicole?"

"Good. Things are pretty busy at the hospital. She, uh, had a familiar face in her neck of the woods recently."

Duke raised an eyebrow. "How familiar?"

"Familiar enough to cause quite the scandal in our little community."

"Jay, you gotta give me more than that."

Jay nodded. "I will. I just have to make sure I cross my T's and dot my I's before giving any more details."

"Fair enough. How's your son?"

Stallard swallowed. "Ah, he's still tryin' to sell his arts and crafts on *Woodsy*."

"I thought he was a youth pastor down in Aiken."

Mr. Stallard drank some coffee. "He is. Still living with three buddies too. I always told him that getting an English major wasn't going to take him anywhere. He's uh.. gonna be spending Christmas feeding the homeless up in Ackerman…" Jay felt his voice drift for a moment and saw a look of concern flash over Duke.

"Well, that should make you and Nicole proud, right?"

"Yeah, yeah. He's gonna do what he's gonna do."

Duke changed the subject. "How're things at Latimer?"

"I'm ready for break," Stallard admitted. "Jimmy Richards wore a 'got gilfs?' shirt yesterday."

Duke laughed. "Isn't that boy a daddy?"

"Yep. Sixteen, and a father of two."

"And the world weeps."

The bearded manager hurriedly dropped off the drinks. "Kit will be with you soon."

Duke grabbed a basket of tea bags. "You keepin' an eye on the psycho?"

"We are. One more wrong move and he'll be expelled without a second thought."

"Good."

Stallard nodded. "He was almost bounced from Advanced Art. His grade dropped to an 80 last week. If he blows the final project, I'll pull him out at the first opportunity."

Duke shook his head. "I'm surprised a boy like that made it into that class..."

"Letting him in was a mistake from the beginning. Rest assured, the moment his grade slips, I won't hesitate to take him out."

Duke checked his surroundings. "Are you worried at all about what Elmer might have to say about all this?"

Stallard looked to his feet. "He has always maintained that he wants the boy out as much as I do."

"Let me know if the man starts causing problems."

"What do you have in mind?"

Averting Stallard's eyes, Duke dropped his voice to a whisper. "There have been… conversations between me and two school board members about making a change if he gets in your way again."

Stallard stayed silent, processing the information.

Duke continued, "It never sat well with me, having a principal who was never committed to the Latimer community. He never gave St. Luke's a real chance. Now look, I know he grew up with that church downtown, but in my honest opinion, being a principal of a school means you need to be a principal that represents your community -- and I'm not sure Elmer is... Anyway."

"Do you all have another candidate in mind?"

"He's sitting right in front of me." Duke smiled. "Keep me in the loop, okay?"

"Will do," Stallard breathed, his eyes wide.

Kit Shields gingerly stepped up to the table. "Hey, guys."

Beaming, Duke whipped two dollars from his pocket. "Hey, Kit. Remember us?"

—

A tapping noise whimpered from the doors of Latimer High School and provided a minor annoyance for Mr. Stallard. A T.V. illuminated his office, and the assistant principal eyed the monitor with noticeable amusement.

Two years ago, concerned parents and members of the community pressured the school to install a new security system. In response, the school installed a single, out of date video camera at the school's entrance. It was because of this "state of the art" surveillance system that Stallard could see junior class president Chad Hinez at the doors of the school. It was a frigid December morning, one where the air tore into bare flesh like the tip of a sword.

Reclining in his cozy office, Stallard watched the student like a vulture over its prey. He told Chad to arrive at 7:30 this morning. The time was 7:22. Stallard's phone vibrated on the desk. For the fourth time, the assistant principal ignored it.

"What can you do?" Stallard asked aloud.

When Jay Stallard was six years old, an errant fruit fly had caused his right eye to swell shut, and it made the principal hypersensitive to their movements. Whether it was on the rotting bird on the sidewalk, the dog poop in the backyard, or that awful creature that wouldn't stop flying around his skull, Jay felt an intense, unreasonable hatred whenever a fly crossed his path.

When he was 12, Jay watched a fly fall into an open jar of pickles.

At that moment, Jay became a collector. Channeling his rage into months of practice, Jay started snatching his prey from the air and clamping their legs between his fingernails. He relished their squeal-like buzz and how they squirmed in his vice-like grip. He'd then rip the wings from their backs and toss their maimed bodies in a jar at the corner of his desk. To his amusement, the wingless flies would crawl over their fellow corpses in search of an escape. It was never long before life deserted the creatures and sent their bodies to the rotting pile below.

Jay did what he could to keep this a secret, but on an unfortunate afternoon during his freshman year, his girlfriend uncovered the mountainous grave on an ill-fated first date. Humiliated and enraged, the boy shattered the jar by a dumpster in the city.

But it was okay.

Mr. Stallard smiled at the motionless, triumphed teenager standing in his monitor. Jay had moved on to better things.

—

Using the glow of twilight streaming through his windows, first year teacher James Austin graded a variety of student drawings on top of a faded wooden desk.

Jay Stallard stood at the door of Mr. Austin's art room and scrutinized Latimer's new hire. Mr. Austin had a full head of brunette hair and a large black cast over his left hand. Austin was young and carried as much acne as the high schoolers.

Wearing a crew cut that failed to conceal his bald spot, Stallard sported a red and gold Latimer football sweatshirt. "Hey, James?" Stallard asked lazily.

The art teacher stood. "Yes?"

Almost a head shorter than Latimer's new hire, Mr. Stallard crushed Austin's hand in a vice-like handshake and held it for an extended time.

"I'm Jay Stallard. I teach freshman and sophomore history and have coached football, girls' basketball, and track for the past six years."

"Don't you run that judo club after school, too?"

Mr. Stallard nodded. "Yep, that's me."

"Wow," Austin murmured. "Kind of a jack of all trades, huh?"

"Uh, sure. Well, I don't know if Principal Murphy spoke with you about this, but Mr. Adams designed the banners for the football team while he taught here."

"Did he?"

"Yes, and he left some big shoes to fill. Anyway, it would be great if you could whip up a banner for us by Thursday night. I'll have someone run through the details with you by tomorrow."

Mr. Austin considered. "Hm, well--"

"We appreciate it," Stallard said, turning to the door.

A curious look on his face, Mr. Austin called out to his colleague. "Jay? Before you go."

"Hm?"

"I have a busy week in front of me, so in return, it would be great if you could have a few of your football players come with me to move the kiln up from the district's old bus barn to my art room."

Mr. Stallard's eyes fluttered. "No can do, sorry. My players have spirit night and our first game to prep for. They're not gonna have time for an errand like that."

"That's too bad, because I don't have time for an errand like yours."

Jay took a step toward Mr. Austin. Keeping his voice calm and precise, Stallard crafted a response. "The art teacher at this high school designed the football banners for the last fifteen years."

"And that teacher retired."

Mr. Stallard took another step, moving toe to toe with his colleague. Donning a smile, Mr. Stallard changed his tone. "James. Maybe Principal Murphy didn't make it clear to you, but the staff you joined here has always taken pride in working as a team."

"I believe Principal Murphy did explain that to me. I believe reciprocity was the word he used."

"Yes," Stallard breathed. "Reciprocity."

Looking down, Mr. Austin bored into Stallard's eyes. "So, will you be the one who moves that kiln here for me?"

Biting his lip, a glare commandeered Mr. Stallard's expression. After toying with the idea of a response, Stallard gave Mr. Austin a slow nod, and strode away from the classroom. "Don't worry about it. I bet STUCO can make something better anyways."

Mr. Austin beamed. "I'm sure they'll do a great job."

—

Mr. Stallard sat across from Principal Elmer's desk, a notepad sitting in front of him. An elaborate painting was hung behind Principal Elmer. A sleeping Black couple laid inside a barred, golden bed, designed to look like a jail cell. Skeleton-like figurines hung from golden bars erected along the bed, whose slow death resembled the nightmare awaiting the couple's awakening. Mr. Stallard narrowed his eyes. What kind of distasteful message was a painting like that sending Principal Elmer's students?

Principal Elmer spoke to Stallard. "When are you meeting with the Social Studies team?"

"Uh, 3. Hoping it'll be quick."

Elmer narrowed his eyes. "Did you schedule it after school for that reason? Is this where you're telling them about the new economics section on the state tests?"

Stallard sighed. "I thought I'd slip it in."

Elmer released a belly full laugh and slapped his knee. "Slip it in? You may want to order Pizza here tonight."

Stallard shook his head. "Always a mess with Social Studies."

"If Mr. H goes on a tangent, send him to me and I'll calm him down."

Mr. Austin stepped into the classroom and greeted Principal Elmer. "Hey!"

Mr. Stallard noticed a wide smile appear on Elmer's face when James walked into his office. Elmer's voice boomed. "James! I'm glad you stopped by."

Standing a head shorter than Principal Elmer, Mr. Austin warmly took the principal's hand. "How can I help you?"

Principal Elmer gestured towards the painting behind him with pride. "*Dreams* has been my favorite painting since my college days. How much did it set you back?"

James smiled. "It was on the house, literally. This summer I painted the home of a widowed family friend of ours. I got into the job knowing I'd be doing it for free, but last weekend she called me and said I was welcome to anything in her collection. I remembered how much you loved the work of Jacob Lawrence, so it was an easy decision."

Mr. Stallard stifled an eyeroll. "Of course James gave Elmer a painting like that," he thought.

Principal Elmer beamed. "You didn't have to do that for me, James. You could have picked something for yourself."

"Trust me -- it was the only one worth collecting."

Mr. Elmer continued, "Know that you are welcome to a trip to the Blue Duck with Victoria and I, on us."

"Well, you know I'm never going to turn down an invitation for free food."

"If you'd rather go anywhere else, let us know. Thank you again for the painting, James."

Mr. Austin waved him off. "It was the least I could do. By the way, Jay?"

Stallard looked up at Mr. Austin. "Hm?"

"Any chance I could have that showcase key?"

Flashing a glance at Principal Elmer, Mr. Stallard slowly went into his pocket and held up the key.

Mr. Austin swiped the key from Stallard. "Thank you."

Two months later, Mr. Stallard would stand in the same room, but this time, he'd look at the painting with a cool, confident smile.

Mr. Austin would be *murdered* here; he could see his blood on the golden bars.

Chapter 22: *The Pride of Latimer*

Cullen yelled in surprise. "Damn!"

Mr. Austin was quick. "I'm going to pretend that I'm really, really old, and that I didn't hear or understand what you just said." The teacher then looked at Tommy. "But Cullen's right."

Mr. Austin had projected Tommy's digital painting on the wall, and the response was overwhelming.

Cullen continued, "You did all of this on a tablet?"

Tommy pointed to Mr. Austin. "Mr. A let me borrow the one Dex used for his documentary."

"It's based off of a real place, I assume?" Mr. Austin asked.

"It's a closed-down factory about a mile behind my home."

Mr. Austin nodded. "What's the name of your painting?"

"The Yellow Ladder." Tommy hadn't put any thought into a name, but the answer flew out of him.

A girl named Mandy chimed in. "Why did you make the dandelion so big?"

Tommy's cheeks reddened. He had drawn a dandelion on the left side of the picture and put it in focus because of the one girl on his mind. "Do you think it's out of place?" the boy asked.

"No," Mandy said; "I think it's beautiful."

"Cool," Tommy breathed, feeling relieved. "Well, dandelions just mean a lot to, uh, me."

"Well, I don't know about you all, but I think we found our first painting for the student showcase!" Mr. Austin said.

Tommy was stunned. "Wait, really?"

"Definitely! Unless anyone in here disagrees?"

The class murmured out their agreement.

Tommy was in disbelief. "You mean, this drawing is going up for the whole school to see?"

Dexter raised an eyebrow. "That's kind of the point of the student showcase."

Tommy let out an awkward laugh. "Sorry, I'm just -- wow."

Mr. Austin beamed. "I'll have the picture printed and posted on Wednesday. Congrats, Tommy."

Tommy couldn't believe it. He only wished Mia were in class today to see it. She had some Christmas event at the elementary school for STUCO, but it was okay -- she would see it soon enough.

—

The morning sunlight glided through the large windows of Latimer's entrance. Standing in the light, Mr. Austin looked down at Tommy. "Do you want to do the honors?"

Tommy's heart quickened. "I would love to."

Taking a breath, Tommy stepped up and hung his painting for the world to see. He still couldn't believe it. This drawing was made by Tommy "Piss Stain" Taint. The kid who was one vote away from expulsion just eight months ago was now hanging his work inside the "Pride of Latimer".

Mr. Austin closed the showcase and sealed it tight. "That's going to be in there for the next quarter, Tommy. Does it feel real?"

Tommy shook his head. It didn't.

—

Tommy stretched out on the cool earth inside the courtyard. The day had passed in a daze. He and Mia now watched the clouds drift by in the cadmium skies, and he was just about to take her up to his painting of the Yellow Ladder. Something he created was on display for the entire school to see, and Mia would be able to see what he made for *her* every day she walked into the school. Tommy could hardly wait to show her.

Mia extended a dried dandelion out in front of her, examining each of the petals from the end of the stem. "Do you have any plans for break?"

Tommy chuckled. "Heh, no. You?"

"Outside of work? Nada. I hate Christmas break."

"Same here. Why do you hate it?"

Mia sighed. "When I was eleven my mom told me that Santa wasn't going to bring me gifts anymore."

"Was she struggling to pay the bills?" Tommy asked.

Mia shook her head. "I wish it were for something so noble. To the rest of the world she acts like she's the #1 Mom, but really, she only loves me when it's convenient for her. She supported me when I supported her interests and only wanted me to work my dream job as long as my dream job was at her flower shop."

Tommy breathed. "I never really got anything for Christmas. Wait, that's a lie. When I was nine, my mom was seein' a dude named Jame Barth."

"Jame Barth?"

"Yeah, that's one of those names that sticks with you. Anyway, good ol' Jame felt guilty that Mom didn't get me anything and snuck me my first swimsuit mag for Christmas."

Mia's tension split into heaves of laughter. "Oh my God!"

"A classy gift from a classy man."

"What do you hate about the break now?"

Tommy sighed. "I end up spending too much time with Thayne's friends and get into trouble. Last year I wasn't allowed to leave the house for the entire break."

Mia thought for a moment. "How do you get through it, Tommy?"

"Christmas? I never expect much, so I'm never disappointed."

"No, not Christmas. Life."

Tommy paused. "Can I give the same answer? You go first."

"How do I get through it? I've put everything on my future." Mia had a bloodthirsty expression. "It's a cutthroat way to live."

"Really?"

The sunset burned in Mia's eyes. "It's all I have. In my lowest moments I tell myself, 'I'm going to be a writer, I'm going to North College, and I'm never coming back here again.' It's my anthem. It's how I get out of bed every morning, and some nights it's how I fall asleep. I can't control my parents, I can't control my friends, but I can control me, and for the love of God I'm getting out of here." Mia sighed. "I *hate* Christmas break. Tommy, when the nightmare of this time ends, where do *you* want to go?"

"Well, that's just it. I have no idea. The closest thing I had to a 'plan' was dropping out last year and selling protein shakes with Thayne. But I dunno. I can't end up like Mom, jumping from job to job and partner to partner hopin' to find that quick million. But not me. I can't stay here. I won't be in Dead Oak for the rest of my life. Last week I was looking at my boxcar and realized that maybe I did have a purpose in this life -- and it made me want to make something for you."

"For me?"

"Yeah, do you want to see it? It's in the student showcase."

"The student showcase? Tommy, I'd love--"

Hot Jazz blasted from Mia's phone, causing the girl to shudder.

"Oh crap. Work alarm," the girl explained glumly, holding up her phone.

"Do you have time to run back in the school? It'd be quick, I promise."

Mia grimaced. "I'm sorry, Tommy. My manager voluntold me to take this shift and I have to pick up my work clothes from Yuki's. This will be the first thing we do when we get back in January, I promise."

Tommy watched Mia sit up and fully appreciated that he wouldn't be seeing her for the next two weeks. A melancholy sweeping over his body, Tommy formed a sentence that sounded like a plea. "Sometimes I think I'm going to die here."

Staring deep into Tommy with her kiwi-colored eyes, Mia extended a dandelion toward the boy. "You're going to find a way out of here, Tommy. You just have to believe."

Tommy took the dandelion from Mia's hand, his fingers trembling.

"Are you sure?"

"Of course," Mia said. "I have a lot more back home."

Tommy exhaled. He would remember this moment for the rest of his life. "Are you going to be okay?"

"Over the break? I'll be at the greenhouse for 28 hours a week to help the time go by. You?"

Tommy nodded. "Yeah, I'll get through."

"Tommy, promise me something?"

"Anything."

Mia spoke. "Can you be my friend?"

Tommy felt a pang hit his heart. "Fr...friend?"

"Yes. There is nothing more in the world I need right now than a friend. Someone I can talk to and listen to about what this world really is. Someone who makes me laugh and dreams with me. Is that too much to ask? Can you be my friend?"

Tommy felt wounded. "*Just* friends?"

Mia reassured. "There's nothing *just* or small about friendship. There's nothing more important to me right now than friends. You and Yuki are why I'm pulling through right now. It's nothing personal. I'm just not wanting to date anyone right now."

The words "right now" caused hope to kindle inside Tommy. He smiled. "Okay. If that's what you need right now, I can do that."

"Thank you."

Tommy looked over his dandelion. "Thank you for everything."

"Be careful with Thayne this break, okay?"

Tommy laughed. "Okay."

Mia glowed back at Tommy. "Merry Christmas, Tommy."

—

Unsorted: Grade Cards

Unsure where Tommy had run to, Lynne cautiously maneuvered into Tommy's room. She opened the rolltop desk and saw a piece of printer paper jutting out from a binder. Realizing it must have slipped past her detection yesterday, Lynne grabbed the paper and digested its contents.

Tommy Tate **Grade Card** **12/18**

Course	Q1	Q2	S1	Grade
Comp Tech	88	102	95	**A**
Speech	92	89	90	**A-**
History	92	81	86	**B**
Algebra II	86	74	80	**B-**
Advanced Art	95	80	88	**B+**
Junior English	90	89	89	**A-**
Astronomy	96	101	99	**A**

Weighted GPA: **Unweighted GPA**

3.71 3.57

"Tommy, you are rocking it! Rock the Artist in You Project and you'll finish up with a 3.8! - Mr. Gordon."

Wiping her eyes, Lynne stuffed the grade card back into the binder and returned it beneath the rolltop desk.

Chapter 23*: The Unjust Judge*

Milk jugs, each with hearts of flame, lined the streets across the older neighborhoods of the city. The patchwork of snow and yellow grass gave a sharp contrast to the golden flame inside the thousands of plastic luminaries. Honoring a Christmas Eve tradition that spanned back for decades, thousands of fires hummed inside the city of Baldridge.

Standing at the edge of the Friendly Acres mobile home park, Tommy hid his hands in the pockets of his suede leather jacket and looked at the flame-tinted roads across the street.

Cocaine Thayne let out a belch behind Tommy. "Why are we out here? It's cold as balls outside."

"You don't have to come," Tommy reminded.

"I ain't tryin' to rile you. I just don't get why you're out here. Didn't you say you came out yesterday?"

"The church sings songs on the two nights leading up to Christmas. I wanted to hear them on both nights."

"Are you plannin' on actually goin' inside tonight?"

Tommy shook his head.

"Whatever boats your float, Tommy. So what're you doin' on the 30th? Scratch that. I know you ain't doin' anything, so you're comin' with me to a party bein' thrown by one of my friends who goes to college at the NC."

"Sweet ass," Tommy said. "I'll think about it."

"Think about it my butt! You're goin'." Thayne turned to the fiery candles that stood on the edge of first street. The fire was an inviting light to the elaborate old city and left the outskirts in darkness. Thayne laughed. "I don't blame 'em for stoppin' there. No one wants to step foot in Felony Acres."

As the last stretch of daylight spilled over the horizon, the two boys crossed the demarcation line between Friendly Acres and the ornate homes of the old city. A gentle glow hung inside Tommy's eyes, and it remained as he gazed into the fire light.

Thayne lit a cigarette. "Your ma still seein' the *Schwann's* man?"

"Nah, that was just a fling."

"Dang, really? How's she holdin' up?"

"Pretty great. We have a freezer full of nuggets that'll last for weeks."

Thayne laughed. "Nice! She made out like a boss. You still have any of those wings?"

"You mean the ones that gave you food poisoning?"

"Them's the ones! A night by the crapper ain't nothin' for some fine cuisine."

"Uh, if you say so. You can have 'em if you want."

"Hell yeah!" Thayne shouted.

The last embers of twilight yielded the light to the thousands of glowing luminaries, which guided the boys through the veins of the old city. They passed a cathedral-sized house that had been dazzled up for the season. An ornamental Santa Claus waved to the rovers of the night, and it sparked a smile across Tommy's face.

Tommy looked to his cousin. "Santa gettin' you anything this year?"

"Screw Santa," Thayne sputtered.

Tommy smirked. "The fat man never got me anything, but I don't got anything against him."

"I hate him."

Tommy raised an eyebrow. "You and your mom are better off than we are. You always get better stuff than me for Christmas."

"You wanna know why that is?"

Tommy's eyes narrowed. Part of him had always wondered. Neither of their moms worked, but Thayne and his mom always had nicer things than he and his mom did.

Thayne looked over at Tommy. "Anyone ever tell you how my stepdad died?"

"It was a car accident, right?"

"Right. Think you was a baby when it happened, but do you know *when* it happened?"

Tommy hadn't, but he was starting to put it together.

Thayne continued, "Christmas Eve. Slid off the Manchester highway after goin' shoppin' for little ol' me. Anyway, we get monthly insurance payouts and will till it dries up in a couple years."

"Holy crap," Tommy breathed. "I'm sorry, Thayne."

"Today's sixteen years to the day since it went down." Thayne turned around to give Santa the bird. "Screw that guy. I coulda used Santa when my stepdad died, and hell, I coulda used him when it pretty much killed my ma too -- Lord knows she ain't been the same since."

Snow began to fall from the skies, obscuring their silhouettes from the neighborhood's sights.

Tommy put his lips together. "Santa never even got to know me. If I was lucky, Mom would make some Chef Boyardee and give me Dr. Pepper on Christmas day."

Thayne grumbled. "Santa got to know me alright. He would get me the best toys on Christmas morning, and then didn't do a dang thing as my Mom sold them to pay the bills. He didn't do a dang thing when my stepdad died, and he didn't do a dang thing when I OD'd last year."

"Well, you're still here, aren't you?"

"What a gift," Thayne responded, throwing his cigarette by an ornamental deer. "Man, what the hell are we even doing out here?"

Tommy snapped, “I said you didn’t have to come!”

“It ain’t that. It’s you, cuz. Why are you even wastin’ your time out here?”

Tommy turned a corner and looked forward. A final line of luminaries aligned themselves like a great hall that led to the Baptist church. Flames dancing in their casings, the glow swayed through the neighborhood street.

Tommy thought over Thayne’s question. “You know, they say the good kids get presents and the bad ones get coal, but what about the kids that get neither presents nor coal? I never had a chance to know Santa, but -- I don’t know -- I like this time of year. I like seein’ people being nice to each other, I like hearing people sing, and everything feels kind of magical.”

“What?” Thayne shouted. “Magical? That don’t cut no ice with me. You told me you came here to *this* bench last night. You know why you ain't goin' inside?”

Tommy bit. “Why?"

“Because you know all those 'nice' people wouldn’t even look at you if you walked in. Those papes would want nothin’ but for you to leave.”

Tommy lifted an eyebrow. “Papes?”

Thayne clarified. “Paper assholes. Those who pretend that the world is better than it is. Them the ones who spend ungodly amounts on gifts that’ll be thrown out in a year’s time. You tellin’ me that’s the meaning on this holiday? To buy a bunch of useless crap instead of helping kids who are actually starving on this pile of a planet? Christmas ain’t meant for us, because we see through the lie - so what are we even doin’ here?”

With Thayne’s bun of brunette hair coming loose at the seams and his hoodie’s deep stains still visible with this light, Tommy wondered if he had a point. “I don’t know,” he said to Thayne. “I’m lookin' for a sign, I guess.”

“One of these days, Tommy, you're gonna realize that all this time the sign was right in front of you, and you know what it is?”

"What?"

"That you should've gone partyin' with me on the 30th."

Tommy hit Thayne on the arm. A line of luminaries encircled the church and radiated the building's stone exterior. Across the doors of the congregation stood the bench Tommy visited during this time every year. A tantalizing aroma of chili and cinnamon rolls wafted through the air and traveled inside the boys' nostrils. Thayne pleaded, "Oh, come on. If we walked all the way out here we should at least grab a plate."

"Nah," Tommy said, "they're collecting donations for some charity. It'd look bad if we didn't have any money."

"What's the frickin' point of a free meal if you have to pay for it?"

"It'd be like goin' to a restaurant and not tippin' the server," Tommy replied.

Thayne laughed. "I never tip the server."

"Don't tell that to my mom. Oh, hey," Tommy added, throwing a pack of cigarettes to Thayne. "Merry Christmas."

"You couldn't get your hands on any 27's?"

"My mom got an extra pack of the stuff she gets."

Thayne could barely stifle his disappointment. "They'll do."

"Whatever, I don't know why you came out, bro. Can you just do one thing for me? Can you sit on the bench and listen to the singing with me?"

"Don't get your panties in a knot. I just don't get you, that's all."

Tommy tried to explain. "I never went to church or had any of those things that families do on Christmas. I've always felt like an outsider this time of year, so this -- sittin' here on Christmas Eve listenin' to Christmas songs -- this is what I have."

Thayne lifted his hands. "Well don't let me get in the way."

Shaking his head, Tommy walked to the bench and stopped in surprise. A plate wrapped in aluminum foil was waiting for them, with a single note attached on top.

Picking up the note, Tommy read through its contents.

"**Come inside if you want seconds. We would love to see you!**

Happy Holidays,

Pastor Jack Akins"

Thayne yelled, "Hot dang! Want to split?"

Standing in disbelief, Tommy nodded to his cousin.

Singing began to echo from the congregation, and the first lines of a Christmas song echoed into Tommy's ears. Sitting beside Thayne, Tommy opened his plate and reached inside. Tommy picked out a massive cinnamon roll and halved it as fairly as possible. As an orange glow nestled itself in Tommy's eyes, he held out a gooey half for Thayne. "Merry Christmas."

Lifting up an eyebrow, Thayne took his half. "Merry Christmas, cuz."

—

Tommy went to bed on Christmas Eve wondering about the morning. Usually Christmas was pretty low key, but after his birthday anything felt possible. Regardless, Tommy was still surprised when his mom barged in the next morning.

"Merry Christmas, Tommy!"

Tommy shook awake and digested his mother's presence. A vibrant and rare smile filled Lynne's face, and a small box occupied her outstretched hand.

Tommy couldn't believe it. "Ah, man. I wish I had gotten you something, too!"

"Don't worry about this, Tommy. I wanted it to be a surprise."

Tommy got to his feet. "Wait!" Running into the kitchen, Tommy led his bemused mother to the fridge. Taking out a plate with cinnamon rolls, Tommy opened the box and looked up at his mother.

"Last night, the pastor of the church gave Thayne and I the leftover rolls they had from their food drive."

Lynne narrowed her eyes. "What were you doing down there?"

Tommy put the roll in the microwave. "Thayne and I just wanted to see the luminaries. Someone had these waiting on a bench for us when we got there."

"Thayne *wanted* to see the luminaries?" Lynne asked, skeptical.

"Well, I did. I wanted to go outside last night and Thayne wanted to see me."

Feeling more content with that answer, Lynne settled at the kitchen table. "Once the roll is done, would you grab me two *beastin' limonadas*?"

"Sure."

After splitting the roll in half, Tommy set both bottles down beside his mother. To his surprise, his mother handed one back to him.

Tommy hesitated. "Are you sure?"

"Positive. Crack 'er open and open up your present."

Tommy tore the wrapping to shreds. The boy had no idea what to expect. It wasn't like his mom had a lot of money, so he doubted that--

"Oh my God," Tommy breathed, processing what he was holding inside his hands. "I don't deserve this," he said as he examined the phone in his palms.

Lynne was beaming. "Oh, yes, you do."

Tommy was dumbfounded. "Why?"

She held up her phone. "After Mitch shelled out for me, I realized I needed to get you one, too. Your teacher, Mr. Austin, called and let me know how you were doin' in school. You earned this one, Tommy."

A painful lump developed inside Tommy's throat. "What a stud. How could you even afford this?"

Lynne cracked open her limonada. "Well, I sold some of my knick-knacks and held back on buying some cigarettes and other things to make up the rest of the cost. It ain't got a great data plan -- like you can't download the internet or whatever -- but you should be able to text and call just fine."

Tommy tried to process if this was even real.

Lynne smiled. "Merry Christmas, Tommy."

Tommy cracked open his limonada and took a swig. He spoke over the lump inside his throat. "Thank you."

Lynne raised her bottle.

Given a newfound courage, Tommy set down his limonada. "So, how are you doin'?"

"How am I doin'?" Lynne repeated. "Honest answer?"

"Yeah." Tommy couldn't think of the last time he had asked his mom this question, but after this morning, it felt right to check in.

Lynne took another swig. "I'm alive, but I don't have to tell you that nothin' has been goin' on for the last few years. Once in a while my old waitressing girls will come by, but it ain't often. I feel like I'm alone here, and I don't think that's gonna change."

"It's gonna get better," Tommy said.

"Will it really? Some days it feels like I'm waitin' to die here, and some days I think I'm okay with that."

Tommy took a swig of limonada. "Have you thought about getting a serving job again?" It was a daring question and not one Tommy had ever risked asking.

Lynne nodded. "Believe me, I have, but we'd lose my disability checks, and if my back went out while I was on the job.... we wouldn't have a home."

Tommy remembered when that happened. It would have been around five years ago now. His mom could barely move, and they didn't have electricity for weeks. Her spina-bifida didn't flare up too often, but it was enough to be a risk if she found work again.

"Have you thought about putting that on your application? Maybe you could find someone who was cool about it."

"Maybe, Tommy. Maybe." She got up to her feet and changed the topic. "Want some ravioli?"

Tommy smiled. "It wouldn't be Christmas without it."

Finishing the bottle of *limonada*, Tommy watched his mother maneuver through the kitchen. The conversation had been short and cut off before Tommy could offer any real ideas, but the boy could not remember a time he felt closer to his mom.

Chapter 24: ***Snakes Everywhere***

Tommy knew it was a terrible idea from the beginning.

The black cat roosted on Tommy's chest and gave off a throaty purr. A slew of text messages laid unopened on Tommy's cell phone, shedding a blue light from the living room table. The boy did not even look at his phone. He knew who they were from, what they were asking and already knew what his answer was going to be.

The days since Christmas had been groundbreaking for Tommy and his mom. They took a trip to the dollar store, cooked multiple dishes of food, and stuck a copy of Tommy's grade-card on the refrigerator. As lush as these moments had been, Lynne had spent the last few nights out of the trailer and had been MIA for the last day.

The isolation had caused Tommy to unlock unwelcome emotions that haunted him in his home for the past few years. The school year had caused these feelings to retreat in the dark canvasses of Tommy's mind, leading them to bide their time until he had nowhere to go but home.

Tommy's phone vibrated against the wooden table, and the boy answered without hesitating. "What's up?"

Tommy considered. "I'm game. I'll be ready at 9:00."

Tommy smirked at Thayne's reaction. "I know the deal. See you soon."

—

Sitting in the passenger seat of the Saturn station-wagon, Thayne repeated himself to his cousin. "Just one hit, Tommy."

Tommy looked at the joint in Thayne's hand. He knew this was part of the deal but being face to face with this decision added a new perspective.

Previously silent behind the wheel, Rock spoke up at this part of the conversation. "This is the gonna be the biggest gosh darn party of the year. Don't be a puss."

Thayne laughed. "Yeah, don't be a puss, Tommy."

His heart racing, Tommy picked up the joint. He had promised, and it was only the 30th, so no matter how messed up he got tonight, he would be fine by the time school picked up next week.

Rock turned off to a huge, blue house sitting beside the dirt road. Pulling into an open space beside the cars draped up and down the grass, Rock turned back to Tommy. "If I wait one second longer, I'm gonna hold you down."

Taking a breath, Tommy pressed the joint between his lips, breathed in and felt his senses overload. The tastes of ash and nasty, flaming garbage filled up Tommy's mouth and burned inside his throat, while a plume of smoke overfilled his lungs and caused the boy to gag.

Tommy wheezed, causing Rock to snicker. "That's a virgin toke if I've ever heard one."

Thayne held out a hand. "Don't be selfish, Tommy. Hand it over."

Tommy obliged. "Does it always smell this bad?"

Thayne and Rock doubled over in laughter. "Like crap, bro." Thayne took a toke and passed it over to Rock.

Rock inhaled and held it back out to Tommy.

Tommy hesitated and felt Rock's eyes cleave him. "Don't hold us up, puss."

Tommy lifted the joint and inhaled again. The taste was even more corrosive, and the cough lasted longer than the first time.

On and on it went.

Despite his best efforts, Tommy hacked with each hit, and Rock laughed every time.

—

The effect hit Tommy before they stepped out of the car, and he had to be supported by Thayne to make it to the house. A crowd of bodies greeted the trio at the door, and they laughed beside Rock when they looked at Tommy.

Making an effort bigger than any he had before, Tommy looked over to Thayne. He wanted to ask why, why the people were laughing, and why so many snakes were inside the house.

There were snakes, snakes everywhere. Long, python-like creatures that slithered up and down the floor. They were kind snakes, though, and parted the floor whenever Tommy took a step. Thayne maneuvered Tommy through a web of bodies and snakes until they reached a room illuminated only by a strobe light. Fear sunk into Tommy. Pulsating bodies rubbed up against his own until a sudden drop put him and Thayne on a couch at the side of the room, and there they sat for what felt like days.

Tommy's right eye slid into his face like butter inside a frying pan. His left slid higher and higher -- until the people, snakes and the world had been tilted off their axles, and then Tommy's body was floating, higher and higher until his body pressed against the ceiling, and there he looked down at the people and the snakes writhing beneath the flashing strobe light.

Tommy slid his tongue over the base of his mouth. His teeth had broken apart and the pieces liquified inside his gums. The dancers in front of him had enlarged like giants in front of the flashing light, and the boy realized the giants were staring at him.

Looking past the snakes, Tommy grabbed Thayne's shoulder. Tommy had to tell him, the giants wanted to turn them in.

"Thayne!" Tommy yelled.

"What?"

Tommy wanted to tell him about the giants, but for the life of him he couldn't remember if giant was even a word.

Thayne repeated himself. "What?"

Something careened into Tommy that turned his world around. Something was wrong. No, everything was wrong. Thayne's eyes were open so wide it looked like he was out of his mind. Tommy had been beside him when he lit up before, and he never had an experience like that. He looked around the room; nothing about the room was right. The giants, the snakes, nothing.

Fear pumped fire into Tommy's veins. There was something else in the joint he smoked, something stronger than pot. Sweat poured down Tommy's face and cascaded like a waterfall before his eyes. He had been deceived. The boy released several short, panicked breaths.

And Rock was the one responsible.

Tommy slammed his hand into Thayne's chest and pulled him over by the shirt. Thayne yelled in surprise. "Tommy, what are you--"

Feeling Thayne's shirt rip inside his hands, Tommy showered spittle in his cousin's face. "WHERE?!" Tommy bellowed.

"Where what, Tommy?"

"Rock!" he screamed.

His fingers trembling, Thayne pointed at a door in the corner of the living room.

Staggering to his feet, people and snakes fled Tommy's footsteps as he trudged toward the door. Tommy was going to do what should have been done years ago. He was going to cave Rock's face in, and nothing was going to stop him. He ran into a table instead, and dozens of cups of beer spilled onto the floor. The giants, all with ping-pong balls, were shouting. The giants were angry and would separate Tommy limb from limb.

Tommy felt Thayne's arms wrap around his body. "I got you," Thayne whispered. "I got you."

A crazed, untempered energy flowed through Tommy. Thayne had to get off of him. Tommy knew he had to get out and get somewhere far away from here. "Get!" Tommy yelled. It was all he could manage.

"Naw, bro," Thayne stammered. "I got--"

Tommy screamed, "I said GET." Given a surge of strength, Tommy slammed Thayne against the wall and watched him crumble to the floor. Pushing through the bodies and snakes that packed the house, Tommy stepped through the front door and into the bitter night. He had to get anywhere but here.

—

Pure energy flowed through Tommy's body and sent him in the night. He sprinted through a tunnel of streetlights woven inside the darkness. Their glows passed by his vision, and their remnants burned in his retinas. The temperatures bit Tommy's exposed hands and numbed his fingers, but the boy was far away from the concerns of his body. He had never run this fast in his life, and he had no plans to stop.

Chapter 25: *The Cool Face of the River*

Rosi looked up mournfully at the North College banner hanging at the top of the old, blue Victorian-style house in the student neighborhood of the city. Loud, drunken voices overwhelmed her hearing. Rosi stepped onto the yellow stairs, matching the blue, yellow and red colors of North College. Two college-aged guys sat in patio furniture, the one on the right giving her a wolf whistle.

Rosi looked to the right side of the porch and scanned the guy. He was shirtless, had a slight gut that hung over his shorts, and was still donning shades despite it being near midnight. He started barking at her.

Rosi spat. "I'm 16, bro."

The guy lifted his hands. "Hey, I was just sayin'."

Rosi pushed open the yellow door of the house and the smell of weed overwhelmed her senses. "If contact highs actually exist, I'm getting one tonight," she thought.

A bunch of college students sat on couches against the walls, and a couple were sprawled out on the floor. Stepping to make sure a wall was behind her, Rosi pulled out her phone. Scrolling to a contact labeled "Dad", she hit call.

A ringing filtered in from upstairs. Turning to a stretch of wooden stairs, Rosi walked to the upper floor and walked to where she heard the ringtone.

She stepped into a room. Multiple guys were lying unconscious on the floor, and the ones who were conscious didn't seem to notice her at all. A wooden table with several dollar bills sat at the center of the room. Her dad was just behind it -- he, too, was passed out on the floor.

Rosi tapped him on the shoulder.

"Dad!"

He didn't move. He was in his mid 30s, and the outline of his handsome, boyish face could still be seen under the wrinkles that now lined his expression.

Rosi bent down and tried to shake him awake. "You locked me out of the house, Dad. Wake up."

Rosi looked at her father's soaking jeans for the outline of the house keys in his pocket. She knew they wouldn't be there. They'd be in his car, which was locked with a code she still didn't know.

A guy's voice spoke from behind her. "You're welcome to stay with me if you need a place."

Rosi turned to see the shirtless bro standing at the door. He was short, and his shades now stood in his grasp.

Rosi stood to her full height and looked him in the eye. "I will stab you in your worthless slab of a face if you ever talk to me again."

The guy smiled. "Really? You got a weapon on you?"

Rosi stepped towards him and did not move her gaze. "You have three seconds to find out."

Rosi began the countdown. "Three…"

He looked at her defiantly and said, "Two."

Rosi was resolute, now close enough to smell the liquor soaked in his breath. She reached into the purse and felt outside of her pepper spray. "One."

The guy put a hand on her shoulder. "I'm just messin' with you, sweetie."

Rosi stormed out into the hallway and threw open the front door to the house. Pulling out her phone, Rosi called the only number she could think of. Adam's voice was on the other side. "Hello?"

Rosi stepped off the porch and walked into the park on the North College campus. "Adam. I need you tonight. My dad, he--"

Adam's voice was angry. "We talked about this. I don't do same-day stuff."

Pin needles pricked Rosi's face. "Adam, please. I was there for you on Thanksgiving, I need--"

Adam yelled through the phone. "Woah! Hey now, I did that for *you.* If you're going to try to guilt trip me, get your facts right."

Rosi began tearing up. "Adam. I *need* you."

Adam took a breath. "Rosi, this is too much for me right now. Coach is having me confront Cullen about his diet, and it's just put a lot on my mind. I'm sorry. I feel bad about this, I really do, but whatever your dad is up to isn't my fault."

Rosi felt him hang up, and the phone hung down at her side. Rosi looked in defeat at the lake set in the middle of North College's Potter Park. The moon reflected on the water, and just in front of it she saw a tumbleweed of hair sitting across from it on the freezing evening.

Rosi breathed out in surprise. "Tommy?"

Tommy turned and looked at Rosi at the shore of Potter Lake. His eyes warm and inviting, he responded. "Hey, Mr. Austin!"

"Mr. Austin? Tommy, it's me, Rosi."

Tommy smiled and looked at the water. "I'm not gonna tell ya what the boxcar is about, Mr. Austin. You can keep asking, but I'm not talking."

Rosi was perplexed. Keeping her distance, she sat about 10 yards behind Tommy. She couldn't explain why, but she didn't feel threatened by him here.

Tommy continued, "So. What brought you here today?"

"My deadbeat dad. What else?"

"I thought your dad was dead, Mr. A."

Rosi looked in the water. "It feels that way sometimes."

"The moon looks good off the water tonight. Do you know that river Langston Hughes was talking about is in this town?"

Rosi asked, "What river?"

"What river? The Kaw." Tommy recited a Langston Hughes poem. "The calm, cool face of the river invites me for a kiss."

Rosi swallowed and looked up at the sky. "How often does it invite you?"

"Every day. Some nights more than others. Tonight was a bad one. My own cousin gave me laced weed. I'm not good, Mr. A."

Rosi mused to Tommy, "I'm not good either. I was locked out of my own home tonight. But you know what's worse than that?"

Tommy looked over at her, an eyebrow raised. "Huh?"

"I've lived there all those years, but it's never been my home. I don't think I know what it feels like to have a home."

Tommy thought it over. "Sounds like you live in Kind Pines."

"Close. Felony Acres. I use my aunt's address to get into LHS." Rosi conceded. "You ever wake up and realize that the things you thought in life were all a lie? We were left to find out these hard truths on our own, and for us, we don't have any fantasies to run to anymore. That's what childhood is supposed to be, right? It's supposed to have all these dreams of light. But it hasn't felt like childhood in a long time."

Tommy cracked up. "Honestly I never really had those dreams. You can't pretend your crap don't stink in Kind Pines."

Rosi changed the subject. "So tell me about this boxcar."

Tommy shook his head. "I was hoping you forgot."

"Nah. The boxcar. Spill." Rosi wondered if this was the same boxcar she saw him go into this August, and she was curious to know more about it.

Tommy took a deep breath. "It's annoying that you keep asking, because the dandelion is the most important thing about the painting, but if you insist. When things got bad last year, I would think about walking behind the boxcar to a ladder and climbing to the top of that ladder."

"Why's that?"

His eyes on the water, Tommy seemed to mull over the answer.

"Tommy?"

"Well… After a really bad day last year, I made a noose I was going to take up there.... Well, after I did it, of course."

Rosi felt her heart race and peered right into Tommy. "What were you going to do?"

Tommy was silent.

"Tommy?"

"Don't worry about it."

Rosi raised an eyebrow. "You know I got to, right?"

Tommy exhaled. "I know, Mr. A., I know! Like, I never actually planned to hurt Adam. It was like this escape I'd go to when he'd come after me, and on bad days…"

"So it *was* just a fantasy?"

Tommy threw a pebble in the pond. "You know the types of things he does to me. The things his entire crew does to me. There are days I don't even feel human."

Rosi felt her stomach fall out from under her. She struggled to find her words. "Well, I'm glad you moved on from all that. Did you throw away that journal when all that stuff hit the fan last year? You know, the one that *wasn't* stolen?"

Tommy swallowed, keeping quiet.

Rosi was stunned. "Tommy, don't tell me you still have it?"

"I do."

"Where?"

"Somewhere safe. Beside the noose."

Rosi looked straight into Tommy. “Tommy, you gotta get rid of those things.”

Tommy shook his head. “You don’t know how easy it would be for him to take it all away again. Some days I feel so close to losing it -- of letting it slip between my fingers and falling back to the same place I was last year.”

“Tommy. You have to throw that all away.”

Tommy laughed. “Who are you to lecture me?”

Rosi swallowed. He was more right than he knew about that, but she pressed forward. “That’s true, but with that journal you’re not going to leave last year behind.”

“I wish it were only last year. That's what no one gets. Five years ago my mom was drugged on pain pills when she said it."

"It?"

Tommy swallowed. "I don't want to talk about this anymore."

Rosi paused. “That’s fine, but one more thing?”

“Yeah?”

“Why’s the dandelion so important?”

Tommy laid out in the grass. “…I haven’t decided yet.”

Rosi seriously doubted that, but she changed the subject. “Well, how are you getting home, Tommy?”

“No. I can’t go home tonight.”

Rosi narrowed her eyes. “I get you, but where else can you go?”

Tommy breathed. “I have one place.”

—

Rosi stood outside the front door of the Riverfront Brewery. She used to go here with her grandma when she was little. Well, that was before she passed. The Riverfront Brewery was *the* special restaurant they would go to. Grandma always said that since even before 1900, it was the #1 spot in the city, and it was always the #1 place that students wanted to go before prom. Rosi looked out at the water. It was beside the Kaw River. She heard it was called the "Candlelight House" by a sailor in the early 20th century, and right now she could see the city lights reflecting off the water.

Riverfront was only about a half mile from Potter Park, but the cold was already overwhelming. Despite being in red gloves, Rosi couldn't feel her fingertips. The lights inside the restaurant were dimmed, and Rosi could see a few workers through the window.

Tommy shivered behind her. "So where are we, Cullen?"

Rosi rolled her eyes. "You were the one who wanted to come here."

Tommy shook his head. "Cullen, I didn't even want to leave Riverfront."

"We're at Riverfront, dummy!"

Rosi turned around and saw Dexter Allen walking by the front area. Rosi waved her arms. "Dexter!"

Dexter stopped and threw his arms up in surprise. He ran to the door and grabbed keys from a keychain on his waist and went to greet them.

"Rosi Williams and… Tommy T? We got an odd couple situation going on here?"

Rosi smiled wanly. "Yeah, I guess. Um, Dexter, I think someone might have given him a roofie."

Dexter's eyes widened. "Oh crap. Really?"

Tommy shook his head and whipped his head to Rosi. "Not roofies, Cullen. Acid."

Dexter took a step to Tommy and waved his hand in front of his face.

Rosi continued, "He says he can't go home."

"Well where can you go, my dude?"

Tommy was quick to answer. "Cullen's."

Dexter shrugged and looked at Rosi. "That's a big ask, Rosi. He's doin' two-a-days over break."

Rosi clarified. “It would only be him. I’m good tonight.”

“My phone’s charging in the back. I’ll see if Cullen’s awake. I’m still here for a couple of hours, but you’re both welcome to crash with me if you need. My parents won’t care.”

Rosi gnashed her teeth. “I think we got to get Tommy to bed.”

Dexter nodded. “I’ll go make the call.”

Rosi watched Dexter run off and stood shivering inside the lobby of Riverfront. It was nice and warm and much better than being outside tonight, but she was still cold. She turned around; Tommy was staring at his feet. She really felt for him and, for a moment, felt a twinge of guilt when she thought about some of the things she had done to him.

Tommy looked up towards the interior of the restaurant. “Mr. A,” he breathed.

Rosi narrowed her eyes. “I thought I was Cullen now?”

Tommy pointed towards the doors inside the restaurant. “Mr. A.”

Rosi turned around and exhaled in surprise. Mr. Austin *was* standing there, beside a tall, stocky and slightly chubby man she recognized as Cam Thomas, the general manager of Riverfront. They were both holding cans of *Whoop @$S* energy drinks, and Rosi saw Mr. Austin lean in and give Cam a kiss.

Rosi gasped. Her mind raced. “Mr. Austin and Cam are a thing? I didn’t even know Mr. A swung in that…” Her mind trailed, and she tapped Tommy on the shoulder.

Tommy turned. “Huh?”

Rosi whispered, “Did you know this? About Mr. Austin.”

Tommy raised an eyebrow and spoke with sincerity. “*I’m* Mr. Austin.”

Rolling her eyes, Rosi turned to see Dexter running to the lobby. Before Rosi could speak, Dexter opened the lobby door and held up a finger.

"He doesn't know you're here. Yes, him and Cam are an item, and he brings Cam an energy drink and helps him close down on weekends."

Rosi nodded. "That's, like, one of the sweetest things I've ever heard."

Dexter turned around, and Rosi saw Mr. A and Cam walk back into the kitchen. Dexter continued, "He helps us close down. It's really nice, but no one finds out about this. Okay?"

Rosi had never heard Dexter speak so seriously before. "Is it really that big of a deal?" she asked. "I mean, it's not 1990 anymore."

"You know what side of the highway our school's on," Dexter retorted. "You ever notice how, every year, LHS graduates tend to come out the first week of college?"

"Well, yeah, it's practically a meme at this point."

"A meme for you, maybe. Perhaps you need to stop and think about why that keeps happening."

Rosi gestured to Tommy. "So what's the plan there?"

"Cullen said he can come. His sister says you can stay too, Rosi."

"How will we get there?"

Dexter gestured behind him. "Our pit cook, Bon, is about to leave. He's a driver on the side and said he could give you a lift with an IOU."

Tommy yelled from behind them. "I got money."

Rosi turned to see Tommy holding his wallet and nodded to Dex.

Dexter stepped to Rosi. "And Rose?"

Rosi looked up at Dexter. "Yeah?"

"No one finds out about Mr. A. Not even Adam."

Rosi nodded. "No one will find out. Not even Adam. I promise."

Dexter opened the door. "You can wait in the lobby. Bon will be out soon."

—

Tamira hugged Rosi the moment she made it through the door. When they stepped back from each other, Rosi saw Cullen approach the door and put his hand on her head. "Where's Tommy?" he asked.

Rosi gestured toward the car behind her. "Passed out in the backseat."

Cullen rolled his eyes. "For God's sakes."

Tamira turned. "You can take the pod, Rosi. How long are you staying?"

"Just tonight. I'll be out early tomorrow morning."

"You sure?"

Rosi felt tears begin to form. "I'm sure."

"Look. I know Cullen and my pa are all about converting Warren's old pod into a bed n breakfast, but we could easily set it up for you. It wouldn't be free, mind you, but it'd be cheap. Are you working again?"

Rosi shook her head.

"It doesn't matter." Tamara said, "I think I could hold 'em off for a couple months till you got on your feet. Cullen would know you'd be good for the money. You ain't safe where you are right now."

Rosi looked to her feet. "Thank you. I'll think about it, okay? Just do me a favor?"

"Anything."

Rosi stepped aside as Cullen carried Tommy inside their home. Rosi gestured toward Tommy. "Don't tell him about me, okay?"

"Don't tell him about you?"

"He got drugged tonight. I don't think he'll remember me, and if he doesn't, can you keep it that way?"

"Sure," Tamira said. "Let's get you inside."

Chapter 26: ***25 Bucks***

Cullen walked into his uncle Warren's room and gently closed the door. It was 7:57 A.M., and Warren's alarm would ring in three minutes. Cullen looked at his uncle. Warren looked strikingly like him, but his uncle's legs were much, much skinnier. Cullen looked at Warren's wheelchair and made sure the wheel locks were in place.

Loud snoring echoed around the room. Cullen looked over and saw Tommy fast asleep behind him. Figuring he better give Tommy a heads up, he shook Tommy's leg and woke him up. Tommy moved his head up from the bed and opened his eyes. He seemed to apply all his focus on Cullen before asking, "Cullen?"

Cullen breathed. "How's your head?"

Tommy lifted a hand to his temple. "It's like my head got beaten like a drum, and snot is cased over my mouth, dude. How, how am I--"

Cullen cut him off. "Here? How much of last night do you remember?"

"I went to a party with my cousin and an a-hole friend of his. We smoked a joint before going in, but neither of them told me it was laced with something heavier."

"That's some next level BS of your cousin. Any clue what was in the joint?"

Tommy shook his head. "No. I kinda panicked once I realized what was happening. I wanted to kill them for doing that to me, but then I, uh, just decided to get out of there, I guess. I don't remember anything after that."

"Well, someone got you a ride here last night."

"Are you serious?"

"Dead serious."

Tommy exhaled. "Do you know who it was?"

The lie came easily for Cullen. "Not sure, but I do know you gave them 25 dollars and told them to keep the change."

Tommy was resolute. "They deserved it after putting up with me. It was only 25 bucks after all."

Cullen raised an eyebrow. "*Only* 25 bucks?"

Tommy looked to his feet. "I know. I know. I just… I don't really want to think about yesterday, okay?"

"Alright."

"Thank you for everything. I would have been in huge trouble without you."

Cullen responded, "Just be smarter about who you get blazed with."

Warren's alarm went off behind Cullen. Cullen clapped his hands. "You ready to get up and around, Warren?!"

Warren, his back still to Tommy, let out a high-pitched answer. "Yes!"

Cullen reached into a wooden dresser and extracted a pair of blue gloves. "Did you have an accident last night?"

"Nope!"

Surprised, Cullen answered, "Nice. Well then let's get you up, my man." Cullen turned back to Tommy, who was looking at them both in a daze. "By the way, Tommy, this is my uncle, Warren. Warren, this is Tommy. Warren, do you mind if Tommy's here while I get your jeans on?"

Warren revealed a toothless smile. "That… crazy jackass… is fine."

Tommy turned to Cullen. "Did he just call me a crazy jackass?"

Cullen pointed over to Warren with a lightning reaction. "Ask him, not me."

Awkwardly, Tommy turned back to Warren. "Did you, uh, just call me a jackass?"

Warren released another high-pitched laugh.

After holding up a pair of jeans that had Warren's approval, Cullen provided explanation. "You were kind of out of your mind last night. I couldn't get you to go to sleep. You woke Warren up a couple of times and eventually I had to take you to the garage. You ended up nodding off around five."

Tommy buried his head into his palms. "I am so sorry-- to both of you guys, but Cullen, don't you have practice this morning? You only got a couple hours of sleep."

Cullen responded mournfully. "I've been livin' off this schedule all year, Tommy."

"That's true. So, my cousin and his crew get me into bad situations sometimes, and I've never had a friend before who could get me out of them. I just want to say thanks, I guess." Tommy looked up to Cullen. "Can I ask you a favor?"

Cullen opened one of Warren's pill bottles and replied to Tommy. "Shoot."

Tommy spoke. "If I ever get in a situation like that again, can I count on you to--"

Cullen opened a bottle of water for his uncle. "No, Tommy. I can't be your rescuer."

"Rescuer? I'm not askin' that, Cullen. I'm just saying, if my cousin gets me into a situation like that--"

Cullen put a straw in the bottle. "Then why are you hangin' with your cousin in the first place?"

"Cause he's family, Cullen. I thought you'd get it."

Cullen shook his head. "I really don't though, dude. Have you ever heard me talk about my older brother?"

"No."

Cullen nodded. "There's a reason for that. I love my older bro. But you know what? He's a sketch locksmith who boosts cars and breaks into houses. Hanging with him is gonna get me in trouble. The rest of my family needs me, Tommy. What would I tell 'em if I got arrested because I was hangin' with my brother?"

Tommy looked at his feet. "Are you okay? I don't even know what I said."

Cullen took off his gloves. "No, Tommy. I'm not okay. I got barely two hours of sleep, remember?"

"Crap. Sorry. I know I should be appreciative that you bailed me out last night."

"You're good, T. But you can't make this a habit, you get me?"

"I won't," Tommy promised. "Is there… any help you need now?"

Cullen nodded. "Yeah, in fact. Could you make some toast for Warren and me? Tamira will show you where everything is."

"You got it," Tommy said, leaving the room.

Warren spoke. "He… seems… nice."

Cullen helped Warren get his shirt on, pulling down the back of it all the way between Warren and the back of his chair. "He's a screw-up, but I like him."

Warren continued, "You, uh, lectured him… pretty good."

"Yeah. He had it coming. He's gonna screw up his life forever if he keeps screwin' up like that, and I'm not gonna be his security blanket." Cullen knelt in front of his uncle. "I won't lie to you. This issue hits me deep. I don't know, I feel like I haven't had any say over my own life since Ma died. I feel like I've been asked to chip in for the family and care for Tamira since I was in the fourth grade. Sorry, I know I shouldn't be complainin' to you."

Warren pushed back, "No, Cullen. You… you've had a grown man's… responsibility… for a long time."

"But I ain't a grown man. I'm still a scared kid who's afraid he and his siblings ain't gonna have heat at night. I was combin' my sister's hair before she went off to kindergarten, and now I'm bein' told to take out a 10 grand loan to go to college next year? Dad said he wants me to be the first in his line to go to college. You know he wants me to use that alumni scholly you have access to at the NC, but, Uncle, I don't know if I want to go!"

Warren replied, "College ain't… goin' anywhere. What would you do?"

"Get an apartment somewhere close. I want to be here till Tamira graduates. But truth be told, I think I just want to figure out what I'd want to do to begin with. Tamira could take your alumni scholly, too. She's been workin' for that."

"Your ma is… smilin' on you, nephew. Whatever you do… she'll be proud."

Cullen exhaled. "Thanks for that, Uncle. Let's get you some breakfast."

When Cullen and Warren moved into the dining room, Tommy had toast waiting for them. Tamira was already cutting up Warren's food and had an annoyed expression on her face.

Cullen spoke. "I see you met my sister, Tommy."

"Yeah, apparently I woke her up last night, too. Sorry."

Tamira flashed a look of annoyance at Tommy. "How long is Dad's shift?"

Cullen stretched out. "It was a 12 hour one. He should be back around noon. You good until then?"

"Yeah, I'll be alright."

Cullen gestured towards Tommy. "Alright, let's bounce." He looked at his family. "See ya."

Warren and Tamira saying bye, Cullen led Tommy out of the home.

Tommy checked the time. "Are you going to have time to drop me off before practice, Cullen?"

Locking up his front door, Cullen nodded. "Yeah, I'll be okay."

“So, if it’s okay to ask, how long have you taken care of your uncle like that?”

Cullen led Tommy to his jet-black Dodge Stealth. “Well, Warren and my mom were twins, and they were pretty much inseparable for their whole lives. Warren was diagnosed with cerebral palsy when he was seven, and my mom helped him out through her life. After Mom passed, my dad stepped up to the plate and took Tamira, Warren, and my screw-up brother Calvin and I back into his life.”

“I had no idea about your mom,” Tommy stated, getting into the car. “I'm sorry.”

“It was a long time ago. Anyway, knowin’ Warren's why I got the job at the care home. Growing up with Warren was one of the best things that ever happened to me. He’s one of the funniest dudes I know.”

“You’re a class act, Cullen.”

Cullen shook him off. “I appreciate it, but Warren’s ten times the guy I am for putting up with Tamira and I’s BS for so long.”

Tommy put on his seatbelt. "Cullen, could I ask one more thing?"

Cullen nodded.

“Is any of this real?”

Cullen laughed. “All real, promise. Drink some water, have some hard candies. Take it easy today, and you’ll begin piecing apart what’s real and what ain’t by the afternoon.”

Chapter 27: *The Lone and Level Sands*

Tommy gave a blank stare to a message on his phone. He didn't know how anyone got his number. He had only given it to a select few, and the idea of a friend betraying him was too much to stomach on the first day back to school. *It's a bad omen*, Tommy's mind concluded. He felt a lot of regret over the party and how hard he leaned on Cullen. He never should have smoked that joint. He never should have let his guard down.

Renaming the contact to "Mystery Asshole" on his phone, Tommy stepped off his bed and lifted Mia's dandelion from his desk.

On the last day of the first semester, Mia had given him the first Christmas present that ever melted his heart. Today, he would return the favor and show Mia her gift in the student showcase.

It would be hers to keep forever.

—

Tommy was sprinting with childlike glee. "I can't wait for you to see it!"

Mia shadowed Tommy's footsteps. "I can't either! I don't think I've ever seen you this happy."

Tommy wended a corner. "I've been waiting all break for this. I hope you like it."

"The fact that you made something for me is the only gift I need."

Tommy halted his footsteps and slid up to the doors of the student lobby. Mia ran into Tommy the moment he stopped.

His heart racing, Tommy turned his head and found himself face to face with Mia. Standing closer than he ever had before, Tommy looked straight into her eyes and tried to whisper an apology.

"S-sorry."

Mia smiled. "You're fine."

Tommy was so close he could smell Mia's mint-coated breath. Feeling his face get hot, Tommy found his footing. "Are you ready?"

"Absolutely."

Thrusting open the doors, Tommy yelled, "Merry Christmas, Mi--"

Tommy gasped. He felt his chest contract in surprise. Tommy's spot for *The Yellow Ladder* been stripped bare inside the showcase.

Tommy breathed in disbelief. "It's gone!"

Mia looked at him in confusion. "Who could have even done this?"

Tommy squeezed his hands into fists. "Someone took it away. This place -- I *hate* this place!"

"Tommy," Mia muttered. She put a hand over his fist. "It's going to be okay."

Tommy's anger began to ebb the moment he felt her touch.

"Let's go talk to Mr. Austin about this," Mia suggested. "He'll get this figured out."

Stomaching his emotions, Tommy followed Mia out of the lobby.

—

With Mia by his side, Tommy stormed into Mr. Austin's classroom. "Did you take down my painting?" Tommy asked, pointing a finger at the teacher.

Mr. Austin looked up from his desk. "Take your painting down? What're you talking about?"

"It's gone. Someone's taken it down."

"I promise I would never take down your work without telling you, especially one so meaningful."

Tommy clawed for answers. "Can you just put it back up then? Maybe somehow the showcase was left unlocked over break?"

Mr. Austin shook his head. "No. I mean, I don't think so. I remember double checking after I locked it up."

"Does anyone else have a key?"

"Well, normally I don't even have a key."

Tommy tilted his head in confusion. "Then who does?"

The morning bell rang, and the teacher left Tommy's question floating in the air. "Don't worry, Tommy. We'll get this figured out. I promise."

—

Tommy sat back in Mr. Demko's 2nd period class and zoned out from Demko's droning in the front of the room. While he couldn't hear Demko, the conversation between Brian and Adam filtered into his ears.

Brian turned to Adam. "Do you know where Rosi is?"

Adam shrugged. "She said she was feeling pretty sick last night."

"Did you two finally become a thing?"

Adam snorted. "Ah, no, she just smokes my pole."

The blunt edge of the statement caused Tommy to flip around, catching Adam by surprise. Adam met Tommy's eyes. "Do you have something to say to me?"

Feeling an edge from the day, Tommy spat. “I don’t know, peckerwood. Did I say something?”

A lunacy hinged itself inside Brian’s eyes. “You better watch yourself, because we’re coming for you.”

“Good luck with that,” Tommy answered.

Adam whispered, “You always talked about killing yourself, Piss Stain. After this, you might actually do it.”

Tommy stuck a finger towards Adam. “Bleed out and die, you thin-blooded douche.”

Adam had an unsettling smile. "We warned you."

—

“I don’t know,” Tommy muttered. He and Mia were sitting on the student patio after school. “I mean, you’d have to factor in that the Justice League is really overpowered compared to the Avengers. Like, it would be really difficult for the Avengers to take down Superman alone. Now, if you pitted Superman against World War Hulk, then things would be interesting.”

Mia raised an eyebrow. “World War Hulk?”

“Yeah, he’s a suped-up version of The Hulk. The angrier he gets, the more powerful he becomes.”

“Huh. Has there ever been a suped-up version of Superman?”

“Oh, yeah. Superman Prime. He’s a golden Superman that’s invincible to just about everything. Don’t even get me started on him.”

“Heh, okay.”

Her voice broke when she said it. Tommy turned; there was an unusual paleness in her complexion, and there was even a puffiness in her eyes that he had missed when she joined him.

“Mia… are you okay?”

"Don't worry about it, Tommy."

"I'm going to worry about it. You're my friend."

"You'll think it's stupid."

"Maybe, but that doesn't mean you shouldn't tell me."

Mia sighed. "I missed my STUCO meeting this morning."

"Is that it?"

"I wish. It's the second strike on my record, and if I get one more I'll be kicked out for good."

"Ah, well, STUCO isn't that big of a--"

Mia cut the boy off. "Tommy, as of this morning I have two-thousand-three-hundred-ninety-two-dollars and eleven cents to my name, and all of it will be spent in my first month at North College. I need scholarships, and Stallard's letter of recommendation can get me those. Mr. Stallard went to the NC, believe it or not. His name carries a lot of weight. Every little bit counts, and it counts for so much."

"I'm sorry."

Mia shook her head. "Mr. Stallard lost it when I talked with him."

Tommy nodded glumly. "I know the feeling."

"He said if I'm late again then I wouldn't be welcomed back to STUCO."

"What made you miss the meet--"

Before Tommy could finish, Brian sat down at an empty space between Mia and Tommy with an apple in his grasp. "Don't let me interrupt you, Tommy Taint."

Mia's eyes were fixed open at their maximum capacity. "Let's go, Tommy."

Tommy's eyes barreled into Brian. "No. I'm not afraid of this tool."

Brian took a bite from his apple. "Well, Mia really used to get cozy with this tool, if you know what I--"

Tommy lifted himself to his feet so fast that it took Brian by surprise. Gagging on his apple, Brian stood like a tower over Tommy. "Me and the boys are coming after you, pizza face."

Mia put a hand on Tommy's shoulder. "Tommy, please. Let's go."

"Yeah," Brian whispered, "listen to your friendzone, Tommy."

Peter Good, moving from substituting Art to after school duties, walked over. "We okay here, boys?"

Mia's touch soothed Tommy's adrenaline. Controlling his breathing, Tommy looked at Peter. "Yeah, we're just joking around."

The explanation sturdy enough for Mr. Good, Tommy felt himself being escorted by Mia away from the patio. Tommy scooped up his backpack and high-tailed after Mia through the lobby, the main hallways, and into the John Wagner Fieldhouse.

Tommy caught his breath. "Mia -- I'm sorry if…" but before he could manage another word, he watched in horror as Mia fell onto the center of the court.

Mia broke down, crying louder than he had ever heard before. Tommy knelt beside her, but no matter what he tried, she could not bring herself to speak.

Part Three: Before the Last Breath

Sitting behind his computer, Mr. Stallard read through the draft of a staff-wide e-mail he had written about tomorrow's hat policy meeting. His only light coming from a sterilized lamp on the right side of his desk, Stallard fixed a typo at the bottom of the message.

A single knock echoed into the office.

"Yes?" Stallard asked.

Mr. Austin stepped inside. "Jay? I was wondering if we could talk about something."

An out-of-character smile curled on Mr. Stallard's face. "Of course. How can I help you?"

Mr. Austin took a seat. "I won't take much of your time. I just wanted to ask you about the student showcase."

"The Pride of Latimer?"

"Yeah. Before Winter Break, I hung up three of my students' projects inside the showcase, but when we got back, the project I selected for the centerpiece was gone."

Stallard looked up at the ceiling. "I see."

"Why'd you take it down, Jay?"

Stallard's eyes flickered. "Well, your student showcase is designed to show your students' best drawings and paintings. And that design was made on a computer."

"A tablet," Austin corrected.

"Sure, but the issue is that it was made digitally."

"I didn't realize you were making the final decisions on my showcase this year."

Stallard interjected. "In a way, I always do. It's why you come to me for the key."

Mr. Austin released a heavy laugh. "Are you actually going to make me go to Jeff for the student showcase key, Jay?"

Narrowing his eyes, Jay looked at Mr. Austin in icy silence.

Mr. Austin nodded. "Alright then."

Jay lashed out, revealing a dagger in his voice that Austin had never felt before. "Are you enough of an idiot to think that Jeff will let you put that monster's drawing at the front of the high school?"

"Still having a hard time getting that monster expelled, huh? You and Randy should detain him again and this time try beating the confession from him."

"And we'd do it in a heartbeat," Stallard confessed. "Maybe you've forgotten, but Jeff was gone at a ritzy administrator's conference that day, and someone had to step up for the safety of our students."

Shaking his head, Austin turned around to leave. "Well, I'll quit bothering you. I know you have an e-mail to send out about whether a headband is considered a hat in this school. I'm sure that will be equally important for our students' safety, huh?"

Stallard reclined in his chair. "James? Before you go. All those long nights you and Tommy have spent alone in your room -- it's touching just how much of a liking you've taken to the boy." Donning a full toothed smile, Stallard took aim. "But I guess he is your type, huh?"

The words hit Mr. Austin like a bomb. His cheeks collapsed. He lowered his voice. "You would lie about something like that just because of Tommy's poster?"

Mr. Stallard smiled. He knew everything about him and Cameron. Hell, his wife was the nurse when Cameron had his heart attack. It was why James took a week of leave last fall. Stallard kept his voice clear and steady and let loose the guillotine. "I'm appalled; you and Cameron isn't a lie, is it? It would just be.... so unfortunate if your secret about Cameron somehow made it to the public."

Mr. Austin stepped towards his desk. "But what you're saying about Tommy is evil."

Mr. Stallard lifted his hands. "Woah, woah, woah. If the community found out that Tommy spent the afternoons studying alone in your room, it wouldn't be *my* fault if they made an incorrect assumption. I hate to think about what the parents would say if they knew about the alone time you and the boy spent together. They might even think *you* wrote that letter to the school board and are why Tommy's back here."

Mr. Austin stared in disbelief. "You're counting on bigotry to end my career?"

"I'm counting on no such thing. All I'm asking is that Tommy's drawing stay out of the showcase."

Mr. Austin put his head down and stormed out of the room.

Watching Mr. Austin retreat, a victorious gleam colored Stallard's baby blue eyes. Doing one last scan of the e-mail about the hat policy meeting, Stallard unchecked Mr. Austin from the e-mail list, and pressed send.

Chapter 28: ***Forsaker***

Without a word, Tommy edited his "Mystery Asshole" contact and changed it to "Adam's boytoy." Expelling a breath, Tommy threw his phone into his backpack and stared through a window of Bus B-45.

Part of him wanted to ask Dex and Cullen about what to do, but he knew what they were going to say. "*You just gotta ignore him.*"

Tommy felt another vibration from his bag. It was easier said than done.

—

Mia spoke firmly. "I don't want to talk about what happened yesterday."

Sitting across from Mia in an isolated corner of the cafeteria, Tommy shook his head. "I can't do that, Mia--"

"Yes, you can. I never want to talk about it again."

Tommy gnashed his teeth. "Fine."

"You don't need to worry about this, Tommy."

"I'm your friend. I'm going to worry."

"I know, but Tommy--"

Tommy held up a hand. "If it was me in that gym, would you have asked me what was wrong?"

"Tommy...."

Resentment flashed in Tommy's eyes. "Do you know how he treats me? You can't stonewall me on this."

Mia took a sharp breath. "Tommy. If I choose not to say anything then I wouldn't be stonewalling. This isn't any of your business--"

"But--"

"Let me finish. I don't need to talk about this. I need someone to be here."

"I would always talk to you."

"If I asked you if you were actually going to kill Adam Augustine last year, would you give me an honest answer?"

Tommy launched onto his feet and was about to storm from the cafeteria.

Mia held up her hands. "Tommy -- please. I'm sorry, that was harsh, but you get what I'm saying, right?"

Tommy didn't know what was hurting him more, the fact that Mia's comparison was dead on or that he may have misjudged him and Mia's friendship. Giving her the dirtiest glare he had ever given her, he planted himself back in his seat.

"Thank you," Mia breathed. "I vowed after my sophomore year that I would never speak to Brian again, and I don't plan on breaking that promise. If he ever comes up to us again, can you ignore him for me, Tommy?"

"So you just want me to stand there?" Tommy asked.

"One of the hardest parts of caring about someone is being there for that person when there's nothing you can say to help. Can you walk away from him, Tommy? Can you do this for me?"

Looking to his feet, Tommy nodded.

"Thank you." The girl held up her phone. "Thank you for talking to me so early today. Know that I'm always a text away."

"You're a true friend for putting up with me," Tommy responded, fighting back tears. "You're the first person who ever has."

"Everyone else has missed out. Have you talked to Mr. Austin about your drawing yet? I'm dying to see it."

"I'll talk to him after school. He said he'd let me know by the end of the week."

Mia beamed. "I can't wait."

—

His hair tousled from the school day, Tommy stepped into Mr. Austin's room.

Cullen was perched behind a desk, ready to greet him. "What's good?"

Tommy shrugged. "I need to talk to Mr. A. You seen him around?"

"What do you need to talk to him about? Anything I can help with?"

Tommy shook his head. "I doubt it. For some reason my drawing was taken from the showcase over the break, and Mr. Austin said he'd look into it for me."

"Really? Well that bougie BS would be thanks to our pal, Stallard."

"I knew it."

"Don't worry," Cullen reassured. "Mr. Austin will take care of you."

Mr. Austin entered the room. "How are we doing, gents?"

Tommy was quick to the point, "Um, well. I was wondering if we could get *The Yellow Ladder* back in the showcase today?"

The teacher grimaced. "Actually, I was hoping we could talk about that in private?"

"What?" Tommy asked, confused. "No, Cullen is fine."

"Are you sure? Because you may not like what you're going to hear."

A chill clamped over Tommy. "What do you mean?"

Mr. Austin shook his head, "It's not going to happen. I'm sorry, Tommy."

Tommy yelled, "Are you kidding me?"

"Tommy," Austin murmured, his voice apologetic, "I will find a special place for it in my classroom, or maybe even another place for it in the school. I'll make this right."

Cullen entered the fray. "Come on, Mr. A, just get it back in the showcase."

Mr. Austin disregarded Cullen's comment. "Tommy, I will make sure that everyone can see it from in here. How does that sound?"

Tommy was beside himself. "Are you really going to let Stallard win?"

"It's more complicated than that."

Tears bled into Tommy's eyes. "Do you know about the things Stallard's said to me? The things he's done to me? You don't even know. He hates me… And you're letting him beat me again."

"I promise I will make this up to you. Just listen to me."

Tommy stepped toward Mr. Austin. "You're trash. You're no different than Stallard."

Cullen stood up between the two. "Chill, Tommy. You're goin' too far."

Mr. Austin put a hand on Cullen's shoulder, and his voice was calm. "I can't allow you to speak to me like that, Tommy."

"That's fine!" Tommy yelled, "because I'm done talking!"

Seeing Mr. Austin sigh, Tommy stormed into the hallway.

Tommy slammed through the door of the Annex. His breathing short and panicked, the boy slammed his hands on the top of a trophy-filled table.

"Breathe," the boy reminded himself. "Just breathe." The boy lifted his fist to strike the table but held it in the air. "It's gonna be okay," Tommy reminded himself. "Mia will understand. She'll get it." Tommy's phone buzzed inside his pocket. Relief filling his body, a hopeful smile filled Tommy's face as he looked at his phone.

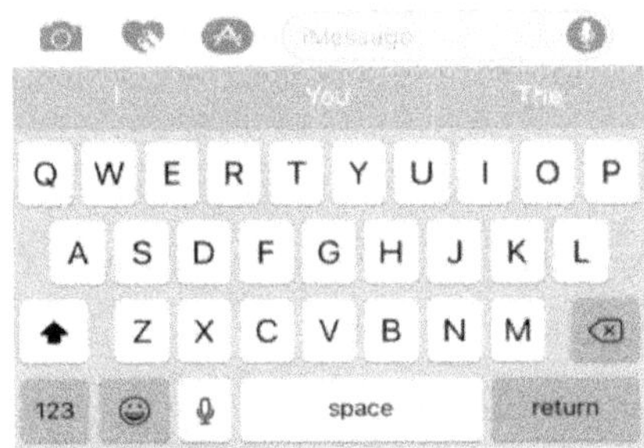

Tommy's hand quivered around the screen, and his face gave off tiny contortions around his upper lip. He released a blood curdling scream and spiked his phone to the ground. He shoved the collection of dusty trophies from the table and watched as they shattered across the tile.

Feeling like he was about to explode, the boy collapsed onto the floor.

Chapter 29: ***The Cheese Stands Alone***

With Tommy's footsteps fading in the hall, Mr. Austin shut his classroom door and directed his gaze to Cullen. Cullen quickly looked away.

"Cullen, have you ever told anyone about Cam and me?" Mr. Austin asked.

Cullen looked up, shocked. "Hell no, Mr. A. I'm not gonna sell you out like that."

"Yeah. I know you won't. I just--"

"No one is going to find out, Mr. A."

Mr. Austin grimaced. "Someone did."

Understanding filled Cullen's expression. "Stallard?"

"And he's holding it over me."

"Mr. A, you have to tell someone."

Mr. Austin shook his head. "I can't do that. If Cam and I became public knowledge, it'd break the community."

Cullen was incredulous. "You're fooling yourself. Parents love you here. They would riot in the streets if they heard about this."

"Jay has friends too, and his are in high places."

"High places?" Cullen asked angrily. "Like people on our janky school board? You're not seein' the big picture! This could go viral. You could start a movement to burn down the Stallards of the world."

"No," Mr. Austin said bluntly. "I don't want to do that."

"But why?"

"I don't want to be a nationwide story. I don't want to be known for my love life. I want to be known for being a darn good teacher. My talent has always been in the classroom, and that's where I want to stay. Besides, do you think the Stallards of the world leave a trail behind? In the end, it's my word against his, and the things he'll accuse me of would tear this community in two. I will not have that be my legacy. I have devoted too much of my life to this for that to happen."

"Tommy may never forgive you," Cullen pointed out.

Mr. Austin sighed. "If he's the person I think he is, he will." He looked over at Cullen. "So, what's your plan next year?"

"You askin' where I'm goin' to school?"

Mr. Austin shook his head. "No. I'm just askin'."

Cullen looked over his teacher. "A guy I know said all teachers are cops."

Mr. Austin shrugged. "I get where the dude's coming from. I am a mandatory reporter, and I used to think the same thing as the guy you know, actually."

"But you're real? I can talk to you about something and you're not going to give me a bunch of sugar-coated BS?"

"Believe me, the BS I give is *never* sugar coated. As long as you're not sharing anything illegal with me, it won't leave this room."

Cullen nodded. "So, I'm thinkin' of not going to school. Would that be so bad?"

"Not at all. What changed your mind?"

"Nothin'. I mean, everything. I don't know. I sorta realized that I don't know if I ever wanted to go at all. Everyone says I should go into nursing or med school."

"It makes sense. You've worked at the nursing home for a couple of years."

Cullen snapped, "But that's the thing. I didn't do it 'cause I wanted to. I did it because I got tired of coming home to no electricity. I was tired of tryin' to care for my uncle in the candlelight. My dad lost his refinery job and couldn't make ends meet with his jobs after that. So I stepped up. I was just 14. The cafeteria in the nursing home needed someone to stock shelves so I stocked shelves. I figured my experience helpin' Warren could eventually lead me to workin' with the people there. By 16 that's the type of care that I was doing." Cullen felt his heart start rushing inside his chest. "Look, I ain't sayin' I don't love my uncle or the people I help out at work." Cullen's voice rose. "I will care for my uncle forever, but am I a bad guy if I don't want this to be my job forever? What if I'm being stupid? Mr. A, I don't even know what I want to do, but if I don't go to college now, what if I never get to go, what if I--"

Mr. Austin put a hand on Cullen's shoulder, and Cullen felt himself calm down almost instantly. Mr. Austin looked at Cullen. "I don't know if I know another student who is shouldering the responsibilities you are for your family. Cullen, you don't have to apologize for wanting to find the person that you want to be." Mr. Austin pulled up a chair. "When I was 14, I was still doin' work for my dad."

"Work?"

Mr. Austin smiled. "House painting. But slightly different from the work I do in the summers. Because when I worked with my dad, my job was to look for weak points."

"Weak points?"

"Garage door combinations written on sticky notes. Spare keys in hide-a-key rocks. Garage openers in parked cars on the street."

Cullen's mouth was agape. "You did B&E's?"

"Nah. Dad gave the combinations to other people. Got paid for it that way. I could always talk my way out of feeling guilty. We painted big houses. The people had more money than they deserved, and the jobs were always done when the people weren't home. No one got hurt. Until I read that one of the families we did got held up at gunpoint."

"What?"

Mr. Austin nodded. "Yeah. I couldn't ignore that, and the responsibility I had for that. I told Dad I was done. I was messed up, Cullen. I realized my whole life and the world my dad taught me had been a lie. I dropped out of high school, got my GED, and by the time I was 18, I was workin' as a carney in a traveling circus."

Cullen laughed. "You were a carney?!"

"On and off until I was 20. You ever been to one of those mirror mazes?"

Cullen nodded. "Of course."

Mr. Austin continued, "I walked through that mirror maze every day. Every day I would stare at my reflections. Hundreds of them. I would look at every single one, wondering which reflection was the person I wanted to be. And three years later, I walked out of that mirror maze thinking I might know. I quit my job and enrolled in North College. I wanted to be the teacher that my father never was. To teach kids that a better world *was* possible. The person waiting for me at the help desk was my future boyfriend, Cam."

Cullen smiled. "Funny how that all works out."

"You never know when it'll happen. But Cullen, you owe it to yourself to walk through that mirror maze. Look at every single reflection you have. Take as much time as you need. Don't let anyone rush you, and don't stop looking until you find yourself."

"Thanks, Mr. A.," Cullen said with a smile. "I better run to basketball practice."

"Still gonna dunk this year?"

"You know it. You gonna be okay?"

Mr. Austin replied, "I'll be alright. You worry about dunking, taking state, and walking through that maze, alright?"

"Thank you, Mr. A."

—

Dexter filled a mug of coffee in Cullen's kitchen. Cullen checked over his duffel bag to make sure he was ready for the night's game. Cullen spoke to Dex. "Thanks for bein' here. You sure you can give me a lift home tonight? We'll be gettin' back late."

Dexter nodded. "Sure am. Mr. A and I are finishing the documentary tonight and watching it with Principal Elmer."

Cullen stood up straight as an arrow. He couldn't believe it. Dexter had talked about this documentary for years. Hearing it was done? He couldn't picture it. Heck, he couldn't even imagine what it felt like to put something together like that.

Dexter narrowed his eyes. "What?"

"Dex. You realize what a big deal this is, right? Bruh, we gotta celebrate."

Dexter shook his head. "After I get that scholly, let's celebrate."

Cullen laughed. "Naw, swerve on that bougie BS." Cullen stepped to the closet by his front door and pulled out a crimson and gold letter jacket. Without hesitating, he tossed it to Dexter. "Here you go, bruh."

Dexter caught his jacket in surprise. "Were you savin' this for me?"

"I wanna say yes, but really I found it a couple of weeks back cleaning out our guest pod and just remembered I had it."

Dexter laughed out loud. "Why were you cleanin' out the guest pod?"

"Tamira's tryin' to get Rosi to move into that pod."

"Adam know about that?"

"It ain't none of his business. He knows what a deadbeat her dad is and apparently passed up on helpin' her out. Besides, she's sayin' she only wants to come if she can pay the $200 a month we askin' for, so it seems like a good deal."

"Alright." Dex looked over his jacket. "I've hardly even worn this since the school shut swimming down, you know?"

"Yeah, I know, and that changes now. You are one of the most thoughtful people I've ever known. But you ain't just thoughtful, you put your thoughts into action, bruh. How much money did you raise for them shelter animals?"

Dexter looked at his feet. "It wasn't huge... I mean, it was--"

Cullen laughed. "Quit BSing'me! How much?"

Dexter whispered, "$5,700."

Cullen punched Dexter in the arm. "$5,700 dollars?! Damn, Dex! When do they announce the winner of that scholly?"

Dexter answered confidently. "Thursday the 17th. Think it starts at 6:40."

"That's right after practice. Mind if I tag along? Got a big game the next day, but I should be able to go."

"You can come if you want to. It's gonna be a real boring fancy-do, though."

Cullen pointed at Dexter. "Put that jacket on, bruh. I ain't gonna argue about it."

Dexter nodded, putting on his jacket. "Fine. But enough about me. You ready for the Panthers tonight?"

Cullen obliged. "Yeah. Isaac Segal from Baldridge got me up to speed. Apparently I'm gonna be up against a 6'8 flopper named Tex."

"You ever gone up against someone taller than you before?"

"Not since sophomore year, but he's a cornfed kid who can't tie his shoes. Isaac said he's slow and stocky and didn't start shooting hoops until high school."

Dexter nodded. "Alright. Sounds like you got it."

Still in her Giraffe print PJ's, Tamira stepped in the kitchen and froze when she saw Dexter. Grinning, Cullen stepped behind Dexter to fill up a thermos full of coffee.

Dexter looked at Tamira. "Mornin', beauty."

Tamira stammered. "I, I didn't know you'd be here, Dex."

Cullen scoffed. "I told you about that this weekend. Remember when you said you couldn't give me a lift home after the game?"

"Guess it slipped my mind."

Cullen shrugged. "Don't worry, we gotta bounce anyway."

Dexter stood up. He was about an inch shorter than Tamira, but it didn't seem to wear on him. "Made a little extra coffee for you. I know you got your ACTs comin' up. You're gonna rock 'em, girl."

Tamira nodded. "Appreciate it, Dex. So what's that letter for?"

"I got second in state butterfly a couple of years back. Cullen's making me wear the jacket because, well, you know your bro."

Tamira smiled. "It looks nice."

Cullen, still behind Dexter, gave the biggest jackass smile he could to his sister, who flipped him off the moment Dexter turned around.

Cullen held open the door for Dexter, who walked outside. When he was out of earshot, Cullen spoke to his sister. "His jacket looks nice, huh?"

Tamira shook her head. "He's still too short."

"Whatever gets you through the night. See ya, Sis."

"Good luck tonight," she said.

—

Released from class for the game right after lunch, Cullen stepped onto the court and saw Adam was already there. "You ready for the Panthers?" Cullen asked.

"Ready as I'll ever be."

"I'm guessing you're already lookin' to the next game?"

"No way, one game at a time. Always."

"Don't play with me. I know you've had an eye on February 18th for a while. You're gonna show your old man how to play the game, remember?"

Adam took a seat in the bleachers. "I remember."

Cullen took a seat beside him. "You ready to take your old man down?"

"He's an amazing dad. He's the reason I found God, play basketball, and drive that Mustang out in the parking lot."

Cullen sat back and gave Adam a discerning look. "You know, in the 7 years you and I have played ball together, I don't remember the last time he came to a game."

"He'd be here if he could. He's a real busy guy, but I'm lucky to have him as a dad. I've been ready for a chance to get that record my whole life. I think every boy is, in a way."

Cullen exhaled. "Me and my pops never had that in our lives. We got kind of a weird story."

"Weird how?"

Cullen thought about it. "He abandoned my mom when she was pregnant with my sister, Tamira. I spent the first five years of my life thinking I'd never know him, but things changed when Ma OD'd on her birthday."

Adam exhaled. "Wow."

"He stepped up after that. He came back in my life and has also helped my mom's twin, Warren. Sometimes I think he did that to repay her. Anyway, is there somethin' more between you and your dad?"

"What do you mean?"

"I just never see him around."

"He works himself to death, but without his job he couldn't have provided for me and my brother. He's put my needs first for my whole life."

"So why're you so keen on doing this on the 18th?"

Adam whispered, "Because...."

Draped over the bleachers Cullen scrutinized Adam's face. His eyes were lost somewhere on the court in front of them.

Cullen nudged him. "Because...?"

"Because I want to share that moment with him."

Brian walked into the fieldhouse. "What's up, Adam? I got our paintball guns ready for the weekend!"

Cullen raised an eyebrow and looked at Adam. "Since when do you paintball?"

Adam dropped his voice to Brian. "Let's talk about it later, okay?"

After watching Brian walk into the locker room, Adam recovered his traditional demeanor. "Ready for the Panthers, then?"

Cullen put an arm around Adam. "Let's go."

Cullen's eyes darted up to the windows of the Latimer Watchtower. He saw a flash of movement behind the windows -- and he wondered who was there.

—

A silence hung inside the Latimer-occupied locker room. They could still hear the roar of the crowd and see the glee on the opposing team.

Cullen strangled the towel inside his palms.

No one would remember his 19 points or 13 rebounds. No one would remember that Devin had the worst game of his life, and of course no one would think of Adam's missed free throws at the end of the game.

Cullen glowered at the sullen faces staring in his direction.

All they'd remember is that a 6'8 kid who couldn't walk straight hit an off-balance shot over him to win the game.

LHS's perfect season was gone.

Cullen got up and walked to the far side of the opposing locker room and heard Coach Hardcastle's voice.

"Armstrong," he called.

Cullen looked at the tall, dark-eyed coach who still had visible stubble on his face.

Hardcastle gestured. "Can I speak with you a second?"

Cullen nodded and followed his coach in the hallway. Cullen's mind raced. "Coach didn't actually blame me for this shot, right? He knows the type of game I just had."

Hardcastle led Cullen to a hallway pasted with green lockers. The moment they were alone, Hardcastle stopped and put a finger in Cullen's chest. The coach growled in Cullen's face, so close Cullen could smell the wintergreen chew in his coach's mouth.

"Pathetic effort today, Armstrong. You need to decide now. Do you want your memory of this year to be wiping old man's asses, horkin' down boneless wings, or winning a state championship? You need to decide what's important to you, son."

Without another word, the coach stormed back into the locker room.

Feeling his energy leave him, Cullen sat against the green lockers. Absorbed in the shock of the moment, he could hear the Panthers celebrating in their locker room from what felt like a world away.

—

Unsorted: February 7th

When I was in 2nd grade Virginia Morgan gave out heart shaped chocolates with inviteations to her Valentine's Day party. I was the only one who wasn't invited. I used to hate Valentine's day. Valentine's day was the first time I felt alone in a room full of people. I've never forgotton that moment, the looks on the other kids and their chocolate smeared teeth. Ms. Padway gave me Jelly Beans when she saw I didn't get a chocolate... I always liked her, I wonder what she's up to now?

I am about to be kicked out of art. Mr. Austin talked to me after class and told me I might need to start staying after school every day but that he was "rooting for me" to "turn things around."

Valentine's day party. Sixth grade, Kayla Reynolds threw away the twix I gave her in front of the whole class. Everyone laughed. Kayla has legit herpes now. So I guess I lucked out there.

But really what is "mouth herpes?" Isn't that just a cold sore? Doesn't basically everyone have that? Now I just feel bad again, and somedays it just feels like there's no escape from this feeling. Because there is no escape from Adam and his band of bros. They follow me everywhere and light up my phone with abuse. Piss Stain. Fatass. Tommy Taint. I never have to wonder who's texting me, because there are no moments I can even breathe without them reminding me about who I am inside. I almost lost it yesterday, so much that

Cullen asked me if I was going to be okay. I wish I could be honest with him. I wish I knew he wasn't broing out with Adam on the basketball court. I wish I could trust Cullen.

Last year. Valentine's. A pink letter was slipped inside my bookbag. The same pink love letters I had been getting for months. But this was no love letter. "Dear, Tommy. Please slit your wrists. Happy Valentine's Day."

I think the hardest thing about Valentine's Day isn't that it makes me feel alone. It's that somewhere along the way it just felt like an ordinary day. But things are better. I see Mia every day now. We walk together between almost every class and spend afternoons outside in the courtyard. She told me she wanted me to be a friend, but sometimes I wonder if we can be more. She grabs my hand sometimes, and just asks to hold it a while before she goes home.

Mia is the first person I've ever been myself to, and the first person that made me want to be myself. And she's given me a feeling that I have never felt before. I love you, Mia.

...And maybe Valentine's Day will feel different this year."

Lynne looked up from her son's journal.

"Poor kid," she muttered darkly. Closing the book, she walked from her son's room.

Chapter 30: *Cartographist*

Tommy's phone vibrated inside his pocket.

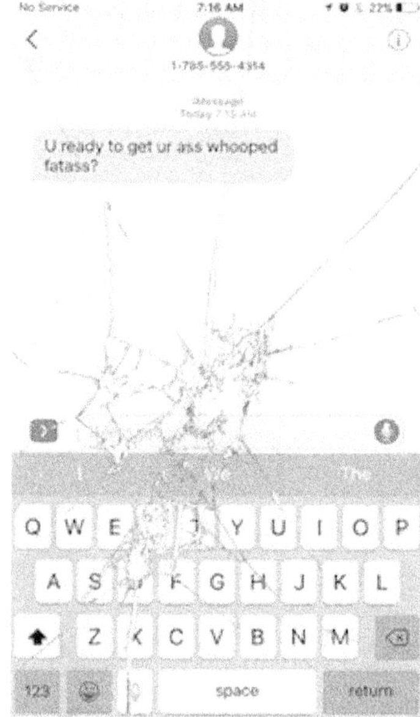

The text hit Tommy like ignited acetylene. Renaming the number to "Asshole #3", Tommy pocketed his phone and looked through the masses of bodies in the hallway. Getting a dirty look from a faceless group of freshmen for stepping into their circle, Tommy searched for his target with a crazed look inside his eyes.

The boy watched them all clear out until he was alone in the hallways. He could see the door of Mr. Austin's classroom. In ten steps he would have been inside; he would have hardly been late. But he couldn't do it. And before he knew what he was doing, he found he was walking out of the school. He went through the doors before he knew what was really happening.

—

Tommy was sitting under the tree when Mia made it out at the end of the day. Tommy looked to Mia. "Did you get everything figured out with STUCO?"

"I think so. It'll take a while to earn back Mr. Stallard's trust, but I should be okay."

"Good."

"What do you think of Valentine's Day?"

"Heh," Tommy said. "It's never really been my thing."

"I think the day is cursed for me."

"Really?"

Mia took a breath. "When I was ten years old, back when my parents still talked to my family on my real dad's side, I got my pa's old German Shephard just before he passed away. Her name was Flora, and she was a mess, Tommy. She chewed up the furniture, peed all over the house, and would howl at 5 A.M. each morning. My stepdad wanted to kill her. One day he hit her so hard it made her ear bleed."

Tommy gasped. "Holy crap."

"I couldn't let that happen to her. That dog meant more to me than anyone. She meant.... Well, she just meant a lot to me. She opened up to me in a way that no person ever had. My love was all she needed. She's so smart, Tommy. She laid down if I held up two fingers, stayed if I held up one, and spoke if I gave her the thumbs up--"

Tommy's phone vibrated in his pocket.

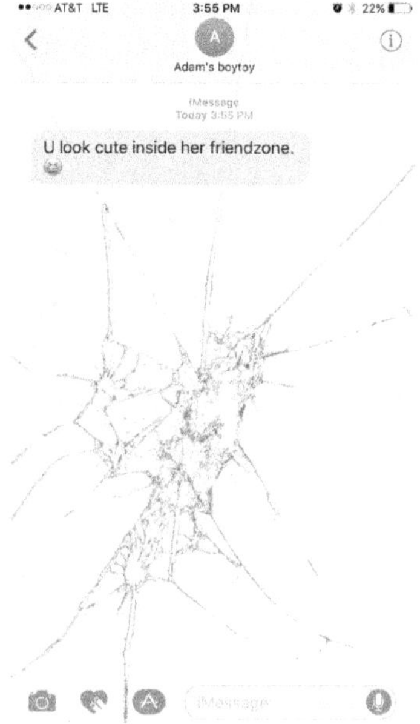

"--but on Valentine's Day over the next year, Flora wasn't waiting for me when I came home. Marc told me through tears that she had been hit with a car earlier that day."

Tommy's eyes darted around the windows of the school. He felt naked to be watched over by Brian from somewhere inside Latimer. Letting out a breath, Tommy found the window from where he was spying on them. The boy jumped to his feet.

Pausing her story, Mia looked up in surprise. "Tommy?"

"I'm so sorry you lost your dog," the boy said. "That must have been really hard. I forgot, I have to run somewhere. I'll send you a text tonight, okay?"

Mia swallowed. "Okay."

Lifting his backpack, Tommy stormed through the courtyard with a cutthroat purpose. This one was for Mia. He was going to end this problem with Brian once and for all.

—

Tommy slammed inside Mr. Dickert's empty classroom, causing Brian to jump back in surprise.

"You're done," Tommy screamed, shoving Brian against the wall. "For all the BS you put me through last year, you were right about one thing: I'm crazy. So let me tell you how it's gonna be. You're going to delete the pictures you have of Mia, and if you ever text me or talk to her again, I'll kill you."

Soaking in Brian's terrified expression, Tommy turned toward the door.

Brian whispered, "She's using you."

"Maybe," Tommy admitted. "Maybe not."

"She is. No one likes you. Being around you makes her feel better about herself."

"You're one to talk. Everyone hates you, Brian, and I'm gonna guess you're hiding from practice because your own team even hates you."

"You don't know what you're talking about."

"Don't I? Did you decide to start cleanin' up port-a-potties rather than playing the game?"

A crazed look filled Brian's eyes. "Did Cullen tell you Coach said that?"

Tommy beamed. "Like I was saying, no one likes you."

Brian yelled, "Well, let me tell you something that bastard didn't tell you."

"Don't call Cullen a--"

Brian screamed, "Shut up, cuck. You don't even know Cullen."

"He's my friend."

Now Brian was laughing. "You wanna know the only reason Cullen talks with you?"

Tommy took the bait. "Why?"

"Because Mr. Austin begged him too. He told the whole team he wasn't your friend, Tommy."

"You're wrong."

"Am I?" Brian asked. "He told us all about your dates at Riverfront. Am I wrong about that too?"

Looking like he knew he had the upper hand, Brian strode toward the door. "You're gonna regret threatening me today, Piss Stain."

Swallowing his surprise, Tommy collided into Brian as Brian pushed through the door. Brian sneered. "See you soon, Tommy Taint."

Tommy's voice tore apart. "Slit your wrists, Brian."

—

The room was still.

A body sat on the bed, its eyes open, arms extended, motionless.

The temptation came over in waves.

His mom had been gone all Saturday.

It was always there. Always waiting for him.

A noose was in Tommy's grasp. He ran his fingers over its thorny threads. It hung behind everything that he did. He wasn't meant for this place, and this felt like the answer he'd been looking for his whole life.

His phone vibrated in his pocket. There was an e-mail from Mr. Stallard.

Advanced Art Stallard, Jay 7:32 PM (Today)

Thomas, You had an unexcused absence in Mr. Austin's class yesterday. As per his class syllabus (see attachment A), this absence dropped your participation grade by a letter and caused your overall grade to fall to a

78. In accordance with Mr. Austin's student contract (attachment B), this grade no longer makes you eligible to continue participating in Advanced Art.

Please report to Mr. Johnson's 1st period Regular Art class on Monday.

Mr. Stallard

Assistant Principal of Latimer High School

Vice President of the Baldridge City Council

Captain of the Neighborhood Watch (Spyglass Division)

Tommy felt his heart skip. He knew this was coming. His grade in Advanced Art had been in free-fall since January, but to find out through the words of Mr. Stallard made him feel barren inside. The boy closed the e-mail and tossed the phone off his bed. He had at least expected Mr. Austin to tell him in person.

It turns out Mr. Austin was as cold as everybody else.

Tommy spat. He had to get out of here, now. He had to find his boxcar.

—

Tommy walked into the night.

Shrill winds screamed in the darkness. The day had reduced last night's snow into grimy patches on the soil. Tommy sighed. Cullen was one of them. He had always been one of them.

He had been so blinded by acceptance that he overlooked the signs. Cullen had been friends with Adam since they were elementary schoolers; why should Tommy have expected anything different?

Stepping near the edges of the blue light, the boy smiled. He needed his boxcar now more than ever.

The light flickered out as he approached. Instinctively, he walked to the black and yellow railcar and lifted himself inside. Pulling out his journal, the boy waited for the light.

This was his lone place of normalcy. The one place where he had any sort of control over his life. His one and only sanctuary.

The light sparked on, allowing the boy to fill his journal like a match to fire.

"I wonder sometimes what kissing feels like. It's not something I thought about for a while, like something I had stuffed away in a time capsule."

Tommy's cheeks reddened. Even admitting this to himself made his heart race. It felt wrong to wonder such a thing, and yet it had been on his mind for weeks.

"But with Mia.... but with Valentine's day. Maybe she will be my first kiss. Maybe--"

A gunshot tore through the air and missed Tommy's face by inches. Looking up in panic, the boy leapt for cover as shots pelted the inside of the car. The sound of gunfire deafening, Tommy watched several cloaked figures approaching the boxcar. A shrill ringing in Tommy's ears, air bled out his lungs and strangled his heart.

The horn of a train echoed in the distance.

The boy gagged for air. *Was this what a heart attack felt like? Is this where I'm going to die?*

A pellet hit Tommy in the face and blinded his eyes, burning him with what felt like acid. As the pain rocked Tommy's senses, Tommy breathed.

It was paint.

Light from the oncoming train streamed inside the boxcar as laughter drifted into Tommy's ears. There was no mistaking this laughter, for he had known it for years. Since the first day of second grade and every day after, he knew exactly who was invading his sanctuary.

"Brian and Jonah," Tommy whispered.

They were close now, only feet away. Feeling the hatred boil inside him, Tommy picked up a broken brick lying to the boxcar's side.

His voice as clear as day, Brian yelled into the boxcar.

"Come and get it, Tommy Taint."

Without hesitating, Tommy spiked the brick in Brian's face.

Chapter 31: ***Deathblow***

"Holy crap!" Adam yelled.

Brian staggered backwards and tripped over the railroad tracks. It's horn careening through the night, the train passed through the tracks and tunneled straight toward Brian's flailing body.

Panic seized Rosi. Sitting in the passenger seat of Adam's Mustang, she leapt out of the car, and screamed.

Brian fell on the nearside of the railroad tracks and the train passed him, missing his body by inches.

Adam, sitting in the driver's seat, paused the gunfire blasting through his speakers and sprinted from his Mustang.

Brian stood up on their side of the tracks and spiked his mask in the ground. "He broke my mask!" Brian yelled, blood rushing down his face. "Piss Stain broke my mask!"

The train rushing beside them, Adam laughed. "Broke your nose too."

Brian snapped, "Shut the hell up, Adam!"

Rosi stepped behind Adam and gripped his arm. Jonah and Devin gathered around them. Jonah put his hand on Brian's shoulder. "You gotta be careful, man. That train almost killed you!"

Brian brushed him off, lashing out at Adam. "Why didn't you tell us that a *train* was coming?"

"How was I supposed to know? Rock didn't mention a train."

"I'm gonna kill Tommy!" Brian yelled. "I'm gonna frickin' kill him."

Rosi stepped back. Brian just might. Rosi had never seen him lose it like this before.

The train roared, dragging its last train car through the demarcation line.

Brian screamed, "You're mine, Tommy Taint!" Sprinting to the boxcar, Brian looked under and inside, but Tommy was gone. Brian punched the side of the car and unleashed a roar of pain. "Where are you!?"

Jonah pointed toward the wheat fields. "Can't have made it far. Want to track him down?"

Brian spat the blood from his mouth. "Let's do it."

Standing beneath the flickering blue light, Adam watched the three run into the night, and Rosi watched Adam. He held the paintball gun lazily and without interest. Instead, Adam focused his gaze on the rusted over boxcar.

"Why would Tommy come here?" Adam asked. Putting his gun over to the side, Adam lifted himself up through the door of the boxcar. He held out his hand and asked Rosi. "Want to see Tommy's world?"

Rosi looked up at Adam, feeling disgruntled. "Why was this so important to you?"

Adam looked surprised. "Eh, it isn't a big deal. You know who Tommy is. He has it coming."

Rosi shook her head. "I'm not asking about Tommy, I'm asking about you! Why go through all this? Make these plans, work with a drug dealer, and for what? Why?"

Adam recoiled. "Do you remember what he threatened to do to me?"

Rosi nodded. "I do -- and I remember you had me leave fake love notes in his locker for a year before that. Oh my God, Adam. All those notes you had me write. Do you remember that? What did that last letter say, the one you had me write on Valentine's Day?"

Adam waved his hand. "I don't remember what it said. I mean, why do you remember? Leave it to a woman to hold stuff over me like that."

"You told him to slit his wrists."

"You wrote those letters, and you didn't seem to mind then."

Rosi pushed back. "But I should have. It was my writing, but your words. You did it just as much as I did! Just like you're doing this today. Cut the BS. Why does this matter to you? I've listened to BS like this my whole life. Dad always said, 'Oh it's just one drink. It's not a big deal.' And don't be like my dad. Don't you tell me this doesn't matter to you. You almost got Brian killed tonight, Adam, and what do you think they're gonna do if they find Tommy?"

Adam looked off in the distance. "You know, I never really understood why you put up with your dad. But now..." Adam moved his eyes to Rosi. "I wonder why he puts up with you."

Searing hot tears overfilled Rosi's eyes. She breathed through her nose and looked Adam in the face. Rosi breathed. "You and me are done."

Adam laughed. Each word as puncturing as the next. "There never was a you and me."

Leaving Adam on his own, Rosi stormed back to Adam's Mustang and slammed the passenger door. Tears flowing down her face, she watched Adam retreat into the boxcar. Adam's phone vibrated from his center. Wiping her face, she looked at the message waiting for Adam from Rock Rustin.

Rosi opened Adam's phone and looked over a text.

It was a picture of Tommy. He was turned around, maybe in his bedroom, and his butt crack was hanging out. Rock's message to Adam said one thing.

"Use it well."

Rosi looked up at the boxcar. Rock was going to get Adam killed and Adam didn't even see it.

—

Adam drove his car through downtown Baldridge. Brian slammed his fist into the ceiling of Adam's Mustang. "That Piss Stain! Where did he even hide?"

Adam snapped, "If you punch my car again you're walking home."

"We should call the police and get him expelled!" Brian screamed.

Rosi laughed. "And say what, genius? He fought back when we came to beat the crap outta him?"

Brian screamed, punching the interior.

Adam slammed on the brakes, wheeling the car over to a gas station. "I'm not screwing around! Stop it. You wanna hitch home?"

For a moment, Rosi noticed a look of pure loathing on Brian's face, and Rosi wondered if they were going to fight. Rosi looked over Brian. Tommy messed him up bad. Brian's nose had swollen into an angry, splotchy purple, ballooning to the size of an avocado. Streams of blood had flowed down his face and stuck to the sides of his chin.

Brian blew out a sigh. "I'm sorry."

Adam started the car. "Make sure you don't get any blood on my car. All the mud you tracked in is enough of a pain to clean."

"I get my nose broken and the cleaning lady tells me I can't even bleed? You laughed when Tommy broke my mask and could have cared less when my gun froze up. I told you this was crap weather for paintball, I told you. Sometimes I don't think we're even friends."

Adam smirked. "Your night's about to get a lot better."

"Oh, yeah?""

Without a word, Adam extended Tommy's green journal back to Brian. "He left this in the boxcar, and you're gonna love what's inside."

Rosi sighed. "All right, that's it for me. Let me out."

Adam opened his mouth in surprise. "Let you out here? All alone?"

"We're in a freaking gas station in 'Latimerville.' I'll be fine."

Brian looked up at Rosi in surprise. "What's with you?"

Rosi looked in the distance. "This thing you're doing now. The thing you roped half of the basketball team into, I don't want anything to do with it. Let me out."

Brian laughed. "What a woman."

Rosi opened the door. "Yeah, that's me."

"You know what this means if you walk out of here, right?" Adam said. "What it means for us?"

"I didn't think there was an *us*." Rosi snapped. "But, Adam, you're going off the deep end, and I don't think you see it. You meet your drug dealer in the fieldhouse, you're barely focusing on hoops, and this god-awful thing you're planning.."

"And?" Adam asked.

"And I think you're going to crash." She took a breath; she would not allow herself to cry in front of him. "Goodbye, Adam."

Adam shrugged her off. "Peace."

Closing the door, she watched Adam speed away in the night.

Chapter 32: *Cowboys*

Tommy stood behind an abyss of expression. "I am an idiot. I am such an idiot."

Tommy had watched Brian's rage with smug satisfaction. Sitting on top of the yellow ladder, Tommy watched the search party meander below before running off in the fields. Adam stayed behind. Tommy knew Adam hated paintball, but Tommy also knew a chance to abuse him caused Adam to make impressive compromises.

Tommy watched Adam disappear behind the boxcar and fought the urge to drop down below. For a moment, Tommy thought about ending Adam there. But there came Rosi Williams. Rosi, the girl who always broke him. Like always, Adam had surrounded himself before attacking in the open.

But now? They had everything. They had absolutely everything. Everything he had written in the green journal about Adam, about Brian, and about Mia. He did not even realize it was gone until he made it home, when he opened his rolltop to write about what happened.

Hot welts dressed Tommy's face and neck. He had not realized how many times he had been hit. It all happened so fast.

He was back to square one. This was last April all over again. They didn't have anything to get him expelled, but they had enough to ruin everything.

Forever his boxcar would be a paint-splattered symbol of tonight. A reminder of what Adam had done and the hell that would follow.

The boy got to his feet and stumbled into the bathroom. It was time to get the paint out of his hair and forget about tonight.

Switching on the light, Tommy looked in the mirror. Horror took hold of his eyes. Splotches of pink, purple and green had been plastered and dried across his father's leather jacket. It was ruined. An ugly, hopeless ruin. His hand shaking, Tommy reached into his pocket and pulled out Mia's dandelion. Its bloom was covered in red paint. It too was utterly destroyed.

Tommy roared. He threw the dandelion across the room and slammed the jacket against the floor; he was never going to wear it again. An angry purpose boiling inside him, Tommy threw his mattress against the wall and retrieved the black journal inside his bed. It was time to burn everything. Time to burn it all down.

He would give Adam and the world one last chance to redeem themselves. One final chance before he went down this road.

The boy looked at the black journal resting in his grasp.

If they didn't, Adam wouldn't make it out alive.

—

Unsorted: Art Project

Lynne struggled to sleep through the night and now had a headache that made sleep impossible. Getting out of bed, Lynne walked to the outside of Tommy's room. He had been closed up in there since she got back on Sunday, and his bus was about to leave.

She was surprised to see a note on his door.

> Got to school early. Caught the early Baldridge bus.
>
> Art Project

Narrowing her eyes, she pushed through the door and looked inside. Strands of dried paint ran across Tommy's desk and was scattered along the floor.

"Messy frickin' project," she mused.

Avoiding the paint, she opened up Tommy's desk and reached for his journal.

Lynne gasped. It was gone.

Her mind raced with concern. "What are you up to, Tommy?"

—

A cold drizzle started falling when Lynne stepped out of her home, causing the yellow grass to glisten on the roadside. Her foundation, eyeshadow, and lip-gloss applied to the T, Lynne walked through the gravel beneath a scarlet umbrella. Walking confidently, she reached the pavement and felt the blisters on her ankles burst. Lynne, unwavering on her destination, felt her hands split open by the end of Green Oak.

"A half mile down, two to go."

Lynne's hair was frozen to her skull by the time she walked up the steps of the city's bus. Her feet throbbing in pain, Lynne limped to one of the back seats. It was just then she realized she'd left her cell phone at home. Despite swearing to herself, she still felt a small victory for making it to the bus on time.

—

Lynne stood in a crowded line at the town's marketplace. Languid expressions and glossed-over eyes covered the people around her.

The clerk yelled, "Next!"

Lynne handed her check to the clerk. This was a monthly ritual she had engaged in ever since she had left her last job, but it was still hard to do. Her eyes wandered out the broad windows of the marketplace, settling on the North College Drive-In. The Drive-In was just across the street and had just refurbished its original, 1950's style sign.

Lynne smiled. It was time for a monthly indulgence.

—

Kit Shields filled up a mug full of coffee. "Here you are, and here's your sugar to go along with it."

Lynne took the sugar. "Thank you. How do you like working here?"

"At the drive-in?" Kit asked, taken aback.

"Yeah, if you don't mind me asking. Are you too busy to chat?"

Kit looked over the empty restaurant. "Oh, I guess I have some time. Do I like it here? Yeah, I do. The doubles are tiring, and Sunday mornings are a little rough, but overall I can't complain."

"I remember Sundays," Lynne breathed. "Worked here for seven years back in the day. Does Ol' Phil still come around here?"

"Oh, God, yes."

Lynne laughed. "That perv would slip me a fifty if I let him 'hug' me after his meal."

"A fifty?" Kit asked. "He only gave me a twenty."

Lynne snorted. "The economy's been tough on everyone."

"I didn't know he was the handsy type when that happened. Our manager Luke takes care of him now, and Phil stiffs him every time."

"In my time, my manager Dave thought it was a hoot and got pissy if I 'complained' about 'easy money.'"

"What a douche," Kit said.

"I heard he left for a job in the city."

Kit smiled. "Are you thinking about coming back? I can get you an application."

"Oh, no. I didn't end on good terms with the owner. He told me I'd never be welcomed back again."

Kit snorted. "Yeah, Lew Wilson is a bit crusty like that."

"I'm actually thinkin' about applying to Riverfront soon. I've heard good things about their management."

"Oh yeah! Cam Thomas is the bomb. My ex works there and thinks the world of that place."

"Really? I might run by today then."

Kit smiled. "You'll make great money. They have a really chill scene."

Hoisting Lynne's platter of Fish and Chips, a giant, smiling man dropped the plate in front of Lynne. "Enjoy!" he bellowed, sauntering back to the kitchen.

Kit looked down. "There are no chips. How are there no *chips* here?"

"You're okay," Lynne reassured.

"That's Charles. He's the productivity manager for all of Lew's properties. He's evaluating Luke today. Charles is clueless, but everybody loves him anyway."

"That's the way of the world," Lynne said.

"I'll be right back. Remind me of your name again?"

Lynne held out her hand. "Lynne."

"It was great to meet you, Lynne. Let me know how things go at Riverfront, okay?"

Lynne beamed. "Will do."

—

Lynne lingered at the entrance to the Riverfront Brewery. She could go in and ask for Cam, just to see how it went. Maybe they would even have a position open for her. It was in such a pretty spot, on the river and all. The only snag would be the transportation there. Lynne's feet throbbed inside her shoes. It was a big snag, she thought, because just walking to the bus stop was exhausting. She'd only be able to work during the day, and she knew the money was never good during the day.

Lynne breathed. Next time. Next time for sure.

Realizing it was getting late, Lynne set course for her sister's.

Chapter 33: *Miasma*

Mia stood back in horror.

This was a nightmare, and *everyone* had seen it. They had hung them in the cafeteria, taped them to lockers. Mia even heard the pictures were inside urinals.

But the main horror was right in front of her.

A giant banner hung in the fieldhouse. It had the photocopied journal entry, one of the many where Tommy professed his love for her, but the worst part was the life-size picture of Tommy that now hung throughout the school. It had him hunched over his bed, with half his rear end out for the world to see.

Mia closed her eyes.

Adam Augustine's voice filtered in from behind her. "Any idea where Tommy is?"

Mia turned around with rage. There was a triumphant look on Adam's face, complete with a smile that made her blood boil.

Adam continued, "Because... this really isn't as fun without him."

Mia stormed past Adam. Grabbing every printed paper on Tommy she could, she stormed out of the gym. Her hands quivered around the copied writings.

"...Mia is the first person I've ever been myself to, and the first person that made me want to. And she's given me a feeling that I have never felt before.

I love you, Mia.

...And maybe Valentine's Day will feel different this year."

Mia shut her eyes. She had to find Tommy before it was too late. Stuffing the page into her pocket, Mia looked for Tommy at every corner in the hallways. Groups of people surrounded the flyers, and their laughter carried through the school.

Taking out her phone, Mia gave him a call.

No answer.

This was devastating. Absolutely devastating, and could drive Tommy to, to… Mia didn't want to think about it. She ran into the school's office.

The secretary, Mrs. Norris, yelled out from behind Mia, "Stop!"

The flyer in her grasp, Mia burst into Principal Elmer's office.

Empty.

Mrs. Norris continued, "Like I was trying to say, Principal Elmer isn't in here. You'll have to speak to Mr. Stallard."

Without hesitation, Mia turned and wrenched open Stallard's door.

Reclined behind his desk, Stallard's eyes were glued to the day's crossword.

Mia slammed the flyer on his desk. "Are you doing anything about this?"

Stallard looked up from his paper. "Believe me, we're doing all we can."

"Really? Because there are still hundreds of these around the school."

Stallard sneered. "Would you like me to pull them down one by one or find out who did it? I'm as concerned as you are. The ink for those flyers alone cost the district hundreds."

Mia's mouth fell open. "The *ink* for those *flyers*? You think that *this* is the problem here?"

"We're getting to the bottom of it, hun."

"How, through reading your comics?" The words left Mia's mouth before she could catch them, but she was not going to apologize. Stallard split her with his gaze, daring her to say more.

"One more word," Stallard warned.

Mia walked toward the door. "You're worthless."

Stallard rose to his feet, his voice breaking into a whisper. "Apologize. Apologize now."

Mia paused, looking at Stallard with disdain.

Stallard pointed at her throat. "Apologize or you're out of STUCO."

He was slightly shorter than Mia, but she had never met someone so imposing in her life. Mia lifted her hands. "I'm out, then." Striding into the hallways, hot tears welled up inside Mia's eyes. She had to find Tommy to let him know it would be okay. Turning a corner, Mia found herself face to face with Principal Elmer.

"Mia! Are you okay?" The principal asked, his voice concerned.

Mia stared. Realizing he was as giant of a man as she had ever met. Mia saw that the principal had dozens of mashed up papers in each hand. It dawned on her that he must have spent the morning pulling them from the lockers. Mia met Principal Elmer's eyes. "Do you want to know who did this?"

Elmer nodded. "Getting this cleaned up is my top priority. I'm on my way to the gym with the custodians now. I can make sure it *never* happens again, but I need to know who did this."

Mia's voice was clear. "Adam Augustine."

—

Mia stepped into Mr. Austin's classroom. Cullen and Dexter were the only ones there. Looking exhausted, Cullen was resting his feet on the desk in front of him.

Mia pointed at Cullen. "Did you know about this?"

Cullen shook his head. "No, I didn't."

"Do you know who on your team was behind it?"

"Yes," Cullen admitted. "Word is Adam put together the whole thing."

"Obviously."

"Naw, you're not hearin' me. Word is they ambushed Tommy at the boxcar he likes to go to and stole his journal there."

Mia's voice got serious. "Who else was with them?"

"What I know from the team is that Devin, Jonah and Brian were there."

"Wow. That's three starters from the basketball team. Be a shame if that destroyed your chances for state."

Cullen shrugged at Mia. "It just might. Someone rolled on them. Adam's with Mr. Stallard now, and if Brian ain't lyin, Adam still had Tommy's journal in his backpack."

"Good."

Cullen continued, with noticeable awkwardness in his voice. "Uh, I should mention, it wasn't only the team there. Rosi was with them, too."

Mia's heart sank. "Really?"

"Seein' as you two were close, I didn't know if I should bring it up."

"I'm glad you did, but I'm surprised you weren't invited." Mia admitted.

"He wouldn't have asked me. Adam knows Tommy and I kick it. It ain't a secret that there's bad blood between him and Tommy, but I never would've thought Adam could've done this."

Dexter nodded. "It makes sense. You don't run with Adam outside of b-ball. You've never seen him outside of the golden boy act he plays on the court."

Cullen raised an eyebrow. "Have you seen him act another way, Dex?"

"Personally? No, but I know a kid from Baldridge who thinks he's a Nazi poster child."

"Why'd he think that?" Cullen asked.

"Apparently him and Adam played in a summer league together."

Cullen breathed. "Adam's a man of many faces."

"He's the golden boy here," Dex said. "He can't risk hurting that."

Mia interjected. "Have either of you reached Tommy?"

Cullen held up a phone. "No. But I reached someone else."

The door opened behind them, and Rosi entered the room. "Hi."

Mia leveled Rosi. "So you just stood by as your boyfriend attacked Tommy?"

"If that's how you see it, I won't argue. But he's not my boyfriend. Adam made it clear he never was, actually, after I yelled at him about the night."

Mia replied, "Well, you're gonna have to do better than that."

"How about this?" Rosi pulled out Tommy's journal and held it for them to see. "Adam panicked when Stallard was looking for him. He asked me to take it," Rosi laughed darkly. "Just two days after telling me we were nothing, he asked me to cover him so it 'didn't ruin the state team.'"

Mia swiped the journal. "That's a little better. Have you talked to Elmer, Rosi?"

"I'm not ready to do that, Mia. I'm sorry."

"This doesn't do anything, then. How many copies did Adam make of this?"

"They're gone." Rosi said, "They threw away everything when Stallard came looking for them."

Mia glared at Rosi. "If that's the best you can do."

Cullen breathed. "Well, I gotta do something."

"What are you going to do?" Dexter asked.

"I don't know yet, but I'll start with Brian and go from there."

Mia nodded. "And I'm gonna find Tommy."

Peter Good opened the door, and the students turned around to see him.

Peter smiled. "Are any of you the teacher here?"

Everyone shook their heads.

Peter breathed a sigh of relief. "Thank God. It took me forever to find this place."

Chapter 34: ***Reimagined***

Adam strode up beside Jonah, Devin, and Brian inside the John Wagner Fieldhouse.

Jonah yelled, "You're alive! Did they find out anything?"

"Course not!" Adam said. "Only a moron would have a journal like that at school."

His nose the size of a small country, Brian laughed. "I can't believe that puss didn't show today. I'm gonna kill him tomorrow."

"Careful about that," Adam warned. "Ol' Elmer is addressing the school about this on LHS News tomorrow."

Concern flashed on Jonah's expression. "He still doesn't think you did it, right?"

"Oh, no, he does, and he probably thinks a few of you were in on it, but there isn't a thing he can do. He doesn't have the journal, and the printer we used didn't need a log in. He did say that he was going to 'keep an eye on us,' so we better watch out, boys." Adam said, casting the threat aside.

Jonah snickered. "Tommy sure did write about you a lot, Adam. You worried he might snap?"

"I'm more worried he has a crush."

Brian lamented at the now-empty space on the gym's wall. "You know, he got out of this way easier than he deserved."

Adam sneered. "What are you talking about? This day is going down in history. Whether it be tomorrow or next year, everyone will remind him that his big, red rear was up for the world to see. This is going to be with him forever."

Brian sighed. "I guess."

Adam changed the subject. "Oh yeah. Grandparents will be goin' to a funeral in Iowa on Thursday. Means I have the house alone on Wednesday night."

Jonah smiled. "You thinkin' a party?"

"Yeah. Nothing crazy since it's a school night, but it could be a good time." Adam put an arm around Brian. "Cheer up, guy. Tommy Taint may have played hooky, but people will blow this up until it's a legend."

But Adam was wrong about one thing.

Hidden inside the Annex, Tommy had been looking down at the court and watched everything through Latimer's Watchtower. Each cadence of Adam's laughter speared through Tommy's eardrums.

Tommy smiled. It was over for Adam.

There was only one thing left to do before he began.

—

Mia sat against the great tree in the Latimer courtyard. A cold sleet cascaded from the sky, covering the grass in a fine gloss.

Tommy approached her from the edge of the courtyard. She rushed to him and threw her arms around him. "Oh, Tommy," she cried. "What happened to you?"

"Adam and Brian. They caught me at my boxcar and stole my journal. It ain't a big deal."

"Ain't a big deal?" the girl repeated. "Tommy, you have to tell someone."

"Who?" the boy asked. "Stallard? The police? You know no one will believe me."

"Principal Elmer. Talk to him tomorrow."

"He already tried with Adam today. It's no use. I ain't gonna be a bitch about it."

Mia looked at him in disbelief. "Be a bitch about it?"

"Be real. Who is Stallard, the school board, and this entire city going to side with?"

Mia nodded in defeat. "Tommy," she breathed, pulling him in again. "I am so sorry."

They held each other for just a moment, but Tommy wished it could be for the rest of his life. When they pulled apart, Tommy whispered, "Did you read the letter?"

Closing her eyes, Mia nodded.

Tommy continued, "So...."

Mia replied, "Tommy… I am lucky just to know you. You are one of the closest friends that I've ever--"

Tommy cut her off. "No. I don't wanna hear it."

"Tommy...."

"We can't go back to how it was. Not after today."

"Don't you like having me in your life? Are you saying you want to throw what we have away?"

"You know too much," Tommy said. "It'll never be normal again."

"I will always be here for you. You don't throw something like that away."

Tommy breathed. "Every time you see me, you'll know how I really feel."

"I thought you were my friend. You promised me," Mia choked. "I didn't think you would let someone like Adam tear us apart."

"You were wrong."

A single tear streamed down Mia's face. She looked angry. Tommy wondered if she was going to hit him. "I was wrong. I never would have thought you were a coward."

Tommy bit into his gums and didn't reply.

Mia shook her head and pulled out her backpack. "I have something for you."

Tommy stood back in surprise. She was holding his green journal.

Tommy yelled, "Where did you get that?"

"Rosi. She broke up with Adam over this, you know."

"She was never dating Adam."

Mia spoke. "That's not the point, Tommy. He went too far on this. There's a lot of people who are with--"

Tommy cut her off, "No. Maybe they're not with Adam, but they'll never be with me. I gotta go, Mia."

"Well, if you change your mind, know that I'll always be your friend. What do you want me to do with the journal, Tommy?"

"Save it, burn it, throw it into the Kaw. It's not me anymore." Giving her a detached nod, Tommy left Mia alone inside the courtyard.

"Ordinary Valentine's Day," Tommy thought. "Ordinary day."

The boy cycled through his agenda and landed on the picture. Before today, he never would have guessed that this person was capable of such a thing. But only one person could have taken that photo, and that was his beloved cousin, Cocaine Thayne.

It would begin there.

—

Tommy charted out his actions. He would have to be meticulous in everything he did, because if it went to plan, he would never be welcome back here again.

Thayne opened his door. "Tommy!"

Drenched from the rain, Tommy smiled. "Hey, cousin!"

Bringing Tommy into a sopping hug, Thayne gestured his cousin inside. "I missed ya, cuz! Come in and dry off."

Grace, planted at the room's corner, spoke to Tommy. "Are you here with your ma? She's s'pose to be comin' down soon."

"No. Can I hit up your bathroom? I had a long walk here."

Thayne stepped in for his mom. "Knock yourself out!"

"Thanks." Maneuvering through the clutter, Tommy tiptoed to the bathroom and shut the door. He knew he would have to move fast. Lynne's upcoming arrival added an unexpected complication to his plans.

Tommy gingerly opened the back lid to the toilet, revealing its inner workings. As expected, a bag of single edge razors floated at the top of the water. He had accidentally stumbled upon this on a morning a few months back; Thayne was hungover and had forgotten to fully attach the lid. Thayne had worn long sleeves for the next two months. This memory caused a twinge of guilt to pull on Tommy's heart.

Taking a breath, Tommy cast away his uncertainty and reached into the bag.

—

Tommy's gaze was transfixed.

Amidst all of his aunt's junk, rotted food and roaches on her kitchen table, there was something that the boy had never seen before. It was an older, worn out golden statue of a Baldridge Brinehawk. He had been walking to Thayne's room when he spotted it, and now he couldn't take his eyes off.

Baldridge Singer of the Year: Jaime Lynne Tate

Thayne walked out to find Tommy. "I thought you were crappin' somethin' awful."

Tommy held out the trophy. "Why do you have this?"

Her voice keener than it had been in years, Grace jumped in from the living room.

"Your ma didn't want it no more. Said she didn't like thinkin' about the Jaime Lynne days. I thought I told you to put that away, Thayne."

"The Jaime Lynne days?" Tommy asked.

"Yup. You got in the way of a lot for her."

Tommy gave his aunt a dangerous look.

Thayne put an arm around Tommy. "Ah, don't worry about all that, Tommy. It all went down years ago." Thayne led Tommy to his room. "I'm happy to see ya, man."

Tommy sat on Thayne's bed. "It's been a while."

"No joke! I was wonderin' when you'd be apologizin' for what you pulled at the party."

Tommy sighed. "Yeah, sorry about that."

"No worries, man!"

Tommy forged a smile. "Yeah.... but I guess there is one thing I want to bring up."

Thayne took a drink. "What's up?"

"Do you remember a picture you took of me? It would have been a while back. I was over my bed, and I think it had my crack in it and everything."

Thayne spat out his beer. "Oh yeah! How did you know about that anyway? I didn't think I showed you."

"You didn't, but whoever you gave it to hung it all over my high school today."

Thayne swallowed. "Wow really? Are you sure it's the same picture? I don't think I gave it to--"

Tommy cut him off. "Don't even try."

"Tommy, I just--"

"Shut up! I know you sent out that picture, just like I know you passed around my number. You have made my life *hell,* Thayne. Just please, please tell me you didn't sell me out for Rock Rustin. Just tell me you care about your own *family* more than that asswipe."

Thayne was silent and looked toward the floor.

Tommy snorted and rose to his feet. "But you aren't gonna rat on *them,* are you? Whatever. I'm done with you being a walking embarrassment in my life."

Thayne jumped up to his feet and looked down at Tommy. "What's eatin' you, Tommy? All my life you and Lynne have walked around like your poo don't stink, but you both are bigger losers than Ma and I ever were!"

Tommy pushed himself past his cousin and walked up to his door. "Well don't worry, because you're never gonna see me again."

Something twisted itself on Thayne's face. "Rock was right about you, Tommy Taint."

Tommy came to a halt and slumped his head against the door. Something had broken inside of him, a levee that had been weakening for the past twelve years. He felt his body awaken and an adrenaline flood pour through his veins.

Tommy turned around and spoke calmly to his cousin. "Let's do that one over."

Thayne raised an eyebrow. "Excuse me?"

"Try again."

Thayne snorted. "I said what I said."

Tommy smiled in a dangerous way. He took a step towards Thayne. "You know all that BS I went through last year, cuz? All the stuff with the letter?"

Thayne nodded. "I know that ain't true, Tommy. I don't know what's got into you, but I know all this ain't you."

"Except all of it *was* true." Tommy stepped toward Thayne and let out an open-mouthed grin. "I'm going to kill Adam Augustine, but first I'm gonna beat you."

He would always remember the wild look in Thayne's eyes, the instant his cousin saw the horror he'd unleashed inside his room. Tommy hit Thayne so hard that it sent him flying against his back wall.

Pain shooting through his knuckles, Tommy looked down at his cousin's body and unleashed the anger he had held for the last 17 years.

Thayne would never be the same again.

—

Tommy rested his right hand on a makeshift bag of ice. It was liberating to unload on Thayne. Deep down, he had always known who Thayne was. Thayne had always trusted Rock before he trusted him. Today hadn't been a spur of the moment decision -- today had been overdue.

Tommy's mind swirled to the razors in the front pocket of his coat. Adam was next.

The front door of his home slammed open, shaking the floor beneath his feet.

Lynne barged into the bedroom. "What in the hell is wrong with you? What did Thayne ever do to deserve that?"

Tommy made his voice cheery. "If you really want to know, Thayne took a picture of my bare butt and sent it to everyone around my school. My classmates thought it was so funny that they hung it up all over the building."

"Oh my God, Tommy. I'm so sorry. Did the school do anything? Oh no." Lynne shut her eyes. "I didn't have my phone today."

Tommy snorted. "Why do you waste your time with Grace anyways? She is a leech on the ass of our family."

"Well." Lynne considered, "If I don't, who will?"

"Why should we care?"

"Tommy?" Lynne asked, her voice breaking, "If I got a car for ya, would you be willing to go to Baldridge next year?"

"Yeah, just like I would have if I got Rock's car last year, but instead you..." Tommy stopped, his voice drifting away.

Lynne spoke up. "I am doing my best. I am doing my *best*, and I think you're about to make a God-awful decision."

"And what would that be?"

"I don't know, but it ain't hard to see the signs. I mean for God's sake, Grace was screaming when I made it to her house. She never wants to see you again. You may have ruined everything between Grace and I today."

The boy laughed. "Big loss there."

"You don't get it! You will never understand the hell Grace and I went through when we were kids! She is my sister. She'll always be important to me."

Tommy smiled darkly. "And what about me? Just where even were you today?"

"You really want to know, Tommy?"

"No."

"I was applying for a job, at Riverfront."

Tommy laughed. "Don't tell me that, not again. I'm tired of hearin' that promise. New job, a double-wide trailer with skirting, a car."

"Tommy -- it's for you--"

Tommy snapped, "Don't say that! Just look at your shoes. You're saying you're willing to walk two miles to the bus stop every day to make it to your shifts on time? What if the bus runs late? What if you stay past the last bus home? You gonna pay 20% of your tips to a driver each night? You've broken all these promises before, then given me *all* these excuses when you didn't get the job. You don't change, Lynne. It's just like how Grace *always* comes before me -- even when her and her worthless son make my life hell! Are they worth that? Are they worth more than your own son, Lynne?"

Lynne closed her eyes. “I am your mom, and you are worth more than anyone to me. I am so proud of the things you’ve done this year, but Tommy -- Thayne and Grace will always be family.”

“Will she?” Tommy asked, reaching under the rolltop desk. “Well, I found this with that loving sister of yours today.”

Pulling his mom’s trophy from the rolltop, Tommy tossed it over to his mom.

Lynne gasped, clutching it from the air like it was her child.

Tommy smiled. “So it means something to you? I thought you said this was a ‘trinket from a yard sale.’ It makes sense you lied, though. Grace told me that you don’t like to get into the “Jaime Lynne Days.’”

“Tommy…”

“You don’t have to lie to me anymore about what’s important to you. I know I ruined your life.” The boy muttered. “Sorry about that.”

“It’s not-- you didn’t ruin anything. I, I just--” Lynne stuttered, unable to find the words. “One of these days, if you keep your head on straight, I will tell you all about the singing, your father, and the Jaime Lynne days. But not today. Not like this.”

“Whatever you say.”

Lynne looked at her son. “I’m worried, Tommy.”

“Don’t worry about me.”

“I have to. I think you’re about to go off like a bomb, and I’m startin’ to think that there might be only one thing I can do.”

“And what's that?” Tommy asked.

“I’m gonna give you one more chance. One more chance to straighten up. But, Tommy, if you do anything like this again… then I’m going to report you.”

The color drained from Tommy’s cheeks. “You'd call the police on your own son?”

"Not the police, but the principal. And I would do it, if it meant I *saved* my son."

Sometime later, the mother left her son to brood in his stunned silence. Tommy listened to his mom move around in the kitchen and eventually wander into her bedroom. It was only after she fell asleep that he felt safe enough to open his phone.

49 new messages.

Giving his phone a look of hatred, Tommy trashed them all. His flake of a mother was turning into a major problem. His home wasn't safe anymore, so long as she's one drunken night away from phoning the police.

Tommy flipped over his mattress and took out a briefcase and his black journal from under his bed. Setting the case aside, he opened the journal to the dog-eared page.

He thought to himself, "It's perfect."

Final Draft: The Murder of Adam Augustine

It would be too easy just to shoot him. Adam deserved more. He deserved something every bit as personal as Adam's abuse had been with him. Tommy toyed with the razors in his fingers. It would need to be public, humiliating, and something that no one would ever forget.

Tommy looked over the necessities.

Razors
Weld Bond
Orange Spray Paint
Adam
Basketball Goal

The razors were already taken care of, and the rest would be in his possession soon.

Tommy thought of the field house. They made this too easy. Like they did before every home game, the school would set up their stepladders beneath the goal, as if they were inviting him to do it.

"All I need is a date."

The boy pulled up the school website on his cellphone, scrolling through the gamedays. Tommy's eyes gravitated to the upcoming match.

"Friday, February 18th: Home vs. The Bobcats

Cody Augustine inducted into the LHS Hall of Fame."

Tommy beamed. It was meant to be. Now Adam's perfect, storybook father would get to watch in horror as his golden son bled out on the floor.

Normally, Tommy would worry that an opposing player would dunk it before Adam, but the Bobcats didn't have a single player over 5'10. Tommy smirked. He'd heard that from Brian from the window of the Watchtower.

Tommy's phone rang inside his pocket.

"Hello?"

Rock's voice crashed in from the other side. "You're dead for what you did to Thayne. Next time I see you, you're mine."

Tommy responded, "If I see your crazy eyes again, I'll put a bullet between 'em."

Chapter 35: ***Adam's Murmur***

Adam Augustine stood in Mr. Stallard's office, his eyes at his feet.

Coach Hardcastle stared down at Adam. "All this BS, Adam. Torturin' Tommy Tate. I know what he did to you, and I got no love for the kid. I wish he was out of our school -- heck, I used to rough up kids like him the same way."

Mr. Stallard nodded. "Those kids never made it in the locker room."

Hardcastle agreed. "I never trusted the quiet ones. But if I had searched you before sending you to Mr. Stallard's office, what would I have found?"

Adam smiled innocently. "Nothing, I promi--"

Stallard cut him off. "You weren't careful here, Augustine. We have heard your name come up too much in all this."

Hardcastle lowered his voice. "If you risked ruining state for us, it makes me so disappointed in your judgment, Adam."

"I don't know who you all have been talking to, but state has always been my top priority."

Hardcastle continued, "Ah really? Did you ever talk to Cullen about his diet?"

Adam locked up, staying silent.

"That's what I figured," Hardcastle muttered. "I thought we were on the same team here."

"…I don't know. I mean, I thought Cullen had been pushing harder lately."

"Oh yeah? So hard that he let a bucktooth kid hit a buzzer beater?"

"Well, if I made those free throws...."

Hardcastle replied, "I'm surprised at you. I thought state was important to you."

"It is--"

"Then cut the bull. Cullen has put his personal life over the team. Want to win state? Then stop messing around and sit him down. Understood?"

Adam nodded meekly. "It gets handled today, okay? But I need your help with something else first."

—

In the locker room, Coach Hardcastle and Mr. Stallard stood outside Adam's locker. Adam opened it up for them to see.

Tommy's leather jacket was hanging inside with a whole pallet of paint on the outside of it.

Mr. Hardcastle snorted. "You steal his jacket too?"

"No. Someone put it here. Check what's inside."

Mr. Stallard looked inside Tommy's jacket. There was a small note, and the handwriting was unforgettable.

"Now that day is here...."

Mr. Stallard stared intently at Hardcastle before turning to Adam. There was real fear inside Adam's eyes, and Stallard could see it.

Adam shrugged. "He broke into my locker. There is no other way he could have done it."

Mr. Stallard nodded. "We'll take care of this. Promise."

Hardcastle agreed. "But remember, do your part."

—

Minutes later, Tommy sat inside Mr. Stallard's office. Stallard smirked. Tommy's hair was sticking out in gravity defying directions, just like it always did. Tommy pointed toward the mass of trophies in Stallard's office. "Did you add a new one of those since last year?"

Stallard glowered at the boy. "Do you know why you're here?"

Tommy ignored the question. "I like it. It really brings them all together."

"Those were all here last year," Stallard said, gritting his teeth.

"No, the silver one on the far left." The boy scanned the front of the trophy. "Second in league softball? Aw, that's cool. I didn't know you played softball."

"Do you know why you're here today?" Stallard barked, trying to take control.

Tommy shrugged. "To talk about your softball highlights?"

Stallard lifted Tommy's graffiti-filled coat from behind his desk. "Are you missing this coat, Thomas?"

Tommy shook his head. "I've never seen that before in my life."

"We both know this is yours."

"I guess I got a coat *kinda* like it, but it doesn't have that crap all over it."

"Did you bring that coat here today?" Stallard asked.

"It's at my cousin's," Tommy said.

"How convenient."

"Double check the tags. I was sure to write 'Tommy' on mine."

Mr. Stallard shook his head. The name on there was "Terrance." But he knew Tommy knew that.

Tommy pointed to the door. "So, can I go?"

Stallard threw the coat across the desk. "Since you're being a little turd, let me tell you what happened. Adam found this in his locker. I know you somehow broke into it. After all, it was only last year when you used the same threat to take Adam's life--"

"You mean--"

Stallard held up a finger. "Do not interrupt me. We already called Adam's family. Adam's grandparents are good people, and they thought it would be better if we got you help here at Latimer."

"I don't know what you're talking about."

Stallard swallowed. Tommy was seasoned, and the boy knew that if he really had any proof here, he'd be in handcuffs. Stallard circled over the thought in his mind and re-strategized. Mr. Stallard spoke. "Do you think this is funny? Well, let me guide you through what happens now. I'm giving you one last chance. If I see anything that remotely looks like a threat of violence against Adam or anyone else in the student body, I swear to God I will have you expelled before that enabling mom of yours can make it back here."

Tommy stood up. "Can I go now?"

Stallard eyed the boy dangerously. "One more move, Thomas. If you go too far again, I'll make sure the police take care of you this time around."

Giving Stallard a slight nod, Tommy strode out from his office.

Mr. Stallard sat back. If the truth be told, he wasn't certain if Tommy was even capable of violence. But that wasn't what mattered anymore. Adam, a student in his school, felt unsafe, and Mr. Stallard wasn't going to stand for that. Mr. Stallard got up from his desk and made his way to Principal Elmer's office. He didn't like getting Elmer involved, but he didn't think he had a choice right now. If Tommy was going to be handled, everyone needed to be united here. Stallard stepped into the principal's office and halted in surprise. Jeff Elmer was sitting behind his desk, beneath the golden bars of his painting while Mr. Austin was sitting in front of him.

Mr. Stallard grinned. "Just the people I needed to see."

"Likewise," Mr. Austin said.

Mr. Elmer took over and looked at Mr. Stallard in the doorway. "It's good to have you here, Jay. James was wondering why you pulled a student from his honors class without talking to him first?"

Jay nodded. "Of course. Correct me if I'm wrong, but I was under the impression that we believed that student safety was the top priority."

"Student safety?" Austin repeated.

"Yeah. I moved him to the Regular Art class so he could have access to Mr. Gee, our counselor. Mr. Elmer, please understand, if Tommy doesn't get help, he's going to be a criminal."

Austin spat. "You lying son of a bitch."

Principal Elmer put a hand on Mr. Austin's shoulder. "Take it easy, James."

Mr. Austin continued, "It was safety when you sat back and let Tommy's picture get posted around the school? No. You threw him to the wolves!"

Mr. Stallard shrugged. "We searched Adam, just like you both wanted, but we didn't find anything--"

"Put yourself in Tommy's shoes. Do you think you would have made it through something like that? Because, I'll be honest, I'd be contemplating suicide right now."

Stallard considered. "That checks out. It's a common struggle for your kind."

Elmer screamed, "Jay!"

Stallard lifted his hands. "Artists."

Elmer looked intently at Mr. Stallard. "I do not want to choose between you two."

"No," Jay whispered. "Please do."

Elmer stood up at his desk. All three men were now standing, sizing each other up in a too-small office. "Then I choose James."

Stallard felt a measure of elation. His mind raced. "This is what I've been waiting for," Stallard thought. "This is what I've been praying for. Elmer sided with this deviant and his pet, the sadistic murderer Tommy Tate. The moment I tell Duke about this, the school board will see to it that Principal Elmer will not return next year. Then I'll be able to--"

Mr. Austin interjected, "No."

Principal Elmer stopped. "What?"

Mr. Austin turned to him. "Choose Stallard. You know what he'll do. He'll spread rumors about me, about Tommy, and about you to the community. He'll do everything he can to ruin you, Jeff, and I won't let that happen. You care about kids, Jeff."

Mr. Stallard stepped so close to Mr. Austin that he could smell his soap.

Mr. Stallard whispered, "And I don't?"

Mr. Austin held his ground. "No. You're an evil person, you know that?"

Stallard stayed silent, probing James' every word.

Mr. Austin continued, "You hurt kids, Jay, and there isn't a worse crime in the world."

Mr. Stallard glowered at Mr. Austin, choking back his response.

Mr. Austin turned to Elmer. "When this year is over, I'm done." Mr. Austin turned to leave, and Stallard stepped aside to let him through.

Mr. Stallard smirked at Elmer. "You may come to regret not having my back there."

Elmer breathed. "Nah. I never will."

Stallard ran his hand over Elmer's desk. "If I were you, Jeff, I'd be very careful over the next few months."

"Shut the door behind you." Elmer yelled, disregarding the threat.

Mr. Stallard took one last moment to drink in the scene. He could see James' blood hanging on the golden bars, and soon this office would be his.

Giving Principal Elmer one last confident smirk, Stallard stepped from his office. It was true, he didn't have a chance to bring up Tommy's jacket to Elmer, but that meant he'd be able to take that on his own. Just as he hoped.

Chapter 36: *Cookie Cutters*

Cullen walked into the locker room with purpose in his eyes. Taking a direct path through the locker room, he picked out Adam and Brian and stepped between them. "Can I talk to you both about somethin'?"

"I don't know," Brian said. "Can you?"

"I can beat the crap outta you. You decide which you wanna do."

Jonah laughed. "Daang!"

Brian's ears reddened. "I was joking."

"I wasn't," Cullen muttered, leading Brian out of the locker room. Checking to make sure they were alone, Cullen turned to Adam and Brian. "The texts to Tommy stop today, you hear me?"

Taking a breath in surprise, Brian backed up against a locker. Adam's look, however, was cool and inscrutable. Brian looked up into Cullen's eyes and tried to keep his composure. "We lose our first game and you hassle me with this? Get outta my way."

Cullen stood as still as a statue. "You ain't hearin' me. The texts stop *today.*"

Brian spat. "Are you two butt buddies or wha--"

Adam cut him off. "Done. The texts stop."

Brian stepped to Cullen. "Well, I'm not promising anything."

Cullen rested his arm on the locker beside Brian, leaning over him like a tower. It was a subtle move, but Cullen could see it sent such a fright through Brian that he lost his train of thought.

Cullen kept his voice calm and measured. "If I hear that either of you text Tommy again, you're gonna regret it. You hear me?"

Brian looked up in defiance. "You, you wouldn't--"

Cullen smiled. "One more word, I swear to God if you say one more word...."

Stammering in fear, Brian released a breath. "The texts stop today, I promise."

"You sure?"

Brian nodded. "Positive."

Cullen continued, "And that applies to next year too. I'm still gonna be around, and I know how to hit you both up."

Adam smirked. "He really has become a close friend of yours, huh?"

"Yeah, guess he has."

"Coach wants us all in the gym for a group meeting." Adam said. He looked at Brian. "Wanna do the thing we talked about in practice today?"

Glaring at Cullen, a look of understanding seemed to fall over Brian. "Yeah. Let's do it."

Cullen turned to Adam. "Alright, we're good. Thanks for figuring that out with me."

Without a word, Cullen led the two back into the locker room.

—

Hardcastle blew the whistle. It was a game of Crimson versus Gold. Devin, C.J. and Cullen vs. Adam, Jonah and Brian. After last week's loss, Hardcastle was looking for a spark.

Devin had the ball for red; dodging Jonah, he bounce-passed the ball to Cullen. With Adam draped over him like a strait jacket, Cullen drove under the basket and put up a shot.

Adam smacked Cullen's arm as he shot it, and the sound had been heard by everyone. Adam's foul sent the ball ricocheting off the rim and into Brian's possession. Cullen looked at his coach. Hardcastle must have been the only one in the gym who missed Adam's foul. On the other side of the court, Brian passed the ball over to Jonah. Lifting the ball high up in the air, Jonah saw Adam streaking toward the basket and lobbed the ball for a slam.

But Cullen was there, and with a leap he knocked the ball out of Adam's hands. In a normal 5 on 5 match, the ball would have been recovered by the defense, but a 3 on 3 game was a different story. Without facing a normal defense, Brian rushed in, recovered the ricocheted ball and evaded Cullen's outstretched hand to score.

Brian turned around to Cullen. "You loafed it on that one."

"What?" Cullen asked.

"Don't worry about it," Brian murmured.

Shaking it off, Cullen got into position as Devin ran back up the court. Devin passed it to Cullen and the 6'6 center drove a shoulder into Adam and scored on an easy lay-up.

"Daang," Brian sneered. "We might not have lost if you played like that the whole game."

"Too bad you were on the bench," Cullen yelled.

Brian reddened. "Still want to dunk this year? Gonna be hard when you're pigging out on wings."

Hardcastle intervened. "Boys! Focus on the game."

Brian looked to Adam, and Cullen almost swore he saw Adam give a nod to Brian, like he was telling him to keep going.

The game resumed, and the two teams traded possession after possession. To Brian and Adam's obvious fury, they trailed Cullen's team 9-7 at the game's end.

C.J. passed it down to Cullen. One shot from Cullen would win the game, but Adam and Brian double teamed him the moment he touched the ball.

Positioning himself over Adam and Brian's outstretched arms, Cullen went up for the winning shot, but the ball was off center by a sliver of a hair. It went in and out of the rim and into Brian's arms. Cullen cloaked himself over Brian, trying to pry back the ball from his possession.

"Nice shot," Brian whispered. "It gave up just like you this year."

"One more word," Cullen warned.

Brian passed the ball off to Jonah and ran to the other end of the court. Cullen felt Brian approach him from behind and whisper in his ear.

"No wonder your mom killed herself when she got to know you."

Hatred filled Cullen's eyes. He didn't know what stunned him more, the fact that Brian knew about his mom or that he was stupid enough to say what he just said. Time slowed, and Cullen watched as Jonah roped the ball to Brian's outstretched hands. Brian looked gleeful as he leapt up to lay it in, but Cullen was waiting.

Leaping up against Brian, Cullen clotheslined his arm across Brian's neck and slammed him to the floor. Brian crashed to the ground, causing his head to smash against the floor so hard that it made the team gasp.

Cullen stepped over Brian's body. Brian looked up at him in submission. "I'm sorry, please don't--"

Hardcastle whipped his arms around Cullen in a bear hug. "What in the HELL is wrong with you?" The coach shoved Cullen from the fray and drove a finger straight into his chest. "I will not have *thugs* on my basketball team! On the line, Armstrong. *Thugs* run suicides on my team."

Cullen moved to the other side of the court in a daze. It was like he was hit with a bolt of lightning. Did coach just call him a *slur*? Cullen looked at the silent amalgam of beige faces on his team. Not a single one spoke up. Not a single one said anything.

"Hustle it up, Armstrong! Maybe we can burn off those wings you've been eating!"

Cullen looked at Adam and saw him glance at Hardcastle nervously. Hardcastle had no one way of knowing about his cheat days, but Adam knew. Cullen looked to his feet and tried to contain his rage. This was who he was "allowed" to be at LHS. He wasn't a CNA. He wasn't a caretaker for his uncle. He wasn't the person who cared for his sister as they grew up together. All he was *ever* supposed to be at LHS was a basketball player. No other dreams were welcome here. Cullen stepped to the line and looked at the cowards on his team with the ugliest look he could muster.

Cullen turned to his coach in defiance and dared him to blow the whistle.

"Wipe that look off your face or it's another suicide!" Hardcastle spat.

"Better give me two then, 'cause this look ain't goin' anywhere."

"Oh, I'll give you more than that!" Hardcastle screamed. "You're now watching Friday's game from the bench!"

Cullen exhaled in surprise. He should have expected it, but the consequence stunned him all the same. He watched Hardcastle spit out punishments and saliva across the court. Somewhere in that white noise Cullen found Brian and pierced his eyes. A part of him couldn't help but feel contrition; Brian shouldn't have got caught up in this. Brian shouldn't have even known about his mom, because Cullen had only shared that story with one other person on this court. Cullen locked with Adam's gaze and saw Adam's eyes widen. Just how long had Adam been ratting on him to Hardcastle? To everyone on the court? Months? *Years*? "Does anyone even care about me here?" Cullen wondered. Or did they only ever care about him if LHS was winning basketball games? Tamira was right to leave. She was right all along.

Hardcastle broke Cullen from his trance. "Any more you wanna say?"

Standing alone, Cullen faced his teammates and coaches staring his way.

Hardcastle put the whistle in his mouth and blared it for the world to hear.

Chapter 37: ***The Lion and the Swine***

Tommy saw the look of ecstasy on Adam's face when he walked into Mr. Demko's classroom, but this time, Tommy smiled in return. After his conversation with Stallard yesterday, he knew he had Adam scared, and when the game comes to a halt on Friday, Adam would know that *he* was the one who killed him.

Tommy's mind went to the noose beneath his bed. And by the time Stallard and the police figured it all out, it would be too late to find him.

Adam looked at Tommy like a beast on the edge of starvation, but this time, Tommy was ready, because no matter what Adam said to him, Tommy knew Adam was scared.

Lynne had called Mr. Elmer yesterday, requesting that Tommy be moved from any classes with Adam Augustine or Brian Miller. Elmer had agreed with the request, and even got the clearance he needed from the other math teacher. A week ago, this deus ex machina would have come at the perfect time.

The poster of Tommy's letter and ass crack was waiting for him inside Mr. Demko's classroom. Adam's laughter roasted Tommy's insides when the boy saw it taped across his desk.

Before being kicked from Honors, before his boxcar, and before Mia, Tommy would have taken it in a heartbeat.

But it was too late.

He gave Mr. Elmer the best lie he had ever delivered. A lie about how he called Adam, and Adam assured him that he had nothing to do with Monday. He told Mr. Elmer how he looked up to Adam, and how he didn't understand why someone like Adam could be blamed for such a horrible thing. Elmer seemed skeptical, but what could he have said?

The golden boy shot first. "You missed it, Tommy. This picture of you was all over the school Monday."

Tommy was silent. Mr. Demko was absent, as he always was at the start of class, but there was no reason to get into the fray. He gained nothing by revealing his hand. Not to Adam. Not to the other students around him.

Adam said, “I wondered if you would show your face today.”

Rosi turned around, meeting Tommy’s eyes. Her assaults always razored Tommy to his core, and he braced himself for another. But Rosi stayed out of it and turned back around to her desk.

Adam continued, “Do you want it back? Because I might know who has it.”

Tommy saw Rosi freeze. Tommy furrowed his brow. Rosi hadn’t told them she’d given the journal up. Tommy looked around. Brian was weirdly quiet too, and seemed disengaged from the conversation.

Tommy kept his mouth shut.

Adam breathed. “Ask me nicely and I can get it back to you."

Being met with silence, Adam moved up to Tommy and lowered his voice. “No, a bitch doesn’t ask. A good bitch begs. Beg for it, Tommy.”

Rosi slammed her fists on her desks and stormed out of the room. Tommy saw a look of surprise flash across Adam’s face. Normally, Tommy would have needled Adam about this, but not today. Tommy needed to hear everything.

Tommy played through the plot inside his mind. It would be too easy. It was already Wednesday, and in two days he’d climb the stepladder before the game to set it all up.

Adam cooed, “Too bad your whore mom didn’t abort you.”

Brian gasped, which caromed off like dynamite in Tommy’s mind.

Adam continued, “Do the world a favor, Tommy.”

Tommy braced for the impact.

“Kill yourself.”

—

"Too bad your whore mom didn't abort you."

Adam's comment blared through the loudspeakers inside Tommy's mind. Adam probably didn't realize how right he was. It would have saved his mom a lot of trouble. She would still be Jaime Lynne. Maybe she would have found someone who would have been good to her. Lord knows it was a tall task for her to find anyone, having had a fat bastard for a son.

Tommy's imagination continued. As tall as a skyscraper, Adam towered over Tommy and screamed it out for the world to hear: *Do the world a favor, Tommy Taint.*

Tommy sat alone inside the Annex and listened to it all again.

Adam whispered in his ear, *Kill yourself.*

"Don't worry, Adam," Tommy breathed, "I just might." The boy looked out to the John Wagner Fieldhouse. "But I'm gonna take you with me."

Tommy went over the list of tools in his black journal.

~~Razors~~

Weld Bond

Orange Spray Paint

~~Adam Augustine~~

~~Basketball Goal~~

He had two things left to get, and Tommy knew where to find them. They were even in the same place.

Guilt bubbled up inside him; even the thought of it felt criminal.

Adam's voice flared up again: *Too bad your whore mom didn't abort you.*

Tommy sighed. Mr. Austin's room would have what he needed.

Do the world a favor, Tommy Taint.

Tommy clenched his fists. Was he capable of stealing -- actually stealing -- from someone like Mr. Austin?

Adam whispered, landing the deathblow. *Kill yourself.*

—

Chipper voices of the student body, the shuffling of backpacks, and chairs scuffling against the floors filtered through the hallways.

Tommy swallowed. He had minutes. After the last bell rang, Mr. Austin went downstairs to the lobby to watch over the halls. On some days, Mr. Austin would visit Mr. Elmer for a while before going back upstairs.

Tommy needed luck on his side today. If he was going to do what he was thinking about doing, getting caught by Mr. Austin would ruin everything.

Tommy breathed. Could he do something like this to Mr. Austin?

The bell rang. Without hesitating, Tommy moved to his feet.

—

Tommy sidled up to the end of the hallway, just in view of Mr. Austin's door. The boy went through Mr. Austin's room inside his mind, through all the drawers, closets and desks. He knew it was a precarious idea. If a student was in the room or if the closets were locked, all bets were off.

Mr. Austin opened the door, and Tommy watched as he walked toward the lobby.

Tommy took a breath. It was now or never. The boy rushed into Mr. Austin's room. Empty, but that wouldn't stop anyone from walking in. The boy threw his backpack in front of him and opened the closet. A row of spray paint canisters stared him right in the eye. He was lucky. Mr. Austin kept the orange paint in the back, so it was possible he wouldn't notice anything was missing until the summer.

Tommy threw the spray paint in his bag and looked at Mr. Austin's desk. If he was caught now, everything would be ruined.

The boy sat behind Mr. Austin's desk and threw open the bottom drawers. An unopened pack of Weld Bond met his eye from the left side. Tommy thrust it into his bag and closed the drawers. It was perfect. It could not have gone any smoother.

Mr. Austin's voice rang out from the doorway. "What's going on, Tommy?"

The boy froze. *Keep it cool*, he told himself, standing at the corner of Austin's desk. "Not much, Mr. A. -- I was just looking for you. I didn't see you, so I was gonna leave a note."

"You're just the person I was hoping to see," Austin said. "I have to run downstairs to the senior lobby but realized I left my phone here. Would you like to talk down there?"

Relief flooded Tommy. Mr. Austin hadn't seen him. "I actually have to run, but I just wanted to tell you sorry."

"Sorry?" Austin asked.

"For not keeping my grades up. For getting kicked out of your class."

Mr. Austin shook his head. "You weren't kicked out. Not by me. I've asked Mr. Elmer to reinstate you, and you'll be back in my room next Monday.

Tommy sighed. "Too little, too late," he thought. There was nothing that was going to stop him now. Putting on the biggest smile he could, Tommy looked up at Mr. Austin. "That makes me so happy to hear. You said Monday?"

Mr. Austin nodded. "The 21st. I'll see you there, okay?"

Tommy nodded ruefully. "See you then."

Chapter 38: ***Dissolved Girl***

The Baldridge Greenhouse was a mass complex of buildings on the northeast corner of the city. It stood on a large expanse between the Kaw River and the Manchester Highway. The destination innate to her high school routine, Mia stepped from her car and stood at the rocks along the river. Brandishing her cell phone, Mia listened to her messages.

Brian Miller's voice, talking from what might be his 50th phone number in the last week, came in from the other end.

"Hey, babe. You're never gonna believe what happened yesterday. Cullen threatened me at practice about bothering Tommy. I know you're trying to be a friend of Tommy this year, which is so nice of you. I mean, that's just you, you know? But here's the thing. Adam took Cullen's side. Adam said I 'went too far' with Cullen. Can you believe that? Adam was the one with beef with Cullen this year, you know? Adam was the one who made me do the things I did to Cullen. Anyway. It made me realize what's really important, and that's you. That's us. Remember when we used to go to skating? That was so much fun. I'm looking at photobooth photos we took there during the good times. You aren't smiling, but it's when you still had that messed up front tooth before your braces. I know you'd be smiling now. Come back to me, babe. Love you."

Mia felt a sick feeling plunge into her stomach after the message. Taking a breath, her mind started to wander. "It's time," she told herself. "Time to let Yuki know."

Her phone still in her grasp, Mia dialed for Yurika.

She picked up on the first ring. "Hey, babe."

"Hi," Mia whispered.

"Is everything okay?"

"Brian's becoming a problem again."

Yurika breathed. "I knew it! I freaking knew it."

"He's dangerous, Yuki. If he loses it again...."

"That's not going to happen," Yurika said. "We have plan B for a reason."

Mia looked at the water flowing over the Kaw River. "I'm not ready to go there... There's no telling what he'll do then."

"No matter what, I'm here for you."

"Thanks. I better get to the greenhouse."

"Love you, girl."

Mia smiled. "Love your face."

—

Mia frolicked beneath the half-lit fluorescent lights in the greenhouse. Her coffee had worn off two hours ago and a discolored exhaustion hung below her eyes, but none of that mattered. She had reached the end of her shift and was free at last. The scent of petunia burrowed itself in Mia's nostrils by the time she reached the register. Looking at the last illuminated screen in the building, Mia punched in her social security number and clocked out of work.

Turning to the inviting world outside, Mia smiled. "Sweet freedom."

Mary Bosworth's single pitched voice rang through the greenhouse. "Mia?! Are you still here?"

Mia clamped her eyes shut; she should have skipped faster.

Adopting a smile, Mia answered, "I am!"

Mary stepped up to the desk. "Thank goodness. Could you translate a call for me? A woman named Gaby called wanting to order baskets for her wedding."

"Absolutely," Mia said, stepping back toward the desk phone. "Line one?"

"You know it."

Mia picked up the phone. "¡Hola, Gaby! Soy Mia. En que te puedo ayudar?"

Mary whispered to Mia, "I need to know the type of flowers she needs and how many baskets she wants."

Listening to the receiver, Mia grabbed a notepad. "Bien, para estar seguros, 20 cestas de petunias blancas con salvia, verdad?" Mia translated Gaby's request and wrote it on the pad for Mary. "Gaby wants 20 petunia baskets with Salvias."

"Wonderful," Mary whispered.

Beaming, Mia gave Gaby the details of the order and congratulated her for her wedding. After saying goodbye, Mia looked to her boss.

Mary smiled. "Thanks a million. How'd she hear about us?"

"Her cousin came to us before and told her we were way cheaper than a florist."

"Her cousin is a smart gal. Thanks again, Mia. Have a good night!"

Mia bid her boss farewell and walked out of the greenhouse. Guided from an orange light in the parking lot, Mia walked out to her red Geometro.

Mia, after fumbling through her keys, unlocked her car and opened her door. Mia smiled. She was free.

An arm slammed Mia against her car and knocked the air from her diaphragm. A large hand covered her mouth and pinned her against her vehicle.

Panic bleeding inside her, Mia turned and looked into the eyes of Brian Miller. She swung her left arm towards his face, but Brian repelled the blow. He was at least six inches taller than she was and absorbed every strike. Brian caught Mia's left hand and shoved it up against the car.

Mia looked up in horror. She was face to face with a monster -- a sadistic and uncontrollable monster -- and he looked like one, too. His nose was purple and swollen, and bruises covered his flapjack-like face.

"Stop fighting!" Brian screamed. "I am done messing around! You have cut me out of your life for the last year! And I promised you what would happen if you did."

Mia froze up against the car.

Brian released a toothy grin. "That'a girl. I didn't think you would forget it. If I move my hand, do you promise not to scream?"

Mia nodded.

Brian moved his hand.

Without hesitating, Mia ripped her keys from her car and crushed them into Brian's swollen nose. Brian staggered back, yelping out in pain.

Mia leapt inside her car and fired up the engine.

Stepping up, Brian slammed his fist against the top of her car. "You whore!" he yelled. "You dumb whore!"

Mia turned from the parking lot and accelerated to the highway.

"You're gonna pay for this!" Brian screamed, his voice filtering into the car. "You're gonna pay!"

—

Mia knocked on the massive, ornate wooden door standing in front of her. Yurika threw open the door and wrapped her arms around Mia.

"Are you sure you're okay with this? I'd hate to keep you up too late," Mia said.

Yurika shook her off. "More than okay. Mr. Negut has basically let us sleep through band after we rocked last week's competition, but truthfully? This is more important than anything we'd be working on at LHS."

Mia looked at her best friend with a heavy gaze. "Thank you, Yuki."

"Our black bean burgers just finished in the oven. I'll make you a plate."

Mia felt like she was going to cry. "I could really use a black bean burger right now."

Yurika looked in Mia's eyes. "We're going to get this figured out."

—

Yurika sat behind her desk inside her bedroom. "How many times has he called today?"

Her phone vibrating in her grasp, Mia tossed it on Yurika's bed. "I stopped paying attention after fifty."

Yurika gasped. "Oh, God."

"It's bad."

"Do you know if the greenhouse has a camera?"

Mia shook her head. "Not in that lot, but Mary is having me park in the delivery section from now on where we have a camera set up."

"You know what? After tomorrow, he'll never speak to you again anyway."

"I hope so," Mia whispered. "I'm just worried. I have no idea what he'll do if he has nothing to lose."

"He'll still have everything to lose," Yurika pointed out. "Basketball, his reputation -- everything. It will be your insurance that he stays away from you."

"What if he doesn't take the bait?"

"You know he will. He's an ass-piston."

Mia giggled. "Isn't that term great?"

"I love it. But no matter what, I'm right here beside you."

"Okay."

Yurika extracted a tape recorder from her desk. "Are you sure you want to do this?"

Mia nodded.

"Let's do it."

"Thanks for this, Yuki. I didn't know who else I could go to."

Yurika nodded solemnly. "At this school? Of course. Us Brown girls have to stick together."

The phone vibrated on the bed. Mia took Yurika's hand, answered, and put the phone on speaker.

Brian exhaled in surprise. "Mia?"

Mia kept her voice level. "Hi, Brian."

"It's so good to hear your voice," Brian whispered. "I never thought I'd hear it again."

Mia cut to the chase. "This is the last time we're going to talk, Brian."

"What?" Brian asked. "You answered the phone just to tell me that?"

"You didn't give me much of a choice," Mia responded coolly. "You've called me maybe 500 times this week."

"Just give me a chance," Brian pleaded. "Just one chance. Please!"

"No."

Brian was desperate. "Please think about it. Can you do that for me?"

"Brian," Mia said, "you don't have a chance."

Brian went silent.

Yurika nodded to Mia, urging her to continue.

Mia continued, "We done then?"

Brian went dark. "No. Not even close."

"Brian, listen to--"

"No you listen to me! I tried to be reasonable and it didn't work, so let me tell you how it's gonna be."

"Brian, I'm not going to--"

"Shut your damn mouth!" Brian screamed.

Mia exhaled, feeling the onset of a familiar storm. Finding Yurika's eyes, she fought the anxiety inside her.

Chapter 39: *The Landlord's Daughter*

Cullen brought a burnt DVD over to Mr. Austin's desk. Mr. Austin looked up at his student. "What'd you think?"

Cullen nodded. "Amazing."

Mr. Austin smiled. "It is, isn't it? I hear you're driving Dex to the Mickey Ryan awards tonight?"

"Sure am. I'll get him there in one piece."

Mr. Austin winked. "You better. Otherwise his parents will be really disappointed." Mr. Austin scanned the room. "By the way, have you seen Mia here today?"

Cullen shook his head. "Nah. She was gonna watch Dex's movie with us, but I haven't seen her around."

"I didn't know if she had something for STUCO. I better get in attendance."

Cullen looked around the room. "So, what's the deal with Tommy in here? You kick him out for grades?"

Mr. Austin shook his head. "I never actually kick students out for grades. As long as they meet me before or after school, or during lunch, I give them plenty of chances to come back."

"So why's Tommy outta here?"

Mr. Austin spat. "That decision went over my head, but I got it sorted out. Tommy will be back on Monday."

"Alright. Mind if I look for him now? I wanna check in."

Mr. Austin nodded. "He'll be in Mr. Johnson's room."

Cullen laughed. "Poor kid. I'll be back."

—

Cullen led Tommy out of Mr. Johnson's classroom and waited as Tommy stepped in the hallway. Tommy's demeanor was off. He was stilted, slow, and looked disinterested when Cullen talked to him.

Cullen looked at Tommy. "How're you holdin' up?"

"Fine," Tommy said.

"Nah, don't do that. Talk to me. How you doin'?"

Tommy rolled his eyes. "Crappy, but I think you know that."

"Well, I talked to Adam and Brian and they ain't gonna be textin' you again."

Tommy shook him off. "Why are you talkin' to me, man?"

"You're my friend."

Tommy stepped to Cullen. "Really? So did you know about Saturday?!"

"Tommy, you know I ain't heard a thing about that. I never would have let something like that happen. We're friends, Tommy, and I'm here if you need me."

"I needed you before Monday. I needed you to say something to Adam before he ruined everything for me. But even if you didn't know what they were planning, you stood back and you let it happen."

"Woah!" Cullen yelled. "Let me tell you how it looked from my end. Every day for the last year I heard about how crazy you were inside that locker room, how you wanted to hurt Adam, hell, how you wanted to *kill* him."

Tommy interjected, "And you--"

Cullen held up his hand. "I ain't finished. How do you think it went over when I started kickin' it with the kid who wanted to murder one of my teammates?"

Tommy looked away. "Did you ever think about asking me about that?"

"C'mon. You wouldn't have said a thing if I asked you."

Tommy swallowed. "Whatever, man."

"Look, Tommy. I know you ain't the monster they all said you were, but you never even talked to me about all that. And crap, say what you will about Adam, but he doesn't deserve that--"

Tommy took another step toward Cullen, and a demonic look seized Tommy's face. Tommy's expression contorted and released a scream, "He does deserve it!"

Cullen was stunned. "That's where we disagree."

Tommy took a step back. "I'm -- I'm sorry."

"I can't get behind you on that, Tommy. I'll be your friend. I'll hit him up in person if you need me to give 'em a scare. But I won't do *that.* When you've moved on from this stuff, lemme know, 'cause I'm here."

"It just came out. I didn't really mean it."

"Good," Cullen said. "We're friends, Tommy. I'm always here for you, man."

Tommy flinched at the word "friend" and looked at Cullen with a purpose in his eyes. "Tell me something, and don't BS me?"

Cullen raised an eyebrow. "Yeah?"

"Did Mr. Austin tell you to start talking to me?"

Cullen paused for a moment. "I'm only telling you this so you know you can trust me. Yes. He did ask that I start talkin' with you during the first week of school, but that's not why I became your friend."

Tommy shook his head and turned away. "Friends aren't a special project."

Cullen watched Tommy go back in Mr. Johnson's room, undeterred. "I know you ain't. You're my friend, Tommy. Let me know when you wanna chill."

"Will do," Tommy offered glumly.

—

Dexter settled into the passenger seat of Cullen's Dodge Stealth. Decked out in a full suit, Dexter looked up to Cullen. "Thanks for the lift."

Cullen looked over to his friend. "You ready?"

Dex exhaled. "Ask me in three hours."

Cullen started the car. "We'll get whatever food you want when we're done. On me."

"Sounds good. Mr. A said the food here was garbage."

—

Four hours later, a silence plagued the inside of Cullen's car. Dexter stared solemnly out the passenger window and watched the lights go by on the Manchester highway.

Cullen shook his head. "You were robbed."

"It ain't no thing," Dex said, his voice a little too cheery.

Cullen spat. "They gave the city's scholarship to Harley Cheeseboro."

"Aw, her mural was solid, though."

Cullen pushed back. "You made a more 'solid' mural when you was a freshman, Dex... If they're gonna shaft you, I would rather they had given it to the urban art designer."

"Yeah! What was her name? Lex? Her whole project was sick."

"Do you know her?" Cullen asked. "I saw she was from Baldridge."

"I know of her. We've never met in person."

Cullen shook his head. "Mr. Austin said Harley had an uncle on the board."

"Yeah. She did."

Cullen turned onto the highway. "Where did Harley even go to school? I didn't even recognize the name."

"It's a private school called, uh, The Heritage Academy? Something like that."

Cullen snickered ruefully. "That checks. Us public school kids ain't ever had a chance. Man, Harley's granddad destroyed the streets I lived on. The amount of people I've seen evicted over the years, Dex. Harley's dad's still the landlord of the houses, but no one's comin' to live there anymore, and they own so much of our downtown. That family has taken so much from the people of our city. They already have everything they could need, but their kids take our town's scholarships away."

Dexter shook his head and looked out the window. "Bro, I think you're more cut up about this than I am."

"Maybe I am. I'm tired of the lie, Dex. Ever since Hardcastle called me a thug."

"I told you that you need to go to Elmer about that."

Cullen shook his head. "Nah, man. Elmer and Hardcastle went to Branson together. Everyone says Hardcastle might be the principal someday."

"You don't know if Elmer would back you, huh?"

Cullen exited off the highway towards Salem Street. "Bruh, I don't know. Latimer is no place for Elmer to be somebody. Man, how could he even get a job here unless he looked the other way about stuff like this?"

Dexter looked at Cullen. "Well, I'll vouch for him about this. He'd wanna know."

"I'll think on it, okay? But it'd be after the season. Maybe after Spring Break. I'm already benched for one game. Hardcastle would bench me and lose substate out of spite if he heard I was comin' to him like that."

"I get that. Hey man, I think I'm too tired to eat out tonight."

"Nah, nah. I know you're feelin' what happened tonight, man -- so we're gonna drink some energy drinks and have some wings at Riverfront."

Dexter laughed. "When was the last time you broke your diet?"

"Ha," Cullen started. "it's been a couple months. Worth it, though. Tonight we eat like kings."

"You've been lookin' cut, bro. Honored you'll spend your cheat day with me."

Cullen turned into the Riverfront parking lot. "It's a good excuse."

"Thanks, Cullen."

The two got out of the car and stepped to the Brewery. Cullen put an arm on Dex's shoulder. "You earned it."

A black-eyed, skinny man in a tank top and wild brown hair approached them. He spoke to Cullen and Dexter. "Remember me?"

Dexter laughed. "Course I do, Thayne. I see you out back once a week."

Under the lights of Riverfront, Thayne did not even seem to notice Dexter's reply.

Cullen tilted his head. Thayne had two black eyes and walked with a strange tilt that made Cullen wonder if he was high. "It's 30 degrees, bro. Why are you in a tank?"

Thayne asked again, "Do you... remember me?"

Cullen breathed. "Tommy's cousin, yeah, you called me an influencer, right?"

Thayne replied, "You still run with Tommy?"

"Yeah."

Thayne yelled, "Tell him he's dead to me. Dead!"

Without another word, Thayne walked between Dexter and Cullen and marched from the Riverfront parking lot.

Dexter turned to Cullen. "Well, that's haunting."

Thinking about his conversation with Tommy from earlier today, Cullen nodded. "Yeah, it is."

—

Unsorted: Tennessee Whiskey

Lynne pried open Tommy's rolltop, clawed beneath his desk, and searched behind his bed. She had to find his journal. Tommy was hitting bottom, and she could feel it. He was on edge, and with what he did to Thayne, Lynne feared that he was just about to explode. She could tell Tommy was afraid she was going to call the police about what he did to Thayne, but there was always a risk that the cops would find something illegal on Grace's property. If she could just find the journal, she could put a stop to everything. There was only one place she hadn't looked. Turning her head, Lynne looked over to Tommy's mattress. It was cliched, hiding your stuff under your bed, but she wasn't sure if Tommy had any other place to hide anything. The woman surveyed the sheet at the top of his box springs. It had somehow stayed together over all these years, and it was empty outside of a single piece of tape in its center. Lynne grabbed the end of the tape and pulled. There was a sticky note sitting in the slot under the sheet. It had a small scrawl of Tommy's handwriting... "Final Draft: Hamartia".

"Well," she thought. "I wonder what--"

Tommy burst into the room and screamed, "What are you *doing*?"

Her mouth hanging open in surprise, Lynne turned to face her son.

"Get out!" Tommy bellowed, storming to his mattress. "*Get out!*"

"Tom--" Lynne breathed. "Tommy."

Tommy yelled, "Oh God, I can smell that whiskey from here. Get out of here!"

"Tommy, I'm sorry. I was just worried about you."

"So you decided to break into my room? Jesus, have you ever thought of just talking to me?"

"Would you even answer me if I did?" Lynne asked. "Dang, Tommy. Reading your writing was letting me get to know you."

Tommy's eyes widened. "What?"

Lynne took a step back, realizing her mistake.

"What did you just say to me?"

Lynne held up a finger. "Now, Tommy."

"Have you been reading my journal?!"

"I just wanted to know you were okay. I just wanted to know the person that you, my son, was growing up to be!"

Tommy snorted. "Sorry to disappoint you."

"But you didn't, Tommy. You've grown up to be such a smart and witty young man. I am so proud of you, and these problems you have are nothing to be ashamed of! In fact, they're completely normal."

"Normal?" Tommy yelled. "You think what I'm going through's normal?"

"Tommy. I need you to listen to me. If Adam's the one causin' this, he isn't anything special. His dad was better at basketball than he was, and he ended up riding the bench in some trash college. He makes a livin' now screwing people over at some used car lot. When Grace got all that money when her man died, Adam's dad sold her a piece of crap muscle car that died 100 miles after she bought it. Jesus, Tommy, he told her he didn't have kids and flirted with her, a woman practically just widowed, to get her to buy it."

Tommy was bewildered. "Why does that matter?"

"Cause Adam don't deserve to have this power over you. If I was still a bettin' woman, I'd guess in 10 years he'd be sellin' pieces of junk like his dad."

"You don't get it."

Lynne sighed. "I'm just tryin' to be a good mom. I just wanna help you."

Tommy released a long, high-pitched cackle, a laugh that cut into her soul.

Tommy caught his breath. "That's something you're never going to be."

"Just let me try, Tommy." Lynne pleaded. "I want life to be easier for you."

Tommy spoke through gritted teeth. "It would be easier without you."

"What?"

"Adam and Brian have been right about you for years."

"What do you mean?" Lynne asked.

Tommy looked Lynne right in the eyes. "You're a deadbeat whore."

Lynne hit Tommy hard across the face, knocking him off balance. Tommy looked up with a grin. "Just how many boyfriends have you brought home-"

Lynne screamed, catching Tommy with a hook across the face. The force was so strong that it caused Tommy to trip back and fall against the bed. Pain bursting through his jaw, Tommy looked up to his mother.

She screamed, "What in the hell is wrong with you? I am your mom."

"You're *worthless*!" Tommy screamed.

Lynne struck him again, sending Tommy spilling on the ground. "Do you know what I gave up for you? What it took for me to raise you?"

Face down on the ground, Tommy released several heaves of high-pitched laughter, causing his mom to look at him in shock. Between heaves of reverberating cackles, Tommy turned to face his mom, a smile wide across his face. Lynne watched in terror as blood oozed out from his mouth.

"I wish you would have aborted me. Then you would have been a singer. You would have been Jaime Lynne forever."

Lynne took a step back and watched in horror as her son released a fit of shrill, inhuman laughter. It left a scar in her mind that would never fully leave.

Tommy watched Lynne retreat to his door. "So go. Go! Be the absentee whore mother who called the cops on her own son."

His laughter tearing through her eardrums like a razor, Lynne bolted from her home.

Chapter 40: ***...Until We Felt Red***

Tommy was surrounded by his symbols of death. His razors were at his left, the Weld Bond to his right, and behind him a noose was carefully tied above his bed. Tommy's imagination had been running through this scenario all night, but, as of now, the boy had no idea if it was even practical.

He looked at a basketball rim lying in his bedroom. It was time to put the plan to the test.

A few months ago, Tommy had spotted this rim sitting behind an abandoned scrap yard near Felony Acres. The rim was still there this morning, and he took the long way to get it home undetected.

Tommy picked up one of the razors from his desk. "Here goes nothing." Shaking the orange canister of spray paint, the boy picked off the lid and sprayed. Before, the boy would have never done anything so reckless in his room, but now that droplets of green and blue paint covered his desk, he didn't think it mattered anymore.

Covering the blade with orange paint, the boy set it on his desk and grabbed the Weld Bond. This was the stuff of miracles. Tommy had watched the Schwann's man mix this to fix broken knick-knacks all around the trailer. There were two separate gels to mix together to make it work, but once it bonded, it was inseparable.

Letting the weld mix in an empty nachos container, Tommy put the mix on the back of the orange razor and affixed it behind the clip of the basketball rim. It was nearly undetectable to the naked eye and was given cover by both the net and the clip of the rim. Sure, it was possible someone would spot it, but since no one had any reason to ever suspect it was there, Tommy doubted anyone would see it.

Giving it five minutes to dry, the boy picked up a basketball at the corner of his room. Exhaling, the boy spiked the ball against the rim. The ball ricocheted around the empty room, bounding off the walls and slamming into Tommy's desk.

Tommy beamed. The razor had stayed put.

Tommy proceeded to slam the ball against the rim in every which way. This would be worthless if the ball popped or the blade fell off, but the blade stuck every time.

Tommy walked up to the rim. Time for the final test. With no hesitation, Tommy seized the rim in a stranglehold.

Without reacting, Tommy felt his skin tear open, sending a burning pain throughout his body. His eyes as alive as a skeleton, Tommy lifted his hand and watched a stream of blood flow down his arm.

Tommy smiled. This would be what murdered Adam Augustine. He could see it now, clear as day. Adam would be in his sanctuary, the John Wagner Fieldhouse. In many ways, the fieldhouse for Adam was just like Tommy's boxcar was for him. Adam would be there, in front of hundreds of screaming fans, in one of the biggest games of his life. Adam would be running to make his famous, one-handed dunk, and when his wrist hit the rim… Tommy knew, there would be so much blood.

Tommy thought of his desecrated boxcar, his vandalized jacket, his most treasured possessions that Adam destroyed for the world to see. Tommy thought of the posters of him around the high school and the laughter of the students as Adam humiliated him for the final time.

Tommy imagined Adam's screams as his blood poured out on the floor of his fieldhouse. Tommy imagined the hundreds in attendance at the game who, in that moment, could only sit back in horror and watch Adam's unexpected wake. He imagined the utter humiliation Adam would feel in those final, helpless moments. Then, and only then, would Adam understand what he put him through. It would be in Adam's sanctuary that he would be executed for all the world to see.

Tommy's mind raced. "And in his last moments, he would know that *I* was the one who killed him."

Tommy knew there would be no way out of this without getting caught. Even without a shred of evidence, Stallard would do everything in his power to make sure he was proven guilty.

The boy looked to the noose above his bed. That was okay, because once Adam was dead, his purpose would be fulfilled, and there would be no reason left for him to stay.

—

Adam stepped to the corner of the John Wagner fieldhouse. A custodian named Roxy drove on a riding floor machine through the gym, and it cast off an orangish aroma that nestled into Adam's nostrils. Roxy gave the boy a subtle nod as she passed, and Adam quickly returned the favor.

Tommy watched Adam and the court from the Latimer Watchtower. Tommy caught his breath and felt the nerves inside him calm. Today was the day. That janitor eventually put the stepladders in place and left Adam alone inside the gym. Tommy exhaled. He had almost been spotted on the way here, which could have ruined everything. However, now that he was in the clear, how fitting it was that Adam was here as he wrote the last page of his final entry.

The Black Journal The Last Day 2/18

I remember the day I met Adam. It was the first day of second grade. Adam came to class late, and his hair had those blonde streaks that all the girls liked. I think my real life started that day, before that nothing counted, I was a tourist in some sort of fantasy.

He walked up to me at recess. Already a foot taller than me and all the other kids, he looked down and called me "piggy."

That's all it took. The cost for my friends to dump me for the new kid. Since then life has never been the same.

To them I've never even been human. I was a piggy, a loser, and then I was Tommy Taint. They said it all so much that they forgot who I was, and somewhere along the way I couldn't remember my own name.

Today I know I am Tommy. I am Tommy Leigh Tate.

And after tonight, they'll never forget it again.

Tommy smiled. He would soon never hear another word from Adam, Brian or Mr. Stallard. Tommy threw the razors inside his bag. The bell rang. *It was time.* He would have to say a last goodbye, and then he could die without regret.

—

An icy mist swallowed up the outside air and reddened the faces of those outside. Mia shivered inside her STUCO hoodie. Sitting limply next to the great tree, Mia stared meekly at the soil.

Tommy looked at her. She looked devastated, but it made her look even more beautiful. In a fleeting moment, Tommy wanted to give up his plans and ask to be back inside her life, but he knew he had come too far for that.

She looked up. "How are you, Tommy?

Tommy sat beside her. "I've been better."

"Same."

"Are you going to be okay?"

Mia nodded. "Yeah, I just have to get through today. How about you?"

Tommy thought it over. "Just gotta get through today."

Mia held up a fake glass. "To today."

"To today," Tommy repeated. "I'm sorry that things went down the way they did."

"It is what it is."

"I'll hate Adam forever for what he did."

Mia's eyes flared. "You did that, not Adam."

"I'm not going to say sorry for how I feel."

"And you shouldn't," Mia said, "but I was here for you, and you were too much of a coward to see it."

Even today, her words scalded Tommy's insides.

Mia continued, "I'm sorry, that was harsh."

"It's okay," Tommy muttered, standing up. "I deserve it."

"Are you leaving?"

Tommy nodded. "I'm ready to get today over with."

"Well, always know that I'm here."

Tommy paused at the edge of the courtyard. "One more thing. I'm sorry I left you when you were telling me about how your dog died. That wasn't cool of me."

"My dog didn't die, though."

"What? You said that your dog--"

"I was *told* that she died," Mia said, "but one day, a group of friends took me out for a picnic at Hunter Park, a pasture park a few miles outside of town. There I saw my dog, my *girl,* playing with another little boy. My parents had sold her off to a farm and told their own daughter that she died."

"Holy crap."

"My childhood ended that day. I never put my faith into the world again."

Tommy shook his head in shock. "I am sorry I didn't listen to you."

"You should be," Mia said harshly. "I needed you to hear me, and you left me."

Feeling like he had nothing to lose, Tommy asked the question that had been on his mind for almost a year. "Why dandelions?"

Mia stared forward. "They are the lights of my world."

"They're pests. Everyone wants to exterminate them."

Mia nodded. "And they still grow anyway."

Contrition chiseled Tommy's eyes. "Best of luck today, Mia."

"You too. And Tommy?"

"Yeah?"

Mia looked into his eyes. "I'm always here."

Tommy sighed. "I know."

—

The dark and cozy astronomy room was home to a class half full of sleeping students. For the second straight day, Peter Good played the same episode from *Space Matters*, insisting it was the only episode Mr. Gordon wanted him to play.

While half of the classroom succumbed to slumber, no one noticed the empty seat in the back of the room -- least of all Peter, who was buried in a reading of *Lost in a Lonestar Outlaw.*

Tommy hung behind the lockers of the freshman lobby. He already thought he had a good chance to go undetected with Mr. Gordon. But with Petey? He hit the jackpot.

He knew he had to be precise with every movement. If anyone spotted him in the gym, he wouldn't have another chance.

Making sure the coast was clear, Tommy stepped into the open.

—

Tommy pushed inside the gym. Dead silence coated the hallways and the interior of the fieldhouse. The boy breathed out in disbelief. Everything had worked; Mr. Good didn't notice he was gone, no one saw him in the hallways, and nobody knew he was in the gym. The gym was darkened and spotless, and the orangish, chemical-laden scent set Tommy's nose ablaze.

Everything was exactly where it needed to be. A single stepladder led up to the basketball goal just beneath the Latimer Watchtower. Tommy smiled. Anyone inside would have press box seats to Adam's murder.

Tommy crushed the temptation. As fun as it would be to watch, the boy wanted to be far away when Adam's body collided with the floor. Everyone would suspect him, and they'd be right, but by the time they would kick in the door to his trailer, it would be too late.

—

Tommy made his way out the gym, but before he was able to leave, the door pushed open, and he was standing face to face with Adam Augustine.

Adam's voice bled with panic. "What are you doing here?"

Tommy looked at the vape pen in Adam's hand. "Why do you have a vape?"

Adam froze, seemingly to weigh the situation. There was a seriousness gripping his eyes that Tommy had never seen before. Adam took a breath and flipped over the vape to hold it out for Tommy. "Want a hit?" Adam asked.

Tommy's eyes widened in surprise. He shook his head. "I don't do it."

Adam whistled. "I would have thought you'd started in middle school. Christ, it smelled like you smoked a pack a day back then."

"That's 'cause of my mom," Tommy said, his brow furrowing in suspicion. "So yeah, I'm gonna go."

"Wait," Adam said, pointing to his vape. "I need to know that you ain't gonna snitch on me."

Something broke inside Tommy. It was something about the arrogance of what Adam said, like Adam somehow thought Tommy owed him here. Tommy reached into his pocket and stepped up to Adam. Adam froze.

Tommy spoke with a strange confidence in his voice. "Let's do that one over."

Adam paused. "What?"

Tommy lowered his voice. "Try again."

Adam breathed. "What are you even doing right now? Cut the tough guy act. No one buys it."

Tommy took another step, this time bumping into Adam and forcing him backwards. Tommy grunted, "One more time."

Adam looked down to his feet. Tommy saw his eyes moving all around his feet, like he was calculating his next move. Adam looked at the court's ceiling. It felt like he was afraid to look at Tommy's eyes. Adam shook his head. "I don't know what you want me to say."

Tommy exhaled. "*Try again.*" Tommy took another step. This time Adam stepped back and bumped against a cart of basketballs on the side of the court. Adam exhaled, and Tommy thought he saw real fear in his eyes.

Adam pushed back. "Who do you think you even are right now? Threatening to blackmail me like this! You, you--"

Adam looked down and met Tommy's eyes for the first time. Adam took a breath. "Look. Just don't tell anyone, okay? You don't know what I got on my plate today. Just do that, and we'll be cool, okay?"

Tommy felt rage take him. "You're a sociopath, you know that? You've made my life hell for nine years, and you think we're cool because you offered me a vape?"

Adam looked at Tommy, his eyes wide. For the first time in Tommy's life, he realized Adam truly was afraid of him. Tommy felt the power of that moment, and knew he was in control.

Adam whispered, "Tommy, I'm…"

The comment hung in the air, long enough that Tommy interrupted. "You know what? We're good, you can count on--"

A fist caught Tommy's face from behind, knocking him to the floor. Having snuck in from the outside doors, Rock Rustin jumped over Tommy's body and pinned him to the ground. Breathing in delight, Rock bludgeoned Tommy's face and watched his blood spurt out across the floor.

Tommy saw Adam's fake fear turn into smug satisfaction, and Tommy saw him turn around to the doors of the fieldhouse and stood guard over Rock.

Rock beat Tommy's skull against the hardwood floor, punch after punch. Rock yelled out savagely and pummeled the life out of Tommy. Delivering a final blow across Tommy's face, Rock raised his fists toward the skies and released a beast-like howl. "That's for Cocaine Thayne!!"

White lights blinding his vision, Tommy fought the urge to vomit. Holding up a hand in submission, Tommy watched as Adam's imposing figure came into focus.

Looking down to Tommy's bloodied, mangled face, Adam spoke. "If you tell anyone about what happened here, Piss Stain, I'll kill you." Smiling in triumph, Adam spat in Tommy's face.

The snot burned against Tommy's open wounds, and the boy fought off the unconsciousness creeping in from the corners of his eyes.

Rock cackled. "Now get the hell outta here."

Released from Rock's hold, Tommy tried to stand but collapsed against the floor. Tommy stumbled forward as Adam and Rock's laughter lashed into his ears. Blood was draining from his nose like a faucet, and only one thought entered Tommy's mind.

He had to erase. Erase everything. They had found two journals of his already, but they weren't getting their hands on any more. Tommy breathed. He was going to die on his own terms, and no one was going to take that away.

Tommy, gaining just enough strength to stand, held open the door. Though he couldn't see him, Tommy yelled in Adam's direction, "Hey, Adam?"

Adam raised an eyebrow. "Yeah?"

"Good luck tonight."

"Thanks," he muttered sarcastically.

"Give your dad a kiss for me."

The comment caused rage to boil up to Adam's face. "Screw you, Tommy Taint."

His legs quivering, Tommy flipped the bird as a last goodbye.

Chapter 41: ***Fire Drills***

Mia's ignition key caused a new, deep cut to run from Brian's swollen nose to just beneath his eye, but it didn't seem to bother him. Mia could see him from outside of the cafeteria. He was sitting with Adam, Jonah, and Devin from the basketball team.

Mia had agreed to join him for breakfast today. He demanded it at the end of their phone call.

Yurika put a hand on Mia's shoulder. "Are you sure you want to do this alone?"

"Positive," Mia whispered.

"I'll be here if you need me, okay?"

Whispering thanks to Yuki, Mia stepped into the cafeteria and blended herself in the breakfast line behind a couple of senior football players. She waited in line beside them until she could hear Brian's table. Mia closed her eyes. "Just breathe," she told herself. "This is going to be okay."

Jonah's voice drifted to her ears. "So who's this mystery girl you said would be joining us today, Brian?"

"You'll see. Let's just say I've been after this one for a while."

She heard Adam's voice. "She's not inflatable, right?"

Brian yelled, "Screw you, Adam! It just so happens to be Mia. Is that so hard to believe?"

Adam responded, "Yeah, it really is."

Jonah spoke. "Good for you, man."

Zoning in on their conversation, Mia stepped out of the line and towards Brian's table.

Brian replied, "Thanks, bro."

Adam looked at him. "You ready to start tonight for Cullen?"

"Hell yeah. I can't wait to--"

Mia crashed through like a wave and slammed her fist at the center of the table. Holding a tape recorder in her grasp, Mia unleashed it for the world to hear.

Brian's voice blasted through the recorder. "You stupid whore. I warned you; I warned you about what I would do to you."

Mia spoke through the recorder. "Brian, please--"

"You don't get to say please! I've waited too long, and you have one more day to change your mind, or else."

"Or else?"

"0695," Brian breathed. "I tried it just last week. Does your idiot dad ever change his combination? If I don't see you at Adam and I's table tomorrow, you'll regret it forever. Do you understand?"

"I understand."

Mia paused the recording and looked Brian square in the eyes.

Brian whispered out in shock, "How?"

"A friend of mine let me borrow her tape recorder. Hope you don't mind."

Stunned, Jonah looked up to Mia. "Did he ever hurt you?"

"No, but near the end of our relationship I got home late after working at Mom's flower shop. When I opened my door, I saw that Brian was sitting on my bed, and he was holding his dad's gun in his hand."

Jonah exhaled. "Brian, what the hell?"

Mia continued, "With a smile on his face, he told me that if he were me, he would never think about fighting him again."

Brian spat. "Bullcrap."

"You really gonna go with that after threatening to break into my house last night?"

"You promised to keep our fights between us."

"And you promised you would never talk to me again. Looks like we both lied, huh?"

Brian shook his head. "I'm a different guy now."

"I don't care who you are now. I already played this for my parents, and if you call me, or try to contact me in any way, I'm sending this to Hardcastle, Elmer, and the police."

Adam whistled. "Jesus. What is wrong with you, Brian?"

Mia turned to Adam. "Oh, shut up, Adam. You better pray your God isn't real. Or you will burn *forever* for what you did to Tommy."

Turning to glance at Brian, Mia stormed from the table, and she heard Adam's voice as she walked away. "What was her deal?" He asked incredulously. Walking from the cafeteria, she found Yuki waiting for her in the hallway. For the first time in what felt like days, Mia smiled.

—

Mia buzzed through the empty school hallways. LHS was about to hold a massive pep rally for today's game, but Mia couldn't sit more than 30 seconds. She was too wired to be stationary -- too electric to be grounded. With Yuki's assistance, Mia had liberated herself from that monster. He would never control her gaze again.

Mia stopped. There was a drop of blood on the ground, and it stood out on the white tiled floor. Raising an eyebrow, Mia pressed forward. Blood drop after blood drop arranged themselves in a crimson pattern through the hallway. Led up to the door of the Annex, Mia opened the door and walked inside. Crying reached her ears, causing her pulse to quicken. Winding through the rows of Latimer memorabilia piled up in the Annex, Mia saw a dreadlocked boy crying beside a window.

"Dex?" Mia asked.

"Yes?" Dexter asked, his voice surprisingly level.

"Are you losing a lot of blood at the moment?"

Dex shook his head. "Not physically."

"Do you know who is? There's a trail of blood leading into this room."

"Whoa, really? I must have missed it. I haven't been too observant today." Dexter turned to Mia. "Did you come in here to cry, too?"

"To cry?" Mia asked. "I wasn't planning on it."

"Well that's too bad," Dexter said, "because today, this here is the designated crying room."

Mia smirked. "Someone should have told me. This has been a horrible week, and I watched *Up* over the weekend, so the tears have been at the gates since."

"Well, pop a squat and cry it out with me."

"Maybe we can cry somewhere else?" Mia suggested. "We should probably tell someone about the pint of blood in the hallways."

"Fair point. Any ideas on where to go?"

Mia thought of the big tree out in the Latimer courtyard. "Are you okay with getting a little chilly?"

"Always."

"Awesome. You know where the courtyard is?"

"Sure do. Give me a moment to get it together and I'll meet you down there."

Mia beamed. "Can't wait."

—

Mia frolicked from the Annex. She weaved through the halls and came face to face with Mr. Stallard, who was following the trail like a bloodhound.

Stallard's gaze skewered Mia's hoodie. "Are you still a part of STUCO?"

Mia stumbled. "Uh, no."

"Then don't let me catch you in that again."

Mia's anger rose. "You act like your words still have meaning to me."

"Excuse me?"

Mia was defiant. "You heard what I said."

Stallard took a step toward Mia. "Let me clue you in, sweetie. For one more year, everything I say does mean something to you, and you will respect that."

"I realize you like to stroke the tiny amount of power you have, but you embarrass yourself when you let it go to your head like this."

Stallard's eyes flickered. "Detention on Monday. Any more and it's an ISS."

"I have to work Monday."

Stallard smiled. "That's a shame. You won't like what happens if you miss it."

"Will I get to read all day in ISS? I'm shaking."

Mia watched as a lever broke inside Stallard's mind. Something caused him to *snap*. He lowered his voice to a cutthroat whisper, and he had a deeper tone to his voice than Mia had ever heard before. "I've run over preppy little girls like you for decades. I could make you a cleaning lady, chica. I'm connected with powerful people at North College, and all it would take is one phone call to make your life hell."

A click echoed from inside Mia's hoodie. Beaming, Mia pulled out Yurika's tape recorder and showcased it to Stallard. "I'm carrying this for a crazed stalker of mine, but it'll work for you too."

His eyes wide in alarm, Stallard took a threatening step toward Mia.

Mia cried out, "One more step and I scream."

Stallard paused. They were beside Mr. Austin's room; it couldn't have been a better spot for her.

"Good," Mia breathed. "Now, you listen to me. I have run over *monsters* like you for my entire life. If I find out that you've disparaged my name to anyone, I will have no problem letting the world know about how crazy you really are." Mia stuffed the recorder in her hoodie. "So I don't think I'll be doing detention on Monday, or anytime for that matter."

"If you think that you can *blackmail* me--"

"No one said blackmail. I just have a feeling that next year is going to go really well for me." Her smile wider than it had ever been in her life, Mia gave Stallard a curtsy and walked away.

Chapter 42: ***Wingless Flies***

Clenching his fists, Stallard flipped around and stifled the panicked emotion inside him. He would deal with Ms. Fernandez later; there were more important things to tend to now.

A trail of blood glistened inside Latimer's empty halls. His movements silent, Stallard moved with a crimson glow inside his eyes as he tracked the scarlet ravine to the entrance of a darkened room. Stallard paused outside the doorway and strangled the handle beneath his adrenalized grip. A ravenous expression over his countenance, the principal pushed inside the Annex. Blood was spattered all over the floor of this room. Feeling panic seize his insides, he flipped out his phone and texted the office staff.

"School Lockdown. *Now."*

It only took seconds. High pitched sirens screeched out as a computerized voice filtered through the school. "Lockdown, lockdown, lockdown!"

Panicked teachers, quickened footsteps, and surprised cries from students joined the alarms in a broken harmony. Stallard was content. The front office did well with that response time. Stallard walked to the two windows in the far corner of the Annex. Looking past the basketball court, Stallard's eyes combed through the outside world. Jay exhaled sharply. A boy sat out in the heavy sleet and was surrounded by a pool of blood.

The figure looked up from the soil and found Stallard staring down at him from the window of the Watchtower.

Stallard's eyes widened. It was Tommy. The boy's eyes were so swollen that Stallard wondered if he could see at all. Blood had flooded down Tommy's nostrils and was frozen to the side of his face.

With the horror of the lockdown around him, Stallard held Tommy's gaze and smiled.

Chapter 43: *The Candlelight House*

Lynne pushed inside of the Riverfront Brewery. It was a typical crowd for 3:00 P.M. on a Friday. Save for a couple men sitting at a table near the windows, it was empty.

Lynne looked at her shoes, mangled from the walk to the bus stop. Her hair was drenched from the sleet. She thought, "Could I do this every day? Is something like this even possible?"

A red-haired man approached her. "Lynne?"

Lynne nodded. "Yes, and you must be Cam?"

"That I am, but don't hold it against me. Were you wanting to talk about a job?"

Lynne responded, "I am, but I don't want to get your--"

One of the men sitting at the table called out to them. "Hey, Cam?"

Cam turned. "Yeah, James?"

Mr. Austin looked over to them. "I know that gal. She's the mom of one of my best students, so treat her well, okay?"

Lynne's mouth hung agape. "Mr. Austin?"

"That's the one. Are you applying for a job right now? I didn't mean to interrupt."

Lynne shook her head and stepped to Mr. Austin's table. "You're alright. Cam was just gonna show me around."

Cam spoke. "But that can wait a bit if you two have something to catch up on."

Lynne stopped outside of Mr. Austin's table and realized he was sitting with Principal Elmer. Understanding met Lynne's expression. "Oh, but I wouldn't want to interrupt anything."

Principal Elmer smiled. "You're not interrupting a thing. Like spin dip? You're welcome to start on ours."

Lynne smiled. She was starving. "I'd love to."

"It's great to see you," Cam whispered to Mr. Austin, kissing him on the cheek. "I'll be back around."

Principal Elmer looked at Lynne. "I want to apologize. Your son has been the target of unacceptable abuse from his peers and even from some of the staff at our school. That practice will not continue in the future."

Lynne took a chip and looked over it in her palm. "Last year I wouldn't have believed you." She turned to Mr. Austin. "He loves you, though. You've been a role model to him."

Mr. Austin looked to his feet. "And I'm sorry to say it'll be my last year."

Lynne put a hand up to her face. "Don't tell me that."

Mr. Austin nodded. "I'm sorry. There are… folks in our building who aren't fond of Cam and me."

Lynne gasped. "What? Are you kidding me?" She whipped over to Principal Elmer. "How can you let that stand in your own building?"

Mr. Austin spoke. "It's not up to him. It's my call. There are people higher than Principal Elmer who would come after him here--"

Lynne interjected, "But there's, like, laws against pushing you out for this, right?"

"Sure. But we live in a state where anyone can be let go 'without cause.'"

Lynne snorted. "The house always wins, huh?"

"Always."

Principal Elmer leaned forward. "But Lynne, we're gonna look out for Tommy. You have my word. Your son will be safe."

Lynne gestured toward Mr. Austin. "But with you bein' gone… my son."

Mr. Austin was quick to respond. "Look, as much as I will miss teacher meetings and professional development…"

Elmer released a belly laugh. "Oh, I'm sure you'll miss the salary, too."

Mr. Austin smiled. “Oh, as much of a headache that teaching can be, I’m not gonna be so far away. I can’t leave the students, Lynne.”

Elmer murmured in agreement. “They’re why I’ll never leave.”

“And they are so lucky to have Principal Elmer as their principal.”

“But they’ll be even luckier because Mr. Austin will still be around. Why we’re here today is to discuss a program that North College has to bring an arts integrated curriculum to our schools. Mr. Austin would get his doctorate, and in exchange…”

“I’d have to work directly with our high schools.” Mr. Austin said.

Lynne beamed. “So if you get it, you’d still be around?”

“Always. I plan to always be there to lead the Mickey Ryan awards, too.” Mr. Austin looked to the window, and for a moment, Lynne thought he might be teary eyed. “It’s hard for me to leave. I am dreading the day that I tell my students, but it’s time. It’s time for a new chapter.”

Elmer’s phone screen lit up. "Uh-oh," he said. "Latimer's on an unscheduled lockdown. If you both would excuse me."

Mr. Austin's eyes widened. "Of course."

The principal put a hand on Mr. Austin’s shoulder. “Just know you have a standing offer to come back next year, or any year, for that matter.” He turned to Lynne. “Let me know if you need anything.”

Mr. Austin nodded. “Thanks for everything.” He asked Lynne, “You planning on being here a while?”

Lynne nodded. “I was.”

Mr. Austin smiled. “Great. I could use a little company.”

Chapter 44: *The Bologna Boat Fleet*

Dexter and Mia sat in the bustling John Wagner Fieldhouse. The players from both sides of the court warmed up as parents and the community filled the stands. The wildness about today's game and the lockdown had infected the parents and students in an equal fashion. It was a false alarm, but it nonetheless created a feverish spectacle building toward the tipoff. It was the first game of sub-state, and though Latimer was predicted to win by 30, one could feel the excitement in the air.

Mia whistled. "That was the best cry I've had in years."

"Wasn't it?" Dexter replied. "I think I'm gonna schedule those badboys more often."

"So there's no chance you can make it out to Cali, then?"

"None," Dexter answered.

"I'm sorry."

Dexter shrugged. "It's not your fault I only applied to a single university."

"Where do you go from here?"

Dexter laughed. "Heh, send some e-mails and hope someone will take me."

"You'll be okay," Mia said. "With your grades and portfolio, any college would be lucky to have you."

"I hope so. But that's enough about me. Are you still thinking about North College?"

Mia snorted. "In spite of Mr. Stallard's promises to ruin me with his sweet hook-ups, that's the plan."

"That tape is crazy. Are you really going to sit on that until next year?"

Mia looked up at the ceiling. "I don't know, I'd publish it after I graduate for sure, but before that..."

"Are you worried about how he'd react?"

Mia sighed. "Worse. I'm worried that people will take his side. I'm worried they won't think it's so bad. You ever worry about that? That there's no one here who will even take something like this seriously? Or even acknowledge it matters?"

Dexter looked to the court. "All the time."

Mia watched Mr. Stallard enter the gym and shake Coach Hardcastle's hand. Mia felt a weight fall over her lungs as she watched him, she whispered to Dex, "I grew up with this assumption that teachers all had to be great people."

Dexter laughed.

Mia smirked. "I know. I was dumb."

"Not dumb. It's natural as kids to assume the best in people -- and there are some amazing teachers out there, no doubt. Mr. A has reached legend status for me."

"But now I wonder, what is stopping a truly bad person, an evil person, from getting a job as a principal? They could do so much damage to so many kids in a job like that."

"If there was any teacher who was actually evil, it's Stallard."

Mia exhaled. As if he had sonar, Mr. Stallard turned and looked her in the eyes, and she held his gaze. She whispered to Dex, "The moment I graduate next year, this tape will burn him down. I will make sure of it."

"Hell yeah. You gonna lie low until then?"

Mia shook her head. "No. I'm applying for STUCO next year, and I'm going to do everything I can to make a real change in this place -- even if it means going straight to Elmer."

"With your status? You could make a lot of changes happen, Mia."

Watching Stallard turn away, Mia changed the subject. "But before all that, do you have any advice before I go on to my senior year?"

Dexter laughed. "I'm not sure if I'm the one to be giving advice."

"I insist," Mia responded playfully.

Dexter looked out toward the fieldhouse. The stands were filled to the brim; the game would start any moment. "You know," Dex said, "you never told me what your book was about."

Mia opened her eyes in surprise. "I can't believe you remembered that."

"How could I forget a title like *Captain Spudz and Her Bologna Boat Fleet?*"

The girl smirked. "Fair point."

"So what's it about? You can't leave me hanging with a title like that."

Mia blushed. "It's embarrassing."

"I insist."

"Argh, okay. It's about a seven-year-old girl named Marisol. Mari loves to go on magical adventures with her imaginary friend Sudha, but one day her parents drop her off at her Aunt Gertrude's for the weekend, and Aunt Gertrude tells her that good girls don't play with imaginary friends. Good girls study. Good girls play the piano."

"Was Aunt Gertrude a fascist?"

Mia's eyes twinkled. "Close to it. Mari starts crying at her dinner table because she won't eat her vegetables and she can't play with her imaginary friend anymore, and that's when Captain Spudz bursts out of Mari's bologna boat to find her imaginary friend Sudha. Captain Spudz leads Mari across the Applesauce Sea and through the French Fry Forest. The two end up going through the Broccoli Jungle where they find Sudha and decide to go on their own adventure. Mari is snapped back to reality when her Aunt Gertrude says, 'Mari, are you playing with your bologna boat? Good girls don't play with their food.' On the last page, Sudha whispers in Mari's ear, 'It'll be our little secret.'"

"That's amazing! Did you finish it?"

Mia shook her head. "With STUCO and everything, I didn't have the time."

Dexter's eyes followed the players on the basketball court, jumping from Adam to Jonah to Cullen. "People tell me that all the time. That they can't do the things they want to do until they graduate, but -- spoiler alert -- life only gets busier from here, and instead of gold stars, STUCO and GPA, we'll be dealing with student loans, apartment payments and full-time jobs. Are you really going to let a gold star get in the way of doing something in this world?"

Mia laughed. "Come on, that's not fair."

"Is it? If I took my state trophy to a job interview, how would the boss react?"

"They'd laugh you out of the building."

"State trophies, straight A's, the honor roll…they're all just repackaged versions of the gold stars Mom put on the fridge."

"But that doesn't mean they don't mean something. Good grades get people into good schools," Mia responded.

"And that's great. But the system preaches that high school is a finish line, and so many believe it. Do you know how many people have come up and told me that high school was the best years of their life? You know how sad that is to me? This place shouldn't be a finish line; this place should be our launching pad. But some never even leave. Look around you." Dexter pointed at the court and watched Adam dish in a layup. "There are kids down there who think these days will last forever, who think they will walk through their entire lives as the gladiators they are now, but do you know how much this will all mean once they graduate?"

"Absolutely nothing."

"Absolutely nothing," Dexter repeated. "This place has made them arrogant for a world that doesn't exist, and they're heading for the slaughterhouse."

"That's grim," Mia muttered.

Dexter chuckled. "Okay, rant over. It's been a rough few days. Can I just ask for one thing?"

"Anything."

Dexter looked into Mia's eyes. "Finish your book."

"You still think so?"

"I didn't win the scholarship, and you know what? Maybe I didn't deserve it. My movie had some issues. I didn't have proper sound equipment, but the hard part about it is that the person who deserved to win didn't either."

Mia smirked. "But you're going to keep going, without a Plan B?"

Dexter considered. "The day I lost the scholarship, Mr. Austin gave me a letter. The letter said I was the closest person to a son that he and Cam would ever have, and that if I wanted, the Riverfront Brewery would eventually be mine."

Mia gasped. "Wow."

"How do I even begin to thank them for that?"

"But you're just going to give that up to go for a pipe dream?"

"Right now we have the luxury to go for pipe dreams. The work I've done for the documentary saved the lives of over a dozen animals, and that's more important than any scholarship could ever be. The doc allowed me to look above the walls of this school. Mia, this is our time. We are without debt or obligation; me making movies in college won't keep me from Riverfront; finishing your book this summer won't stop you from a future career. There are thousands of little girls and boys who need Captain Spudz to look up to. What would Sudha say?"

Mia laughed. "Okay! You win."

"Damn straight," Dexter said, dropping the mic.

Out on the basketball court, Principal Elmer took the floor. "Hello, everyone! We would like to thank you all for coming out today. Before we get started, we'd like to recognize an incredible person in this district's history. Cody Augustine, if you could join me out on the court."

At equal height with Elmer, a man with dyed blonde hair walked onto the court. The Latimer crowd screamed out and lifted themselves to their feet for him.

Elmer continued, "And now, it gives me great pride to welcome you into the Latimer Hall of Fame. To present you with the honor, we were lucky enough to find someone you may recognize."

Lifting himself from the bench, Adam held up the hall of fame plaque and walked out to his father. His palms shaking, Adam extended it to his dad.

With the crowd roaring, Cody took the award and gave them a lazy wave.

"And without further ado," Elmer announced, "let the game begin!"

Chapter 45: ***The Real Stories of LHS***

Cullen felt the tremors from the crowd, his teammates, and saw a nervousness grip Adam that he had never seen before. Adam walked over to him before the game began.

Adam patted Cullen on the shoulder. "If there was anything I could do to get you playin' today, I'd have done it."

Cullen shook him off. "Don't act like my friend, Adam."

Adam looked up in surprise. "Is this about what Brian did in practice? Dude, I'm sorry. I had nothing to do with that."

"Do you really think I'd forgive you if you sprinkled on some BS with me? You know, I really thought we had something when I told you about my mom. You were one of the few people I ever told about that. How long did you wait before spoonin' that to Brian?"

"I wouldn't tell him. Brian... Brian's an a-hole."

Cullen laughed. "Do you even know you're lyin' to me right now? I hate Brian, but at least he has the balls to say these things to my face. You're just the chicken-shit who gets off on hiding behind Brian and ratting to Hardcastle."

Adam stammered, "I don't even -- I don't even know what you're--"

"I just wanna know why. Why would you go to all that trouble?"

"You really want to know?"

Cullen raised an eyebrow. Tip off was in one minute, but there was something in Adam's voice he had never heard before. It was cool and confident yet plagued by an undeniable lust. Cullen nodded. "Yeah, I wanna know."

"You're lazy, and it's going to cost us state."

Cullen laughed out loud. "Y'all so bougie. Adam Augustine, who hasn't worked a day in his life, is callin' me lazy?"

"Sorry I like b-ball more than wiping old people's buttholes!" Adam shouted. "I have put my life on the court."

"And I respect you for it, but some of us ain't so lucky. You make fun of my car sometimes. Talk about how you'd waste me if we ever raced, and you're right, you would, but you know who paid for my car? I'll give ya a hint. Some of us don't have a rich daddy who buys us toys whenever he feels guilty."

"Screw you!" Adam yelled. "It's not my fault that my dad bought me a Mustang."

"I ain't blaming you, but I've worked for everything that I have, and until you can say the same, you best shut your mouth about my work on the court."

The refs blew the whistle. The game was starting.

Adam smiled. "Well, I'm gonna enjoy the court today. Have fun on the bench."

Cullen smiled back. "Hope it works out for ya."

Cullen watched Adam step to half court and stand across from the tallest person on the Bobcats, a 5'10 kid named Evan Smith. Cullen snorted. Even the tallest person on the Bobcats should be zero match for Adam.

The official whistled and threw the ball up towards the skies. Adam tipped the ball into Devin's outstretched hands. Devin drove up the court and stopped at the three-point line. Spotting Adam open in the corner, Devin flung the ball to his teammate.

Adam caught the ball and looked up at the basketball goal. Cullen narrowed his eyes; Adam rarely attempted a three, but today felt different.

Without hesitating, Adam took a shot.

It was an airball, missing everything before falling into Evan's outstretched hands.

—

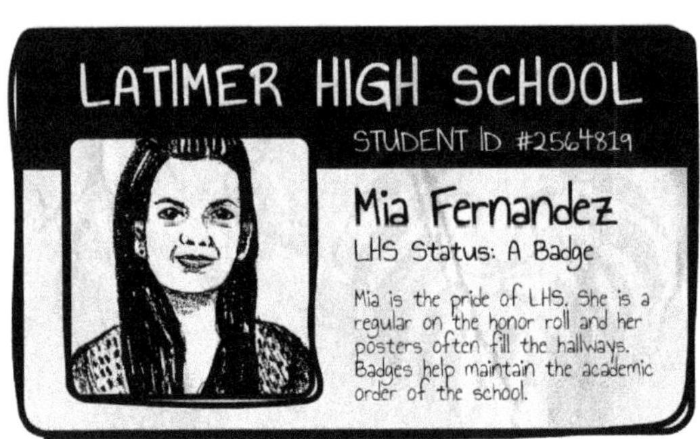

Mia and Dexter sat back in amazement. Everything was going wrong for Latimer. Adam had missed every shot he had taken, and the team was getting dominated beneath the basket. Latimer was down by six coming out of halftime.

Mia looked at Cullen sitting on the bench. They were within earshot of the players and coaches, so Mia dropped her voice to a whisper. "Shame they couldn't put Cullen in right now."

Dexter snorted. "Think Hardcastle would rather lose than play a 'thug.'"

Mia looked at the court darkly. "I hope we lose then."

She watched Devin pass the ball to Adam. Facing the basket at the far end of the court, Adam drove the ball inside before dribbling against his foot, making the ball roll on the floor. Evan scooped up the ball and drove towards the opposite end, weaved through Adam and Devin, and laid the ball in the basket without a struggle.

Hardcastle clapped his hands. "You're alright. Lots of time left, Augustine." Mia saw Hardcastle turn around and immediately shake his head. Coach stopped at Cullen, who was sprawled out in a relaxed fashion in his seat.

The coach yelled at Cullen, loud enough so everyone could hear. "Are you enjoying this?"

"Nah, Coach," Cullen said flippantly. "I just wish there was something I could do."

Hardcastle stepped over Cullen. "Well there isn't, and you only have yourself to blame."

Mia looked over at Dexter and whispered to him, "You really think he'll keep Cullen out all game?"

Dexter looked over the crowd. "If he keeps Cullen out of this game and we lose, it'll ruin his reputation here forever."

Mia smiled in awe. "Hardcastle won't be able handle that heat, will he? All of his status, his degree, his name in this community… None of that matters. Cullen's got him here. We're going to lose, and Hardcastle's never gonna show his face in town here again."

Dex snorted. "Nah, my man Armstrong has all the leverage. Hardcastle's gonna fold. I'll give him ten minutes."

Mia looked at him in surprise. "Really? Want to put money on it? Winner buys the other a limeade tonight."

"Be sure to get me a strawberry limeade after Cullen leads the comeback."

Mia relished the moment. She looked at Stallard, then at Hardcastle. For all they liked to talk, it was their student, Cullen, who had all the power on the court right now. Seeing this gave her a feeling of empowerment she never felt before.

Smiling, Mia turned to Dexter. "Deal. If Cullen gets us a win, I'll buy him one, too."

—

Coach Hardcastle traditionally put out an extra seat to allow Stallard "courtside seats" for games. Today, Mr. Stallard got in his seat early -- he wasn't going to miss Latimer's blowout -- but it had not gone to plan. Mr. Stallard had a front row seat of Hardcastle's quips to Cullen throughout the third quarter. Stallard gritted his teeth. The only way Latimer won was if the two could compromise.

At one point in the game, Stallard whispered to Cullen, "You know, I think if you apologized, Hardcastle will let you back in."

Cullen turned to Stallard and had a gigantic smile on his face. "Apologize, huh? That's funny."

Mr. Stallard felt anger surge up inside him. He couldn't remember the last time students were so disrespectful towards him in a single day. Stallard sighed, changing his tactic. "It'll be a shame if this was your last memory with this team."

Cullen nodded. "Shame if it was yours too."

Mr. Stallard looked at the court. Cullen wasn't wrong.

By the end of the third quarter, the fieldhouse sat in a stunned silence. With twenty seconds left, Latimer was down by 10 against the Bobcats.

Everyone had stood witness to Adam's worst game of his career. He had only four points and only made one shot of the fifteen he'd taken from the floor.

Coming into the game, Mr. Stallard wondered if Hardcastle recognized just how important Cullen was to Adam's success. Cullen's size and strength on the inside allowed Adam to move freely around the court. It's possible he thought Cullen being on the court wouldn't matter today.

"For Pete's sakes," Stallard thought. Adam couldn't even handle the fun-sized Bobcats. He was getting mangled out there. Stallard watched from the bench as the Bobcats sank an uncontested three and extended the lead to thirteen.

Screaming in frustration, Adam caught the ball and slammed it against the court. A referee pointed his way and said, "Do that again and it's a technical."

Stallard heard Hardcastle sigh. The coach had lost control. Stallard could see sweat glued across his face. Yelling for a timeout, the coach gathered his team.

Hardcastle pointed to Adam. "Take a blow, Augustine."

Adam began to protest. "Coach, I'm--"

"That ain't up for discussion. Grab a seat and get your head on straight." Hardcastle gritted his teeth. Stallard already knew what his move was, and that Hardcastle fought it from the game's beginning. But the stakes of today were too high.

The coach swallowed. His pride was running out of time. "Armstrong!"

Cullen raised an eyebrow.

Hardcastle sighed. "You're in."

"That's what I thought," Cullen muttered. Throwing off his over-shirt, Cullen jumped up and joined the huddle.

Coach took out his whiteboard. "Devin, you're going to take the ball to the top of the key and loft it into Cullen. Cullen, with your size advantage you'll attract an immediate double team. When you do, C.J., I want you to run along the top of the three-point line and I want Jonah to set a pick to break you free. Cullen, be ready to pass it out to C.J. so he can take the shot."

Hardcastle looked over his team. "We ready? Lions on three. One-two-Lions!"

The team broke, and Cullen ran out onto the court with a vigor inside his eyes.

Stallard sat back. This was the first time Cullen hadn't worn an undershirt beneath his jersey. Stallard remembered when he brought in Cullen and his dad and demanded Cullen cover his tattoos under his jersey. Cullen had covered them every game since, until today.

Now out on the court, Cullen looked Stallard right in the eyes and grabbed both of his tattoos, as if he was daring Stallard to say something. Stallard gave Cullen this -- if LHS pulled this off, people were going to remember this game because of Cullen. LHS had a whole quarter left and they weren't exactly playing the Harlem Globetrotters.

C.J. inbounded the ball to Devin, and as directed, Devin sprinted to the top of the three-point line. Devin threw it inside to Cullen, who caught the ball. Though he was directed to toss it back out to C.J., Cullen looked up to the basket and saw he had an open lane. His eyes wide, Cullen dribbled toward the basket.

Stallard raised an eyebrow. This wasn't the play design. Cullen was supposed to pass, but now soared into the air, and with the eyes of the crowd upon him, he ripped his arm back and slammed the ball inside the rim. Stallard gasped. Hardcastle had ridden him the whole year because he was too big to dunk the ball, but today was the day that changed.

The crowd was electrified from their stunned stupor, lifting to their feet and releasing a roar down upon the court. Cullen pumped his fist high into the air. Looking to his teammates, Cullen yelled, "We're winning this dang game!"

A horn rang out through the court, signaling the end of the third quarter. Breathing in his excitement, Cullen turned to their new side of the court and stared at the goal sitting beneath the Latimer Watchtower.

—

Tommy sat against the back of his trailer. A deep blue consumed the skies, and thick clouds released white flakes like those inside a snow globe.

Tommy lit a match, illuminating his bruised-up expression. Thick streams of dried blood had stuck over Tommy's chin, and his right eye was swollen shut with purple skin. Tommy breathed. He deserved this. He had seen the monster he was inside. The words flashed before his eyes -- the planning and the painstaking effort he had poured in to murdering another human being.

He felt the blood crusted over his face. It all made sense. Of course Rock was Adam's dealer. It was how Adam knew so much about his family, his life at home, and how Adam was *always* a step ahead of him. "Well," Tommy thought darkly. "Until today."

The boy knew the game would be starting at any time. He could imagine the crowd, the players, and the energy. The boy thought back to the afternoon. The goal beneath the Latimer Annex, the rim, and the razor.

Thinking of Adam and his father, Tommy let out a sigh.

Mr. Stallard was vindicated. Tommy had no right to be at Latimer. If only Stallard had succeeded last year. If only he had swayed the school board to expel him. This whole year had been nothing but wasted time. To have his hopes so high, to only have them stolen. To be betrayed by Mr. Austin, and to be reminded of who he was by Adam Augustine.

Tommy felt the falling snow burn the wounds on the side of his face. All this year had done was prove everybody right. He thought of Cullen, Mia and Dexter. They had been better friends than the boy ever deserved, and everything could have been different. He felt pain seize his heart when he thought of Thayne. He could never forgive himself for what he did to Thayne. It wasn't Thayne who deserved that, it was Adam. Adam deserved to die. Adam had taken everything from him. He had taken away his chance to be anything but a piss stain.

For years, Adam had told him what a monster he truly was, and Adam was right. Tommy clenched his fists. It would all be over soon.

The boy's thoughts turned to the game.

—

Rosi screamed in delight. The fourth quarter was domination -- absolute domination. LHS had dominated the Bobcats inside and outside, and the Bobcats had not scored for the last five minutes. Evan drove inside and put up a shot, but it had zero chance; Cullen leapt high and blocked the ball out of the air, causing the crowd to explode. Rosi looked at the clock. Latimer was down four with four minutes left. This game was theirs. Rosi watched Cullen lead the team to the other end of the court. The Bobcats had been relying on their players slipping inside for easy lay-ups, but they had no prayer against Cullen -- he swatted away their shots with ease.

Just minutes later, Rosi watched Jonah's three swish through the basket. They were only down one with over two minutes to go. She had never heard the crowd like this before. She could feel the ground shaking beneath her feet. This comeback would be talked about in this town for the next decade.

Evan drove the ball up the court. The Bobcats were confused and in disbelief. Evan held the ball up to the skies, looking for someone to pass it to. Cullen read his mind. Evan and the Bobcats needed to eat time, and Cullen watched Evan's eyes connect with his teammate's. Evan threw the ball in the air, but Cullen had read it the entire way. Stepping out in front of his opponent, Cullen stole the ball and sprinted toward the basket.

Cullen had told Rosi that sometimes his friends watched the games from the windows of the Annex, calling it their personal press box, and as Cullen sprinted towards it, she wondered if there was anyone there now. Rosi smiled. This would be the moment that people talked about. The moment that everyone remembered from the game.

Leaping into the air, Cullen slammed his hand into the rim, and released a scream that silenced the entire gym.

With all eyes on Cullen, Rosi watched in horror as Cullen's body hit the ground.

Chapter 46: *The Wayward Bus*

Guided in the darkness by the orange city lights, Lynne and Mr. Austin followed a set of footprints in the thin layer of snow. The city bus was waiting at the bus stop, and the two paused before entering.

Lynne looked up to Mr. Austin. “I guess this is where I leave you.”

“Yeah,” Mr. Austin admitted, “but this bus goes until 3 A.M on Fridays. I’ll let them drop me off back here.”

Lynne smiled. “I appreciate the company.”

A few stops later, the bus took an extended stay at the shoulder of the Manchester highway, and there it had been for the last ten minutes. A group of muscled college guys had joined the bus in the last rotation, and fifteen minutes ago one had puked all over the bus.

The driver, angry and rolling his eyes, dropped sawdust over the liquidy vomit. He looked over at Lynne and Mr. Austin. “How did I get stuck with the *Sweetheart* route?”

Lynne turned to Mr. Austin. “You know, why is this called the Sweetheart route at night?”

Mr. Austin laughed. “It’s from the N.C., college students usually can’t find privacy… but on a big empty bus driving the entire city like this?”

Lynne snorted. “Oh my Lord. Are you speaking from experience?”

“If you saw how awkward my existence was in college, you’d know that wasn’t the case. But hey, it's *your* turn to tell your story. I don’t care to talk about myself when I’m sober, and the wine’s wearing off.”

Lynne turned to Mr. Austin. “What do you wanna know?”

“You just applied for Riverfront; where were you before that?”

Lynne sighed again. “Well, the answer is pretty personal.”

“And I haven’t been being personal?”

"Ah.... alright," Lynne said. "Truth is I haven't worked for five years. I have a kind of spina-bifida which makes serving hell on my back. The last time I served, I dropped a full tray on a swanky group of assholes and laid on the ground for over an hour."

"That sounds horrible."

"One of the worst days of my life. As I laid there, I watched this bunch of douchebags walk over me and into another party table in the restaurant. Not a single one asked if I was alright. In fact, they were all pissed because some of the food got spilled on 'em. They demanded a free meal and a new server, and they was out of the restaurant before I was."

"What a bunch of monsters."

The bus driver switched the bus into drive and pulled out onto the highway.

Lynne continued, "What I hated the most was that group didn't even treat me like a person. They treated me like a piece of garbage, and I swore that I wouldn't let anyone treat me like that again."

"So, why are you going back?"

Lynne put a hand over her mouth. "Because I let down my boy."

Without thinking, James put his hand on her shoulder, inviting her to continue.

Lynne obliged. "For the last five years, he's watched his own mother give up on life, and the worst part is that sometime in there I stopped even thinking about my own boy." Lynne shook her head. "It took a fight, the worst fight we have ever been in, to wake me up to that, and he said some awful things. Things that I didn't deserve. But he's seventeen, and can you imagine if we were still judged for the things we said at seventeen?"

Mr. Austin smirked. "I'd have never found a job."

"I mean, he had no right to say the things he said, but he does have a right to have a mom that he can look up to. I just worry there ain't time. I worry that it's too late for me to say sorry, that it's too late for me to make things right…"

Mr. Austin considered. "You know, my own father was a raging alcoholic who was abusive to me, my mom and my siblings. To this day he's the reason no one in my family speaks to me, but in my 27 years when he was alive, it would have never been too late."

Tears welled up inside Lynne's eyes and ran down her face.

For the second time that evening, the bus driver stopped at the end of his route and breathed into the microphone. "Route Blue, Friendly Acres."

Lynne smiled. "I suppose I better take this one. Thank you for talking with me tonight."

"Of course," Mr. Austin said. "Good luck with everything. It's never too late, Lynne."

Wiping the tears from her face, Lynne walked out of the bus with her head held high. She was two miles away from seeing her son again. Lynne smiled. Two miles away from a new beginning.

Chapter 47: ***Sun of Nothing***

Coach Hardcastle blew a gasket. "That foul was flagrant! That was *flagrant!*" Cullen looked at his arm as the team nurse did several tests on it. The nurse had a streak of gray in his beard and looked through his thick rimmed glasses at Cullen's arm before looking up at Cullen. "Looks like your wrist hit the rim pretty good. With any luck, this is only a wrist contusion. Honestly, I'd be more worried about your back after that fall."

Cullen nodded. "Yeah, that's what hurt the most." Cullen looked at the opposing bench. Evan had collided with him before he leapt to the rim, and everyone seemed to think it was intentional. Angry parents rained boo birds down on the refs, with some promising that refs would need to leave the country if Latimer lost the game. Right now custodians were wiping down the floor and the basketball rim at Hardcastle's request, but Cullen knew there was nothing wrong with the rim or the floor. Adam had dunked on it a thousand times, but on his dunk, Cullen got shoved in the air by Evan, which caused him to collide against the rim and fall on the hardwood court.

Hardcastle walked up to Cullen and the team nurse. The nurse spoke. "Cullen has a wrist contusion and landed hard on his back, but we'll only know the true extent of his injury after an MRI."

Hardcastle breathed. "We'll be in the clear if that's the case."

The nurse said, "He wants to stay here until the game ends, is that alright with you?"

"Yeah, an extra 90 seconds ain't gonna hurt no one."

Cullen looked at the scoreboard. Despite the foul, he had miraculously made the shot, putting them up for the first time that game.

An official ran to Hardcastle from the court. "Alright, we wiped down the court and the basketball goal like you asked. Everything looks good."

Hardcastle turned to his bench. "Augustine, you're in."

From the opposing sideline, Evan gave Cullen a wink, something that sent pure anger through his body.

Turning around, Cullen grabbed Adam by his jersey. "If you blow this, I'll kick your ass with one hand!"

Hardcastle nodded. "You heard the man! Now let's go out and win! "

—

Dexter and Mia waited out in the Latimer parking lot. With Rosi by his side, Cullen stepped from the school.

Mia shook her head. "What a crazy game!"

"How's the arm?" Dexter yelled.

Cullen looked at the makeshift sling over his right arm. "They just think it's a wrist contusion from how it hit the rim. That little tool Evan shoved me as I was in the air. Honestly, my back hurt more when I landed."

Mia breathed. "We were terrified. The whole crowd was."

"Ah, I'm alright. Just happy we won."

"That was the best finish I've ever seen." Mia said.

"With any luck I'll be back in time for state."

Mia was still amazed over the game. "Dex and I were worried we were going to blow it, but Adam came out of nowhere to block that last shot."

Rosi sighed. "And his dad wasn't even there to see it. He left at halftime. Adam prepared all year for this game. He was going to beat his dad's record, and his dad didn't even stay for the whole game."

Cullen looked at his feet. "Yeah. Wish I could feel for him, Rosi, but I can't. Adam even ducked out of our team celebration in the locker room."

"I hear you. Sometimes I think Adam's destined to become his dad."

Mia changed the subject. "I'm worried about Tommy. Anyone hear from him?"

Everyone shook their heads.

Rosi looked at the group. "If someone can, please tell him I'm sorry. That would mean a lot to me."

"Well, if you really want him to hear it, one day you'll have to tell him yourself." Cullen said.

"I know, and I will."

Mia pushed back. "Math is the worst part of the day for him, you know that?"

"I know, and I know I'm a reason for that. But I won't let Adam or Brian hurt him in there anymore. I promise."

"I'll let him know, okay?" Cullen said. "But I don't want to tell him if you're not up to hold your end of the bargain."

Rosi was firm. "I'm up for it. Adam's BS in math stops *today.*"

"Good," Cullen said. "You ready for your move?"

"I am. Tamira is helping me get the last of it moved to your pod this weekend."

Dexter looked at Cullen. "So you're really gonna come back for state, then?"

"That's the plan. But know I'm only gonna win it on my terms. I'm never doin' a damn thing for Hardcastle ever again. By the way y'all, Dex and I were gonna hit up Riverfront if y'all wanted to join."

Mia beamed. "I'm there. And limeades are on me."

Cullen took a moment and watched his friends walk back to their cars. There was someone missing, though, and Cullen hoped Tommy was okay.

Chapter 48: *Bleak*

Tommy's body convulsed on top of his bed. It wasn't Tommy Taint, it wasn't fatass, it wasn't even Piss Stain that cut him the deepest.

It was the words from Mia, because she was the only one who saw him for who he really was -- a *coward.*

Tommy pulled out the razor from the pocket of his jeans.

He *didn't do it.* He hadn't planted the razor. Tommy now knew that he could have never done it. Despite the planning and the journals. It was all a fiction and pretending any differently would be a fantasy.

Mia had been right. He was a coward when he let go of Mr. Austin, Cullen and Mia, and he was a coward to let his rage for Adam make him throw everything else away.

Tommy threw the razor against his wall. After everything that Adam had done to him for the past decade, he couldn't do it. But Adam was right. He had shown Tommy the evil he was capable of; he was going to use Adam's condition to *kill* him. Just even having a thought like that showed how awful he truly was. Tommy knew now that it was never because of Adam. Adam would have never treated Tommy this way unless he had permission, unless he was encouraged to do so – and Latimer had encouraged Adam from the moment he walked into Tommy's second grade classroom. It was Tommy's second grade teacher who pretended not to hear when Adam called him piggy. It was his middle school choir teacher who held back a laugh the first time Adam called him Tommy Taint, and it was all those faceless people who joined Adam's chant of "Piss Stain Taint" in the high school hallways. He saw them all in Stallard's victorious smile as he looked down at him from the annex window today. Of course, Stallard would smile, he always wanted Tommy bloodied, because he *wanted* Adam to win.

Tommy shook his head. He had a real chance to do something this year, and he had let everything slip away. His friends, Advanced Art, and worst of all, his mom. He had listened to Adam and Brian and used their words against his own mom. That was the most cowardly move of them all.

Tommy watched the rest of his life flash before his eyes. It would be spent here, scraping by in Red Oak. He was his mother's son. He would exist off check to check and partner to partner to numb the time away.

Tommy lifted himself to his feet. Not him. He had let life torment him for too long. It was time to finally take control. Tommy picked up the razor. He had to erase the evidence of today. He didn't want anything about the plan to be a part of how he was remembered. Taking a breath, Tommy pulled the noose from under his bed and threw it beside his desk.

Opening the black journal, Tommy carved his suicide note and bared it for the world to see. He had thought and dreamed of writing this note for years, and now that he was finally here, the writing flowed out across the paper. After reading it over, he tore out the last two pages of his journal and left them on the dining room table for his mom to read.

He doubted his death would haunt Lynne for long. How could it? After all the horrible things he had said to her, his death would probably be a relief. She would be free of him, and she could be Jaime Lynne again.

Throwing on a hoodie, Tommy pinned the black journal between his arm and his body and walked from the trailer. Kindling a match, Tommy set the black journal on fire. No one would ever find this journal. If he could control anything, it would be that people never thought he was serious about killing another person.

Tommy smiled, thinking of Mr. Stallard. Well, some were a lost cause.

Tossing the fiery journal into a metal dumpster at the end of his road, Tommy swung the noose to his side and walked to his boxcar for a final time.

The blue light flickered out the moment Tommy made it to his boxcar, welcoming him back. How right it would be, to get out of here above the place where Adam destroyed his sanctuary. It was pitch black around Tommy's surroundings, but he found the yellow ladder without an issue. Throwing the noose over his shoulder, Tommy climbed the yellow ladder and walked to the platform above his boxcar. Reaching out blindly, Tommy found a bar to tie his noose against.

The boy tied a knot so tight that they'd have to cut it off, and without hesitating he fitted the noose over his neck. A vengeful look upon his expression, Tommy tied it so tight that he began to choke. The boy climbed up the safety fencing and looked down at the world below. For the first time in his life, he was the one in control, and no one could take that away. There was a comfort to that, knowing that he would be the one to end it all.

This had been waiting for him for his entire life. Since the day he had walked into second grade, he knew he was never meant to be here. His own mom had confirmed that just five years ago. He remembered her words, each one still echoed in his ears. There she laid, drugged-up and wrapped in a cocoon of blankets after her back went out at the drive-in, and she stared at him through corpse-like eyes. "It all would have been so much easier without you. My life ended the day you were born."

Tommy swallowed. He was a glitch in the system, a mistake his own mom had acknowledged. He had known from that day that he was living on borrowed time. He knew on that day that he'd one day remedy this mistake. Today was that day. If only he'd acted sooner, he could have saved himself and those who knew him so much time. In an instant it would all be over, and he'd be somewhere new.

The horn of a coming train echoed in the distance.

The boy's body was still. His eyes open, arms extended, motionless.

Tommy smiled. He'd found his way out of here.

The blue light flickered on and flashed inside his eyes for the last time.

—

Unsorted: The Last Day

Blisters split open on Lynne's feet, and she whispered encouragement to herself to keep going. "It's never too late. It's never too late."

Lynne crossed onto Green Oak and felt blood ooze from her chapped upper lip. "It's never too late."

She moved into a near run once she reached Red Oak and threw open her front door with a smile on her face. "Tommy!"

The black cat stared at her, meowing at Lynne in reply.

"Tommy?"

Looking confused, Lynne stepped into the living room, and that was when the note met her eyes. Her fingertips trembling, Lynne read through Tommy's journals of the day in utter shock.

Tommy Tate	The Black Journal	2/19

I committed suicide last night. I have seen the life in front of me and it is one I do not wish to live. I was just not meant for this life.

Mom I'm sorry for what I did. I'm sorry I was the monster they always said I was. I'm sorry you wasted your time on a piss stain like me.

I am sorry to everyone who believed ~~I was worth a shi~~ in me. I just don't belong here. I am not meant for this life.

Tommy Leigh Tate

Mascara-cloaked tears ran down Lynne's face and splashed against the wooden floor. A passing train roared in the distance; it shook the trailer and echoed in her eardrums. Placing her son's crumpled note back on the kitchen table, Lynne unleashed a wounded scream.

—

Tommy breathed out in denial. In the blue light he found Mia's paint-splattered dandelion folded on his shoulder.

He despised Mia for fooling him into thinking he had another purpose in this world. Tommy smashed the dandelion in his fist. He wanted his last act in this world to be him choking the life out of Mia's dandelion. He hated her for what she did to him.

And yet…

"No!" Tommy thought. He had to do this. It was preordained. He was meant to go out this way.

The train passed by below. Tommy closed his eyes. This was his way out of here.

Mia's voice rang inside his ears: "Anything is possible for you, Tommy. You just have to believe."

Hot tears bled from Tommy's eyes. Despite Adam, Brian, Mr. Stallard, and everything he had been through at Latimer; he could see Mr. Austin, Dexter, Cullen, and his mom brightly inside his eyes. He could see the afternoons where he dreamed beside Mia in the courtyard, and he could see the dandelion in his grasp.

Even after everything, he couldn't do it.

The boy felt the edges of his noose. There was no way to untie it; the rope was too tight around his neck. Tommy didn't know what he was going to do. His mind raced. "Am I going to die before I have a chance to live again?"

The boy snorted, and then laughed harder than he had laughed in months. The noose was so tight around his neck that every heave brought him pain, but to laugh at all made the feeling worth it. He had remembered the razor lying inside his pocket, and the fact that this razor would be what saved his life was difficult for Tommy to comprehend.

Tommy slipped the sharp edge of the razor out against the rope and began to cut his way to life.

—

Purple bruises puffed out from Tommy's neck. The rope and the razor rested in his left hand, and though he wasn't sure why, the boy planned on keeping them for a while. Stepping onto the gravel of Red Oak, Tommy saw his front door hanging open in the breeze and heard his mother's cries inside.

Lynne was doubled over on a kitchen chair, and a stream of tears flowed from her eyes. "Please, God, No. Please, God, bring him home."

Tommy spoke. "I'm home, Mom."

Her mascara stuck across her face, Lynne looked up in surprise. Her boy was standing in the doorway. His nose was swollen, his right eye puffed shut, and there were angry splotches around his neck. The two rushed into each other's arms and held each other in the center of the room.

Chapter 49: ***Way Out of Here***

Sitting in the hallway, Tommy looked up from his math homework. "What the hell is an imaginary number?"

Mr. Austin pulled out a set of keys. "Isn't gazillion imaginary? I dunno, last time I took math cell phones were the size of cinderblocks."

"Ah, well," Tommy breathed, "he lets us grade our homework anyway, and I say this is worth a B."

Mr. Austin put a key in the student showcase. "I'm going to pretend I didn't just hear that."

"What do you care? You'll be out of here in two months!"

The teacher turned to Tommy. "That's true, but I'm every bit your teacher until these months are over."

"You'll always be Mr. Austin to me." Tommy said.

"That means a lot. Leaving my students has been the hardest part of this."

"You're really going then?"

Mr. Austin nodded. "It's time. The system has worn me down, and the students deserve someone who can give 100% to the job."

"You at 70% is better than most at 100."

"That's kind of you to say, but for my sanity, it's time to move on."

Tommy nodded. "I get it, but you really think I can get through my senior year with Mr. Stallard?"

"Principal Elmer's contract got renewed at the board meeting yesterday. As long as he's here, you're gonna be okay. Just don't internalize next year, Tommy. Lean on your friends, your mom, and go to Mr. Elmer if you need."

"I won't close up again. I promise."

"So do you have any plans for tonight?" Austin asked. "It's the first Friday of Spring Break, after all."

Tommy checked the time. "I'm catching a ride in a few minutes. Cullen and Dex are throwing a party tonight. They're signing their lease for an apartment and they've invited a lot of people to celebrate."

"Sounds more fun than what I'm up to. I'll be meeting a few fancy-do people at the NC about my PhD work."

"I'm happy Dex got everything worked out at North College."

Mr. Austin nodded. "I knew he'd find a way. That kid is too talented to not be recognized by somebody. Is Cullen still sky high?"

"After state? You know it."

"If I were the MVP at the state tournament, I would be too."

There was a time when Tommy dreaded the idea of the basketball team winning state because it meant *Adam* would win state. But Cullen invited Tommy to the game with Dexter and Mia -- and once the game started Tommy found himself wanting to cheer for his friend. Tommy was so happy for Cullen.

Mr. Austin turned back to Tommy. "Are you ready?"

Without hesitation, Tommy handed *The Yellow Ladder* to his teacher.

Mr. Austin took the painting and centered it in the showcase. "Beautiful, isn't it?"

"I'd say."

While looking at the painting, Tommy noticed his reflection off the doors of the showcase. It was March 18th, a month past what was going to be his last day. He was happy it wasn't. His face was almost cleared -- the purple marks on his neck were gone, and all that was left was a little pink splotch beside his eye.

Mr. Austin looked at Tommy. "I'm sorry it took so long for me to do this."

"You don't have to say sorry," Tommy said. "I wouldn't have cared if it never went up at all."

Mr. Austin stepped back. "I had to see to it. Principal Elmer handles the key now and he'll make sure that for the next two months, everyone who steps foot in this high school will see something *you* made."

Tommy swallowed. It didn't feel real.

Mr. Austin shut the showcase. "Are you going to be okay next year?"

"Are you kidding? I'm counting down the days until you're outta here."

Mr. Austin laughed. "Life is good, then?"

Tommy nodded. "As good as life can be. I have more friends than I've ever had before, and both Dex and my mom wanna help get me a job at Riverfront for the summer." Tommy unzipped his backpack. "And of course, I still have to turn this in. Mia and I finally came up with a title."

Tommy held a slip of paper to Mr. Austin.

Submission for the Mickey Ryan Awards

Title: Komics for Kids

Applicants: Mia Fernandez & Tommy Tate

Advisor Signature: James Austin

"I love the name," Mr. Austin said.

"It was all Mia. I'm so happy you're able to come back for this."

"It's all thanks to the program Principal Elmer hooked up for me."

Tommy stepped back a moment. He had thought about this moment for the last month, but it didn't make what he was about to say any easier. Tommy sighed, "I need to confess something to you."

"Confess?"

Tommy nodded. Reaching into his backpack, he pulled out the can of orange spray paint and Weld Bond and held them out for Mr. Austin.

Tommy's voice broke. "These are yours. I stole them from your room. I was going to use them to do a very bad thing."

Mr. Austin took the items with a stunned expression.

Tommy was speaking at a rapid-fire pace. "I understand if you can't forgive me for this. I know I broke your trust."

"Did you hurt anyone with these things?"

"No. But I was going to."

"Did you do anything that you can't undo?"

"No. I didn't go through with it. But Mr. A., with everything that I wrote last year, there was a time when I thought I could actually *do* it."

Mr. Austin kept probing. "Will you ever go through with a plan like this?"

Tommy looked up at Mr. Austin. "No. I promise."

Mr. Austin nodded, processing the information.

Tommy continued, "Are you angry with me? Do you think I'm a monster?"

"I'm hurt. I won't lie about that."

Dread hit Tommy's insides. "I don't know if I'll ever forgive myself. For this. For what happened with my cousin and I. He told me what I did to him was unforgivable, you know? I think I might agree."

Mr. Austin held up his hands. "I can't speak to what happened between you and your cousin, but I can speak to what happened to us -- you're forgiven. And no, Tommy. You're not a monster. Not even close. I'll need time to process this, but we're okay. What worries me more is hearing you talk about how you can't forgive yourself. If I never forgave myself for the scams I pulled in high school, I would have turned out like my father. Tommy, do you want the real reason why I'm leaving this job?"

Tommy nodded.

"Because now I can finally say that the love of my life, my future husband, is Cam Thomas. I've wanted to share my true identity for longer than I could remember, but I couldn't here. I can now, and it wouldn't have happened if I chose to stay. Do you know how liberating that is? To now be able to fully be the person that I am? I don't know the person that you want to be, Tommy, but the world needs to hear your voice."

Tommy felt himself become choked up. "I don't know what I want to do with my life, and I know things will be rough along the way. But as a wise person once told me, 'it's a bleak road,' and I'm going to do everything I can to overcome."

"I believe in you, Tommy."

The boy beamed. "My ride's here. I better skidaddle."

Mr. Austin looked up to see Cullen, Dexter, Mia and her friend, Yuki, approaching from the hallway. Stepping up to the showcase, Mia saw *The Yellow Ladder* for the first time. Smiling wider than she ever had before, she looked to Tommy. "It's gorgeous. It was worth the wait."

Tommy breathed. "In the summer it'll be yours."

"Are you sure?"

"I've never been more sure of anything."

Without a word, Mia brought Tommy in for a hug. Tommy closed his eyes. For a while he didn't think they'd be friends after what happened between them in February. After everything, Tommy was never going to take her for granted again.

Cullen spoke up behind them. "You know, I coulda gone for a hug, too, but whatever. It's fine."

Smiling, Tommy hit Cullen on the shoulder. "All you have to do is ask."

Mia looked at Dexter. "We have a lot to look up to if we're going to match your senior year."

"Want my advice? Have Yuki write about your project. It'll get the whole town behind you."

Yurika laughed. "Thanks, Dex. I won't lie, another scholastic award would be great for my resume." She looked at Tommy. "If you're interested, I'll give you my number."

Tommy smiled, "That'd be great." The boy turned to Dexter and brought him in. "I'm sorry about the scholarship, Dex. But you know what? Screw California. With your documentary, you've already done more than half the jerkoffs in Hollywood."

"Nah, Tommy. Whatever you do will be great next year. I won't be surprised at all if you surpass me."

Mia laughed. "Dex aren't they showing your movie in the park and having an adoption day this Saturday?"

Yurika nodded. "Yeah. I wrote the advertisements for it."

"Even *if* we manage to win, we're not topping you, Dex," Tommy said.

Mr. Austin butted in. "Take it from me, Dexter. You might not have a trophy, but what you did was more impactful than any project I've *ever* overseen."

"It was golden, Dex," Cullen said.

Tommy looked at them. "Will you two be ready to live together next year?"

Dexter tapped Cullen. "Eh, I guess it won't be so bad living with this guy for a while."

Cullen joked. "We'll make due."

"I hear you got a new job, Cullen." Mr. Austin said.

"Yeah, I'm gonna be working with the kids at *Boys and Girls Club* this summer. Already been told they're interested in keepin' me longer. We'll see."

"Those kids are going to love you."

"That means a lot to hear you say, Mr. A. I learned a lot this year watching you. You made me think this might be what I was meant to do."

"You're going to do amazing things, Cullen." Mr. Austin said.

Tommy soaked in the moment. He looked at his friends in near disbelief. He couldn't believe that it was less than a month ago that he actually thought about going through with his plan with Adam. He knew now it never would have worked. If the razor had fallen off, or if it had been noticed at any time, Stallard would have found a way to expel him that instant. Tommy felt his stomach drop. What he didn't even realize was that Cullen started dunking, too. If he *had* planted the razor, Cullen might have… Tommy couldn't even think about it. He looked at his friends one more time. He never would allow himself to hurt someone like that again -- losing Thayne was hard enough. If he had acted out on his plans about Adam, he would have lost everyone else, too. His entire life he had yearned for a way out, to get away from the crushing feeling he had at Red Oak, at school, and about the world in general, and as he stood back to appreciate his friends, he realized that they--

Mia yelled at Tommy, breaking him from his thought spiral. "Tommy! Earth to Tommy! We gotta boogie. We can still catch happy hour at Riverfront before we hit up Dex and Cullen's tonight."

Everyone enthusiastically expressed their approval and Dexter pulled out his keys. "I got my truck. Let's roll!"

Tommy turned around and smiled at his teacher. "I'll see you around, Mr. A."

"Take it easy, Tommy." Mr. Austin said.

Feeling at peace, Tommy followed his friends out of his high school.

Bleak I

II Benjamin Honeycutt

Beyond Bleak - The References in the Novel

Chapter 2:

Van Gogh, Vincent. *The Starry Night.* 1889, Museum of Modern Art, New York.

The Holy Bible, *The New King James Version,* Luke 10:25-37

Bishop, Rudine S. *Free Within Ourselves: The Development of African American Children's Literature.* Westport, Conn: Greenwood Press, 2007. Print.

Chapter 5:

Anderson, Maxwell. *Anne of a Thousand Days.* Dramatists Play Service, 1950.

Chapter 8:

Steinbeck, John. *The Grapes of Wrath.* New York, N.Y.: Book-of-the Month Club, 1995. Print.

Chapter 9:

The Holy Bible: *The New King James Version,* Luke 11: 5-8

Chapter 11:

Jackson, Shirley. The Lottery and Other Stories. 1st pbk. ed. New York: Farrar, Straus and Giroux, 1982. Print.

Chapter 13:

Shakespeare, William, Mowat, Barbara A. Werstine, Paul. *The Tragedy Of Macbeth.* New York : Washington Square Press, 2004, c1992. Print.

Mastrosimone, William. *Bang Bang You're Dead.* Showtime, 2002.

Chapter 14:

"Cheech and Chong's Up in Smoke." Paramount Home Entertainment (UK), 2003.

Shawnna - American Rapper

Martin, George R. R. 2011. A Game of Thrones. New York: Bantam Books.

Chapter 17:

Bing Crosby (with the Andrews Sisters), Mele Kilikemaka, The Voice of Christmas

Chapter 18:

Leone, Sergio, Director. *The Good, the Bad and the Ugly.*

Chapter 21:

Lawrence, Jacob. *Dreams #1.* 1965, New Britain Museum of American Art.

Chapter 23:

The Holy Bible: *The New King James Version,* Luke 18: 1-9

Chapter 25:

Hughes, Langston, 1902-1967. Suicide Note, The Collected Poems of Langston Hughes. New York: Knopf: Distributed by Random House, 1994.

Marsh of Swans, Dreams of Light, From Ashes Beneath, 2017

Poppe, Maddie, Don't Ever Let Your Children Grow Up, Songs from the Basement, 2018

Chapter 27:

Pak, Greg, et al. *World War Hulk*. Marvel, 2008.

Johns, Geoff. TALES OF THE SINESTRO CORPS SUPERMAN PRIME #1. DC Comics, 2007.

Chapter 29:

Cormier, Robert. *I Am the Cheese: A Novel.* Pantheon Books, 1977. Print.

Chapter 32:

The Colour, The Devil's Got A Holda Me, Between Earth & Sky, 2007

Chapter 37:

Lieber, Todd M. "Ralph Ellison and the Metaphor of Invisibility in Black Literary Tradition." American Quarterly,

vol. 24, no. 1, 1972, pp. 86-100. JSTOR, www.jstor.org/stable/2711916. Accessed 26 Sept. 2020.

Chapter 46:

Steinbeck, John. *The Wayward Bus*. Heinemann, 1990.

Bleak:

Special Thanks to Beverly Daniel Tatum, whose work *Why Are All the Black Kids Sitting Together in the Cafeteria?* was a constant source of reflection for me and made a major impact on this work and in my teaching.

Thanks to Kimberly Geswein, who created the font, "Annie Use Your Telescope," used for Tommy's handwriting and *Bleak*'s front/back matter. Thank you to the creators of the "Pacifico" and "Permanent Marker" fonts, both used in the novel.

Cover dandelion images licensed through user emielcia on canstockphoto.com, spine dandelion licensed through user Dole.

Thank you to my father. It was an incredible honor to include your designs of the student ID pictures throughout Bleak.

All texts created and sent through Apple's iMessages platform

Thank you to Jeremy Gulley for providing Spanish translations for Chapter 38.

Music Credits

The music I listened to was a constant source of inspiration for me in the 15 years I spent crafting this work. The title *Bleak* is itself a reference to Opeth's track on their 2001 album, *Blackwater Park*. I listened to the track during a very difficult time in my young adult life, and it was in the track's final chorus that the ending of this work finally came to me. Opeth's *Bleak*, Portishead's *Cowboys*, Jimi Hendrix's *All Along the Watchtower*, and Porcupine Tree's *Way out of Here* helped me survive during some of the toughest parts of my life, and those tracks, as well as those referenced in my chapter titles, were instrumental to this novel finally getting published.

Chapter 1: Song of I - Steven Wilson ft. Sophie Hunger
Chapter 4: Keep Your Eyes Peeled - Queens of the Stone Age
Chapter 6: All Along the Watchtower - Jimi Hendrix
Chapter 14: Bolt Cutter - Doomtree
Chapter 15: It Was a Good Day - Ice Cube
Chapter 17: Wicked Game - Chris Isaak
Chapter 19: ...and the Great Cold Death of the Earth - Agallloch
Chapter 21: Dreams - Fleetwood Mac
Chapter 26: 25 Bucks - Danny Brown ft. Purity Ring
Chapter 28: Forsaker - Katatonia
Chapter 29: The Farmer in the Dell - Einstein Baby Lullaby Academy ft. Marco Pieri
Chapter 30: Cartographist - Purity Ring
Chapter 31: Deathblow - Deftones
Chapter 32: Cowboys - Portishead
Chapter 33: Miasma - The Black Dahlia Murder
Chapter 34: Reimagined - The Contortionist
Chapter 35: Adam's Murmur - Cynic
Chapter 36: Cookie Cutter Bitches - Snow Tha Product
Chapter 38: Dissolved Girl - Massive Attack
Chapter 39: The Island: Come and See & The Landlord's Daughter - The Decemberists
Unsorted: Tennessee Whiskey - Chris Stapleton
Chapter 40: Until We Felt Red - Kaki King
Chapter 41: Fire Drills - Dessa
Chapter 47: Sun of Nothing - Between the Buried and Me
Chapter 48: Bleak - Opeth
Chapter 49: Way out of Here - Porcupine Tree

About the illustrator

SHELBY MILLER

Shelby Miller is a teacher and graphic designer living in Lawrence, KS. She has her BA in Graphic Design from the University of Kansas, MA in Elementary Education, is a 200 hr certified yoga teacher and enjoys finding creative ways to use her skills together. After starting her passion of traveling in college, and working with schools around the world, Shelby has developed a passion for non-profit work and continues to pursue ways to serve the global community.

About the Author

Benjamin Honeycutt grew up in a rural community in south-central Kansas. After graduating from the University of Kansas, Ben moved out to Colorado with his partner, Natalie. He is now a middle school 21st century learning teacher and the Chief of Operations for a non-profit called Open World Cause. He was inspired to get into education after the years of targeted abuse he experienced in school. Ben works every day to help students find their purpose.

benhoneycutt.com

www.ingramcontent.com/pod-product-compliance
Lightning Source LLC
Chambersburg PA
CBHW070641310726
48982CB00001B/360
* 9 7 8 1 7 3 5 8 6 5 3 7 9 *